# PRAISE FOR JL

MW00655532

## THE KENNEDY GIRL

"Fashion, elegance, and espionage… From the walls of U.S. power brokers to the glamorous fashion houses of Paris, historical-fiction fans will love this behind-the-scenes take on one of the most famous names in politics. Dazzling and intriguing, this novel will captivate readers right to the delicious end."

—Kirsty Manning, international best-selling author of *The Paris Gift*

"Paris, 1960s fashion, glamour, romance, *and* espionage? Yes, please. *The Kennedy Girl* is a skillfully crafted and well-researched Cold War mystery about a young woman who thinks she's going to Paris to model at the glamorous House of Rousseau only to find out much more than a job is on the line. Julia Bryan Thomas impresses with her layered, captivating characters and vivid, fully realized European settings while maneuvering through the complexities of gender, war, and international intrigue. An engaging escape!"

—Emily Bleeker, Amazon Charts and *Wall Street Journal* bestselling author

"*The Kennedy Girl* has all the ingredients of a great novel: intrigue, espionage, fashion, and Paris. Like her cast of characters, Julia

Bryan Thomas's writing is bold, colorful, and fearless. Absolutely riveting!"

—Erika Robuck, bestselling author of *The Invisible Woman* and *The Last Twelve Miles*

## THE RADCLIFFE LADIES' READING CLUB

"In 1955, four young Radcliffe students—Tess, Evie, Merritt, and Caroline—gather at the Cambridge Bookshop to explore the scope of a woman's life using the words of Brontë, Wharton, and Virginia Woolf as their guides. As each young woman discovers what ambition, love, and independence mean to her, friendships shift and evolve until the group's bond is shattered by violence and betrayal. This endlessly charming—at times heartbreaking—novel weaves a gentle spell on the reader. You will never want to leave the Cambridge Bookshop."

—Mariah Fredericks, author of *The Lindbergh Nanny*

"*The Radcliffe Ladies' Reading Club* is a loving, engaging tribute to female friendship and to the intimate power of books. It paints the struggles of four young women in living, blooming color as they come into their own in 1950s Cambridge, Massachusetts, a world that has only begun to crack open the door of opportunities for women. Tess, Caroline, Merritt, and Evie want more than they are being offered—more education, truer love, greater freedom—and they make mistakes as they pursue their dreams. They stumble. They fall. But, like the heroines of the books they love, they stand up and try again. Join the Radcliffe Ladies' Reading Club and dive into this passionate, emotionally rewarding story. You'll be glad you did."

—Mary Anna Evans, Benjamin Franklin Award–
winning author of *The Physicists' Daughter*

"When Alice realizes her dream of opening a bookshop, she doesn't anticipate the crucial role she, her books, and her wisdom will play in the lives of four first-year college women. Though from vastly different worlds, Caroline, Evie, Merritt, and Tess take on the challenges and temptations of their new independence together—until an incident drives them apart, revealing emotions and biases they don't recognize, even in themselves. Julia Bryan Thomas's elegant prose and compelling storytelling take us back to the heady early days of college and remind us of the joy of discovering books and making new friends, and the painful awakening that can prevail. *The Radcliffe Ladies' Reading Club* is an engrossing story of literature, friendship, and lessons in compassion learned and shared. I loved every heartbreaking, empowering, unexpected, and uplifting moment of it."

—Penny Haw, author of *The Invincible Miss Cust*

"A story of female freedom and constraints that doesn't shy away from the trauma—and joy—that faced U.S. women in the 1950s."

—*Kirkus Reviews*

"Relevant now... A good fit for enthusiasts of historical fiction centering young women, New England settings, and college nostalgia."

—*Booklist*

# FOR THOSE WHO ARE LOST

"Julia Bryan Thomas has ensured that readers of *For Those Who Are Lost* will never forget the children of Guernsey displaced during World War II. This is a captivating and complex story about family, about deception, about flawed characters in inconceivable circumstances, and about the power of love to both damage and heal."

—Kelly Mustian, author of *The Girls in the Stilt House*

"This richly layered story about losing, finding, and forgiving unfolds when a Nazi threat to an innocent island off the coast of France is imminent. Desperate action is taken, and children are sent into the unknown where destinies are altered. Then the isolation and pressures of a tedious war beget heartaches and heroes. *For Those Who Are Lost* is riddled with secrets and sins for the sake of survival. Kudos to Thomas for a poignant and compelling read."

—Leah Weiss, bestselling author of *If the Creek Don't Rise* and *All the Little Hopes*

"*For Those Who Are Lost* is a surprisingly suspenseful novel, fraught with the tension of intersecting lives in impossible circumstances.

The literary momentum pulls the reader forward at an ever increasing pace toward a poignant ending."

—Audrey Blake, *USA Today* bestselling author of *The Girl in His Shadow* and *The Surgeon's Daughter*

"A sure bet for readers of personal war stories and those who want to know, 'What about the women and children?'"

—*Booklist*

"What a compelling story of love, courage, and forgiveness. Highly recommended."

—Historical Novel Society

ALSO BY JULIA BRYAN THOMAS

*The Radcliffe Ladies' Reading Club*

*For Those Who Are Lost*

 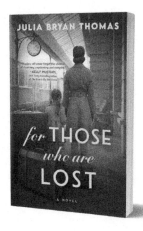

# THE
# KENNEDY
# GIRL

## JULIA BRYAN THOMAS

sourcebooks
landmark

Published by Sourcebooks Landmark, an imprint of Sourcebooks
P.O. Box 4410, Naperville, Illinois 60567-4410
(630) 961-3900
sourcebooks.com

Cataloging-in-Publication Data is on file with the Library of Congress.

Printed and bound in the United States of America.
POD

*In memory of my grandmother,*
*who instilled in me a love*
*of books and writing.*

What chance did I stand between the Communists on
one side and the Establishment on the other?

—LEN DEIGHTON, *THE IPCRESS FILE*

# BEFORE

Espionage. The very word is French. It stems from *espionner*: to spy, to peer, to peek into the dark recesses of life. In the best circumstances, information is used to solve a puzzle, to improve lives, to keep a community or country or world safe. In the worst, however, it can be deadly.

Being fluent in the language, he was familiar with the root of the word when he was recruited from the campus of Georgetown University in Washington six years earlier. Afterward, he discovered that DC-area colleges have long been breeding grounds for the nation's intelligence agencies, tapping some of the best and brightest minds in the country. It was flattering, in retrospect, but if he'd known, he might have gone to Stanford.

The CIA has very specific requirements for its agents. They make their pitches based on an intimate knowledge of a subject's life: their finances, alcohol use, criminal record—or lack of one—and predilections of every sort. Their appeals are then made based along the lines of ideology, patriotism, or religion, although it is just as easy to ensnare a potential agent on the basis of ego or greed. In certain scenarios, blackmail or coercion is necessary.

He was an ideological soul. That's where they got him. He believed in the concept of good over evil, in the triumph of democracy over fascism, that Franklin Delano Roosevelt and Winston Churchill had the world's interests at heart when they set out to defeat Hitler during World War II. And the creeping menace of the Cold War, which threatened to undo all the good that had been done, stuck in his craw.

His training took a year. Espionage, he learned, is conducted at five different levels. First comes the planning stage, where ideas are tossed out to see how to get to step two, collecting data. Information is found in a myriad of ways, through both public sources, such as newspapers and archival material, and unofficial means, including informants and stolen secrets. The information is then subject to processing: putting it into a digestible format so that the fourth stage, analysis, can occur, which is the process of turning information into intelligence. The final step, dissemination, is when that intelligence is successfully handed over to the government.

The first few years, he did his job with precision, learning to separate emotion from the cold-blooded truth: that the Cold War wasn't merely an intellectual pursuit but a brutal, deadly one. However, he didn't anticipate the turn it would take in 1960 with a fashion house, a beautiful girl, and an oncoming collision with disaster.

He was an ordinary man with ordinary dreams, until one day the government changed that for him. Because once someone becomes an agent of the federal government, their life no longer belongs to them. It belongs to a higher entity, and the old dreams and old life fall away as if they never existed at all.

# PROLOGUE

Later, she couldn't say how it happened—how a twenty-year-old girl from New York with no money or connections became involved in an international affair—but it happened all the same. Nor could she say how she, Amelia Jocelyn Walker, found herself standing over the body of a man with a revolver in her hand and a hastily repositioned pin in her pillbox hat.

Mia looked at the body sprawled at her feet and then at the gun, which was still smoking. Although she hadn't expected anyone to die, there was no doubting her role in these terrible events. The acrid smell of gunpowder filled the room, and she lowered the weapon in her hand as she debated what to do.

She didn't want to admit it, but her current circumstances had come about the way all girls are made unwitting accomplices in crimes: trusting people in a world where no one can be trusted. For the world in 1961 wasn't the beleaguered decade of the forties, when the war had been the focus of everyone's lives, nor was it the quiet rebuilding of lives in the fifties, when Americans aspired to some sense of normalcy.

The decade of the sixties was an entirely different beast, even at its onset. People coming of age in that era were aware of the Cold War lurking in the background of their lives, East versus West. Yet over time, as is so often the case, the American people became inured to the distant threat and relegated it to the back of their minds. After all, there were more immediate things to think about. Fashion was changing. Harper Lee startled the literary world with her masterpiece *To Kill a Mockingbird*. Civil rights demonstrators began to stage sit-ins at lunch counters across the country. America was in the process of moving from the conservative presidency of Dwight D. Eisenhower, a steady anchor of the nation during the 1950s, to the notably younger and more progressive administration of John F. Kennedy.

By 1961, most women were more interested in the life and fashion of their new First Lady than in international politics, Mia included, though she could perhaps be forgiven, being only twenty at the time.

Now, however, the body in front of her demanded her attention. Sliding the Colt .32 neatly into her pocketbook, she glanced up, catching her reflection in the mirror. She almost didn't recognize the face staring back at her. Of course, there were the familiar deep-brown eyes and wide lips, her chestnut hair pinned in a flawless chignon. Apart from slightly pink cheeks, she looked completely normal. But there was a veneer of sophistication and hardness that had never been there before. Her clothing was the only thing that was out of place. The blue Jacqueline Kennedy tailored skirt and matching jacket was meant for lunch at Les Deux Magots or strolling along the Seine, as if she were in a Deneuve film. Instead, she was standing over a body in a flat she had never been in before.

Mia made a quick calculation. A man was dead, a man who had trusted her. She bent over him, checking his pockets to see if he had anything that might link him to her, finding nothing. Then she stood, making certain nothing in the room was out of place. After slipping on her gloves, she turned off the lights and opened the door a crack before stepping into the corridor and locking it behind her.

She didn't hurry as she walked to the staircase, then made her way down four flights of stairs. In the lobby, where the concierge was handing over a packet of mail to one of the residents, she locked her eyes on the door and went toward it with as normal a pace as she could manage. Outside, she turned left, toward the Jardin du Luxembourg, trying to calm her nerves. It was a fine morning. The sun was shining, and the blustery wind, which had terrorized Paris just the day before, had blown its way toward Strasbourg and into Germany, leaving behind a perfect summer day.

She strolled along the Rue des Écoles, looking at it as if for the first time. The windows of the buildings she passed were open as

Parisians welcomed the good weather, pots of geraniums in riotous reds and pinks dotting the balconies. Passing the Sorbonne, she noticed a crowd of people coming and going. Mia had long wanted to go into one of the buildings and look around, envious of the stacks of books the students carried under their arms. Life held untold opportunities for them, she thought, wondering what she might have studied if she'd had the chance. Now, of course, it was a moot question. She was there to do a job, and then a job within a job, and it was too late to think of anything else.

A couple of blocks away, she spied a patisserie and went inside. It was a relief to be off the street in a nearly empty shop, although she knew that nowhere was truly safe. Opening her pocketbook, she ordered coffee and a croissant. She placed a handful of francs on the counter as the man handed her a small paper sack and a cup of coffee, which she proceeded to carry to the park.

She found a quiet area in the shade of the chestnut trees, where she sat in one of the ubiquitous green metal chairs. Steam rose from the coffee, which she did not sip. She might look composed on the outside, but inside her rib cage, her heart was racing. Setting the cup on the ground, she opened the bag and removed the croissant, which she proceeded to feed to the pigeons clustered at her feet. Then she took the revolver from her pocketbook and slipped it into the bag, crumpling it up as small as it would go. She rose from her chair and found an empty rubbish bin, tossing it inside.

Mia wandered through the gardens, wishing there was someone

she could talk to who could help her make sense of what had happened. None of her fellow models at the House of Rousseau were reliable, and none of the men, however genial and accommodating they had been, were trustworthy, either. Even her roommates were not above suspicion.

She thought of speaking to Madame Fournier, who lived in the apartment next door. The older woman kept to herself, as most of their neighbors did, although it was clear she did not appreciate having a trio of young women in the adjacent flat who were prone to late nights and constant socializing. At the apartment where she had grown up in New York, Mia was used to busybodies and the gossip that arose when so many people lived in a single building and had expected such from the woman next door. Madame Fournier, however, did not pry or scold them, as the concierge sometimes did. She was polite, if frosty, in her demeanor.

But of course, Mia couldn't speak to anyone without putting them in danger, and neither could she suddenly flee back home to the United States. She would be found as surely as the sun rises in the morning. There was still another piece of evidence to dispose of, and she had to buy some time one way or another to figure out what to do.

Because one thing she knew for certain: her life depended on it.

# 1

---

The day she arrived in Paris, the colors were so strong and sharp that it was as if Mia had lived the first twenty years of her life in black and white. Everything was a feast for the eyes: vivid-yellow ranunculus in flower-shop buckets, electric-orange vespas and bistro chairs tucked under tables at each corner café, red Métro signs at the entrances of the underground railways. And the doors. She had never seen anything like them: deepest burgundies, delicious but indescribable French blues, jade greens—all worn and peeling but so stunning she could hardly take her eyes off them.

She was being driven by a young man named Luca Rossi, who worked for the House of Rousseau and had announced he would be escorting her around Paris for the foreseeable future. When he met her at the airport, she was taken aback by his dark, Italian good looks, but he was so down to earth that she overcame her usual reticence and got into a car with him.

"How was your trip, Miss Walker?" he asked, changing lanes smoothly in the clog of traffic congestion. "Or may I call you Mia? Everyone at the House of Rousseau becomes great friends, working so closely together."

His accent was thick, but his English was impeccable. His hair, while longer than she was used to, was freshly cut. His jaw was strong and his Roman nose commanding, but it was his dark, piercing eyes that drew one in and demanded attention.

"Mia's fine," she replied, trying to stay awake. "I'm sorry. I'm a little tired. I didn't sleep much on the airplane."

"Not to worry," he said, concentrating on the road ahead of him. "Everyone is exhausted after an international flight. But tomorrow you'll feel better, and we can really see the sights of Paris."

"What's it like, working at Rousseau?" she asked. "And what about my roommates? Do you know them?"

"Rousseau is an exciting place to work," he replied. "Something is always happening. And both of your roommates are wonderful girls. You'll like them both."

Mia leaned back in her seat, watching automobiles zipping past as Parisians went about their business. She wasn't used to traveling in a car, particularly not one so small. At home, she either took the bus or walked, her world limited to the apartment she had shared with her father until he passed away a few months earlier and the bakery where she tended the counter and swept the floors. Now she was in France. It was incomprehensible to her that her life had changed so monumentally in only a matter of weeks.

"How did you know where to pick me up?" she asked.

"Theo told me when you were expected," he answered. "He said you were coming from New York, so I knew where to find you."

Mia stole a glance in his direction. "Do you know him well? Theo, I mean?"

"Of course," Luca answered, holding the steering wheel loosely despite the speed at which they were traveling. "He's an excellent employer."

Theo Gillette, who worked for the fashion designer Marcel Rousseau, had appeared in the bakery where Mia worked just a week earlier. She had noticed him come into the shop several times and assumed he was new to the area. One day, as she was leaving work, she found him waiting nearby. Some of the other girls from the bakery had been approached by men, but Mia had never expected it to happen to her. He was twenty years older than she was, at least, with blondish-brown hair combed back and a neatly trimmed mustache. His suit was of an elegant cut, the likes of which they rarely saw in their neighborhood, and he smiled as she approached. She tried to think of something to say to discourage him, but he began before she could even speak.

"I want to offer you a job," he said, preempting her protest.

"A job?" she repeated, shocked. That was the last thing she'd expected him to say. "What sort of job?"

This was not the way proper young women found work. Everyone knew that. They stood in lines at department stores and restaurants and offices, filled out the appropriate paperwork, and waited through a long series of rejections before something was finally offered to them. Jobs—and certainly good jobs—were not offered at the drop of a hat by a stranger on the street.

"I'd like to sit down with you to discuss it," he said. "There's a coffee shop around the corner if you are available now."

Mia shook her head. "I'm not interested."

"Ten minutes of your time," he replied, holding up his hands. "That's all I need, and then you are free to go."

Perhaps it was the knowledge that the funds in her bank account were dwindling or the fact that she was struggling to find a smaller apartment, but she found herself falling into step beside him.

"My name is Theo Gillette," he said. "May I ask yours?"

"Mia Walker."

"Miss Walker, I think you will find that this meeting will be worth your time."

"Ten minutes," she insisted.

They walked around the corner to the nearest diner, where he held the door open. Even though it was only four o'clock, the place was nearly full. He followed her to a table by the window and held out her chair. Mia sat, clutching her handbag as he took a seat across from her. He reached into his coat pocket and extracted a thin envelope, then pushed it toward her. There were no markings on it of any kind.

"What is it?" she asked.

"Open it and see for yourself."

Inside, Mia found a single slip of paper. She pulled it out, blinking when she realized what it was: an Air France ticket from New York to Paris. The date on the ticket was just over a week away.

"I can't take this," she said, stuffing it back into the envelope and sliding it toward him. She couldn't leave the country with a strange man for any reason. It was uncomfortable enough just sitting in a café with him. However, he made no move to take it back.

"I represent Marcel Rousseau, a fashion designer in Paris," he said. "We discover models all over the world, most of them from ordinary walks of life. When business brought me to New York a few days ago, you caught my eye."

"I don't understand," she replied.

"I want you to come to Paris and work for the House of Rousseau," he said. A waitress arrived, and he ordered two cups of coffee. When she left, he turned his attention back to her.

"Do you have a passport?"

"Well, yes," she stammered. "But I've never used it."

"Then now is your opportunity to do so."

"I'm no model," she argued. "I have no experience, for one thing."

"We'll train you," he answered. "Many of our models come to us with no previous experience."

"Why me?" she asked.

"You have the look, Miss Walker," he continued, folding his hands. "I knew it the moment I saw you."

"I can't," she replied. She could imagine what her father would have said. "My life is here."

That life, however, had become unstable. Her father was gone. Money was tight. She was going to be forced to move to a smaller apartment by the end of the month. Still, she couldn't cut all ties and go to Paris with a total stranger, even if it were a legitimate offer. This was the place she knew and where she would find a way to start over. There was no other choice.

"You'll make a wonderful model," he said, interrupting her thoughts. "You fly to Paris next Friday morning. At the airport, you will be met by my assistant, who will take you to the apartment you will share with a couple of other models. You won't have to pay rent for the first few months, and you will receive a reasonable salary as well."

"This is too much," she protested.

"It's your opportunity, Miss Walker," he answered. "It's a chance that every girl in New York would die for."

"But I don't know anyone there."

"You'll have two roommates who are about your age. Maeve has been with the House of Rousseau for a couple of years and Elisabeth for almost a year and a half. They'll help you find your footing." He looked at her for a moment. "This is a job, Miss Walker, nothing more. And I, for one, think it is a job that you will do very well. More than well, in fact. I believe you have the potential to become the face of the House of Rousseau."

He stood. Mia took the envelope from the table and held it out to him, but Theo Gillette shook his head.

"If you cannot bring yourself to go to Paris," he said, "then cash in the ticket. But personally, I will hold on to the hope that I will see you in a week on French soil."

He gave a small bow and then left, leaving Mia shaken. She wasn't rich and she wasn't beautiful—certainly not model material. After a few minutes, she tucked the envelope into her pocketbook. She would go home, pack up as much of the apartment as she could, and search the classifieds for a smaller place, one she could afford on her own. When Theo Gillette came back to the bakery, she would return the ticket. No self-respecting young woman would take something worth so much from a stranger.

But he did not return to the bakery the next day, or the next. Every evening, she looked at the ticket, wondering how anyone could possibly leave such a valuable sum with someone they didn't even know. She imagined that most young women in her position would have cashed it in immediately without even caring whether he would come back or not. But still, she waited for him to return.

The apartment looked emptier by the day. In fact, it was almost unrecognizable. She donated her father's clothing to charity and sold his books, eight or ten at a time, to bookshops. She gave most of the kitchen supplies to the young couple who lived on the floor above her and brought the plants to the rooftop garden they shared with the rest of their neighbors. It was difficult to part with so many memories, but there was no other choice. Things had changed, whether she wanted them to or not. Holding on to the past wouldn't bring her father back.

The past, however, had its own complications. She was reminded of them again when sorting through her father's things and she came across a file she had never seen before. With shaking hands, she opened it and flipped through the contents. She lifted a card and then slapped it back inside, taking the entire thing down to the incinerator of her building to destroy it forever.

The following day, she found a one-room apartment several blocks away. It was small, but there was room for a bed, a chair, and a bureau. The kitchen was even tinier than the one she was leaving, with counter space barely large enough to hold a plate, but the rent was affordable, and above all, it was clean.

At the end of the week, however, Mia realized Theo Gillette wasn't coming back to get the ticket. She decided to cash it in, after all. There was no sense wasting perfectly good money because of her pride. With only two days until it had to be used, she walked to the bus stop. She glanced at a newsstand and saw that Jacqueline Kennedy had made the cover of another magazine. She bought it, tucking it under her arm, and then took the bus to the airport and found the Air France counter. She opened her pocketbook and placed the ticket on the customer service desk.

"I'd like to cash this in, please," she said.

The clerk, a thirtysomething woman in a crisp airline suit with a matching neckerchief, nodded and took the ticket, then flipped through a book. Mia shifted her weight nervously, wondering if the woman thought she had stolen it. Girls like her didn't have the money for such an extravagance.

"The ticket value is three hundred and seventy-five dollars, miss," the clerk pronounced.

Mia gasped as the woman opened a drawer and took out a stack of twenties, counting them out on the counter. It was practically a fortune. Her rent could be paid for six months. She could fill her kitchen with food. She could take her time and look for a new job. Perhaps she could even think about what she wanted out of life.

She stared at the clerk, suddenly uncertain about what to do. Girls like her were not offered modeling jobs in New York, much less France. Models came from a different class and background. Some worked in the theater or had special training. They didn't tend the counter in small bakeries. Mia was seized by doubt. She wasn't the sort of person to take chances, but if she stayed, she would be giving up her only opportunity to see Paris. It might not be a legitimate offer. But even if it weren't, she reasoned, she could spend a couple of days in France and then come home. She could start over a changed person, one who had seen the most famous city in the world. She glanced at the magazine in her hands, at Senator Kennedy's wife, making a snap decision. After all, Paris had changed Jacqueline

Kennedy, the woman she admired above all others. Perhaps it could change her, too.

She looked at the clerk and shook her head, realizing in that moment that she was going to go. She had enough in her bank account for a ticket home if it all went horribly wrong. The apartment was practically empty, and the room she had planned to rent held no appeal.

"Wait," she said, holding out a hand.

The clerk stopped counting the bills and gave her a look. "Yes, miss?"

"I'm sorry," she murmured. "I've changed my mind."

The woman returned the money to the drawer and slid the ticket back across the desk. Mia took it, wondering if she had the courage to follow it through. She dropped it into her pocketbook and snapped it shut.

Walking back to the bus station, she was shocked at what she had just done. But instead of fear, she felt a surge of something unfamiliar, something akin to hope, the first time she had felt it since her father died. She would see Paris, even if just for a couple of days. An experience like that could change a person's life.

When she arrived home, she took her father's suitcase and opened her closet, mulling over what to pack. She decided on a handful of dresses and a green jacket with a matching skirt. Then she went to the desk and pulled out a manila folder of clippings. The pages torn from newspapers and cut from glossy magazines were photographs of John F. Kennedy's wife, which Mia had collected since the senator had decided to run for president.

Jacqueline Kennedy embodied everything she admired most: elegance, grace, and refinement. Yet she wasn't just beautiful. There was an intelligence in her eyes that set her apart, a spark of determination. Mia sifted through the clippings until she found her favorite. In it, Mrs. Kennedy was standing behind her husband, watching him speak to reporters. Although she stood at the side of the photo, she dominated the picture. Mia wondered what she was like in person. Even though she would never meet her, she longed to have the poise of the politician's wife.

She slid the clippings back into the folder, looping the string around the cardboard buttons to secure them. Then she put the folder into her suitcase and finished packing. An hour later, she stood in the empty apartment, questioning her own judgment. She was taking an enormous risk, but her father used to say that everyone was entitled to at least one mistake. Hers, if she was making one, would be Paris.

Now she had arrived in France. As Luca sped through the city, Mia leaned back against the seat, feeling drained. The last weeks of her father's life had been taxing. Until this moment, she hadn't realized how exhausted she was.

"How did you know who I was at the airport?" she asked, glancing at Luca, trying to take her mind off her fears, which were starting to get the better of her.

"You looked a little lost," he admitted. "Like I was the first time I tried to navigate this place."

"Where is the apartment?" she asked, wondering nervously what her roommates would be like. She had never lived with other young women before. She clutched her handbag, mentally counting the money she had brought with her in case she had to find other accommodations quickly.

"It's in the Latin Quarter, not far from the Sorbonne."

"The Sorbonne?"

"It's one of the universities in Paris," he answered, brushing his hair back with his fingers. "A lot of Americans study there. You'll love the area. It's right in the center of things, perfect for exploring."

Ten minutes later, they arrived in front of a yellowing limestone building on the Rue des Écoles. It was tall, with a zinc-gray mansard roof and black iron railings on the balconies of each window. Narrow chimneys rose from the top of the building under a cloudless sky. Luca wedged the Citroën into a parking space and came around to open her door. She stepped out of the car as he retrieved her case, suddenly nervous as the reality of what she had done finally hit her. He pushed his hair back from his eyes and smiled.

"Your flat is up there," he said, pointing to a window on the third floor. "You'll like your roommates. And I'll be back tomorrow to show you around Paris if you like. I'll see you most weekdays, of course. I usually chauffeur the three of you to work and make certain you are delivered safely to your doorstep each evening. The rest of the time, I run errands for Monsieur Rousseau."

Mia nodded, following him to the door of the building. He opened it with a key, which he then handed to her. She slid it into her pocket as they walked into the foyer. The entry had an ancient glass chandelier and a striking black-and-white-patterned tile floor. The staircase was wide and circular, with moldings and gleaming brass rails, though the wallpaper was peeling at the edges. Luca took her suitcase and headed up the stairs, leaving Mia no choice but to follow.

They trudged up three flights. At the top, a small underfed black cat slithered in front of a door, stopping to glance up at her to determine if she was friend or foe.

"Friend," she murmured in response to the unverbalized question, reaching out a hand to touch his soft fur. He leaned into her hand. "Do you have a name?"

When the door opened, the cat skittered down the hall and out of sight. A young dark-haired woman of Mia's age stood there, and she reached out and took the suitcase from Luca.

"You're the new girl!" she exclaimed with a strong Irish accent. "I'm Maeve Kelly. We were hoping you would make it."

"Mia Walker."

"I'll say goodbye here," Luca said, stuffing his hands into his pockets.

"Thank you for driving me," Mia replied.

He nodded. "I'll see you in the morning to give you a proper look at Paris, when you can really appreciate it."

He waved as he went down the stairs, whistling an unidentifiable tune. Mia turned and followed Maeve into the apartment, wondering if she had made the right decision. Perhaps it was exhaustion or the surreal feeling of being in a foreign country for the first time, but she couldn't begin to imagine what her life would be like the following day, much less six months from now. Only time would tell. But one way or another, she had begun a new chapter of her life, however long or short—this time as an American in Paris.

# 2

---

Rain beat steadily against the windows, rousing Mia from a deep sleep. She stirred in the dark room and sat up, wondering where she was. Then it came to her: she was in Paris, in a flat with two young women she had met only the day before. Her stomach tightened, her nerves getting the better of her. What was she thinking, coming all the way to Paris without any idea of what was going to happen? Propping up on one elbow, she watched the rain as it coursed down the windowpanes. She couldn't tell what time it was, so she reached for her handbag and opened it, pulling out a gold pocket watch that had belonged to her father. She lightly ran her fingers over the face, thinking of her parents. The chain had gone missing years ago, and her mother had threaded a ribbon through the bow. Even after she'd died, her father had never replaced it. Now that they were gone, Mia always kept it with her to remind her of them both.

She sat up, checking the time. It was six thirty in the morning, although she realized that, according to her body clock, it was past noon, and she was starting to feel hungry. She got up and opened the door. From the sound of things, neither of her roommates were awake. Then she remembered it was Sunday morning, and they would probably sleep in late. After shutting the door again, she sat on the bed. The room was small, but it was a roof over her head. A tall wardrobe stood across from the narrow bed, which was layered with blankets. A bedside table had enough room for a book, and a small desk stood to the side of the tall French doors. Mia walked over and opened them, glancing down at the street below.

This, she thought, was Paris. Tall pale limestone buildings. A café just across the road, with tables and chairs outside under the awning, where restauranteurs were preparing for a busy day. Delivery vans were dropping off merchandise at the markets. Mia watched the activity for a while and then closed the French doors.

She lifted her suitcase onto the bed and pulled out her things one by one. First, she placed a photo of her parents on the desk. Then she opened the wardrobe, hung up her dresses, and placed her shoes on the shelf below. There were four small drawers on one side, and she put her few things in the top one, wondering if she would be there long enough to fill any of the others.

Then she tucked the suitcase under the bed and went into the kitchen, finding the larder empty. She poured herself a glass of milk, wondering what they did for food. She was accustomed to cooking for her father, but there was no evidence that any meals had been made here for some time. She returned to her room and crawled back into bed, watching the rain. After a few minutes, she burrowed under the blankets and closed her eyes, listening to the distant echo of car horns and trucks going past in the street. It was not unlike her apartment in New York, and she fell asleep to the familiar, bustling sounds.

When she awakened, she reached for her father's watch. It was past nine. She got up and went out onto the balcony. The rain had stopped, and the air smelled of something she couldn't identify. Although she still didn't hear Maeve or Elisabeth stirring, Paris had woken from its slumber, and the day had begun. Luca hadn't mentioned what time he was picking her up, but she decided to get dressed. When she was ready, she went into the sitting room as Maeve came out of her bedroom, slipping on a robe.

"Good morning," she said. "I was just about to make some coffee."

"I would have made it myself," Mia said, pointing to a contraption on the counter, "but I've never used one of those before."

"It's a French press," Maeve replied, taking a closer look at her. She smiled. "You're already dressed. Are you going somewhere today?"

"Luca is coming over," Mia answered.

"Ah. You're about to see the sights of Paris."

Maeve scooped coffee into the metal filter and plugged in the kettle. Then she threw herself into the pink armchair and stretched her hands above her head. "Wasn't the rain nice? I always sleep better when it rains. It reminds me of home."

Mia nodded, sitting across from her. Her roommates were near her own age, yet they both seemed so worldly and self-assured. She wondered if she would ever feel that way, if living in Paris would change her usual reserved behavior. However, she doubted it. Ingrained habits were hard to change.

"What are you doing today?" she asked.

"Nothing, if I can help it," Maeve replied.

"How about coming with us to look at the city, then?" Mia asked.

She wasn't used to being alone with a man, especially one as attractive as Luca. Perhaps it was because she had spent the last two years caring for her father, but men had never been part of the equation. She had been focused on one thing: trying to help him get well.

Maeve shook her head. "That sounds too much like work. I love doing absolutely nothing on Sundays. Don't tell me you're one of those conscientious types who is up at the crack of dawn, raring to go."

Before she could answer, Elisabeth came into the room. Both of them were striking young women. It was no wonder they had been chosen to model for the House of Rousseau. Maeve had curly black hair and sharp gray-green eyes that matched her personality, but Elisabeth was more classically beautiful, with elegant features and warm hazel eyes. Of the two, she was more approachable, and Mia instantly felt comfortable with her. Elisabeth flicked a blond lock behind her shoulders and smiled.

"Is someone making coffee?" she asked.

"The water's about to boil," Maeve answered.

"You're up early," Elisabeth remarked, turning to Mia. "Must be the time change. I thought you'd sleep away the day."

"I hope I didn't wake you."

Elisabeth smiled. "Oh, don't worry about that. We sleep like the dead. Wait until you've worked here for a while. You'll see what I mean."

She grabbed a banana from a bowl and went over to the window, looking down at the street below.

"How long have you been with the House of Rousseau?" Mia asked.

"A year and a half, I think, but it feels like forever." Elisabeth turned to Maeve, who was unplugging the kettle. "Don't you think so?"

The Irish girl nodded. "I can hardly remember doing anything else."

"What's it like?" Mia asked. She had no idea what happened at a fashion house or what a modeling life would entail.

"You've never modeled before?" Maeve asked.

"No," Mia admitted.

"You've been thrown in the deep end," Elisabeth said. "I don't blame you for being nervous. I was, too, when I started."

"It's a whirlwind life," Maeve remarked. "There will be fittings, and practices, and modeling events. But don't worry—we'll be there to help you figure everything out."

"Do you like working there?" Mia asked.

"Of course," Elisabeth replied. "I can't imagine what sort of life I'd have if I'd stayed home in Sweden. I would probably be working in my brother's antique shop, or maybe in a restaurant. Nothing as fabulous as modeling."

"Do you miss home, though?"

"Not really," she answered. "But I'm lucky. I can visit a few times a year. I suppose it will be harder for you to get home to see your family back in the States."

"I don't have any family," Mia replied. "My mother passed away when I was young, and my father just a few months ago."

"I'm sorry," Elisabeth said. "You know, you'll have to come to Sweden with me sometime. You'd love it."

"Which part of the country do you live in?" Mia asked.

"I'm from the south, near Copenhagen. Some of my friends live there, so I always visit when I go. I'll take you with me next time. Maeve came home with me for Easter, and she really liked it."

"I did," Maeve said. "Here. Try this."

She handed Mia a steaming cup, waiting as she tasted it. Mia grimaced. It was stronger than any coffee she'd ever had before. She set it down quickly, and Maeve shook her head.

"She's not ready for your coffee yet," Elisabeth remarked, smiling. "It took me ages to be able to drink it. Now I don't want anything else."

"I should finish getting ready," Mia said. "Luca should be here soon."

In her room, Mia looked down at her dress, hoping it was

acceptable. She scrutinized herself in the mirror, wondering what Theo had seen in her that had caused him to bring her all the way to France. Maeve and Elisabeth were glamorous—stunning, even. She was an ordinary girl with nothing to recommend her.

"Stop," she said, looking at her reflection.

She couldn't start out with so little confidence, or she would surely fail. Straightening her shoulders, she applied a layer of gloss to her lips. Then she reached for her father's watch but realized it wasn't on the table.

Mia looked down at the floor to make certain she hadn't dropped it. She would never be able to forgive herself if she had broken it. After checking inside her handbag, she set it on the table and bent to look under the bed.

It wasn't there. She searched every surface, pulling the blankets from the bed in case she had dropped it, but it was nowhere to be found. A feeling of panic came over her. That watch was her final link to her father. She had carried it with her everywhere since he had passed away. She went into the sitting room to ask if either of the other girls had seen it but found she couldn't even form the question. She couldn't accuse them of taking it when she hadn't even been there for twenty-four hours. Besides, she hadn't seen or heard anyone go into her room. It had to be there somewhere.

There was a rap at the door, and Mia took a deep breath, resolving to pull the room apart later. Of course she would find it. Perhaps she had placed it in the wardrobe, or it had fallen inside a pillowcase.

Something like that couldn't simply disappear from the room. Trying to regain her composure, she opened the door to find that Luca was waiting.

"You're here," she said, unexpectedly relieved to see him.

"I hope I'm not too early," he answered.

"Not at all," Mia replied, shaking her head. "I've been up for ages."

"She's an early bird, this one," Maeve said.

"Not really," she protested, although it was true. Working at a bakery had made an early riser of her. She turned to Luca, feeling flustered. "What are we going to do today?"

"Let's make it a surprise," he said. "Come on."

Mia grabbed her pocketbook and scarf and followed him down the stairs. He led her down the street to his car and held the door open.

"Sorry I couldn't get any closer," he said. "Parking is often difficult here."

"It's fine," she said, tying the scarf under her chin.

"The first thing everyone wants to see is the Eiffel Tower," he said, backing out of the small space. "So we'll head there first."

He pulled onto the street so quickly, she had to grab the dashboard. Luca shifted gears, maneuvering around the other cars with skill. Mia steadied herself, watching him weave in and out of traffic.

"Are you nervous?" he asked, his eyes on the road in front of him. "About coming to France, I mean."

"I suppose so," she confessed.

"Don't worry if it takes a while to adjust to things," he replied, glancing at her. "I'm sure everything is different here than the life you've been living before, but you'll get used to it. Everyone does."

"How long have you been here?" Mia asked.

"I moved here from Milano with some friends almost five years ago," he replied. "It's fun to see the world, no?"

Ten minutes later, the Eiffel Tower came into view. As they got out of the car, Mia stared up at the wrought-iron lattice, so familiar from books and pictures, unable to believe she was seeing it now with her own eyes. This was why she had come to Paris. It was even more impressive than she had imagined, and her eyes traveled up with the elevator as it rose from street level.

"Would you like to go up in it?" he asked as they made their way through the crowds.

People milled about everywhere, sunning themselves on the park grounds, standing in line for tickets, eating ice cream from vendors with *Glace* signs above their counters. Shielding her eyes with her hand, she looked up at the brave souls who stood on the upper deck of the tower. It was dizzyingly high.

She shook her head. "Maybe next time."

"Of course," he said. "I was going to suggest ice cream, but I bet you are ready for some proper food."

Mia nodded gratefully. "Actually, I am."

"There's a café just a few minutes' walk from here."

He took her hand, and they made their way through the crowd, past a large colorful carousel where a long line of children waited for a turn. Then he led her down a quiet neighborhood street, and soon they were standing outside a café. They took a table outside as a waiter in a white jacket came over to offer them a menu. Luca waved it away, ordering in rapid-fire French.

"I ordered a couple of American hamburgers," he said, when the waiter had gone. "I thought you might want to ease into French food slowly."

"Thank you," Mia replied. "How did you learn to speak French so well?"

"I went out with a French girl for a while," he said, shrugging. "And the longer I stayed here, the more I improved. Speaking of French, your lessons will start tomorrow, in case you didn't know."

"Lessons?" Mia said, looking up. "What do you mean, 'lessons'?"

"You'll be working with Madame Laurent," Luca replied. "She helps all the new girls. Over the next couple of weeks, you'll be learning some basic French and touring some of the cultural sites around the city."

"What's she like?" Mia asked, finding herself disappointed that Luca hadn't been assigned to the task.

"She's wonderful," he said. "Everyone loves Madame Laurent."

"Does that mean I won't start work at the fashion house right away?" she asked. She had been nervous about seeing Theo Gillette again, but now she was being handed off to another stranger.

"That's right," he answered. "They ease you into it."

*So many changes*, she thought. And nothing was what she had expected it to be.

After lunch, Luca pushed back his chair.

"Come on," he said. "There's something I want to show you."

They wandered back toward the Eiffel Tower, where he led her to a line at the edge of the river.

"This is the way to see Paris for the first time," he said. "By boat."

Within minutes, they were gliding down the river. Luca pointed out the sights one by one: the Musée d'Orsay, the Louvre, Notre Dame, famous places she had seen in schoolbooks. She couldn't help feeling overwhelmed by it all.

"I can't believe I'm here," she confessed. "I almost didn't come, you know."

"I'm glad you did," he replied, leaning over the railing. "Paris is the most beautiful city in the world."

They cruised for most of an hour, having gone up the Seine and turned around, leisurely making their way back again. When they disembarked, they walked back to the car.

"Just one more thing to see today," he said, "and then I'll take you home."

He drove down a few quiet streets. Mia took off her scarf and tied it around the handle of her pocketbook. She couldn't imagine a more perfect day. It hadn't been a mistake, she thought, taking a chance on Paris, whether she decided to stay or not. A couple of minutes later, he pulled in front of a tall building. Then he turned off the engine and smiled.

"*Eh, voilà!*" he said.

"What is it?" she asked. As far as she could tell, it was just another handsome French building. Paris was full of them.

"This is the House of Rousseau," he answered.

Mia stared at him for a moment and then looked back at the name affixed onto the building. She tugged at the handle of her door, stepping onto the pavement.

The wide double doors were painted a shiny black, with two tall topiary trees on either side, and the windows flanking them were large, each designed with a pair of gray chairs and a gown on display between them. In the window to the left was an evening dress of pale-blue silk on a headless mannequin, a strand of pearls wound about its throat. Mia had never seen such a stunning dress in person. It was even harder to imagine that someday, she might wear one like it. She stood before it for a few minutes and then went over to look in the other window.

There, the mannequin was dressed in the most exquisite wedding gown she had ever seen. It had a high neck, with lace on the bodice and sleeves, over a satin dress. Underneath the lace, it had a sweetheart neckline, curving down delicately, with a full skirt cascading from under the narrow waist.

A pair of pearl-encrusted slippers stood on the floor next to the dress, as if the bride had slipped them off for a moment. She could imagine a lucky young woman taking a long last look in a mirror before reluctantly allowing her mother to unbutton the satin buttons on the back of the dress and help her take it off, never to be worn again. It was a dream of a dress, simple in style, yet of such elegant lines that if one were to wear it, or even see it, it would never be forgotten.

She hadn't made a mistake trusting Theo Gillette after all. She was going to be modeling for a prestigious French fashion house, changing her life in the most unimaginable of ways. She stared at the gown, transfixed, before she realized that Luca was standing beside her.

"It's nice, isn't it?" he asked.

"It's the most beautiful thing I've ever seen."

He stood so close, she could hear him breathing. A ripple of something indefinable went down her spine. Until this moment, Paris had seemed as unreal as a fairy tale. Now the world suddenly seemed large, looming with possibilities.

"Just think," he said. "Soon, you'll be wearing some of these beautiful gowns yourself."

She nodded, not trusting herself to speak. A week ago, she was sweeping floors in a Brooklyn bakery, and now she had just experienced the most wonderful day of her life. She only wished her father were alive so she could tell him about it.

They drove back to the flat in silence, lost in thought. When they arrived, she stepped out of the car and smiled.

"Thank you, Luca," she said. "This was a perfect day."

"This was nothing," he answered. "Just wait until tomorrow when you meet Madame Laurent. That's when your education will truly begin."

He waved and was gone before she could even reply.

# 3

---

The flat was empty when Mia arrived. She went straight to her bedroom to look for the pocket watch when something shiny caught her eye. Snatching up the watch from under the bedside table, she breathed a sigh of relief, turning it over to inspect it for any damage. Fortunately, there was none.

She must have dropped it, although she was certain she had looked there. Of course, that had been hours ago, and she was so tired that she might not have been paying attention. Mia resolved to buy an alarm clock and she would tuck the watch away for safekeeping. She couldn't take any chances with something so irreplaceable.

Still, she wouldn't want either of her roommates in her room looking through her belongings. Some things were meant to remain private. It had been wise to destroy her father's file, she realized. The past was behind her now, and that was where it had to stay.

A key turned in the lock, and she followed the sound into the sitting room, where Elisabeth and Maeve were letting themselves in. They each carried a bag, which they deposited in the tiny kitchen.

"How was your day?" Maeve asked, unpacking one of the bags and setting things onto the counter.

"I've never seen anything like it," Mia replied, coming over to give them a hand. "Paris is such a beautiful city. And we went by the fashion house, too. I can't believe I'm going to be working there."

"I knew you'd love it," Elisabeth answered.

"Tell me about the job," Mia said. "Do we work Monday through Fridays? Are there regular eight-hour days?"

"Sometimes," Maeve answered. "But it's an erratic business. Some days are full, with fittings and practicing on the catwalk; others are study days, when we learn about the garments we're going to model. We find out as much as we can about each outfit we wear so we can describe them for the customers."

"Occasionally we get a day off here and there, which is nice," Elisabeth added. "It makes up for the times when we have an evening event. I think you're going to enjoy it."

"I know I do," Maeve replied. "I was working as a secretary in Dublin, and I have to tell you, nothing compares to the freedom and fun we're having here."

"Come on," Elisabeth said, placing the groceries on the counter. "Take a look at this, Mia. We've decided not to let you starve. We went to the market on the corner."

"We don't keep a lot of food in the flat, since there isn't much room," Maeve admitted. "We go out for dinner most evenings, so we usually just keep a few things around, mostly fruits and vegetables."

"And bread and cheese," Elisabeth said, nodding. "And of course, there's wine."

Maeve laughed. "Always wine."

Mia watched as they made a tray of food and placed it on the trunk in the small room. She and Elisabeth sat on the sofa and Maeve in the armchair across from them.

"Luca says that I will be starting lessons with Madame Laurent tomorrow," Mia said, taking a carrot from one of the plates. "Who is she? What's she like?"

"She's the most interesting person I've met in Paris," Elisabeth answered, setting her wineglass on the table. "She knows everything about the city. Spending time with her is my favorite thing I've done in France."

Maeve nodded. "None of the other houses have someone like her, who not only works with the designers but with the models as well. She usually gives you lessons for a week or two, sometimes longer."

Elisabeth poured Mia a glass of wine. "It makes the transition to a new job in a new city much easier. Monsieur Rousseau wants all his girls to understand who we are in the scheme of things."

"In other words, we're not just typical models," Maeve explained. "We're women who understand the importance of fashion and the value it holds in the world, like art or music or theater."

Mia was impressed. A week ago, she had no idea what she was getting herself into, but suddenly, she knew it was important— something she could be proud of, if she worked hard and took the time to learn her craft.

"Did you have a nice time exploring?" Maeve asked.

Mia nodded. "We took a cruise on the river."

"It's a beautiful day for it," Elisabeth answered.

"It's Paris," Maeve replied. "Even if it's raining, it's beautiful."

Mia began to relax. She had been living a solitary life for far too long. Even when her father was alive, she was shut away from people her own age. There was a whole world out there, she realized, and now she was going to be part of it. The thought was both exciting and terrifying, even though she had already done the difficult task of traveling across the ocean in search of a fresh start.

"I meant to tell you, we have a few people coming over tonight," Elisabeth said.

"Who?" Mia asked.

Her roommate shrugged. "I've asked over a few girls from Rousseau so you can get acquainted. And we may have a couple of theater friends who will stop by."

"I'll set out the champagne glasses," Maeve said. "We have to celebrate our newest arrival."

Mia looked at the small room. "This is lovely, but how do you manage to have guests?"

Elisabeth laughed. "It's Paris, Mia. Everything is possible. And when it gets too crowded in here, we drift out into the street and find a nice place for a drink."

By seven o'clock, the flat was full, and Mia had taken up a position near the wine bottle, where she poured a glass for everyone who wanted a refill, giving herself time to take everything in. People flitted around the room like dragonflies, lighting here and there for a moment, discussing art, literature, and music. Elisabeth put a record on the stereo, and strains of "It's All in the Game" reverberated around the room as a suave older man walked up and leaned against the counter next to her.

"I haven't seen you before," he said, raising a brow. "Are you a new Rousseau girl?"

"I start in a week or so," she replied.

"Rousseau knows what they're doing, that's for sure," he said, looking her up and down. He lit a cigarette and held out the silver case for her to take one but pocketed it again when she shook her head. "I'll bet you need someone to show you around Paris."

She shifted her weight uncomfortably, wondering how to answer him, when Maeve sidled up next to them and set her glass on the counter.

"Don't worry, Antoine. She's seeing the sights, all right." She made a shooing motion with her hands. "Besides, a girl needs a little experience before she's ready for you."

He shrugged and walked away.

"Thank you," Mia said. "I had no idea what to say to him."

Maeve glanced at the wine bottle. "By the way, don't be so generous with the wine. Just pour an inch at a time. We want to make it last for a while."

Mia nodded, chastened. Guests came and went, but the party carried on for three interminable hours. When the final visitor left, she kicked off her shoes and turned to her roommates, ready to help clean up the flat, but both Elisabeth and Maeve said good night and went to bed. Mia stared at the wineglasses strewn about the room before rounding them up and rinsing them in the small sink, hoping against hope that it wouldn't be a regular occurrence.

The following day, armed with directions from Elisabeth, Mia made her way to a building a quarter mile away. She found the address easily. Tall wrought-iron gates stood ajar, allowing her to walk into the courtyard inside, where there was a large tree-filled garden. Wood violets and peonies bloomed in the shade between gray wooden benches. After she had taken a few steps inside, the noise of the city seemed to fade away. As she stood admiring it, a woman came out of the building and walked over to her.

"You must be Mia Walker," she said. "I'm Vivienne Laurent."

"It's very nice to meet you, Madame," Mia replied.

Madame Laurent was perhaps forty, an attractive woman with perfectly coiffed blond hair and a pale linen suit. On her left wrist, she wore a thick gold bangle.

"I see you like our little garden," she remarked.

"It's lovely."

"Won't you come inside?" she asked, gesturing toward the house behind her. "We must get acquainted."

Mia followed her into the building. Madame Laurent's flat was on the second floor, and they went up a large marble staircase and through an open door. Mia followed her inside the room, which was unlike anything she had ever seen. The tall ceilings and woodwork were painted a warm white. The doors were made of pine, the brass knobs newly shined. Expansive bookshelves were filled with books and art, plush sofas and chairs were gathered around the marble fireplace, and large gold-framed mirrors hung on the walls. Blue and white jardinieres were filled with plants, bringing life to the room. It was simple yet elegant, perfectly arranged to draw one in.

Madame Laurent was as sophisticated as her flat. She was slight and tall, making Mia wonder if she had perhaps been a model herself once. Madame gestured for her to sit in a chair next to her, where she lifted a teapot to pour two cups of tea. She handed one to Mia and indicated the cream and sugar bowls, but Mia shook her head.

"I imagine everything must seem very strange to you right now," Madame said, taking a sip from her cup.

"It is," Mia replied. "I feel like I have fallen into an entirely new world."

"A world I believe you will enjoy," Madame Laurent remarked. "And if you agree, we shall spend a little time together for a few days to let you learn a little something of our country. Is this your first trip abroad?"

"Yes, Madame."

"For many of the girls I work with, it is their first opportunity to see Paris, and we want to give you some context so that you may appreciate what it means to represent our lovely city."

"That's very kind of you."

"I love it, in fact," Madame Laurent continued. "One might say I am a proud ambassador for France."

They finished their tea and set their cups on the tray. Mia smoothed her skirt. She couldn't help feeling like she was interviewing for the position, even though it had already been given to her.

"This is my usual plan," Madame said, folding her hands on her lap. "We meet here for an hour or so each morning to teach you a few basic French phrases and vocabulary that will make your life easier. And then we will venture abroad and educate ourselves about the world around us."

"Yes, Madame," Mia said.

"Then we shall begin," Madame replied, nodding. "First, we shall discuss the proper way to greet someone."

She handed Mia a notebook to make notes, and they worked for about an hour. She taught her several basic phrases, asking her to repeat them over and over. Eventually, she brought out a tray of sandwiches and a fresh pot of tea.

"We must have sustenance," she said. "There is a lot of walking involved in learning about our city."

After lunch, they gathered their things and left the building. Everywhere Mia looked, she saw something unexpected. People bicycling home with baguettes in their baskets, impossibly small cars navigating narrow lanes, the bustling culture of outdoor cafés, shops with curiosities in the windows that she had never seen before. As they crossed the bridge facing the cathedral, a violinist played for a small audience, and along the waterfront, artists were focused on their easels, making renderings of Notre Dame in chalk or oils. The city was vibrantly alive. New York had a bustling culture, but this was different. All around them was a greater zest for living than she had ever experienced before.

Notre Dame was as impressive up close as it had been when she had seen it from the boat with Luca the day before. They approached the west side of the building, where there were three arched doorways below two immense towers with a round stained glass window between them. Hundreds of yards above, perched on the side of the building, gargoyles stared down, daring them to enter.

However, Vivienne Laurent was not the sort of woman to be daunted by the staring eyes of gargoyles. Mia followed the Frenchwoman through the doors, music echoing through the chamber. As they made their way down a corridor, Madame Laurent pointed out the significance of the statues and stained glass windows. Mia could hardly take it all in, wondering how she of all people had been chosen by Theo to come to France for this extraordinary adventure. The education she had received in a mere two days had already changed her life. After they finished touring the cathedral, Madame led her back outside.

"Do you see this?" Madame Laurent said, pointing to a round circle of stone set into the pavement in front of them. It had a star in the center and bore the legend, *Point Zero des Routes de France.*

"What is it?" Mia asked.

"This is the point from which all travel is measured in France," she replied. "Take a coin and drop it onto the star, and you may make a wish."

Mia took a penny from her bag and held it tightly, wondering what she could possibly wish for. She couldn't have her parents back. She didn't want to resume the life she had been living before, which now seemed dull compared to Paris. Life had been so turned upside down over the past few days that she couldn't think of a single thing to wish for. She tossed the penny onto the star anyway, watching Madame's satisfied nod.

On the second day, they visited the Jardin du Luxembourg. A grand building stood on one end of the extensive grounds, near a fountain where children were casting boats from side to side. The gardens were uncrowded, but small groups of people strolled about the grounds and sat in the shade of the towering elms that dotted the landscape. Madame Laurent and Mia walked through the park, scattering pigeons as they went.

THE KENNEDY GIRL · 47
"This is the Palais du Luxembourg," Madame said as they approached the building. "It was once the house of kings. Louis XIII and his mother, Marie de' Medici, lived there. Later, during the French Revolution, it was used as a prison, and then it became the residence of Napoleon Bonaparte, who appreciated its finer qualities. Two years ago, the Palais became home to the French Senate. Now you are looking at the building where state business is conducted."

"I can't believe I'm here," Mia confessed. "Although I have to admit, I'm not sure I'm model material. I don't have any experience. It doesn't seem fair that I've been given an opportunity like this."

"I can already tell by looking at you that you made the right decision," Madame Laurent remarked as they walked down the path. "You have an elegance about you. Give it just a little time, and you will see what I mean."

The following day, they visited the Louvre, returning twice more to explore the museum to its fullest. But there were other museums to see as well. Mia was especially taken with the gardens of the Musée Rodin.

"And what of this?" Madame asked, drawing her attention to a statue to her left as they explored the grounds. "Do you recognize this sculpture?"

"It's called *The Thinker*," Mia replied, relieved that she knew the answer. "We learned about it in school."

"*Oui, Le Penseur*," Madame Laurent said. "This is the sculpture garden, which I find particularly peaceful. I like to walk through it in silence and allow myself to absorb the beauty of it all."

For two weeks, they worked on her French, explored the city, and added to her once-minimal knowledge of art, architecture, and design. It seemed as if Mia had been destined to meet and be educated by Madame Laurent, who served as a private finishing school of sorts for a young woman who had never expected it whatsoever.

In the evenings, when Maeve and Elisabeth were often out, she pored over her notes, repeating the now-familiar phrases to herself until they felt natural. She could greet Madame in French, "*Bonjour, Madame Laurent. Où allons-nous aujourd'hui?*" She could ask about the time and the weather, and order basic items from a menu. She learned her *gauche* from her *droite* and could ask for help in shops, all the while soaking up the masters of painting and sculpture and design.

At the end of the two weeks, she went through the courtyard and knocked on Madame's door.

After their lesson, Madame brought a tray of small quiches and placed them on the table.

"I'm afraid today is our last day together," she said, lifting the teapot and pouring tea into two delicate porcelain cups.

Mia leaned forward. "Our last day?"

She had forgotten that Elisabeth had told her to expect only a short time with Madame Laurent. The last two weeks had been the best of her entire life, cocooning her in Madame's world of culture and gentility.

"Not to worry," Madame continued. "I've saved something wonderful for last."

"I can't believe our time is over," Mia said. "I've loved every minute of it."

"You're a very good student, Mia," she replied. "I've worked with several of Monsieur Rousseau's girls, and you have been the most eager of them all. Of course, now you will be in the business of learning about fashion. But before you do, we shall have one more exquisite day enjoying Paris."

"Can you tell me about Monsieur Rousseau? How long ago did he start the firm?"

"It's been fifteen years," Madame Laurent answered. "He's a creative genius. I've been privileged to work in various positions at Rousseau, but in recent years, he offered me the chance to work with his newest models, which I love to do."

"What do you know of Theo Gillette?" Mia asked. "He's the one who hired me."

"He's been with Monsieur Rousseau from the beginning," the woman replied. "His expertise at running the business leaves Monsieur Rousseau free to concentrate his energy on fashion and design. The House of Rousseau, like all the best fashion houses, is a well-oiled machine."

"I can't wait to see it," Mia said, wondering if she would fit in and feel comfortable working there. She wanted to ask more about Madame Laurent's experiences at Rousseau, but the older woman suddenly stood.

"Come, we must make the most of our final day together."

After lunch, Madame called for a cab, and they were driven across the city to Montmartre, where they stopped in front of a structure the likes of which Mia had never seen before.

Small metal railway cars traveled up and down a steep incline on the hill.

"This is the *funiculaire*," Madame said. "And we are heading to the Sacré-Coeur."

They climbed aboard and Mia clung to a rail as the car jerked into motion. It took less than two minutes to reach the top, where they found themselves on a large balcony overlooking the city. She could see the Eiffel Tower in the distance, as well as a thousand monuments and buildings. Behind them loomed the Sacré-Coeur, an enormous white structure with three domes, one of the loveliest things she had seen in Paris.

Madame Laurent was not inclined to talk, allowing Mia to enjoy the view. After they sat on the steps for a while, they toured the cathedral slowly. Then Madame led her down a small street, where they browsed at leisure, looking in bookstores and stationery shops and a *chocolaterie* with a dizzying array of bonbons and confections far too perfect to eat.

"I love seeing Paris through the eyes of a young person," said Madame Laurent. "It's like being young again myself."

Mia had once read that Jacqueline Kennedy had spent a year of college living in Paris, and she found herself wondering if the senator's wife had experienced a day as perfect as this, overlooking the entire city from the butte of Montmartre, which seemed too magical to be real. But of course she had, Mia thought. The Jacqueline Kennedys of the world had good educations and trips abroad and opportunities not offered to ordinary girls like her. Yet here she was, Mia Walker, standing—literally—on top of the world. Even Jackie Kennedy couldn't have wished for more.

"I don't want this to end," she murmured to Madame.

"Ah, but all good things come to an end, *chérie*," Madame Laurent replied with a shrug. "And you are now ready for the journey ahead of you."

The words sounded almost ominous. A cool breeze blew in from the south, ruffling the hems of their skirts, and Mia wrapped her arms around herself until the sun came out from where it had hidden behind a cloud. A few moments later, the breeze fell away as quickly as it had come.

Madame Laurent was right. Tomorrow was coming, whether she was ready for it or not.

# 4

———

Mia had almost forgotten Theo Gillette. Learning basic French phrases and walking the city every day with Vivienne Laurent had been so all-consuming that she had hardly thought of him since her lessons had begun. She was also trying to adjust to living with roommates, whom she liked, although they invited people over more often than she wished. Artists and models filtered in and out of the apartment—a few outrageous, most harmless and entertaining, but certainly more society than Mia was used to. Of course, things were bound to be different. Now it was time to concentrate on why she had come to Paris in the first place: to do a job for a man who had changed her life with an offer she couldn't refuse.

At the end of the day, it didn't matter if Paris was beautiful or had the best museums in the world or how difficult it might be to assimilate into a culture different from her own. The only thing that mattered was whether Mia could handle the job for which she had been hired. So she awoke with some trepidation over her first day of employment at the House of Rousseau.

She got up early, staring out the window long after she dressed, waiting for her roommates to stir. Even when they stayed up late playing Sinatra on the stereo and mixing weak martinis for their guests, Mia never slept in. As usual, she didn't leave her room until she heard Maeve get up and begin to make coffee in the kitchen.

"What time is Luca picking us up?" Mia asked as she buttoned the blouse she had chosen for her first day of work. As soon as she was earning a salary, she would have to buy some new clothes. "I want to be ready on time."

"Usually around nine o'clock," Maeve answered. "He'll honk when he gets here. But don't worry. He's used to us making him wait."

Mia glanced at the clock. "It's already after eight. Don't you need to get ready?"

Maeve shrugged. "It won't take that long."

Mia grabbed an apple from the bowl and cut it into pieces. She wanted toast, but the last time she'd made some, Elisabeth had commented on her habit of slathering on butter. Diet restrictions were something she hadn't considered when she'd agreed to the job. Besides the French lessons she had been given by Vivienne Laurent, there were other things she had learned as well: how to hold a fork, how to take small bites of food to savor it rather than simply bolting it down like she was used to, how to take one's time and do things properly, as a Frenchwoman would. She had been raised by a single father who'd paid little attention to the way things were supposed to be done, and nothing in her school years had addressed the lapses in her overall education. She wondered if things would have been different if she had grown up with her mother. After two weeks observing Madame Laurent, she had learned that there were protocols to follow, proprieties to observe, and most importantly, the obligation to stifle one's impulses. She had come to France thinking herself a respectable person, but even in so short a time, she had become all too aware of her shortcomings.

"Are you nervous about meeting Monsieur Rousseau?" Elisabeth asked, pouring coffee.

Mia paused her knife over the apple. "What if he takes one look at me and sends me right back home?"

She could just imagine how she would feel with a $375 hole in her bank account and no prospects whatsoever.

"He's not going to send you back," Elisabeth replied. "You're one of us now."

Mia had been happy at the bakery, grateful that she could take care of her father, never considering what else she might like to do. Now things had changed. She wanted to live in Paris and learn everything she could about the fashion industry. If she had known what sort of life she would be living when Theo offered her the job, she would have seized the ticket in front of her and agreed at once. It was clear now that she had needed something to care about, and nothing was more interesting than immersing herself in the world Madame Laurent had opened up to her.

When Luca arrived, she followed Maeve and Elisabeth down the stairs and got into the car, where he was waiting.

"How is everyone today?" he asked, flashing his usual smile.

Mia felt a small pang of jealousy as Elisabeth sat in the front seat next to him.

"A little hungover," Elisabeth admitted. "How are you?"

"Fine, as always," he replied.

"It's too early to be this chipper, Luca," Maeve murmured, slipping on her sunglasses.

Mia sat forward, watching as they passed through the streets. Every day, it became easier to get around. She recognized shops and cafés in their neighborhood and had even managed to buy a few things at the corner market just the day before. It was daunting to move to a foreign city, but Paris wouldn't be unfamiliar forever. When they arrived at Rousseau, she followed her roommates up a set of stairs and into a room, where several other young women were waiting.

"Miss Walker?"

Mia looked up as Theo Gillette approached. He smiled, giving her a small nod.

"I'm pleased that you decided to join us," he said. "I hope you enjoyed your time with Madame Laurent. She said you were a very good student."

"She's very kind," Mia replied. "And Paris is such a beautiful city."

"Excellent," he pronounced. "Today will be another training day for you. I'd like you to shadow one of our assistants so that you can learn your way around the building and see the different departments in action. That's the easiest way to familiarize yourself with what we are doing. Then, tomorrow, you will join the rest of the models. There will be dress fittings and other activities to acquaint you with your job."

"Yes, sir," she replied.

"This is Diana Larson," he continued, nodding at the woman who came up behind him. "She will be showing you around and allowing you to familiarize yourself with the various departments."

"Will I meet Monsieur Rousseau?" she asked.

"I'm afraid he's in meetings today," Theo answered over his shoulder as he walked toward the staircase. "It will have to wait for another time."

Diana gestured toward a door, and Mia followed her to the staircase. Like Theo, she appeared to be American, but Mia didn't want to ask. The woman was a few years older, with a slight build. Her long dark hair was styled away from her face, falling just below her shoulders. Her dress was attractive enough and yet not one that would be remembered even a minute after leaving her presence. Perhaps that was the point; the couture of the House of Rousseau must take precedence in all things.

"Come this way, please," she said, nodding at Mia.

From the moment she stepped inside the building, it was clear that the fashion world was more complex than Mia realized. She was shown into the atelier, where much of the actual sewing took place. The room was a hive of activity, with a half dozen people discussing plans and designs. Miss Larson and Mia did not interrupt them, nor did the seamstresses seem to notice their presence.

"This is the place where every creation begins," Miss Larson said in a low voice.

It was fascinating to watch them in action. Mia stood at the side of the room, observing the designers, who made sketches of various couture designs. Drawings, along with snippets of fabric and lace, were pinned to a board on the side of the room, allowing them to imagine a garment in various shades, or with one neckline or another. The types of skirts and the fullness of each were being debated by a couple of men in one corner, arguing the merits of box pleats versus pencil skirts and A-lines. It was clear Mia had taken for granted all that went into creating a single dress.

"Let's go to the next room," Miss Larson said after a while. "This is where you will find structure couture. See if you can understand how these garments get this designation."

Inside the room were a few tables, where people were using both sewing machines and hand-stitching to create the bodices of the gowns. Mia wandered among them, watching each one.

After several minutes, she turned to Miss Larson and pointed to a bodice that was lying on a table.

"Here," she said, pointing to the seams of the garment. "I think this is what you mean by 'structured couture.'"

"Very good," the woman said, lifting the bodice. "There are thin rods of plastic sewn between the seams that allow a bodice to stay up on a woman's body without using straps. This is called 'boning' because they become the bones of the dress. Now we will look at unstructured couture."

They went into the next room, where the difference was evident at once. Unstructured couture had a romantic, uncorseted look, a loosely cut dress that allowed it to flow gracefully as one walked.

Mia touched the hem of a garment, looking at Miss Larson. "This looks like it belongs to a Greek goddess."

"Aphrodite could do no better," Miss Larson replied, nodding.

They spent more than an hour observing as both types of garments were pieced and sewn. Watching them come together before her eyes seemed like a form of magic.

"There's something I'd like to show you," Miss Larson said, leading her up a flight of stairs to a chamber at the top of the building. "This is the cutting room."

Away from the busyness of the atelier and workrooms, the cutting room stood alone. Six women worked individually at their stations, cutting silks and linens for garments, working slowly and carefully to make certain not to waste a single meter of fabric. The only sound was the shearing of fabric and the rustle of the transparent paper patterns that guided each steady and disciplined hand. The room, with its large windows overlooking the rooftops of Paris, seemed nothing less than a sanctuary. Mia and Miss Larson lingered for a while and then went downstairs to a floor with doors leading to several rooms. Miss Larson opened the first, and Mia followed her inside.

"Here, we have *passementerie*," she said.

Already Mia could see that this was her favorite room of the studio, a collage of every sort of decorative trimming. Jars of buttons lined the shelves: flat, shank, toggle, stud; those covered in fabric to match the exact color of a dress, others made of pearl or zinc alloy or metal. Some were fashioned of exotic shells or glass or even semiprecious gems. There were hundreds of them, all different, each eye-catching for their color and beauty. There were ribbons of every type, as well as tassels, cords, and trim in every color. She wandered among the bins of rosettes and ropes of braided trim.

In the next room, she was introduced to *plumassier*, the art of using ornamental feathers in design. A young man sat at a table, fashioning an exotic hat unlike anything Mia had ever seen before.

"Sergei, this is Mia Walker," Miss Larson said.

"Mademoiselle," he replied, nodding.

The room was full of bins, showing off the dizzying array of color, size, and textures of his feathers. Mia wandered the room for a few minutes and then sat next to him, watching as he worked. His fingers nimbly flew across a garment as he pinned feathers into place. He glanced up, impressed by her interest.

"*Plumassier* is the real star of haute couture," he said without pausing his work. "The right placement of feathers can change the entire look of a garment."

In the corner, Mia saw a prime example: a white gown with a dusting of feathers over one shoulder. She walked around it slowly, realizing that without the embellishment, the dress might even seem plain. However, no one would forget the gown he'd created. It would stand out at any event. Lucky was the woman who would get to wear it.

In the final room, three women were working on broderie. Their needlework was quick but precise as they created by hand eyelet, lace, and embroidery. At the end of the tour, Diana Larson led her downstairs to the first floor, where Mia paused on the landing.

"Is there another set of rooms down there?" she asked, nodding toward the basement.

"Nothing but storage," Miss Larson said. "That's where the boxes and leftover items are housed, which are often distributed to charities."

They passed a door where several models were whispering and laughing among themselves. The girls stopped when they went by, looking Mia over before they scattered to different rooms. Once again, she glanced at her dress, aware she wasn't as sophisticated as any of them.

However, the fashion house was a world within a world. Each room housed a variety of artists who employed entirely different skills. Tailors, designers, seamstresses: it took an army to make a single gown. Mia had once been in the garment district of New York and seen a factory of women at work on ready-to-wear. It was little more than a sweatshop: harsh conditions, dim lighting, no air other than a few open windows. Women hunched over sewing machines, stitching a collar or a hem. They were paid by the piece, although not much, and there was no incentive to take one's time and make it perfect.

The House of Rousseau was a repository of craftsmanship, each department believing their contribution to be the most important to the final product, which would find its way to the wardrobe of the wife of a president or a millionaire, or perhaps an actress starring in the latest show. It was a world where every part of the dress represented a highly evolved art, and only the best would make it in a Rousseau design.

Over the next few days, she was introduced to the essence of her job. She met with stylists and tailors; she was given her first lessons on how to walk and demonstrate a gown; she was sent for a photo shoot and instructed on how to pose and show off her best side.

"You were meant for this life!" Elisabeth said one evening as they were looking through magazines together, discussing the current trends in fashion.

"She's right," Maeve said, nodding. "You're a quick study, Mia. Aren't you glad you took a chance and came to Paris?"

In fact, she was. By the end of the week, she knew the building inside and out. This place, which had been unknown to her a week ago, was beginning to feel like home.

"Mia, a group of us are going to a restaurant after work," Elisabeth told her at the end of their shift on Friday. "Want to come along?"

"I'm a little tired," she replied, relieved that for once, they wouldn't have an apartment full of strangers all evening, as they had for the last three days. "I think I'll make it an early night."

"Are you sure?" asked Maeve. "We deserve a night out!"

"I'm sure," Mia answered. "Have a good time."

When they had gone, Mia decided to walk back to their flat. The area where they worked led to noisier boulevards, where traffic swirled around her. She made her way in the right direction, avoiding the stream of cars and trucks racing by, but after several minutes, she realized she had wandered into an unfamiliar area.

It was a crumbling, decrepit part of Paris. Some of the buildings had smashed windows; broken glass littered the street. Few people milled about, but those who did, approached her, hat in hand. Wind whistled down the alley, stirring debris. She quickened her step as she made her way through, trying to get to a familiar street.

It was hard to believe they were two sides of the same coin: the perfect Paris she had experienced until now and the unseemly one she had stumbled onto on her own. After all the beauty she had witnessed over the past few weeks, she had never imagined that there was an unsavory side to the city.

But perhaps, she thought, she had only seen what she wanted to see. Unfortunately, that was a thought she would have again in the not-too-distant future.

# 5

Chantal Fournier had her secrets. All French women did, particularly if they were seventy-four years old and, one might think, invisible to anyone younger than forty. She had moved to her flat on the Rue des Écoles nearly fifteen years ago after a disagreement with her family and had never looked back.

In some ways, this was better—the anonymity of the city, being yet another faceless person on the street and, particularly, in her building. She kept to herself, preferring not to rub shoulders with many of her neighbors except for Aurélie Bernard in 4B, who, at age eighty-six, was past her prime and in need of whatever emotional or physical support Chantal could provide. That said, Madame Fournier was all too aware that no one was taking care of her. Not that she was elderly or that she needed to be taken care of. At least for now, she was an independent woman.

Chantal's apartment, 3A, was one of the largest and nicest in the building. When she moved in, she had hired contractors to paint the crown moldings and rebuild cabinets. She brought nothing with her from her grand house in Normandy and furnished the space simply, with a long sofa and comfortable chairs, tall bookshelves, and a round wooden table she had found at the flea market on the northern edge of Paris. She used the table not only for dining but also to conduct her correspondence. It was a round pedestal table made of mahogany, of a generous size and sturdily built. It brought her enormous satisfaction, as did the thought that its unknown provenance would have irked her husband, Noel, to no end if he were still alive.

Everything from the Normandy house had either been relegated to them from his ancient relatives or, if not, chosen by Noel. Though she'd lived there since the day they married, it had never felt the slightest bit as though the house or anything in it had belonged to her. When he finally died and she wanted to clear out some of his books, his sons—well, yes, also *her* sons—had such a tantrum about her moving their father's things that she picked up her handbag and left the house without a word, never to return. If one has outlived a domineering husband, one is not required to extend the privilege of making all one's decisions to his sons.

It was Tuesday morning. Chantal washed her face, applied her lipstick carefully, and fashioned her favorite blue Hermès scarf about her throat *à la française.* Taking her mesh market bag, she folded it neatly into fourths and tucked it into her small blue handbag.

Tuesdays were set aside for exploring, followed by a trip to the market for fruits and vegetables. Like Madame Bernard, her groceries were delivered once a week, but she preferred to choose certain items herself to make certain they were the freshest, ripest produce to be found in all of Paris.

Chantal never simply opened the door to her flat and proceeded out into the world. *Mais non.*

She listened at the door, made certain there was no movement or sound to be heard on her floor, then opened it a crack to peer into the corridor before stepping out and locking it behind her.

It wasn't that she was afraid of people or that she couldn't speak to anyone. Indeed, she was the eyes and the ears of the building, aware of each and every tenant and their purpose in living in her building on the Rue des Écoles. However, she had little desire to interact with anyone. In her opinion, that generally brought poor results. So, while she was curious about everyone who lived there and interested in their comings and goings, she had no intention of inflicting their person onto herself. Now and then, when she saw one of her neighbors, she gave them a curt nod and went about her business.

Once outside the door of the tall limestone building, however, she was an entirely different person. The person, perhaps, that she might have been had she never married Noel. She held her head high and made her way through the narrow streets of the 5th arrondissement until she reached the Petit Pont, then walked halfway across. She paused in the middle each time she went over the bridge and caught her breath at the beauty of Paris, watching the vessels cruising up and down the Seine and the activity that swirled around Notre Dame. She rarely went into the church, thinking it mostly for tourists, who flocked in great numbers to see it when the weather was fair. Instead, after she had reflected for a moment, she walked across the bridge, turning left to go to the Place Dauphine on the northwestern side of the Île de la Cité, a pleasure she reserved for an especially fine day.

The Place Dauphine was one of the oldest public squares in the city. From its western side, the Eiffel Tower could be seen towering over the Champs de Mars; from the east, the Louvre. In spring, the square was covered in tulips, and in fall, golden leaves from chest-nut trees littered the ground. Of all the parks in Paris, the Place Dauphine was her favorite, and worth the walk to get there. There was no amount of distress in life that could not be cured by sitting in that spot, on her favorite bench, listening to the whistling of the wind and the lapping of the water against the shore and the church bells tolling every hour on the hour.

The Sainte-Chapelle stood behind her, and after a while, she budged from her spot to go inside. After her eyes adjusted to the dim light, she went up to the vestibule table, where she took a candle and lit one, placing it among the others. She wasn't religious, although she had a sort of faith, but she liked sitting in a pew and gathering her thoughts. It was the one place where she allowed herself some introspection. There were things of which one must be forgiven, she knew, and this was the place to do it. Sins, however one meant not to do them, popped up as often as wildflowers in unmown fields, particularly impatience and unkindness and the hate that stewed in one's heart. She didn't want to hate any longer, when it came to that, although living among other humans sometimes made that a difficult proposition. But still, she could light a candle and hope for the best, along with the rest of humanity.

Afterward, she wandered back toward the bridge to carry on with her errands, absolved, at least in her mind, for a few days. Surely nothing sinister could stir the pot of restless emotion before she was back in the Sainte-Chapelle, lighting another candle and laying down her thoughts about Noel and his ungrateful children, and often herself.

In no hurry, she made her way across the Pont Neuf and into the 6th arrondissement. It was a good day for walking. The smaller streets had little traffic, leaving her plenty of time to browse shop windows. Of course, she didn't need anything. She was seventy-four years old. She had spent a lifetime among beautiful things and walked away from it all in a fit of pique. Even after she'd furnished her Paris flat, she bought only the essentials one needs to cook and clean and conduct a life. The only splurge she allowed herself was collecting books.

She had taken to reading again, books she hadn't read since she was an adolescent. They seemed to have greater meaning to her now than they had even as an impressionable girl. She ached with the Count of Monte Cristo at the unfairness of his suffering, and cheered for him when he acquired a fortune and decided to exact revenge on those who had wronged him. Madame Bovary was also more enlightening at this age. As a girl, she had hoped for Emma to find true love and an escape from the troublesome aspects of life, but now she could see that the young Frenchwoman was never to find happiness in the arms of a man. If only she'd been informed of this sooner, she might not have swallowed arsenic and could have perhaps found happiness within herself.

That was what Chantal intended to do. She found a bookshop and went inside, browsing for a few minutes, but came out empty-handed. *Eh bien,* she thought. She hadn't found anything new to bring home, but she was in the middle of a Dickens novel, anyway. One mustn't force oneself to read something until the moment was right. It was satisfying to know that Oliver Twist and Fagin were waiting for her on the mahogany table. Even more so that she couldn't recall how it ended.

She peered in shop windows until she came to a stop in front of a toy store, where small metal cars just large enough for a toddler to climb inside caught her eye. Jean-Louis would have loved the shiny red and blue cars, and Jacques as well. She could see them in her mind's eye as clearly as if it had been yesterday, their wisps of pale hair and pudgy fingers and delighted smiles, always happy and playful. They had been the joy of her life. But now they belonged to their wives and families, as it should be, with opinions that had not originated from her. In the years before Noel died, they had no time for her apart from frequent criticisms, which she had escaped by getting on a train for Paris and never looking back. And she didn't unless shiny metal toys were wagged in her face. But this was not a moment for introspection, so she turned away from the store and continued on her way.

The *boulangerie* Poilâne was busy when she arrived, and the queue was long. Chantal found her place in line, jostling others around her if she herself was jostled, the Frenchwoman's unspoken language to safeguard her position in a queue. However, she felt no impatience here. She loved the smell of baking bread and watching the bustle behind the counter of vigorous young assistants who took orders and handed out round loaves of sourdough and brioches and baguettes to willing hands. She also appreciated having the opportunity to consider which items would be going home with her that day. Taking her mesh bag from her pocketbook, she ordered a baguette and two *pains au chocolat* when it was her turn, barely resisting the urge to hold them to her nose when they were handed over the counter. Even a bouquet of roses never smelled so good.

Her final stop would be the tiny market in the square not far from her building. The bread was light, but heavy vegetables and fruits were not, so she always purchased them last. Monsieur Seydoux, the proprietor, was eighty now, but his age did not prevent him from leering and paying her far too much attention when she stepped across his threshold, as he had for the last fifteen years. As usual, she pretended not to notice him as she wandered over to the bins to test the firmness of the aubergines and the freshness of the onions and tomatoes. When she had found the perfect specimens, she went to the counter and took out her francs, not making eye contact until the last second.

"Ah, Madame Fournier," he said with a sigh. "And what are you making this fine day? Ratatouille? An omelet, perhaps?"

"I'm making parmigiana," she replied. "As you know, it's best when the aubergines are fresh."

"*Mon dieu*," he said, glancing toward the heavens. "That sounds wonderful. I haven't had parmigiana in such a long time."

She ignored the blatant hint for an invitation, which he did every time she came into the shop. Instead, she gave him a cold smile.

"You should make one soon," she answered, taking her bag and turning. "*Au revoir*, Monsieur."

She lifted a hand as she left, making her way down the street, thinking how her life in Honfleur had been so different. She'd had a maid to clean everything from the crystal chandeliers to the seven bedrooms in the eighteenth-century manor. Another, Beatriz, ran errands and went to the markets and peeled potatoes in the kitchen. Of course, Simon, the gardener, took care of the grounds, and Monsieur Gasquet took care of the horses. She had very little to do for the most part, except to wander from room to room, looking for imperfections: the ripped hem of a curtain, a stain on a chair. She hadn't grown up intending to be a chatelaine or, in fact, with the aim of looking for a rich husband. She had always hoped to marry for love. However, love can be as capricious as the night sky, a changing thing, with the moon in different quadrants based on the time of night or the season. Her life had been unexpectedly lonely, despite the busyness of her day-to-day existence. The one thing she managed to do each day that brought her pleasure was cook.

Chantal had always loved preparing meals. In fact, the best part of her marriage had been when she created some delicacy or another and presented it to Noel. He treated each meal as a ceremonial occasion, arranging his napkin just so, sitting perfectly straight in his chair—a consequence of his mother swatting his hand when he slouched as a youth—and leaning slightly back as she brandished the plate in front of him. Taking his knife and fork, he did not begin to eat immediately, but inspected the dish for color, temperature, and presentation, like a senior inspector of Michelin stars. Then he would take the first bite, savoring it for a minute or more. The rest of the family watched until he finally nodded in satisfaction, and then and only then could they begin.

Irked slightly by the memory, she went into her flat and began to work in the kitchen. She had only just lit a candle that morning. It was too soon to think of Noel and allow herself to become irritated once again.

She built the parmigiana with as much precision as Gustave Eiffel had built his tower, layering the aubergine between layers of mozzarella and her famous tomato sauce, the recipe of which she would leave to no one when she died. She dotted the layers with basil leaves, using more cheese than she preferred because it was Madame Bernard's favorite dish. Then she placed it in the oven and set the timer.

An hour later, she took the parmigiana out of the oven and let it cool before cutting it into pieces. She set aside some for herself and then put two generous portions onto a plate to take to Madame Bernard. She went upstairs, noting that the air was cooler in the stairwell, as if the outer door below was open, although she could hear no movement in the hall.

"Madame," Chantal called, tapping on the door. She waited a moment and then let herself into the flat. "Guess what I have brought you tonight?"

The old woman lay on the sofa, propped up with pillows. Chantal set the plate on the table and then walked over to her.

"Do you need to get up for a few minutes?" she asked.

"No, *chérie*," Madame Bernard replied, shaking her head. "But perhaps you could help with the cushions."

Chantal plumped and rearranged them, then cleared the table next to the sofa to make room for a plate.

"Are you hungry?"

"What did you make?" the woman asked, sniffing the air.

"I made your favorite."

Madame Bernard smiled, revealing a couple of missing teeth. "I have been dreaming of your parmigiana, Chantal. You're an angel."

Chantal put a portion of the meal onto a plate and brought it to her with a serviette and a fork. Then she covered the rest and stored it in the petit *réfrigérateur*. She took a few minutes to wash the cups and plates and straighten the kitchen before going back to check on Madame.

"You don't have to do that, you know," Madame Bernard remarked. "Annelise will be here tomorrow."

"I know," Chantal said, nodding at her friend. "I just like to help. Is there anything else I can do for you?"

"Put on the radio before you leave, *chérie*, if you would."

Chantal turned on the radio—not too loudly, the way Madame Bernard liked it. Then she brought the woman's glasses and set them atop the book she was reading.

"Good night, Madame," she said. "I'll see you on Thursday."

"Thursday," Madame Bernard answered, nodding.

Chantal slipped out into the hall, making certain the door was locked behind her. Then she went back to her flat to have her own supper.

There was a letter sitting on the table, unopened. Chantal had been looking at it for nearly a week. It was important not to rush pleasures. The anticipation of reading it was as much of a delight as the actual act. Each day, she glanced at the envelope with her address written in the dear, familiar hand, and smiled. Today, she would open it.

She received a letter once every three or four weeks and then let it sit on the table, awaiting the perfect moment to read it. If she grew impatient, she could read all the others that had preceded it. These, she kept in a basket under the table, not visible to anyone who might come into her flat but close at hand should she need to remind herself of their presence.

She cut herself a helping of the parmigiana, scraping off the excess cheese, and poured a glass of wine, bringing both to the table, where she would allow her eyes to linger on the letter a final time before she opened it and read the contents. It was her favorite day of the month, the day she allowed herself this pleasure. The next two days would be spent thinking of how best to reply.

But before she could pick up the letter and enjoy it with her wine, she heard something in the hall. She got up from the table when she realized that someone was standing outside her door.

She opened it, curious, and found her newest young neighbor, the American, surrounded by boxes and bags.

"Is everything all right?" she asked.

The girl looked at her, as skittish as a deer. "I tripped on the stair, Madame. I'm sorry I disturbed you."

Chantal bent down and began to pick up some of the boxes, and the girl did the same before taking her key from her pocket and opening the door to her flat. Chantal followed her and stood at the threshold as the girl took her things inside.

"Really, I'm sorry," her young neighbor repeated. "I've just had such a long day."

"What is your name?" Chantal asked.

"Mia Walker. And you're Madame Fournier."

"Yes." She looked at her for a moment. "Are you certain you're all right?"

"I'm fine," she said, nodding. "Or I will be, when I get out of these shoes."

Chantal handed over the rest of the packages and turned to go. "Thank you, Madame," the girl said. "I appreciate your help." "*De rien*," Chantal replied.

She went back to her own flat and took up the letter that she had almost opened, placing it back on the table. The moment was interrupted, so she would wait for another time to read whatever had been written inside. Instead, she poured herself a second glass of wine and went to the window, watching dusk fall on another Paris day.

Her thoughts drifted back to the young ladies in the flat down the hall. They were models, of course, ridiculously attractive, with a social calendar that would rival that of Brigitte Bardot. Two of them had lived there for most of the past couple of years, and now the American had joined them. They were beautiful girls, and it was obvious why they had been chosen to model for the House of Rousseau. Their flat, however, appeared to have a revolving door, as they entertained more often than Chantal would have liked. She had not been inside it since they had moved in, and the American had hardly left the door open wide enough to make any observations at all. Of course, if she really wanted to see what was inside the home of three frivolous young women, she could always use a key. The flat had previously belonged to Monsieur Dubois, and he had given it to her to feed his parakeet whenever he was out of town. She had never returned it, of course. Why should she? Who knew if she might need it again?

# 6

Jackie Kennedy's face stared back at Mia, a face she knew as well as her own. It was affixed with cellophane tape to the inside of her wardrobe at eye level, placed there to remind her of the importance of the poise required in a job like hers. After several weeks in France, she had already learned more than she'd ever imagined. Until now, fashion had never interested her. Like any young woman, she liked browsing shop windows, admiring a pretty dress or a well-styled heel, but clothing had never been an important part of her day-to-day existence. Now, however, she could name a host of design elements that she had never heard of before, qualities that made all the difference in the cut of a dress or coat or in the structure of a handbag or pair of pumps.

The women she observed on the street in Paris caught her eye far more often than anyone had at home, where ordinary dresses and sweater-and-skirt ensembles were the ubiquitous daily wear of thousands of young women as they managed their workaday world. In France, where folding a scarf was an art form, details were important. The slit of a skirt or the trim on a sleeve could make an outfit stand out, but even more crucial to the overall element of style was the bearing these women displayed while wearing their clothes. Their confidence, whether wearing couture or off-the-rack clothing, was different than anything she had seen before. They wore their hair styled in chignons or freshly done waves; accessories were effortlessly matched to their clothes. In fact, Mia had heard Theo say that a French woman would rather have a minuscule wardrobe of simple, elegant clothing than a closet full of haphazardly chosen items like most of their American counterparts. She had even begun to edit her own things, letting go of some of the older pieces and choosing more classic items one at a time. She still preferred color—as opposed to the French girls, who wore more somber tones—but for the first time in her life, she was paying attention to the cut and design of clothing she found in her budget, and she was starting to develop a sense of style.

Few young women had the opportunity to learn so much about the fashion world. Theo's offer had come at the perfect time, saving her when she was facing not only a personal crisis but also a financial one, and she valued the education she had received from living for a few weeks in a foreign country. It was more than she could have ever dreamed of.

"We're cutting your hair," Julien told her one afternoon. He was one of the best stylists at Rousseau. "It's time for you to look the part."

Mia sat in the chair and looked nervously in the mirror at her hair, which fell halfway down her back. "I've never had it styled before."

"Trust me," he said. "You'll see the difference."

In a few minutes, she was transformed from an ordinary American with long straight hair to a vision with shoulder-length waves.

"I don't even look like myself," she murmured when he was finished. "I can't believe it, Julien. I'm a whole new person."

"You are now a Rousseau girl," he replied, nodding.

Afterward, she was taught the basics of maquillage, the art of using makeup to its perfect advantage. The face that stared back at her in the mirror was a more sophisticated one than before, and she carried herself more gracefully from all the sessions spent practicing how to walk, how to turn, how to show oneself off to the best advantage. She had felt clumsy and incapable of elegance in the first few weeks, but somewhere along the way, she discovered her inner French girl.

Those French girls, Miss Larson said, never try to copy style but used it as a starting place from which they developed a sense of individuality and a true sense of self. They preferred their fashion to be understated rather than overstated, as their American counterparts preferred, which gave them an edge when it came to natural sensuality and beauty. Mia could already see the advantage of working and living with girls from all over the world. It had begun to shape her vision about herself and her own looks.

"Paris agrees with you," Maeve told her when she saw her new style. "And has anyone told you that you look like Jacqueline Kennedy?"

Mia was flattered by the comparison. For the first time in her life, she was coming into her own. It was thrilling to live in a new city and start a glamorous new life. Everything was beautiful: the clothes, the cafés, the twinkle light–studded riverboats gliding up and down the Seine. She couldn't believe Theo had given her a chance to experience it for herself. And now she was being compared to Jackie Kennedy. It was too good to be true.

However, if she were honest, not everything was perfect. One of her gloves had gone missing, for one thing, and she hadn't forgotten how her father's pocket watch had gone missing for a few hours. She was still uncomfortable mingling with strangers as well. A photographer, who had been professional during a shoot, had been overly familiar with her one evening at their flat. Mia wanted to gain confidence in her social interactions, but the truth was, she relished her time alone.

Her favorite time of the week was weekend afternoons, when Paris belonged to her. At midday, she grabbed her pocketbook and stepped into the corridor of her building, where she heard a scratching sound. She paused and listened for a moment before pulling the door shut behind her. Then she heard it again. It was the cat, sitting under the console table a few feet away. Mia bent down to look at it, and as she did, the door to Madame Fournier's apartment opened.

"Is everything all right?" Madame asked.

Their neighbor was perfectly attired as always, her rose-colored lipstick matching her crisp silk blouse. Her mouth, however, was pinched into a frown.

"It's the cat," Mia replied. "I've seen him several times. Does he belong to you?"

Madame Fournier shook her head. "He belongs to the building, I'm afraid. Some of us take turns feeding him."

"Where does he sleep?" she asked, hoping the creature had a permanent home. He deserved more than a peripatetic existence scooting from console to corners in search of a place to hide.

"Wherever he pleases," Madame said, dispelling her hopes. "Sometimes he stays with Monsieur Lindsay on the second floor."

"Does he have a name?" Mia asked.

"I'm afraid we have never been properly introduced."

With that, Madame Fournier turned and closed the door behind her, leaving Mia to wonder whether she was talking about the cat or about her. She shook her head, reaching down to pet him, but he slinked away before her hand even touched his fur. Perhaps it was because he was French, she thought. Or because some of the people in this building were prickly.

Mia went downstairs and onto the street, feeling better the moment she stepped outside. It was a fine day. She had a book in her handbag and the sudden desire to eat something, so she made her way to a café that she had discovered the previous week. It was called *Les Coccinelles,* which, according to her Larousse dictionary, meant *ladybugs,* perhaps because people flitted in and out throughout the day. There always seemed to be a table outside under the awning, and she sat in the shade, taking out her book.

The waiter approached and took her order. Her French was still at a beginner's level, although she made herself practice as often as possible.

"Mia?" a voice called behind her.

She turned and saw that it was Natalie Simpson, one of the other Americans from Rousseau.

They had been introduced once but seldom had the opportunity to speak. Natalie and the other American, Jane Goldman, had a different schedule than Mia and her roommates. Their work was done in cycles, she discovered. Some weeks were a flurry of activity as preparations were made for an event or a showing; others were slow, leaving them at loose ends waiting for a call.

"Natalie," she said, trying to hide her disappointment that someone had found her when she was hoping to be left alone to read.

"This looks cozy," the girl said. "May I join you?"

"Of course," Mia said, sliding her book back into her bag to make room.

"What are you up to today?"

"Not much," Mia admitted. "I just ordered lunch."

"Jane's gone out on a date, and I didn't want to sit home alone," Natalie said. "I'd love to get something myself."

"Do you live nearby?"

"Eight or nine blocks from here," Natalie said. "I can't believe my luck in finding you just now."

The waiter brought two cups of coffee to the table and took Natalie's order. Mia studied the girl sitting across from her. They were roughly the same age. Natalie's hair, which was a few shades darker than her own, was pulled back and tied with a ribbon. Her eyes, however, didn't seem as demure as the rest of her appearance.

"How do you like it so far at Rousseau?" Natalie asked when he had gone.

"It's wonderful," Mia replied. "I can't believe we get to work in such a glamorous place."

"And the clothes. I feel like I've died and gone to heaven."

"What do you know about Theo?" Mia asked. She rarely got to speak with the man who had brought her to France. In fact, she had gotten the impression that he was never to be bothered.

"He hired me last year," Natalie replied, evading the question. Perhaps she didn't know any more than Mia did about their enigmatic employer. "I was going to school in London with some friends, and he made me an offer I couldn't refuse. I mean, who would turn down the chance to model in Paris?"

"What happened to your friends?"

Natalie shrugged. "They've gone back to California now. They finished the term and decided they had seen enough of Europe. One is engaged, and the other got a job as a clerk in a law firm. I'm pretty sure she's looking for a rich lawyer to marry."

"What about Jane?" Mia continued. "How long have you known her?"

"She was hired a couple of years ago. She was staying with friends in Switzerland, and they stopped in Paris for a few days. In fact, she had gone into Rousseau and got to talking with Theo. The next thing she knew, she was a Rousseau girl, too. To tell you the truth, I don't entirely trust her. I complained about something once, and he mentioned it to me later. If you ask me, just keep your opinions to yourself. That's the only advice I'll give you.

"That was a great party at your flat last week," Natalie went on. "I met a musician there. We went on a date a couple of days ago, and I'm hoping he calls again. Maeve and Elisabeth know the most interesting people."

"It's a never-ending party," Mia agreed, hoping she didn't sound bitter. She always seemed to find herself pouring wine and trying to avoid being picked up by a strange man. For one thing, they were all so much older.

"Have you been sent on any evening engagements yet?" Natalie asked, interrupting her train of thought.

Mia looked up as the waiter appeared with their omelets. "No, I haven't."

"Well, it's coming," Natalie said. "Get ready for it."

"What do you mean?"

"Nothing, really," she said, sprinkling pepper on her eggs. "Sometimes we're asked to model some of the gowns in social settings. If anyone asks you what you're wearing, just tell them it's a Marcel Rousseau."

Mia lifted the edge of her omelet with a fork, wondering why it looked different from its American counterpart. She hadn't been fond of the food so far, that was for certain.

"What do you do at these events?" she asked, trying not to think about her lunch.

"Let men buy you drinks," Natalie answered. "Dance a little. That's all."

Mia looked up. "Are you serious?"

"It's not that bad," Natalie said. "It's all in a day's work."

"I love Paris," Mia said. "But I didn't expect that to be part of the deal. Women are more than just objects to parade around in pretty clothes."

"I won't tell anyone you said that."

Mia started to reply, but Natalie was staring intently at her plate. Until she'd taken this job, she had always been free to voice her opinions. It was going to be difficult to keep them to herself. Natalie seemed to be hiding something, although she couldn't imagine what it might be. In fact, when she thought about it, several things had seemed off to her during her first couple of weeks at Rousseau. Conversations were cut short when she came into a room, looks had been exchanged between Maeve and some of the other models after Theo had spoken to them, and there was a lack of congeniality among them all. She had wondered if it was her imagination, but now she was reconsidering the situation.

The rest of the conversation was flat, making her afraid she had said too much. When they finished their lunch, they parted ways, and Mia walked down to the river and sat on the steps. She hadn't lived far from the Hudson, yet she'd rarely gone there. But there was something different about living here. Perhaps it was the need to get out of the flat, or because everything in France was new and exciting.

She took out her book but didn't manage to read more than a page. There were too many distractions. The occasional boat went past, and pedestrians crossed the bridge over her shoulder, couples walking arm in arm on a mild afternoon. Watching them, she wondered what it was like to be in love. There certainly wasn't a better place for it. Everything about the city seemed to have been designed for lovers. Eventually, she headed back to her flat, finding Elisabeth there when she arrived.

"What have you been up to?" her roommate asked.

"Sitting by the river," Mia said. "It's so quiet down there. Where's Maeve gone?"

"She had a couple of errands to run," Elisabeth replied. "I decided to wash my hair so we can go out later."

"Do you know anything about Madame Fournier?" Mia asked suddenly.

"Not really," Elisabeth replied. "But she's very standoffish. Why the interest?"

"I was just curious," Mia answered. "I saw her in the hallway this morning. We've hardly spoken to her."

"Who knows?" Elisabeth said, shrugging. "You'd better start getting ready. We're going to hit some clubs tonight, I think."

"We aren't going to a restaurant?" Mia asked.

The biggest difficulty she had encountered was the lack of normal food. She was slender enough when she'd arrived in Paris, but while her dress size was in the acceptable range, she was encouraged to diet anyway. One of the tailors had once pinched the back of her arm and raised an eyebrow, leaving her mortified. She had begun inspecting her body for unsightly pudges and started eating less each day. Maeve and Elisabeth were inconsistent when it came to meals, preferring a martini and an apple to actual food. The one exception was Saturdays, when they relaxed and did their best to forget the week by consuming contraband items like pastries and thick cuts of quiche from the local café. Mia had never obsessed about food, but that was before she was living on a near-starvation diet.

"I don't think so," Elisabeth said, interrupting her thoughts. "One of my friends found a great jazz club. He says we should give it a try."

"I'll get ready," Mia replied.

She took a shower, and when she went back to her room, Maeve was standing there.

"Is everything all right?" she asked, uncomfortable that either of them would go into her room without asking.

Her roommate turned around and smiled. "I brought you a dress to wear tonight."

A gold-colored dress with a matching belt hung on the wardrobe, and Mia exhaled, scolding herself for being so suspicious. "I love that dress. Thank you."

It fit her perfectly, but when she came in to submit herself for inspection, Maeve turned up the collar and then sent her back to reapply her rouge.

"You're too pale," Maeve complained. "You need a little color."

Mia went to the mirror and tried again. After she had passed the inspection, the three of them went downstairs and made their way toward the river.

"Where is this place?" Mia asked.

"It's not far," Maeve said. "On the Rue de l'Arsenal."

They walked along the cobblestones of the Île de la Cité and then onto the Right Bank, their heels clattering on the pavement. The laziness of the afternoon had given way to an energy as dusk fell, and people scurried to take advantage of the good weather. They'd been walking for twenty minutes when Maeve suddenly turned and stopped.

"It's just ahead."

Mia fell into step behind them as they approached the club. Lights were strung across the entrance, and music could be heard coming from inside. The room was smoky and dim, with a jazz band playing at the far side of the room.

Maeve was immediately swept into a conversation, and Elisabeth followed her, but Mia hung back, moving closer to the band. She found a table and sat. The room was dark and intimate; the music was good. She was listening to the second set when a waiter approached her with a drink.

Mia took one look at it and shook her head.

"I didn't order anything," she said.

"It's from the gentleman over there," he replied, leaving it on the table.

She turned her head but couldn't see in the dim light. In other circumstances, she might have left it sitting on the table, but the long walk had gotten the better of her, so she lifted the glass. A moment later, a man appeared at her side, smiling. He pulled out the chair next to her and took a seat, placing his hat on the table next to his drink.

"May I join you?" he asked.

He was American, tall and lanky, older than her by a half dozen years. His hair was cropped short, the back so crisp, she wanted to reach out and touch it. Mia looked down, shocked by her own response. She pushed the martini away, afraid to take another sip.

"I'm Philip," he said. "What's your name?"

"Mia," she replied.

"That's unusual," he answered, studying her as he lifted his own martini. "I think I like it. What do you do?"

She wasn't certain how to answer. Saying she was a model in training sounded ridiculous.

Besides, it might give him the wrong impression.

"I'm here for a while with my friends," she said, like she were one of those girls who traveled around Europe going to clubs, living a carefree life. Of course, nothing could be further from the truth.

"Ah," he replied, as if that explained everything. Then he smiled. "Aren't you going to ask what I do?"

"What do you do?" she echoed.

She wasn't used to talking to men. She suddenly realized it took skill to do it well, which made her wonder if it was expected of them by Monsieur Rousseau. Natalie had mentioned social engagements, after all. She was still not happy at the thought of being used.

"I run a company in Chicago," he replied. "I'm here on business for a while. Since I've been stuck in meetings all day, I'm looking for a little pleasant distraction."

"There are lots of things to do in Paris," she replied, in case he was referring to her as the distraction. "Have you been to the museums yet?"

"I wasn't thinking of museums."

She turned toward the band as they started the next number. The saxophone player had stepped up next to the singer and started a melancholic solo.

"I see you like jazz," he said, leaning a little closer.

Mia nodded. "I like it, but I'm certainly not an aficionado."

"That's the beauty of it," he continued. "Anyone can enjoy it. You know, Paris has been home to jazz since the twenties. Sometimes, I imagine what it must have been like to have heard Louis Armstrong or Dizzy Gillespie back in their heyday."

She nodded. "My father had some Louis Armstrong records when I was growing up. I suppose that's why I like it."

"He was the best," Phillip said, raising his glass. "To Satchmo."

She raised her glass but didn't lift it to her lips. Looking around the room, she spied Elisabeth talking to Maeve.

"Thank you for the drink," Mia said, standing. "It looks like my friends are ready to leave."

"Are you sure you won't stay?" he asked. "I can always walk you home later."

"I'm sorry, but I can't."

He nodded. "Maybe I'll run into you again sometime."

"Don't knock museums," she said suddenly, leaning closer. "I'd try the Louvre. It's got something for everyone."

She walked over to her roommates, aware he was watching her as she left the table.

"Are you ready?" she asked.

Elisabeth nodded. "This place is boring. Let's get out of here."

Mia followed them outside, where Elisabeth turned to her.

"I saw that man you were talking to," she said. "He looked nice. Did you give him your number?"

"For God's sake, I hope so," Maeve added. "You need a little excitement in your life."

"I have plenty of excitement," Mia protested. "There's a lot to get used to, you know. Before I came here, I was taking care of my father, not having a life."

Maeve shook her head "Well, it's time to have one now."

They went to two more clubs before Maeve finally grew tired, and then they headed back to their flat. Mia was wobbly from the three martinis she had consumed and wanted nothing more than to go to bed. In her room, she kicked off her shoes, her feet throbbing from walking so far. She slid off the belt and then undid the buttons of the dress before tossing it over the chair. Then she slipped on her nightgown and opened the French doors a crack, peering down below. The street was quiet. Nothing could be heard but the muted bark of a dog in the distance.

She felt snug in her small room in the Left Bank, but her doubts were growing. Perhaps she wasn't cut out for living in Paris after all. It was difficult making small talk with people she didn't know, and frustrating to have to field men and bored roommates when she would have preferred to listen to the music all night.

Mia sighed, walking over to her wardrobe. From the bottom drawer, she extricated her bankbook. She had only managed to save sixty-five dollars. She was receiving a regular weekly check from Rousseau, but it would be a long time before she would be able to find another place to stay. She was going to have to adjust, one way or another.

She put her bankbook away for safekeeping and crawled into bed, too tired to think any more. Tomorrow she would take a shower and wash the smell of smoke out of her hair, but tonight, she would simply lie there, relieved to be home in bed. Worries, she knew, could always wait until tomorrow.

# 7

---

August in Paris was hot and steamy. The temperature had risen above eighty; the humidity was unbearable. Residents fled to the countryside for the weekend, or the entire month if they could, abandoning it to tourists with Polaroid cameras and Bermuda shorts and binoculars strung about their necks as if they were on safari in Africa. Mia's building was noticeably quiet, and even Maeve and Elisabeth abandoned their frenetic social life and spent time indoors with the windows flung open, fanning themselves with old copies of *Vogue*.

To think that she herself could be on the front of a fashion magazine was still a shock. Just that week, Theo had mentioned that she was being considered for a cover in the fall. Changes had been coming at a rapid pace, without giving her time to adjust to them.

When she wasn't at work, Mia spent most of her time in her room, the French doors opened as far as they would allow, lying in her slip on the cool sheets. Business was slower at the House of Rousseau as well. Spring and fall, when the collections were released, were the busiest times of year, and in between events the models were loaned out to department stores and charity shows, as well as for the odd social occasion. Some days were more hectic than others, but for the past couple of weeks, everything had come to a standstill.

The telephone rang. Maeve had gone to the dentist, and Elisabeth was shopping, so Mia dragged herself from her bed and the book she was trying to read to answer it.

"*Allô?*" she said into the receiver.

They had taken to answering the telephone in French, even though the callers were generally one of their friends or someone from work. Of course, if someone replied in kind, they quickly switched to English. Mia had read somewhere that Jackie Kennedy spoke the language fluently, but that was a high bar. Even Maeve, who spoke it better than any of them, couldn't completely master her verbs.

"Mia," Luca said on the other end of the line. "I'm running an errand out of town today, and I wondered if you would come along with me. I could use the company."

"Where are you going?" she asked.

"I'm headed to a vineyard about an hour and a half south of Paris to pick up a case of wine for Monsieur Rousseau," he replied. "The drive won't be so long if I have someone to talk to. Besides, you haven't seen much of France outside of the city."

"I'd love to," she answered.

"What?" he asked in mock surprise. "You don't have to think about it first?"

"No," she said, picking up her sandals, which were by the door. "I'm glad you asked me. It sounds like just what I need."

"I'm not far from your flat. Meet me downstairs in ten minutes."

She went into her room and flung open the wardrobe, taking down a new outfit she had just purchased the week before: a sleeveless green flowered dress with a fitted bodice over a flared skirt. When she'd bought it, she thought it too pretty for everyday wear, but it was perfect for an occasion like this. Slipping it over her head, she managed the zipper on her own. She grabbed her straw bag and a hat and was downstairs in five minutes.

"You're ready!" he called out when he pulled in front of her building, obviously pleased that she hadn't made him wait.

"Ready," she replied.

He jumped out of the car and opened her door before climbing back behind the wheel and pulling onto the street. The top was down, and she was glad she had a scarf tucked in her pocketbook. He took the corner quickly, but she was used to it by now. He was an excellent driver. It was no wonder Theo had hired him. When they got on the highway, she turned to him and smiled.

"We're picking up a case of wine, are we?" she asked.

"We are," he said. "Just wait till you see this place."

"Theo really has you doing everything, doesn't he?" she asked.

"The variety is what makes this job fun," he replied. "I could never be happy shuffling papers in a stuffy office somewhere. I need to move around. What about you? What did you do before you came to Paris?"

"I worked behind the counter in a bakery," she answered. "I've never had the chance to think about what I wanted to do. And then suddenly, Theo was there, making me an offer that changed my life."

"Well, I, for one, am glad he did."

In New York, her entire world was encapsulated in ten blocks, from their apartment to the bakery to the hospital where her father had undergone radiation treatments and ultimately died. She'd known little of the world around her, and certainly nothing of what it might be like to live somewhere else, let alone Europe. The fact that she was doing it now was still incomprehensible, but here she was, speeding across the French countryside with a man whom she hadn't even known two months ago. She had always been too cautious, probably as a byproduct of her childhood. But with Luca, she could simply let go and allow someone else to handle the decisions.

They made small talk, none of it important, although she was aware of the intimacy of sitting alone in a car with him. Too often they were squeezed together with her roommates and shuttled noisily to the House of Rousseau without any meaningful conversation.

"Tell me more about you," she said, glancing in his direction. "I know you're from Italy and that you run errands for Theo and escort us around, but I'd love to hear more about your life growing up."

"It's not that interesting," he answered.

"No, really," Mia pressed. "What was life like back in Italy?"

"Well, I have great parents," he replied. "My father is a carpenter. I spent a lot of time in his workshop when I was growing up, and he was always crafting chairs and tables, selling them in the local markets. I can make a pretty good table myself after working with him for so long. If I get bored here, I can always go into the family business."

"And your mother?" Mia asked. "What is she like?"

"She was raised on a farm in Northern Italy. Her family ran a dairy and produced a variety of mascarpone, which is still my favorite of all the cheeses." He glanced at Mia before turning his attention back to the road. "She's a happy woman. She loves her family, she loves cooking, and she's crazy about my father."

"How many brothers and sisters do you have?" Mia asked.

"Two brothers, three sisters. My mother always said it was a perfect ratio of boys to girls. I'm the second youngest of the family." He paused for a moment. "What about you? Tell me about your family."

"There's not much to tell," Mia answered, shifting in her seat. "My mother died when I was eleven. She was beautiful, with dark hair and enormous brown eyes. Whenever someone spoke to her, she stopped everything and focused on whatever they were saying. It made you feel important. And I seem to remember she was always laughing. My parents were a good match, as a matter of fact. She adored him."

"And your father?"

"He was quieter, more introspective. We were much lonelier after she died. He seemed to lose his lighter side. I loved him, of course, but I often feel like I raised myself. He didn't have the skills to manage an eleven-year-old. Instead, I looked after him."

"He has passed away?"

"A few months ago," she answered. "He was ill for a couple of years. I did everything I could to make him comfortable, but I constantly felt like I was failing, and he finally gave up. He didn't have the strength to fight it anymore."

"I've always felt there was sadness about you," he remarked. "It's difficult to lose parents when you are so young. It must be very intimidating to be going through such a major change in your life right now: a new country, a new job, new people around you. At least when I came to France, my family wasn't far away. I can reach them in a few hours."

"They sound nice."

"They are," he said. "But I suppose if it's what you're used to, you take it for granted."

She had been so consumed by the constant activity, she rarely let herself think about her parents. The truth was, she was still grieving, which was probably the reason she was having difficulty adjusting to the social aspects of her new life. For a moment, she thought of confiding in him about the difficulties she'd experienced—things going missing, the stress and strain of trying to be perfect, the problems with talking to men—but something held her back.

"What do you do in Paris when you're not working?" she asked, trying to change the subject.

"This and that," he answered. "My friends and I play music, smoke too much, and hit the clubs once in a while."

"What do you play?" she asked.

"A little guitar," he replied. "What about you? Do you play an instrument?"

Mia shook her head. "I took piano lessons when I was young, but that didn't last long. I never took up anything else."

"Do you miss your friends?" he asked. "Your old life in New York?"

"I miss my father," she said. "I miss his books spread out everywhere and the way he liked to tell me about what he was studying. He was a natural teacher. Do you go home often?"

"As often as I can," he told her. "Paris isn't the real world, you know."

Mia turned her attention to the road in front of her. If Paris wasn't the real world, she didn't know what was. Right now she didn't have anything else. No one in New York was waiting for her. Her friends had fallen out of touch during her father's illness because she was never free to get together. Thinking about Luca's large close family suddenly made her feel more alone than ever.

Luca pointed to a sign. "We're in the Loire Valley now. It's one of the prettiest areas in France."

The scenery was stunning. Rolling hills and beech trees went on for miles. The traffic melted away, and everything was silent and still, no sound but the crunch of their tires on the road as they kicked up a trail of dust behind them. The villages they passed seemed abandoned. If there was life going on inside them, it wasn't visible to the outside world, apart from the occasional fluttering of lace from a blue-shuttered window. Mia wanted to get out and explore, but of course, they were running an errand for Theo, and she couldn't ask Luca to play tour guide. One day, she would take the train to one of them, perhaps, and wander in and around the churches and buildings on her own.

"I've been to this vineyard a couple of times before," he said. "It's a family-operated business. They never let me get away without having a meal with them. I hope you're up for meeting everyone."

"It's fine," she said, wondering what it would be like to have friends and connections in different towns and villages and be a welcome guest at each one. Although, if anyone could, it would be Luca.

He pulled off the highway and into one of the towns. It looked like a painting by Cézanne, with its deep green hills and houses clustered around a church with a tall steeple towering over them. Cloud-white anemones had sprung up along stone walls and at the base of towering poplars. Few cars were on the roads, and even fewer people were walking around the village. After they passed through the town, Mia was mesmerized by the tall graceful sunflowers dotting the fields.

He drove for another fifteen minutes and eventually turned in at an entrance with a tall iron gate. The letter *P* was written in script on it, and Mia turned to him curiously.

"Is this it?" she asked.

"This is it," he replied. "The Perdreau Vineyards. Jean Perdreau is the owner. He runs it with his sons."

"Perdreau," Mia repeated.

"It means *partridge*," he said. "You'll see what I mean. Their wine labels are embellished with a drawing of a partridge surrounded by feathers. It's one of Monsieur Rousseau's favorite wines."

"What about you?" she asked. "What's your favorite?"

"Well," he answered, leaning closer, his face just inches from hers. "I prefer the Italian wines, of course. But that's just a little something to keep between us."

Mia turned away, coloring, but he didn't seem to notice, concentrating once again on the road in front of him.

He took the turns down a long winding drive and pulled up in front of a large building. Mia could see a rambling stone house in the distance, wondering if they would be able to get close enough to inspect it. They got out of the car, and she followed him to the building, where he leaned into the open doorway and called out a greeting. Mia hung back as an older man in a straw hat came out to meet them. He had a grizzled gray beard and mustache, and rumpled clothes that showed he had been hard at work, but despite it, his smile was one of the most attractive she had ever seen.

"Luca Rossi!" he roared. "How good to see you today. Let me guess… Marcel Rousseau is ready for another case of Perdreau."

"You are correct, sir," Luca said.

"And who is this young lady?" the Frenchman continued, raising a brow. "You've never brought a girl here before."

"May I present Mia Walker, who also works for Monsieur Rousseau," Luca replied. "She's new to France, and this is her first time to visit the Loire region."

"Miss Walker," their host said, taking her hands in his. "What a pleasure it is to have you here today. Have you ever been to a vineyard before?"

"No, Monsieur," she answered, taken aback by his attention.

"Well, that will not do," he replied, letting go of her hands. "We must rectify this situation at once."

He called to someone in the building, and a younger man who resembled him—obviously his son—came up to shake their hands. The young man grinned as he approached, his eyes never leaving Mia's face.

"Luca," he said, before turning to Mia. "And who, may I ask, is this?"

"This is my friend, Mia Walker," Luca replied. "Mia, this is Jean's oldest son, Victor."

Mia murmured a reply and took a step back. He had his father's good looks, but there was something discomfiting about the way he looked at her.

Perdreau gestured toward the fields. "As you can see, we've begun the harvesting process. You should take our guest for a walk around the vineyards and then join us up at the house for the midday meal."

"We'd be honored, sir," Luca replied. "Come on, Mia. Let's let them get back to work."

He led her away from the building toward the fields, where vines were bursting with grapes. As they approached, she could see the trunks were bowed and straggly, the leaves and branches weighed down with the dark violet-colored fruit, which were planted in dozens upon dozens of rows. Mia followed Luca as he wandered among them, occasionally stopping to inspect the large heart-shaped leaves and touching the soil at the root with his fingers.

"I thought grapes were harvested in the fall," Mia said, tilting her head back to enjoy the sun. Her entire body was thrumming with warmth.

"*La vendage* is a process, both here and in Italy," he replied. "The vineyards will have their people picking them over a couple of months, from August to October. At the end of the season, there is a festival to celebrate the bounty of the harvest."

She nodded, wandering slowly among the vines, brushing her hand gently up against the burgeoning grapes. Never for a second had she imagined so beautiful a place. Looking across the field at the men hard at work, it seemed so much more than a profession; it was obviously a passion. Away from the glare of the city, the vineyard seemed to exist in a world of its own.

Luca bent down and took a handful of pebbles. He stood and held them out for her inspection, running a finger through them.

"What is it?" she asked, moving closer.

"Limestone," he answered. "The best vineyards keep it at the base of the vines. It absorbs water and then releases it as the soil needs it."

He put them back at the base of the vine and dusted his hands together. A tractor pulled a cart between the rows as the men worked, filling boxes with fruit. Luca took one of the vines in his hand and pointed to the root.

"They're clipping the bunches at the vine," he said. "Sometimes a vineyard will want to trim them as close as possible to the branch; others are not as precise. You can see from the growth here that Perdreau is very particular about how his vines are treated."

The murmur of voices rose over the field, and she could hear the men talking. It was clear they were discussing the ripened grapes as they inspected the leaves and the quality of the fruit. She walked the length of the vineyard, wishing she could stay forever.

Luca stood on the other side of the row, and he fell in step with her, parted only by a section of vines ten or twelve feet high. She smiled as he was obscured by leaves and vines for a second and then appeared again, studying her intently. He stepped through an opening between the vines, and suddenly he was standing close to her, far closer than he had ever been, even in his tiny automobile.

His jaw was taut, his eyes focused on her own. For a moment, neither of them moved, his lips mere inches from hers as they stood in the shade of the vines. Suddenly, a blackbird startled them as it flew near their heads, chuckling as he made his landing on the vine just above.

"We should go back," Luca said suddenly. "They'll be expecting us."

Disappointed, she nodded, following as he led her toward the house. They walked around the back, where two women were setting out bottles of wine and setting the table with candles and earthenware dishes. A young boy came outside, carrying a large bowl of antipasti.

Perdreau's wife came out to greet them, kissing them on both cheeks, and introduced them to her family. Mia was swept into the kitchen, where she was handed a plate of small round loaves of bread to set on the table.

The kitchen was dark and cool, with a tile floor and walls, and pots bubbling on the stove. Children darted in and around the women cooking, stealing a piece of bread or a spoonful of jam before drifting outside through the green doors once again. Mia watched as Madame Perdreau skillfully drained the pasta and stirred the sauces. The women were barefoot, and she longed to kick off her sandals and stand on the cold tiles, which she knew were a welcome respite from the heat. They didn't speak English, but that wasn't an impediment to the bonhomie they extended. One of the sisters tied an apron around her waist; another handed her a spoon. She listened to the hum of their chatter and was guided to stir the sauce slowly until the meal was ready. When Madame Perdreau removed the pot from the stove, Mia untied the apron, draped it over a chair, and followed everyone outside where Luca was waiting.

Fig trees, heavy with ripened fruit, surrounded the enclosed space, and everyone took a seat.

Luca sat on her left and Madame Perdreau on her right, handing her a plate of bread to pass around the table. There were dishes of nuts and olives and sausage, alongside platters spilling over with cheeses and fruit. A huge bowl of pasta sat in the center.

They lingered for a couple of hours. Mia listened to the conversation, confined primarily to the purchase of new equipment, the number of people who worked in the vineyard, the family business, and the method of wine making. When at last the party began to drift away one at a time, she offered to go with Madame back into the kitchen.

"No, no," the older woman said, before rattling off something in French.

Luca walked over to her, his hands in his pockets. "She said to thank you for the pleasure of your company. I'll just be a few minutes. I'm going to take care of the case of wine for Monsieur Rousseau."

"I think I'll have another look at the vineyard before we leave," Mia said. She turned to Monsieur Perdreau, who walked up to join them. "Thank you for your hospitality, Monsieur. And please thank your wife for me as well."

The older gentleman smiled. "It was our pleasure. Let us hope this will not be your last visit. You are welcome anytime."

"*Merci*, Monsieur," she replied.

She walked to the edge of the field, staring out at the vines before her. It was easy to imagine living here, picking grapes and making savory sauces, perhaps even creating a life. She was glad she had come with Luca, or she never would have had this experience. It was one she would never forget.

Suddenly, she was aware that someone had come up behind her. Smiling, she turned to say something to Luca when she realized it was Victor Perdreau, his lips twisted in a smirk. She looked past him to see if Luca was there, but he had disappeared with Monsieur Perdreau.

"I'm going back now," she said, trying to walk around him.

He put out his arm to stop her. "Don't go on my account, Mademoiselle. We haven't had the chance to get acquainted."

"We're about to leave," she insisted.

"Why the hurry?" he asked, stepping closer. "I can see you like our little vineyard."

She turned to go back to the car, but he stopped her, grabbing her wrist.

"I just want to talk," he said.

"We're leaving."

"Nonsense. Stay for a while."

"Mademoiselle!" Jean Perdreau called, interrupting them. "Come and have a final taste of this wine."

Relief flooded through her. Victor stepped back, allowing her to follow their host. Her heart was beating faster than normal, but she took the glass from Jean and sipped the wine. Before she could turn to see if Victor was still behind her, Madame Perdreau beckoned her to come and fill a bucket with grapes to take home.

From the fields, she could hear Luca speaking in a raised voice to Perdreau's son, although she couldn't tell what he was saying. It escalated into an argument. Mia couldn't make out the conversation, but she saw Luca glance around before handing something to Victor.

Monsieur Perdreau made no comment and did not appear concerned, but her muscles tightened until Luca finally reappeared.

"Thank you for a memorable afternoon," Luca said as they shook hands with the Perdreaus.

"Yes, thank you," Mia echoed.

On the drive home, it was clear the spell was broken, the day spoiled. Luca concentrated on the road, and the conversation was confined to the weather and the state of the traffic heading back into Paris.

"What happened with Victor?" she finally asked, afraid their argument had been about her.

"What do you mean?" he snapped in a brusque tone. "Nothing happened."

Something had changed between them, although Mia didn't know what it was. She wondered if he had seen her with Victor, but surely if he had, he would have realized that the younger Perdreau's attentions were unwanted.

He focused on the road in front of him as Mia wondered what he was keeping from her. Of course, everyone had their private concerns.

She grew cold as she thought of her own. Whatever was bothering Luca, she decided it had nothing to do with her. Everyone was entitled to their secrets.

They sped along the highway as dusk began to fall. She kept her eyes on the road like Luca, trying to understand what had happened between them, the moment where he had almost kissed her left unspoken, though not forgotten.

# 8

---

The first time he saw her, he knew she was the one. She was just an assignment at the time, one with all the requisite model characteristics: attractive, tall, and willowy. But there was something else about her that caught his attention and wouldn't let go.

The sadness, perhaps. The way she was unaware of how attractive she was. The hesitation before she did anything, lest she do it wrong. It was endearing if one was sentimental, but of course, he wasn't. He'd seen her some time before he approached her, following her and tracking her movements, noticing to whom she spoke on the rare occasions she put herself out there. There didn't seem to be many people she was close to. Her body language attested to that even among her acquaintances. He could see that from the way she nearly always leaned away from others during a conversation instead of leaning in. She'd been shut off from people for a long time, from what he could tell, and nothing could have been more perfect. It was as if she had been primed for what he needed her for, molded by life not to trust anyone and yet, at the same time, possessing a desperate need to trust.

There was so much he could tell about her, even from the beginning. She would fall in love easily, despite her reserve, a quality he had to use but not abuse, for she was not the object, only a tool. He wasn't trying to break her, although she would probably break anyway. He doubted she had the strength to withstand the things she was going to have to face if everything went to plan.

She was everything his organization had been looking for, a rare combination of beauty and reserve. She was rough around the edges, of course, but nothing that spending a few months in a fashion house couldn't fix.

He liked following her in the early days, getting to know her routine. Within a couple of weeks, he knew the exact shop windows that would catch her eye and the sort of cravings she had when she was hungry. She liked bananas better than apples but would sneak a rare bit of chocolate from time to time. In shops, she lingered over the pocketbooks rather than clothing. She was attracted to bright colors yet never left the shop with her first choice. It was easy to see she was trying to be sensible, figuring out what it meant to receive an actual check for services rendered and how to deal with it when she did. However, unlike a lot of girls her age, she spent less time shopping and more time wandering in the parks and by the river, making it harder to get near enough to read her mood. She even found her way to the Père Lachaise once in the first couple of months, a place most girls her age wouldn't go near on a dare. Of course, he knew she had recently lost her father and was dealing with pent-up emotions despite her cool exterior.

He had always thought it an odd place to wander, that cemetery. She stepped outside on a rainy day, and he followed at a discreet distance as she slipped and stumbled over the cobblestones, eventually closing her umbrella when the rain let up. It was a poky, dark place, full of leafy narrow lanes and hidden corners. The cemetery handed out maps, but they were impossible to read. None of the paths jibed with the street names. He'd taken one when he'd followed her in but tossed it on the ground in a pile of wet leaves, although he noticed she struggled to make sense of hers. It didn't really matter if he had a map or not. His only job was to get to know this girl: her quirks—like perching on a hundred-year-old grave to have a brief cry for her dead father—as well as her habits. Somehow, quite extraordinarily, she found her way out of the maze, stopping at the exit to remove her shoe, which had rubbed a blister on the back of her heel, leaving a trickle of blood running down her foot. She wiped it with a handkerchief and then slipped the shoe back on before setting off again for parts unknown.

Getting to know someone without their knowledge was a tricky business, but one that he enjoyed. It was a skill, learning more about someone than they even knew about themselves. There were people who would dismiss her as insignificant, of course. There was her youth to be considered, after all. Others would compartmentalize her as a beauty, which she was, and believe her to be as dull as a butter knife.

He began to see otherwise. Yes, she had the simple desires of any nineteen-year-old, and it was clear that she was excited to see the world for the first time outside of her small childhood experience. But she had other interests that piqued his curiosity, which led her right into his grasp.

She was intelligent, always on the hunt for things to learn. She haunted the library, trying her hand at French books but giving up when her language lessons weren't up to the task. Instead, she turned to newspapers. One of her favorite pastimes was picking up a copy of *Le Monde* or *Le Figaro,* using a pocket dictionary to help her decipher the words. She was persistent in her attempts to learn the language, as difficult as she found it. It might have been easier for her if she had been a student like so many of the other young Americans in Paris at the time, but a lack of money or direction, combined with a unique opportunity to have a glamorous job obtained with little or no qualifications, prevented her from even contemplating such a notion.

One of his favorites of her qualities was her cautiousness toward others and a refusal to get close to anyone. Paradoxically, she was suspicious of her roommates but not of the general public, having the opinion that the French were a harmless, perhaps eccentric bunch of people rather than the suspicious isolationists that they are. He wasn't French, but he shared their feeling—not to mention it suited the work he did.

He was getting a PhD in Mia Walker, for better or worse. He wasn't without feeling, but the truth was, it didn't pay to get too close to a target. She was a tool, nothing more. And yet, there was something there, something that happened the first time he had the occasion to speak to her. And for some time afterward, neither of them were quite able to say what exactly that was. Oh, it wasn't like that, of course. Or maybe it was. But all that changed the day he was told that she was expendable. He belonged to a team who was working toward a goal, and the players, himself included, had little value in the long term. It was unfortunate when innocent young women got involved. But, come to think of it, how innocent is anyone, really? Mia Walker had her secrets, the same as everyone else.

He should know. He buried them for her.

# 9

---

It was pouring rain, the dark Parisian sky lighting up in brilliant streaks of lightning, thunder rending the air. Chantal Fournier walked to her window restlessly, opening it a few inches to gauge how bad the storm was. It had already been coming down for hours. Surely it would let up soon. She glanced at her watch. It was almost ten thirty, and she had an appointment in an hour, which gave her time to take care of a few matters.

The first was the cat, whom she had seen in the corridor earlier that morning. He never went outside during inclement weather, preferring to find places to sleep away the day. Sometimes Chantal wished she could do the same, but she never allowed herself to vary from her daily routine. At her age, it was important to maintain the rituals that kept one productive.

She opened her door, stepping into the empty hall. Stooping

down, she peered under the console where lamps lit the hallway, knowing it was a place where the cat liked to hide when he was on the third floor. Occasionally, she found him on the fourth when she was visiting Madame Bernard, and she suspected her friend was one of the residents of the building who allowed him to lap a bowl of milk from her best faience dish. Madame Bernard had a soft heart—that was her problem. The cat was a pest, and the residents of the building were pests as well, none of them taking responsibility for the creature. However, if she didn't look for the cat, Madame Bernard might just be tempted to do it herself, and her friend was far too frail to go hunting for a wayward feline who was loose in the building.

The cat was not in any of his usual hiding spots. Leaving her door ajar, Chantal went down the stairs to search on the second floor. Monsieur Lindsay, an Englishman who had retired to Paris after a career in banking in London, was also known to feed the little beast, but she didn't see a saucer outside his door. She went up and down the hall, but the cat was nowhere to be found. Chantal turned and went back to the third floor, but as the door of her apartment came into view, she realized with a start that one of her neighbors was standing in the doorway. It was the American, the one she had spoken to before. She was formulating a reprimand when the girl turned around and faced her, the cat in her arms. Chantal was surprised at her relief.

"Where did you find him?" she asked, walking up and taking him from the girl, who relinquished him reluctantly.

"He was scratching at my door," the girl replied.

"He is probably hungry."

Chantal walked past her into her flat, putting the creature on the settee and walking into the kitchen for a saucer, which she filled with milk. The girl was still standing in the doorway when she returned.

"Come in, Miss Walker," Chantal said, setting the saucer onto the tile floor.

The cat jumped from the cushions and went over to inspect the contents.

"Thank you, Madame Fournier," she replied. "I'm sorry to bother you. I know he's not your cat, but I've seen you feed him a few times, and we don't have any milk right now. He sounded so hungry."

"Won't you sit down?" Chantal asked.

She was aware of the responsibility she had to attend in less than an hour, as unconventional as it was, but she needed to know more about this girl, and this was an opportunity to ask her a few questions.

"Thank you," Mia said.

Chantal sat down in the armchair across from her. "How are you enjoying Paris?"

"Very well, thank you," she replied. "I like working at the House of Rousseau."

"You're very young to be in a foreign country on your own."

"I'm nineteen. That's old enough."

Chantal raised a brow. "Old enough to get into trouble."

In fact, she was thinking of herself and the trouble she got into at nineteen. Marrying Noel, for one thing. Her parents had pushed her into marriage, thinking only of her future financial security. Well, she'd certainly had that, and it hadn't made her happy. She looked at the girl in front of her, wondering what sort of mistakes she would make. Of course, she had already made an enormous one, even though she didn't realize it yet.

"I promise you, Madame, I am not here to get into trouble."

"Of course you aren't," she replied, folding her hands in her lap. "I was thinking more of myself at your age. How do you find your roommates? Are you settling in all right?"

The girl hesitated for a moment. Chantal was pleased to see that the American wasn't blindly following the others without a thought.

"They're nice," came the bland reply.

"If somewhat adventurous," Chantal observed, thinking of their late nights and noisy visitors. "Although I suppose that is merely a byproduct of being a model in Paris."

"*Oui*, Madame," Mia said, obviously at a loss for how to answer.

"Who is the young man who drives you around?" she asked. "I've seen him on several occasions. He's a handsome fellow."

"His name is Luca Rossi," the girl answered. "He also works for Monsieur Rousseau."

"He must be well acquainted with Paris to be so confident behind the wheel."

"He is."

She defended him rather quickly, in Chantal's opinion. Perhaps she was starting to have feelings for him. Chantal turned her gold bracelet on her wrist and then decided to end the interview. One must get information slowly, gaining her trust.

"It was nice of you to rescue the cat," Chantal said, standing. She could not be late for her appointment. "He doesn't like to go outside when it's wet. I will make certain he eats something."

"Thank you," Mia answered. She stood and walked to the door, turning back as she reached for the handle. "I love your flat, Madame. You have so many books."

"All in French, I'm afraid, or I would loan some to you," Chantal replied. "But there are a couple of good lending libraries that have books in English, if you are interested."

Mia brightened. "I'm very interested."

"I'll write down the addresses and leave it in your mailbox."

"Thank you, Madame. That's very kind of you."

Chantal nodded and watched her leave. When Mia had gone, Chantal walked over to her desk and sat down, taking a piece of stationery and a pen to write down the two addresses. It was important to keep one's promises, no matter how small. Then she jotted a few observations onto a second piece of stationery. When she finished, she took out the basket of letters, pulling out the most recent one.

It was more urgent than the others she had received before. Ordinarily, they brought her enormous pleasure, but this one demanded something of her that she wasn't prepared to give. She pulled it from the envelope, read it once again, and then replaced it, setting it aside. Even if she wanted to do something about it, she couldn't do it now. However, this wasn't the moment to dwell on such matters. She had to leave if she wanted to be on time for her appointment.

Taking the two handwritten sheets of paper from her desk, she proceeded to fold one and tuck it into her pocketbook. Then she put on her raincoat and went downstairs, putting the other—a list of bookshops—in the slot of Mia's mailbox.

The rain had lessened to a drizzle. She opened her umbrella and walked leisurely for three blocks, taking a circuitous route, lingering in front of shop windows and occasionally wandering inside to look at the wares. One was an infants' clothing store. She picked up two or three of the garments, wondering briefly if she had any new grandchildren, before setting them down again. When she stepped back out into the street, she checked the reflections in the windows to make certain that no one was following her. Of course, a seventy-four-year-old woman was not a likely target of suspicion. It was easy enough to explore the neighborhood without arousing anyone's attention.

After twenty minutes, she found herself in front of a patisserie and stepped inside, appreciating the cool, dark interior. She folded her umbrella and went to the back of the restaurant, where there were few customers, and when the waitress arrived, she ordered a cup of tea and a ham-and-watercress sandwich, spreading her serviette over her lap to wait. When the tea arrived, she added a dash of milk and one cube of sugar, stirring it slowly.

The man sitting at the table behind her pushed back his chair, accidentally brushing her arm with his elbow. She kept her eyes fixed on her cup and saucer. She opened her pocketbook, took out the folded piece of paper, and slid it onto the table. The waitress appeared with the sandwich, which she ate in slow, methodic bites. When she was finished, she folded her napkin and stood.

She didn't look at the young man. Instead, she left her money on the table and walked out of the shop. She wandered along the street, stopping at a *fleuriste*, where she paused to browse the selection of flowers. The roses were perfect, but she wanted something different, eventually deciding on pale-orange ranunculus, which were wrapped by the clerk in ivory waxed paper and tied with string.

Back in the street, she noticed the man from the café walking just ahead of her, a paperback novel in his hand, the paper she had written tucked between the pages. Satisfied that she had done her duty, she crossed the street and went a different way, heading back to her flat.

Flowers were one of the loves of her life, and whenever she was feeling distressed, she treated herself to the most appealing ones she could find. In her kitchen, she unwrapped them as carefully as possible, took a pair of gardening shears from a basket on the shelf, and trimmed them at precisely the correct height for the round vase she had decided to use. She snipped excess leaves from the stems, arranging them carefully, appreciating the slight variation in the colors of each bloom.

One of the things she had learned when she first moved to Paris was how to compartmentalize her life. Here, in this flat, it was important to keep her focus on positive matters. If she was troubled, she went to her usual bench in the Place Dauphine. This was the spot for pleasantness only. Therefore, thoughts of her young neighbor, while they crept into the corners of her mind, were banished entirely. There was only so much one could do, anyway, and the way to make the best of any situation was to do whatever one could and then try not to worry about things she couldn't control.

As she brought the flowers into the sitting room, there was a knock at the door. Chantal placed the vase on the table and proceeded to open it, finding, to her surprise, that Monsieur Lindsay from the second floor was standing on the other side.

"Monsieur," she said.

He had never come to her door before, and she couldn't imagine what he might want from her. The entirety of their interactions consisted primarily of nodding to each other in the hall and occasionally muttering a hasty "Bonjour" as they passed.

She knew he was a widower—she had learned that much from the concierge. She also knew he had a son who came once or twice a year from London to visit, although he never stayed long. Monsieur Lindsay was gentlemanly and polite, the most she expected from any man, and he was on her good side because he kept his hallway tidy and he kept to himself. An enigma, particularly when one is clean with proper manners, was a good thing.

She opened the door and invited him inside, wondering if he was going to speak to her about the cat. Surely he knew as well as anyone that the creature was happy with his nomadic existence, a regular flâneur, sweet-talking his way into everyone's kitchen. Or perhaps purring. But that was another matter.

"Do you have a moment, Madame?" Monsieur Lindsay asked.

His face was so serious, she was almost worried.

"Bien sûr," she replied. "Please, have a seat."

She couldn't remember the last time anyone had been in her flat, and certainly not two people in a single day. She had the sudden feeling that he was involved in the same matter she was. Her fears, however, were dispelled when he began to speak.

"Madame, I appreciate what a good neighbor you are," he began, sitting back in his chair. His back was straight, and he looked almost aristocratic.

"As are you," she murmured.

"In no way would I ever wish to spoil the excellent working relationship between us, you understand," he said.

"Of course," she replied. "I feel the same."

"I have given this the utmost consideration for some time, and I have come to the conclusion that I must ask you a question."

"What is the question?" she asked, wondering if she should be concerned. However, the look on his face was so genuine that she couldn't imagine anything serious being wrong.

"I wondered if you might consider having dinner with me one evening."

He looked relieved to have gotten the question out, and it took all the poise she possessed not to laugh. He was a fine-looking gentleman, of course, as respectable and good as any she had known. But he was a handful of years too young to be asking for the privilege to dine with a seventy-four-year-old woman. In fact, until that moment, she had no inkling that women of a certain age were asked anything of the sort.

"Well," she began, but he interrupted her before she could continue.

"I do appreciate the delicacy of us living in the same building," he replied. "It's just that one does not often meet a woman of your stature and bearing. I lost my wife many years ago and never expected to want to break bread with another woman. You, however, have made me wish that I had not chosen such a severe penalty for myself."

She was nearly speechless, rising from her seat. "Would you care for a cup of tea, Monsieur?"

"No," he said, standing. "I won't put you to any trouble. I think if we deepen our friendship, it is wise to do it outside of the sphere of our small world. That way, it will not cause any embarrassment should you not wish to continue the acquaintance."

"I cannot imagine not wanting to continue our acquaintance," she protested.

"But?"

She couldn't continue. How could she say that her age was a barrier to his request, not to mention the personal matter she had revealed to no one?

"I shall take your kind offer under consideration," she said.

It was the best she could do. Ordinarily, she would have put a hasty end to it and not thought twice about it, but she had no desire to hurt his feelings. Besides, it wasn't an easy decision. She couldn't resist a glance at the letter whose urgency had complicated her life.

"Thank you for your time, Madame," he replied, bowing.

"You are too kind."

When he had gone, she prepared dinner for Madame Bernard and took it upstairs. The old woman was looking frailer each time she saw her. She dreaded the day that Madame did not reply to her knock at the door. Although she knew her friend was much older, she wasn't ready for change. But one thing Chantal knew: change doesn't wait until one is ready for it. In fact, it usually happens at the most inconvenient time of all.

# 10

---

"Mia, would you come down to my office for a moment?"

She looked up at Theo, who had suddenly appeared in the doorway of the studio. One of the designers, Franz, was kneeling at her feet, pinning the hem of the gown she would be wearing the following afternoon for her first Rousseau fashion show.

"Take your time, Franz," Theo said as he walked to the door. "There's no rush. You want to get that hem right."

For some reason, Mia was nervous. Theo had never been anything but polite to her, but still, he made her uncomfortable. She could navigate her way around Luca and Elisabeth and usually even Maeve, but Theo was the one person she couldn't quite hold her own against. Perhaps it was the fact that apart from Monsieur Rousseau, he was the chief authority figure in their small world. Also, she had rarely noticed him calling anyone else into his office, and the one thing she hated more than anything else was to be singled out.

Franz took his time pinning the rest of the hem, unaware of Mia's nerves. Eventually, he stood and unzipped the garment, then held it away from her heels as she stepped out of it. She went to the changing room in her slip and slid her own dress over it, fastening the buttons as high as they would go. Then she brushed her hair and inspected her lipstick before walking downstairs to Theo's office. He answered at the first knock.

"Come in."

Mia turned the knob and went inside.

"Sit down, please," he instructed.

She sat in the chair in front of his desk, folding her hands in her lap, making certain she was sitting up straight. Posture, she had learned, was one of the most important aspects of her job, the one quality a model could not ignore. He came around his desk and sat on the edge, crossing his arms.

"How was the fitting?" he asked.

"It was fine," she answered, trying to read his expression.

Of course it was fine. Franz was the best at Rousseau. Mia wasn't certain what else she was supposed to say, unless Theo had merely asked to put her at her ease.

"Your first modeling opportunity is tomorrow," he continued. "How are you feeling about it? Are you ready?"

"Perfectly ready," she said, aware that a show of confidence was expected of her. "We've practiced a dozen times and I've made notes, which I go over at home."

"Well, don't overthink it," he answered. "You'll do fine. I've seen your practice runs."

"Thank you," she replied.

"This is an important event," he continued. "As you know, the House of Rousseau has been selected from among many fashion houses for the show tomorrow, which benefits the hospital charity fund. We are always delighted to have the opportunity to participate. Are your gowns all finished?"

Mia nodded. "All except for the last one. Franz decided to let the hem down an inch for a little more drama."

"He knows what he's doing," Theo said. "You know, Mia, I've noticed you're serious about your work, which happens to be the reason I've asked you to come in and see me today. I want to talk to you about something."

"Yes, sir," she replied, sitting up a little straighter.

"Perhaps some of the other girls have mentioned that there are social occasions now and then when we send our models out to be seen against the backdrop of Paris nightlife."

"I've heard something about it," she replied.

"Tomorrow night, there is just such an occasion, and I would like to send you to be the representative from Rousseau."

"Of course, Monsieur Gillette," she said.

She couldn't possibly tell him that she was uncomfortable in social situations and that she had no interest in pursuing attention for the sake of Rousseau. It was clear that if she wanted to keep her job, she would have to pull herself together and do it.

"You'll be introduced to a gentleman at the charity event tomorrow," he continued. "He will be your escort at a club later in the evening. Miss Larson will provide you with the dress we've selected for you to wear. Your primary duties are to relax and be charming. And, of course, if anyone asks about the dress or even looks interested, you simply tell them it is from the House of Rousseau."

"Yes, sir."

"Good," he said, standing. "We'll talk more tomorrow."

Mia stood, smoothing her skirt. She had been dismissed. She went back upstairs to gather her things, feeling irritated. She had left the only life she had ever known for a serious career in fashion. It never mattered how busy they were; she could handle fittings and photo shoots and studying the designs day and night, if necessary, but she had no interest in being paraded around at social events. She didn't even like the parties that Maeve and Elisabeth liked to host.

"Are you ready?" Elisabeth asked as she joined them. Her friend looked especially radiant in a red dress with a paisley scarf around her neck, the perfect image of a model in Paris. As far as she knew, neither Elisabeth nor Maeve seemed to do this sort of engagement, but then, she hadn't been in Paris that long.

"Ready," Mia murmured.

"We're taking the Métro tonight," Maeve remarked, holding the door open for them as they left the building. "Luca's been sent on another errand."

"By the way, I've been meaning to ask you something," Elisabeth said as they walked down the street. "Has something happened between the two of you?"

"Of course not," Mia replied. "Why?"

"You've been quiet for days," Maeve answered. "It started right after you spent the day with him."

"I haven't been quiet," she protested, aware that she had indeed been upset after their day out together. He'd nearly kissed her and an hour later was barely speaking to her. "It's probably the weather. These muggy days are so uncomfortable."

"Well, that's certainly true," Elisabeth said. "Thank goodness fall will be here soon."

"If I were you, I'd steer clear of him," Maeve warned as they made their way to the closest Métro station. "He's too much of a ladies' man for the likes of us."

Elisabeth didn't bring it up again, but Mia realized she was going to have to get better control over her emotions. The most important thing was to focus on her career. The last thing she wanted to do was jeopardize her position.

The following day, Rousseau was abuzz with activity. Like all the other models chosen to work for this event, Mia would be wearing three separate outfits, and everything was being refitted to make certain they were perfect. She also had meetings with the hair and makeup teams to discuss her look, something that could be modified when she wore the final garment in the show.

In her excitement, she had only eaten a few bites of the salad she ordered at lunch. By the time the show was about to begin, she would have been hungry if it weren't for the accompanying nerves. However, that was quickly forgotten as the professional side of her, one she hadn't known even existed, began to take over. In the moments before she was to walk out to model the first dress, something came over her that she had never experienced before. She held her head high and relaxed as she awaited her turn. This was something she could do.

The second turn on the runway was easier than the first, and by the third, she was convinced that Theo Gillette had known what he was doing when he had chosen her for this job. After all the models had completed their final walk down the runway, they were to mingle among the guests, who would be bidding on the dresses.

She was wearing her favorite of the three ensembles, a midnight-blue gown with narrow straps, and a satin cape, which she removed for effect as she walked about the room. Elisabeth and Maeve were already in conversation with two of the women who had come to see the collection, and Mia looked up to see a gentleman walking toward her.

"Mademoiselle," he said, giving her a mock bow.

There were a few other men present, but he was by far the most attractive. Tall, with brown hair combed neatly back, he brushed a hand over his thin mustache to disguise his smile.

"Monsieur," she said, bowing slightly, lowering her eyes.

"What a lovely gown you're wearing," he said, gesturing at her with a finger. "Tell me about it, if you would."

She took a step back and began to deliver her remarks. "This is a silk evening dress, featuring a scooped neck and a fitted bodice as well as a kick pleat in the back. It has been paired with a swing cape in matching midnight-blue silk, lined with a coordinating shade of blue so that it may be reversible, making it twice as practical for the modern woman. It can be worn with or without jewelry, although one might pair it with a fine pendant for an added layer of elegance. Today, the designers have chosen a three-strand pearl bracelet and pearl-drop earrings for a refined effect."

He laughed. "Nothing at the House of Rousseau is practical. It is purely frivolous. In the best way, of course."

"As you say, Monsieur."

"Does it have a back zipper?" he asked, smiling.

In answer, she turned and lowered the coat below her shoulders, allowing him to see for himself. Then she turned around and faced him again, looking him squarely in the eye.

"Do you have any other questions, Monsieur?" she asked.

"This is a stunning combination," he remarked. "The dark-blue dress and the flush of your cheeks. One might be carried away with the loveliness of it all."

"I'm glad you like the dress, sir," she replied.

"Let's just say I'm a big fan of Rousseau," he said. "Not to mention beautiful models with eyes the color of espresso."

"Thank you, Miss Walker," Theo said as he walked up to join

them. He nodded at the gentleman before turning to Mia. "You may wait in my office."

She smiled, relieved to be able to escape. She was the only model who had been approached by a man. All the other girls were speaking to middle-aged women who were shopping for themselves and their fortunate young daughters. She opened the door to Theo's office and went inside, wondering why he wanted to speak to her again. This was her first event, after all, and as far as she knew, it was successful.

A few minutes later, Theo came in and closed the door behind him. She stood stiffly by the window, afraid to sit lest it wrinkle the gown.

"You did a wonderful job," he said, walking over to his desk and picking up a stack of mail, glancing through it. "Miss Larson has the dress you'll be wearing to the event this evening. Luca will drive you to a private home, where you will join a cocktail party in progress. The gentleman you just met will act as your escort for the event."

He put the mail on the desk. "These are very polite affairs. You will not be expected to talk a great deal. Limit yourself to one glass of wine, if you would. Even less, if possible. It's important to appear to partake in the festivities without allowing yourself to become even mildly intoxicated. Our models are held to a high standard, as you know. Your purpose is to show off the dress to its best advantage and nothing more. Afterward, Luca will be waiting outside for you. Do you understand?"

"Of course."

"There's just one more thing," he continued. "One of the people you'll be introduced to is a man by the name of Szabo. He will ask you what street you live on, and you are to reply, 'I live on Rue de Meuniers, number 46.' Repeat that for me, please."

"I live on Rue de Meuniers, number 46," she said, furrowing her brow. "But, of course, I don't."

"We're merely directing him to a warehouse for him to view certain items without letting anyone else know," he said. "It's important that you get it right. Could you repeat it for me one more time?"

"I live on Rue de Meuniers, number 46."

"Perfect," he replied. "Represent the House of Rousseau well for us tonight."

She nodded, completely bewildered. Something was going on, although she had no idea what it might be. Natalie had warned her about evening events, but no one had said anything about passing cryptic messages to complete strangers. She didn't completely believe Theo's explanation, but then again, she didn't want to lose her job. As long as she wasn't being asked to do something dishonest, she would go along with it for the time being and keep her eyes open. And if something crossed the line, she would quit. There was no other option.

That evening, she was driven by Luca to an elegant building on the

Right Bank. As he stepped out to open her door, Mia alighted from the car and turned to look at him.

"Is this a common occurrence, Luca?" she asked, gesturing at the building.

Luca narrowed his eyes. "Is what a common occurrence?"

"Do all the models do evening events?"

He paused for a moment before answering. "A few of them do. I think it has to do with letting the gowns be seen. It generates business."

"But Elisabeth or Maeve don't—at least, not as far as I have seen."

"No," he admitted. "I suppose it means you're the hot new model. Monsieur Gillette probably wants to make certain that everyone important gets a look at you."

Mia raised a brow, doubting that she was important enough to warrant the attention.

"I'll be here when you're ready to go," he said, circumventing any further discussion of the issue.

She nodded and rang the bell. The door was opened by a woman who greeted her politely. When Mia walked inside, she noticed the men wore tuxedos and the women were clad in various evening attire. Champagne flowed freely, and waiters wandered among the crowd with trays of canapés held over their heads, the aroma of salmon and goat cheese and arancini filling the air. It reminded her that she hadn't eaten since lunch, and even then, it had only been a few bites. However, she couldn't possibly eat anything while wearing an evening gown. A waiter came by and offered her a glass of champagne, which she accepted, taking only the occasional sip.

She looked about the large room, nodding as she saw the gentleman who was her escort for the evening. He set his drink on a tray and moved toward her. He was an elegant man, his skin as tan as if he had just come from the beach in Saint-Tropez.

"Miss Walker," he said, taking her hand. "I'm afraid we weren't properly introduced. My name is Jack Carr."

"Pleased to meet you," she replied.

She glanced around the room, thinking the scene reminded her of old films, where everyone wore glamorous evening clothes and drank copious amounts of champagne. A pianist tinkled the keys of a baby grand, playing a familiar tune. She hadn't thought for a moment that a world like this really existed.

"That's another lovely gown you're wearing," he remarked. "The House of Rousseau is lucky to have you."

"Thank you, Mr. Carr."

"Call me Jack, please. And may I call you…?"

"Mia," she replied.

"A name as lovely as you are," he answered. "Let me introduce you around."

He offered her his arm and led her around the room, introducing her to dozens of people. She listened intently for their names, although no one was named Szabo. She wondered who he was and if he would approach her soon. An hour later, she found herself glancing at the clock.

Her shoes had begun to pinch, and she was still holding a half-drunk glass of champagne, wondering if she could possibly make her way to the door and leave the party. Jack Carr had excused himself to speak to the host, and she knew Luca was waiting outside. Just as she had made up her mind to leave, a short burly man with dark hair came up to her and smiled.

"Are you enjoying your evening, Mademoiselle?" he asked.

"Yes, thank you," she said, wondering how it was getting so easy to lie.

"That's a beautiful dress you are wearing," he continued.

"It's from the House of Rousseau," she replied, pleased that she had finally gotten to do what she had come here to do, advertise the fashion house by means of her gown.

"They have a lovely collection this year," he answered. "My wife will be very interested."

Mia smiled. "I'm glad you think so."

"I'm Jozsef Szabo. Are you from Paris?"

"No," she answered, noting his name as she shook her head. "I'm from New York."

"New York is very nice," he replied. "Tell me, Mademoiselle, what is your address, please?" She had waited all evening for the question but was shocked when she finally heard it. Taking a deep breath, she answered in a low voice.

"I live on the Rue de Meuniers, number 46."

For a moment, he said nothing, but before she could reply, he smiled.

"What a lovely part of the city. It was wonderful to make your acquaintance, my dear."

He nodded and then bowed before immediately turning away. Mia stared after him, confused. She looked around for Jack, but he was nowhere to be seen. She waited another ten minutes, but when he did not return, she assumed that she was free to leave. She set the warm champagne on a nearby table and made her way toward the door. No one else spoke to her as she slipped from the party undisturbed.

"How was your evening?" Luca asked when he opened the door of his car. His voice was so stilted, he might as well have added "Miss Walker" to his question.

"Fine," she replied, surprised at his tone. She wanted to say *Long and boring*, but it wasn't good manners to complain to fellow employees of Rousseau.

"We're lucky to have good weather," he remarked. "These engagements can be difficult in the rain."

Luca was once again silent on the ride home, other than a brisk "Good night" when they arrived at her building.

There was no sound when she let herself into the flat, no light coming from under Maeve and Elisabeth's door. Something about the evening left her unsettled. She changed into a nightgown and crawled into bed, deciding to talk to Elisabeth about it in the morning.

Elisabeth was already out when Mia got up, and she had no desire to talk to Maeve about her reservations. After breakfast, she grabbed her scarf and headed for the door.

"Where are you going?" Maeve asked, coming out of her room.

Her roommate's hair was disheveled, but she looked to be in a better mood than she had been the previous day.

"Out for a walk," Mia said. "It's the best way I can think of to burn calories."

Her answer, while a lie, satisfied her roommate. The truth was, she was headed back to Madame Laurent's flat. She needed advice from someone who wasn't caught up in the day-to-day activities of Rousseau and was removed enough to look at the situation objectively. Were evening events and passing messages a normal part of a model's routine? Luca had called her the hot new model, but despite her new look, she still didn't feel the part. She had no desire to be singled out for things that made her feel uncomfortable, but she couldn't bring herself to talk to anyone about it.

It was an overcast day, and although she had worn a cardigan, she wished she had brought her raincoat with her. She hurried down the block and crossed at the corner, turning right until she had made her way to the gate with the familiar courtyard behind it. However, when she reached out to open the gate, it was locked.

Mia pushed at the gate again. During the two weeks she had come to see Madame, the gate always stood ajar. She looked around, wondering what to do. The bench, which she had often admired, was there, as usual, and muted fall blooms had been planted around the trees and shrubs—a sign that summer was over.

She looked up at the windows of Madame Laurent's flat, but although it was a gray and cloudy morning, the lights were not on. Perhaps she had another student and was showing her around the Louvre or the Musée Rodin, although when Mia had been under her tutelage, the French lessons and discussions about etiquette and poise had always come first.

She was suddenly nudged aside by someone with a key, who turned it in the lock. It was an older gentleman in a rush to get inside before it started to rain.

"*Pardonnez-moi*," he barked in a gruff voice.

"Excuse me, sir," Mia said. "Is Madame Laurent home?"

"Madame who?" he asked.

"Vivienne Laurent," she said more loudly, to be heard over the wind.

"I know of no one by that name," the gentleman replied.

He stepped through the gate and attempted to pull it shut behind him, but she reached out and took hold of it, momentarily impeding his movement.

"The woman in the flat on the second floor," she persisted, pointing to the window she had looked out of on a dozen occasions.

He followed her gaze to the window and then looked at her once again.

"I have no idea who you mean," he said, narrowing his eyes to examine her closely. "That flat has been empty for over a year."

Mia stepped back in surprise. In response, he slammed the gate shut and walked away, leaving her to try to make sense of what had just happened. She had been in this building, the one enclosed by this very gate, with this garden bench nestled under this willow tree. She stared after him, prickles coming up on her arm. Fat drops of rain began to fall, but still she didn't move. If the gate weren't locked, she would have followed him into the building to check Madame Laurent's apartment for herself. Instead, she was left standing outside the courtyard in the rain. She knew one thing, however: she couldn't ask Maeve or Elisabeth about it. They would only dismiss her concerns. Luca had deflected her questions, and Theo Gillette was formidable and remote. No, she couldn't mention her worries to anyone. Her instincts told her she could trust no one at all.

# 11

---

There's a trick to following someone. It helps to have one of those faces that nobody ever remembers and an average personal description. Not too tall, not too short; no mustache or identifying features; no glasses or noticeable tics or eye-catching habits. Anyone trying to describe him would probably have said he was an ordinary-looking fellow of average height with a friendly smile. Which was why he rarely smiled when he was on the prowl.

Some say you can't follow someone you have already met, but the truth is that most people aren't suspicious. They don't expect to be followed. He had to do a few things differently, but in his book, anyone could be followed at any time without their knowledge if one had the right skills.

Like the previous weekend, when he'd had her in his sights on a Sunday morning. It was one of her favorite times to walk around

Paris. Her roommates were late risers, but she hadn't gotten over the habit of getting up early. She frequented a patisserie, in no small part because she had worked in a bakery before coming to France and subconsciously longed for the familiar scents of flour, sugar, and coffee. It no doubt reminded her of her father and the life they'd had together before he died.

Some of his sort were sympathetic or even sentimental toward their marks, but he wasn't one of them. Everyone experienced loss in their lives; in his line of work, it was a given. One wouldn't be doing what he did if one had come from a life where there were big family gatherings and regular barbecues. It's the tough things in life that mold a person—or maybe even stunt their growth—allowing them to be the kind of person who does what he did for a living. He was a fast operator, always on the prowl for information. The upper echelon of his department preferred to keep him moving, which suited the wanderlust he felt most of the time. Stay busy, keep active, run down targets, neutralize threats, prevent World War III. All in a day's work.

It was a Sunday morning, not too early. She stepped out of the front door of her building just after nine. The plant he had there was standing in the lobby, barely visible to someone on the outside if one didn't know what to look for. He waited until she had gone at least a block before he leisurely started after her.

To follow someone, it's important to get to know their habits. He blended in with the crowd, such as it was on a lazy Sunday morning, when the average Parisians were either in a cathedral somewhere for mass or at home in bed, reading the newspapers. But there are always people out and about in Paris, a mix of tourists trying to make the most of their last few hours before a flight, or people walking their dogs or taking a constitutional before the shops are open and the young crowd comes out to spend their hard-won francs on the latest trends.

Mia Walker wasn't the sort to spend money. He knew this from experience, but he also knew precisely how much money sat in her bank account, as well as the fact that she had used very little of it. She was either worried about failing at her job—a reasonable assumption, from everything he knew of her—or she was saving for something in particular. Perhaps a combination of both. Either way, she didn't seem as at home as some might have been after a few weeks in a new town at a new job, which explained her restlessness and desire to get out of the flat to have time to figure herself out.

She suddenly stopped some distance ahead and swiveled back toward him. Whenever a target turned around for whatever reason, he moved close to a group of people, looking like he was part of their conversation. It was the ultimate camouflage in the middle of a city. He turned his face away slightly, though he kept her in his peripheral vision until she reversed course and kept going in the original direction. Perhaps she had forgotten something and decided it wasn't worth going back for.

It was always easier to trail her on foot, but at times, he used his car, always keeping the vehicle pointed in the opposite direction and watching her through the rearview mirror. A car was handy because he could keep a change of clothes close by. It was amazing what a different-colored jacket or shirt made when one was trying to fool the eye. He was an expert at keeping his distance and playing it cool. Occasionally, he even paid locals to follow his target. Someone would always want to make a buck. Of course, he had people keeping watch while she was in her building, and it was his job at the moment to do the trudging around Paris to clock her every movement.

She walked another quarter mile or so until she came to a café. He was pleased because she'd chosen one that was fairly busy, and there were plenty of places to sit and watch her without being noticed. She carried a book with her most of the time but often became so engrossed in the activity around her that she rarely stopped to read. She was more likely to pull it out in the park, where it was quieter and there were fewer distractions. But who could blame her for being taken with the pastime of people watching in the most famous city in the world? One could see everything here if they stuck around long enough. He certainly had.

He fished a notebook from his pocket and jotted a few notes. Then he lifted the pen and held it at a certain angle, as if deep in thought. In fact, he was snapping photographs. He had quite a few of her already, but it was always good to catch some little nuance or expression he hadn't noticed before.

She stayed a good long while, but he didn't mind. It was nearly forty-five minutes before she stood, paid the waiter, and then turned back in the direction of her flat. He bent his head, pretending to write something so he wouldn't catch her eye, and after she had walked part of the way down the street, he went up to the waiter who had served her.

He was fluent in five languages—six, if you count Farsi, which he didn't. It was a truly difficult language, and while he could decipher it enough to go undercover, it wasn't a natural fit. He spoke French and Italian like a native, along with Russian, German, and Dutch. He asked the waiter, who was German, what she'd ordered, holding out a bill, which the man quickly slipped into his pocket.

"Just a croissant and a coffee," the man said.

"If she comes back, see if she orders the same thing," he told him, giving him a conspiratorial wink.

It paid to have as many sets of eyes as possible on the person one is following to gather information, no matter how obscure. Every detail told a story about someone's personality. For example, the croissants. If she ordered something different every time, she was adventurous, perhaps even willing to take a risk. If she always ordered coffee and croissants, she was playing it safe. Plain and simple.

He was an effective asset, the facts of his life buried deep in some bureaucratic file, as Mia Walker's would be in a few years' time. That is, unless she didn't survive the nuclear explosion that was about to rock her life. Not literally, of course, but it might as well be. She would never recover from it.

# 12

---

Vivienne Laurent's disappearance was a mystery. During her training, Mia had been to her flat nearly every day for two weeks, and she knew the address was correct. There were a few things that were troubling her, and she had hoped for some reassurance from the older woman. Maeve was frequently dismissive of her concerns, and Elisabeth never seemed to take anything seriously, but this time, she would have to talk to them and take her chances.

"I tried to go to see Madame Laurent," she said when she returned to the flat, sitting down across from the two of them. "But when I went to her flat, she wasn't there. In fact, I was told it was empty and no one lives there."

"Why did you want to see her?" asked Maeve, flipping the pages of a magazine. "Your training is over."

Mia looked from Elisabeth to Maeve, noting their impassive

faces. "I wanted to ask her about something Theo said about evening events."

"What about them?" Elisabeth asked, shrugging. "This is a creative business, Mia. We're supposed to be seen out and about to advertise the designs and to keep the name of Rousseau on everyone's lips. It's harmless fun and a chance to meet new people."

"I just wanted the benefit of her wisdom," Mia argued. "An outside perspective. It was so unsettling to find the gate locked."

"You've forgotten the address, that's all," Maeve answered, just as Mia had predicted. "But the truth is, our time with her is over. We have more important things to think about now."

Mia knew she couldn't argue with them further. She had taken a huge leap of faith coming to France and trusting an entire world of strangers. But Madame Laurent wasn't her only problem. She had been glossing over concerns about her job. How had Theo Gillette shown up at a bakery in New York and decided to offer her a position that took her across the ocean to another continent? Why had he singled her out to deliver information to strangers? She wanted answers, but she wasn't in any position to get them. She had two choices: either she packed her bags and went back to New York or she could focus on her job and proceed with caution.

She loved working at Rousseau, learning about the world of fashion and design; the proximity of silks and buttons and bows, all begging to be touched; even the first trip she had made down a runway. It gave her a sense of purpose she had never experienced. She was part of something bigger than her, something that mattered. Even if the average woman couldn't afford a Rousseau gown or coat, the fashion house was part of the phenomena that influenced current trends. Something she wore in a show one fall would be translated to the overall fashion look of the season, ending up in many different forms.

Clothing meant something to people. To her and people like her, who had never had enough money, it was merely something practical with which to clothe herself. And yet, even when finances had been the most pressing consideration, she had still occupied herself with time spent picking out the prettiest color or the softest fabric. Fashion transcended mere serviceability. It inspired, consoled, and pleased the people for whom it was meant. Someone's day could be improved by wearing a favorite blouse or tying a scarf around one's neck. Now she was a part of this world, too.

Mia decided that for the moment, she would stay, the perks of the job outweighing her concerns—at least for now. She pulled a sketch pad from her bag and flipped through the pages. Lately, she had been drawing the designs she'd been allowed to wear, trying to remember the details. Her drawings had been rough at first, but she was learning to use a lighter hand so that she could erase her mistakes when she had drawn a skirt too long and disproportionate to the dress, or when the details weren't quite right. She considered it homework, another way of understanding the role she was chosen to play at this time of her life.

An hour later, Mia looked at her watch. It was only eleven, but she was hungry, not having reached a balance of eating less to stay thin and eating enough not to starve. She stood and walked back toward her favorite café. Agnelli's was an Italian restaurant, but the menu had French dishes and even a few American ones as well—not that she could eat them.

She found a table and picked up the menu, deciding on the salad. As she waited for the waiter, she glanced at the other diners under the awning. It wasn't crowded, just a few older women lunching with friends and a lone man sitting a few tables away. Mia studied him for a moment. He seemed familiar. She frowned, trying to remember where she had seen him before, when she realized he was the American who had tried to buy her a drink at the jazz club where they had gone a couple of weeks earlier. She had been rude to him that evening, she recalled, hating the whole idea of going to clubs and being dragged into the social scene.

He hadn't noticed her. In fact, he sat there, reading a book intently—*The Sun Also Rises*, if the cover was any indication—and she realized that perhaps she had been hasty in dismissing him simply because he had shown an interest in her. It was lonely living in a foreign country, and he wasn't the only one to sit behind a book in a public place, having no one to talk to. She did it nearly every day herself. Rising from her seat, she went over to his table.

"It's you," he said in surprise, closing the book and setting it on the table. "Mia, right? I didn't think I'd see you again."

"I think I was rude to you the evening we met," she admitted.

"I'm not accustomed to accepting drinks from strangers. I came over to apologize."

He smiled and stood, holding out a chair.

"I'm not the sort to hold grudges," he replied. "Besides, you were absolutely right. It can be a little dicey, talking to strangers in bars. You never know what their intentions are."

"Maybe I should have asked you."

"You're sounding a little more confident than you did last time we met," he observed. "Can it be you're getting your footing here in Paris?"

Mia tucked a lock of hair behind her right ear. "I certainly hope so. You said you were in business, didn't you?"

"That's right," he answered. "My company sells machine parts, and I'm based here for a while, handling sales in the European market. I've been in Berlin and Amsterdam since I saw you. But I have to say, Paris is pretty great, isn't it?"

"It's the most beautiful place I've ever seen."

He looked up and cocked his head in the direction of the kitchen. "I think I should warn you, the waiter is headed our way. I was planning to order lunch. You are welcome to join me if you don't want to eat alone."

"I'd be delighted," she replied.

"I do have one question for you, though," he said, setting the menu aside.

"What is it?" she asked.

Philip was handsome in an ordinary way, with a pleasant face and a nice smile, not slick and hard looking like Jack Carr. Once again, she noticed his hair had been freshly cut and he smelled of lemon soap. His blue shirt was open at the collar, and the sleeves were rolled up to just below his elbow. She found herself leaning forward in anticipation.

"Do you trust me?"

The look on his face was serious, yet she could detect a mischievous glint in his eye. In spite of herself, she smiled.

"Not in the least."

He laughed. "Good for you, but I'm going to order for both of us anyway."

She sat back, watching as he chatted with the waiter effortlessly, wondering if her French would ever improve to his level. Perhaps it was all the distractions in her life, but she had seemed to have reached a plateau and had not been able to progress any further.

"Your French is perfect," she said when the waiter had gone.

"What about you?" he asked. "Are you learning the language?"

"I'm trying, but it's difficult. I can't seem to remember all the tenses," she said. "What did you order?"

He smiled. "You'll have to wait and see. Tell me more about you. When you said that you were with a group of friends, I just assumed you were only in Paris for a few days."

"I didn't tell you the truth," she answered, glancing down and then back at him again. "I wasn't sure how you would take it."

"That's cryptic," he replied. "Don't tell me: you're an under-world spy."

"I'm a model," she answered. "I've been in Paris for a few months learning the trade and working for one of the fashion houses here."

"That's impressive," he said.

From the look in his eye, she could see that he meant it. For some reason, his approval mattered. Some people would have considered it a frivolous enterprise, an occupation for an empty-headed girl without any other skills. But she had already learned the importance of the job and how a good model was an emissary of sorts. They brought a measure of beauty and elegance into the world. Some might think a model's life was frivolous, but all the Rousseau models she knew took their job seriously, and she certainly did as well.

"How did that come about?" he asked, genuinely curious. "I mean, clearly it's a job for a beautiful woman, and you certainly qualify there. But it doesn't seem like an easy field to break into."

"I was offered the job back in New York," she answered. "Anyway, that's enough about me. Did I see you're reading *The Sun Also Rises?*"

He turned the book over so she could see the cover. "Guilty as charged. It's one of my favorites. I've been thinking about it since I'm staying here in Hemingway's old stomping grounds. When I found it in a bookshop last week, I took it as a sign that I needed to read it again."

"You believe in signs?" she teased.

"Don't you?" he countered. "We've had one just now ourselves. We've run into each other again."

Just then, the waiter arrived with bowls of vichyssoise and two salads, along with two glasses of chardonnay. She hadn't planned to eat anything more than a few leaves of lettuce, but the aroma of the soup changed her mind.

"Have you tried this yet?" he asked. "It's potato-leek soup. It's the best part of coming to France. I'm addicted to it."

They talked between bites. She watched as he tore pieces from a baguette, shaking her head when he offered some to her. She shouldn't even be having the soup, but she had been on a strict diet for too long.

"Have you been to any more clubs?" he asked.

"Too many," she replied. "My roommates can't seem to stand an evening at home."

"You're a homebody, then?"

"You make it sound so boring."

"No," he protested. "It's not boring at all. In fact, I find it kind of refreshing."

"What about you?"

Philip gestured to the waiter to refill their glasses. "I like getting out to hear music from time to time, but on the whole, I'm definitely a homebody. There's nothing better than a good book in front of a fire."

"Sounds perfect," she admitted. "I like modeling, but I'm starting to realize I need to think about what happens next."

"Here or back in the States?" he asked.

"At home, of course," she replied. "This won't last forever. What about you? How long will you be in France?"

"A few weeks, at least," he said. "Maybe longer."

"Your family must miss you," she remarked, imagining his wife and children back in the States.

"I don't have much family," Philip replied. "Apart from a crusty old aunt in Cincinnati."

Mia looked up, surprised. His life wasn't all that different from hers, then. They were both alone in the world.

"What are you doing this afternoon?" he asked after the waiter had taken their plates.

"I'm afraid I've got a dress fitting this afternoon," she admitted. "What about you?"

"I was going to suggest a walk in the park, but since you're busy, I suppose I'll have to go over my sales figures and get those sent to my company."

Mia sighed, wishing there was a reason to prolong their meeting. She felt like she could talk to him forever.

"Will I see you again?" she asked.

She hadn't meant to say the words out loud. To her relief, he smiled.

"Just say when." He reached into his pocket and took out a notebook and a pen. "Here. Write your number down for me."

She took the pen and scribbled her number, her hand brushing his when she handed it back.

"I'll call you," he said, standing. He picked up his book, and she stood as well. "Have a good time at your fitting."

"I will."

He walked down the street without glancing back. She watched until he turned the corner. Never in her life had she been as tempted to follow someone as she was in that moment, but it had been bold enough to ask if she would see him again. She couldn't run after him, too.

# 13

———

Mia left the café feeling better than she had in ages. Philip had asked for her number, and she knew he would call. She hadn't looked forward to anything so much in her life.

She spent an hour at Rousseau being fitted for another gown, and when she was finally released, she walked to the open-air market on the Rue Mouffetard. When her father was alive, she cooked simple meals, but the abundance of fresh fruits and vegetables in France made her more interested in cooking than she had ever been before. The colors were luscious, the smells intoxicating. She lingered over the cheeses, interested not only in the variety but also the way they were packaged with a wax coating or paper, some even wrapped in chestnut leaves and tied with string.

As she wandered, she thought of Philip, wishing he were there beside her. She could imagine the two of them browsing the market side by side, discussing which cheese went best with which wine and how to make a roast chicken. She lingered for a long time before she went back to the flat.

"Where've you been all afternoon?" Maeve asked. "We're going out, you know."

"I went to the market," Mia replied.

Maeve raised a brow. "Did you forget we have plans?"

"Of course not," Mia said, although she would have preferred to wait by the telephone for Philip to call. "I'll find something to wear."

Evenings out were starting to run together in her mind, some spent with her roommates and other Rousseau models, others where she was simply a bauble on someone's arm, touting the fashion house or passing on cryptic messages from Theo, all in the name of advertising their brand.

More than once that evening, her mind wandered from the conversation around her to the hour she'd spent with Philip. She'd never felt so attracted to anyone before. He was good-natured and uncomplicated, and she tried to imagine his life back in the States. There was still so much to learn about him.

"Wake up, daydreamer," Elisabeth teased. "Do you want another drink?"

"No, thanks," Mia replied as she swirled the cocktail in her glass. "I'm still working on this one."

She was tempted to tell her about Philip but changed her mind. Elisabeth was a good listener, but it was too soon to mention him to anyone. He hadn't even called her yet, and she wanted to savor the conversation they'd had until he did. She finished her martini, relieved when they finally went home so she could go to bed.

The following morning, her head was throbbing. She opened her handbag, looking for a bottle of aspirin, when she saw a slip of paper had been tucked inside. Mia frowned, unfolding the message. She read it through once, and then she read it again.

*Mia Walker, you have been found out. Today at twelve o'clock noon, you are to go to the shop at 37 Rue de la Bûcherie. Do not speak to the proprietors. In the room upstairs, you will find shelves of books on the right-hand side. Take the fourth from the left on the second shelf. There is a message for you inside. Follow the instructions precisely as they are set out. Do not disregard this warning.*

Mia shuddered, wondering what it meant and how a note like this had gotten into her bag. Someone had made the wrong assumptions about her, if they believed she was involved in something untoward. Her life was no different from any of the other models'. In fact, it was far tamer. She had to be coaxed out most of the time. Many of her peers were living the high life, as far as she could tell, trying to find themselves rich husbands, French or otherwise, although there was no harm in meeting people in a new city, sipping a glass of champagne or a martini. She had no skeletons in her closet, nothing for which she could be reproached.

She wouldn't go. After all, it might even be a practical joke. Perhaps Maeve was even more mean-spirited than she thought and wanted to scare her. But if it wasn't, why should she put herself in a dangerous position like that? On the other hand, curiosity was getting the better of her, and the Rue de la Bûcherie was only a few streets away. She remembered the street but couldn't recall which shop was at number 37.

She left the flat with the excuse that she was going to mail a letter, though if anyone paid attention, they would realize that in her time in France, she had written to no one at all. However, neither Maeve nor Elisabeth questioned her about it. As far as they were concerned, her life was too boring to comment upon.

As she neared the building, she realized the address belonged to an American bookshop she had found a couple of weeks earlier. Le Mistral was one block from the Quai de Montebello, which ran along the bank of the Seine. The exterior was painted a dark teal green, and inside it was a jumble of books and ephemera, with barely enough room to turn around. A man and woman sat behind the counter and ignored her when she came in, caught up in a disagreement. Mia went to the back of the shop, stopping when she came to the staircase. She went up a couple of steps before she realized someone else was coming down. The stairwell was so narrow that she had to retreat to allow him to get past. A young man with a scruffy beard clambered down the steps, his head in a book, oblivious to the fact that she had to move to make room for him. She waited to see if anyone else was coming, and when she was certain there wasn't, she made her way up the stairs.

At the top, just as the note said, was a room full of books. Although she had been in the shop twice before, she hadn't realized there was an upstairs chamber. It was a small claustrophobic room, with books on either side and a lone window allowing in sunlight. Someone had written a message on a note card, stating *Lending Library—Take One, Leave One*, and tacked it onto one of the shelves. Looking around to make certain no one had followed her, she went to the second shelf on the right and took down the fourth book from the left.

It was out of alphabetical order—that was what she noticed first. Then she looked at the title, pulling it off the shelf. It was an Ian Fleming book, one of the early James Bond novels, *Diamonds Are Forever*.

Mia slipped it into her bag. Then she went down the stairs, past the arguing couple, and back into the street, where across the cobbles was a *bookiniste*, one of many on the Left Bank selling tattered volumes and postcards and oddities in their open stalls. She hurried past a row of them and found a secluded bench where she could sit and look for the message in the book.

The novel, though it had only been published a few years before, had yellowed, weathered-looking pages. She flipped through them until an old torn train ticket fell onto her lap. She lifted it, studying the date, which read *1956*, the same as the publication date of the book. Turning it over, a time and place were scribbled in the margin: *13:00, Montmartre Stairs*.

There were no other instructions to be found. Mia stared at it, wondering what to do. She was in no mood for a wild goose chase around Paris. She had done nothing wrong, certainly nothing for which she could be blackmailed.

It was ten minutes past noon. Mia made a quick decision. She stood and walked quickly to the closest Métro station, where she studied the map before buying a ticket. She followed the signs to Line 12 and waited until the train arrived. She didn't have to wait long before she heard the screech of brakes as it came into view. After it came to a stop, she boarded the train. It wasn't crowded, but still she didn't sit, preferring to stand clutching a rail as the train began to rumble along the tracks.

Trying not to attract attention, she studied the people in the train car. No one seemed to notice her, and she breathed a sigh of relief. This was simply a joke. It had to be, she thought.

She would get off the train and walk up the Montmartre Stairs and sit on the steps of the Sacré-Coeur, just as she had done with Madame Laurent. Then she would go into the church, light a candle, and make her way home.

It wasn't a simple journey. She had to change trains twice on the way there. When the final train jerked to a stop, she disembarked, wondering if she should take a taxi home. She rarely took one because of the expense, but it was unnerving to trek across the city for reasons she couldn't begin to fathom. She walked up the steps from the Métro, relieved to be aboveground again.

The Montmartre Stairs, which were depicted on postcards in every newsstand and shop in Paris, were daunting when viewed from the bottom. The funicular, which stood beside it, was tempting. No wonder people took the railway conveyance instead of trudging up hundreds of steps. The Sacré-Coeur towered over them, casting its shadow on the steps below. Although she could see tourists at the summit, the street level was nearly abandoned. Mia glanced at her watch. Although she had rushed to get there, it was already past one. Taking a deep breath, she went up the first ten steps before turning and looking around. There was still no one in sight.

When she had gone up another few steps, she heard a car arrive near the foot of the stairs. Turning, she saw a burly man in a dark suit jump from the vehicle. Her heart began to pound as he bounded the steps two by two, and though she turned and started to run, she was no match for him. In seconds, he had taken hold of her arm and was marching her back to the foot of the steps.

"What are you doing?" she demanded.

He didn't answer. When they reached the car, he pulled open a door and shoved her inside, sliding in beside her. The driver hit the accelerator before the door was even closed. She tried to jerk away, but the man beside her held her fast, his fingers biting into her arm. The car swerved around a corner, and she was thrown against the opposite door. She reached for the handle, but he pulled her back.

"Let me go!" she cried.

He made no response. His head was shaved, and he smelled of

strong cologne. Every time the driver took a corner, he was jolted against her, and the smell began to make her nauseous. A few minutes later, they arrived at the back of an unmarked building, and the driver opened the door, grabbing her other arm as she got out of the vehicle. Before she realized what was happening, he had tied her arms behind her back. She screamed, but there was no one around to hear. The area was abandoned.

"Let's go," he said in a gruff voice. He spoke English, but it was clear it wasn't his first language.

He unlocked the door, and she was dragged into a cavernous room, empty but for a few chairs and a table. Then he pushed her into one of the chairs as the driver tossed her pocketbook onto the table. She tried to get up, but a hand came down on her shoulder, forcing her back down. A moment later, a door swung open, and a third man approached. Like the others, he was in his forties, also dressed in a suit and tie. He walked up, acknowledging none of them. Instead, he took her handbag and dumped the contents onto the table. He went through everything, item by item.

"State your name," he said at last, finally looking at her. Like the first man, she couldn't quite identify his accent.

"Who are you?" she demanded, her heart pounding. "There's been some kind of mistake."

"No mistake, Mademoiselle," he replied. "I can assure you that if you don't cooperate, you will be punished. State your name."

"Mia Walker."

"Who is your employer?"

"I work for the House of Rousseau."

"Who is your contact person?"

"What do you mean, 'contact person'?"

"Who recruited you?"

Mia frowned. "The manager, Theo Gillette. I believe he chooses all the models who work for Monsieur Rousseau."

The man came around the desk and sat on the edge. He crossed his arms. "I'm not talking about who recruited you to model for the fashion house. Who do you pass information to? Who is your contact person? I want the names of everyone involved."

"Involved in what?" she asked. "I don't understand."

He turned to the man who had grabbed her from the Montmartre Stairs, cocking his head toward the table. "Turn it on."

The burly man walked over to a projector, which made a sudden noise as it sputtered to life. Images began to appear on the wall behind her. Some were blurred by movement, others were clear. She leaned forward, studying them, when she realized she was looking at images of the man she had spoken to at the first soirée to which she had been sent. She racked her brain for a moment before coming up with the name Szabo. A minute later, her own face came onto the screen. She was walking with a wineglass in one hand, circling the room. Mia suddenly had trouble breathing.

"How…?" she began, struggling to free her arms.

"You were being filmed," he replied, studying her carefully. "Do you recognize this man?"

"Yes," she admitted.

"What is his name?"

"I don't know," she lied. "He didn't tell me. How did you get this?"

"You're not here to ask questions, Miss Walker, in case you didn't realize it. You're here to answer them. Now, tell me his name."

He moved toward her, and she recoiled in her seat, struggling to free her wrists. The rope was chafing against her skin.

"He didn't introduce himself," she said. "He started talking as if we were already in the middle of a conversation. I thought he had confused me with someone else."

"What did he ask you?" the man pressed.

She tried to breathe, but her breaths were coming too quickly.

"The same thing everyone else asks," she said, starting to feel faint. "He wanted to know the address."

"Your address?"

"No, not mine, although I don't know if he thought it was or not," she answered. "They all ask for it."

He went completely still for a moment before he spoke. "How many of them have you spoken to?"

"What is this about?" she asked.

"How many?" he growled.

"Four," she said in a panic.

"Tell me the address."

Mia looked at the other two men in the room, the driver and the man who had forced her into the car. Even if her hands had been free, she couldn't get around them and out of this room. She ran through her options. She could either tell him or not, but even she didn't know the significance of the address she had been told to give out. She had assumed it was a warehouse that belonged to the House of Rousseau or something as harmless. For a split second, she thought about making up an entirely different address, but she realized if they came back empty-handed, they would take it out on her. She had no choice but to tell them the truth.

"It's the Rue de Meuniers, number 46," she replied. "But I don't know what is actually at that location."

"Then what did he ask?"

"I don't remember."

He walked a few steps in the other direction and then turned around, rubbing his chin. Mia could tell his patience was about to run out.

"Let me get this straight," he said, coming to stand a few feet away from her. "Theo Gillette sends you out and tells you to give this information to all the people who ask for your address."

She realized at once that she had just put Theo's life on the line, and perhaps even Luca and the other models. She was going to have to find Theo and warn him.

"Can I go now?" she asked. "I've told you everything I know."

"How long have you been with Rousseau?" he asked, ignoring her question.

"Since June."

"And how long have you been delivering these messages?"

"I didn't realize they were messages."

He grunted. "What did you think they were?"

"Theo said they had a warehouse where particular customers were directed to see additional lines of clothing."

"And you believed him."

"Why shouldn't I?" she asked.

However, her bravado was a mask. She'd known deep down that something was wrong at Rousseau, and now she was facing the repercussions.

No one answered. One of the men came up behind her and pulled a bag over her head. Mia screamed but was suddenly slapped, wrenching her head to the side as her face began to sting.

"Don't move," he said.

She tensed as she heard them walking away. Seconds later, the door opened, and she could hear footsteps as they went out, closing the door behind them. Mia held her breath, wondering if they had all gone or if one of them had stayed behind. To do what, she wondered. Would she make it out of this room alive? She began to hyperventilate, but she forced herself to take a deep breath and evaluate her situation.

She struggled against the ropes around her wrists, but it was no use. She tried to stand, but with her arms looped behind the back of the chair, it was impossible. Instead, she began to rock the chair from side to side until it tipped over to the right, landing on her shoulder.

She lay there, stunned, for a few seconds, catching her breath, trying to absorb the pain from striking the concrete floor. After a moment, she inched her way up until her arms were free of the chair and she could sit up on the cold floor.

She was alone in the warehouse, as far as she knew, but the clock was ticking. Her arms were tied together, and she had a bag over her head. Still, she had to get out of there somehow.

Suddenly, the door opened again, and someone walked up to her, his shoes clattering on the cement floor. She recoiled as she felt him moving behind her, where he proceeded to pull off the bag. The sudden light was blinding, and she shook her head for a second, trying to see. As she did, he bent down in front of her, so close that they were face-to-face. Mia gasped as Philip's features came into focus. He was the last person on earth she expected to see.

# 14

Global thermonuclear war was not a foreign concept to Mia. She knew about the race to create bigger, fiercer bombs engaged in by the East versus the West. Atomic bombs had existed for most of her life, most famously deployed by the United States on Hiroshima, Japan, on August 6, 1945, and again three days later on Nagasaki, resulting in the deaths of more than a hundred thousand Japanese, which resulted in their surrender and marked the end of World War II.

She had learned about it in school from her history teacher, Mr. Haddon, who had lost a brother at Pearl Harbor and who was determined to teach his students about the devastating effects of war. Kyle Haddon had been a mere eighteen years old when he perished at the U.S. naval base in Honolulu on December 7, 1941. His life had hardly even begun. The class of 1958 had been told his life story, just like the seventeen classes preceding it. Kyle had been a talented young man with serious dreams, an athlete whose hero was Jim Thorpe, the first Native American to win an Olympic gold medal. Kyle had been president of his high school class and a member of the football team as well as the track team. After pursuing his goal of enlisting in the U.S. Army, he planned to go to medical school, with dreams of becoming a pediatrician. The retelling of his enlistment, service, and cruel death at Pearl Harbor had a profound impact on a classroom full of high school seniors who themselves were about to embark upon their own lives. Mr. Haddon drummed into their heads the names, dates, and facts, ensuring that they would never forget the ramifications of the first and only use of atomic bombs as a means of war. His lesson was simple: if people understood the horror of what really happened, they could stop it from ever happening again.

Yet Mia knew that was not to be the case. A cursory reading of newspaper articles on the subject made it clear that the Soviet Union and the Western allies were hurtling headlong into the Cold War, trying to develop the most sophisticated warfare known on the planet. Some maintained that nuclear proliferation was all in the name of deterrence—that another atomic bomb would never be dropped again on the face of the planet—but it was a race all the same. The Soviet Union and the United Kingdom had already created nuclear bombs; France and possibly even China were nipping at their heels. From the headlines, one might assume that one day every country in the developed world would have an arsenal of atomic weapons, possessing the capability to annihilate all human life on the planet.

172   •   J U L I A   B R Y A N   T H O M A S

The frightening part was that, like Pearl Harbor or Hiroshima, an attack could come at any time, ending life as one knew it. The fear instilled in her by Mr. Haddon of their future being snatched away at a moment's notice on the cruel whim of the enemy made her eschew political news as much as possible. Like so many others, she had comforted herself with the myriad distractions the world offered, hoping for a quiet, civilized *Leave It to Beaver* life. Hadn't she thought as much when she imagined what Philip's life back in the United States was like? Hadn't she imagined herself a carefree wife and mother, tying on an apron to make a tuna-noodle casserole for her husband, who came walking through the door at five o'clock, briefcase in hand, ready to plant a kiss on her cheek?

Somehow, that image lurked before her as she stared up into Philip's eyes in shock. For a full minute, neither of them spoke. Then he knelt behind her and untied the ropes around her wrists.

"What are you doing here?" she finally choked out, reaching for her pocketbook, which was lying a few feet away.

His eyes darted around the empty room. "We can't talk here. Come on."

Holding out a hand, he helped her up from where she was crouching on the floor and pulled her along behind him. She expected him to go for the door, but instead, he went in the other direction, to a staircase at the far end of the building.

"Philip," she began.

He stopped and shook his head before turning around and

leading her up the stairs. She struggled to keep up as he pulled her along, his long legs taking the strides more quickly. On the next floor, he leaned against the wall and then checked both ways to make certain no one was coming. He still hadn't let go of her hand when he nodded, cocking his head to the right. He pulled her around the corner and down a series of corridors until they came to another staircase. This time, they went down. He took the steps slowly, listening for any movement. When they reached the bottom, he turned to face her.

"We're going to have to make a run for it," he said in a low voice, letting go of her hand. "I know you want answers, but we have to get out of here first. Crouch as low as you can and follow me to my car. Do you understand?"

"I do, but—"

"There's no time for *but*s right now."

He eased open the door and she followed, ducking as low as she could to be obscured by the other cars around them. He weaved in and around several vehicles and then looked at her before sprinting across the pavement to his car.

Mia knelt there, paralyzed. She was tempted to run in the other direction, but if she tried to escape on foot, he had the advantage of having a vehicle to run her down. She didn't know what to do. The one person she thought she could trust above all others could be just as dangerous as the thugs who had abducted her. Suddenly, the door of the building banged open, and she made a break for it, running toward Philip's car as fast as she could. He flung open the passenger door and she scrambled inside, pulling it shut behind her. Jerking the car into gear, he pulled out of the parking lot, leaving a trail of dust behind them.

Philip drove erratically for several streets until he turned down a small alleyway. Mia looked out the rear window and saw they were being followed.

"What's going on?" she demanded, bracing herself as they took a sharp corner.

He didn't answer, zipping in and around the dozens of vehicles speeding around them. At one point, their pursuer came within a car's length, and Philip swerved left suddenly, turning off onto a narrow side street. They hurtled through the city for half an hour when he finally parked and got out of the car. She had no choice but to follow him.

"Where are we?" she asked. It wasn't even the most pressing of her questions.

He ignored her remark and led her through the entrance of a small dark building. Soon they were going down dozens and dozens of steps, leading to the dark, airless tunnels beneath the city.

"Philip," she said, stopping on the bottom stair. "Where are we?"

"The Catacombs," he replied. "It's an underground cemetery from the 1700s."

"You have to tell me what's going on."

Philip shook his head. "We can't talk here. Even the dead have ears."

He pulled her around a corner, where they came face-to-face with a wall of skulls and bones in the dimly lit room.

Mia turned her head, repulsed. "I can't do this."

"You can do anything," he answered. "If you'll just trust me a little longer, we will get out of here and I will tell you everything."

They wandered through the silent passageways. Mia noticed Philip kept looking around them to make certain they hadn't been followed. He didn't stop, however, and she was pulled along behind him. Twenty minutes passed before they finally emerged into daylight. However, instead of taking her back to his car, he walked her several blocks to a quiet tree-lined street and into a dark café. He went up to the counter and ordered two cups of coffee and then led her to a seat in the back.

"You're in danger," he said as he sat across from her. "You've gotten mixed up in a perilous situation, whether you know it or not."

"What are you talking about?"

"You're being used by a group called the Alliance," he answered. "It's a coalition of several Eastern European countries trying to steal nuclear information from the United States and the Soviet Union. I want to know how you ended up in that warehouse today."

"I found a slip of paper in my handbag this morning with a warning on it. It gave me instructions to go to Le Mistral. I was directed to a book with instructions to go to the Montmartre Stairs. I was forced into a car and taken to the warehouse."

"Do you still have the note?" he asked.

"I think so," she answered. She opened the bag and extracted the note, handing it to him.

"How did you get this?" he asked.

"I don't know," she replied. "Someone must have put it in my bag last night. My roommates insisted I join them for a night out, and we went several places. I'm sure I put my handbag down at one point or another."

"What was the book you were supposed to find?" Philip asked.

She opened her bag again and pulled it out, giving it to him.

He raised a brow. "This is ironic."

"What do you mean?"

Philip shook his head. "I need to ask you some questions first. How did you get involved, Mia?"

"Involved in what?" she demanded.

The waiter came and put two cups of coffee in front of them, the steam rising as he walked away.

Philip gave her a long look. "You're part of an espionage ring."

"An espionage ring?" she repeated, shocked. "How can that be possible?"

"You tell me. Did you know when you were hired in New York by Theo Gillette that you were going to be used to pass information to enemy hands? The House of Rousseau has been under scrutiny for some time by the U.S. government to determine how involved they are in the operation."

"Theo's a criminal?"

"He has fallen under suspicion," Philip replied. "If we're correct, he's not only recruiting for the fashion house, but fronting an underground organization."

"Is the whole House of Rousseau involved?" she asked.

"As of now, we don't have that information, but we have two likely targets inside the company, and you were caught sharing information with one of the highest-profile operatives in the Alliance."

"Which two people at Rousseau are targets?"

"I can't tell you that at this time," Philip said. "It appears to be an aboveboard business. They employ designers and craftsmen and actually put out a product—but someone, likely Gillette, is running an illegal spying operation out of Rousseau. Until you were identified, we didn't realize that he had decided to use models to pass information to the Alliance."

"You mean when we are asked to attend social occasions on some man's arm whom we've never seen before."

"If you are used to pass information, then yes."

"You know I didn't intend to get involved in criminal activity," she said, anger bubbling to the surface. "And what about you? Who are you, anyway?"

"I work for the United States government."

Mia crossed her arms. "How do I know that's true?"

"You have two choices, Mia. You can either take it on faith or trust me until you're proven otherwise. And it doesn't matter if you were aware of it or not. You've broken the law. You've committed a crime against the United States government."

"Unintentionally, if that's true," she argued. "Who kidnapped me? And if you're saying that Theo Gillette is involved in illegal activities, then how did I come up on anyone's radar?"

"Gillette is only one of many different entities racing to get information. You were obviously spotted, and it confirmed their suspicions about him."

"What do you mean, 'different entities'?"

"Every antidemocratic country in the world is rushing for a shot at nuclear information. There are networks all across Europe and Asia. It's critical that you do not tell Gillette what happened today. Otherwise, your usefulness will come to an end."

"My usefulness to whom?"

Philip didn't answer. They sat at an impasse, their coffee growing cold. Philip read the note again and then folded it and put it in his pocket.

Mia balled her hands into fists. "If you can't tell me who is involved, or even who you are, who am I supposed to trust?"

"Right now, I'd say you can't trust anyone."

"What am I supposed to do now?" she asked.

"That's easy," he replied. "You go home, do your job, and you'll be given a way to report back to me when anything suspicious occurs."

"What if I just leave?" Mia asked. "There's no way I'm going to stay here and get even more involved in something so dangerous."

"You can't leave, Mia," Philip said. "You're already implicated. They'll find you no matter where you go. Nowhere is safe, not New York, not anywhere."

"A person can get lost in a city of more than seven million people."

"If they have the right connections," he conceded. "And you most definitely do not."

Mia stared at him. "You're saying this is hopeless."

"Actually," he replied, "it's not. You're going to work for the United States government and assist with the identification and location of various members of the Alliance."

"What if I refuse?" she asked.

"You've been caught passing information to parties working against the interest of the U.S. government, which means that you can be subject to arrest and incarceration for espionage. Instead, you're being offered the chance to help your country."

"I won't do it," she replied. "It's too dangerous."

"We know about your father, Mia."

She felt as if she'd been struck. "What do you mean?"

"He lost his teaching position a few years ago when it was discovered that he had been a card-carrying Communist in his college days," Philip replied. "During the McCarthy era, he was found out and ostracized by his peers. You're the daughter of a Communist."

"No," she argued, her cheeks burning. "He always regretted his decision. He was sorry he had ever gotten involved with them."

"Does it matter?" Philip asked. "This is not the sort of information that you want to go around."

She tried to breathe. "That's blackmail."

"It's merely a fact."

Mia saw his resolve in the clench of his jaw. The damage was done. Her father had made his mistakes and it had changed their lives forever. She had hoped that by burning her father's card and papers before she left New York, she had put it all behind her, but she hadn't counted on the interference of the U.S. government.

"What happens if I agree?"

"Then we put a plan in place for you to monitor who you're being asked to talk to and what you're instructed to tell them."

"How can I go back to Rousseau now?" she asked. "If we don't know who is involved, it would be dangerous to work among a group of potential spies."

"Do any of the girls you work with seem suspicious to you?"

"I don't think so," she answered. "Everyone seems focused on ordinary things."

"What about your roommates?"

"Well, Maeve is difficult," she admitted. "She always seems to have an agenda."

"Then you should keep a close eye on her, not least for your own safety." He stopped and looked at his watch. "Listen, we have to get you back to your flat before they become suspicious. You've been gone for hours."

"What will I tell them?"

"You could say you've taken a lover."

Mia blushed. "That's ridiculous."

Philip stood. "It's not as ridiculous as you might think. Besides, it's a ready alibi if you need it."

Mia got up and looked him squarely in the eye. "Why did this happen today? I don't know anything. Anyone can tell you that."

"You're wrong," Philip replied. "You probably know much more than you realize. Here."

He held out a piece of paper.

"What's this?"

"Instructions. Take the Métro to the Eiffel Tower, then take a taxi back to your flat." He held out a twenty-franc note and waited until she took it. "There's a box in the broom closet on the ground floor of your building. If you have information to pass or you need to reach me quickly, leave a note in there."

"What if they kidnap me again?"

"You're being watched at all times," he answered. "Trust me, you're an asset and we need to keep you in one piece."

Mia took a deep breath. "When will I see you again?"

"Don't worry," he replied. "I'll be seeing you plenty, even though we won't be talking. I've got my eye on you. You'd better get going."

Mia nodded. There was nothing left to say. She stepped out of the café and took the closest Métro to the Eiffel Tower, as she had been instructed. She was exhausted when she finally reached her building, still baffled by everything that had happened. Someone had involved her in a crime, likely Theo. Philip wasn't a random businessman in Paris, either; he was stalking her, and everyone else at Rousseau, to investigate the possibility of crimes and wrongdoing. Some of the other girls she worked with were potentially involved, and she had no idea who. She couldn't trust any of them.

"Where have you been all day?" Maeve asked when she walked into the flat. "I swear, you just dropped off the face of the earth."

Her roommate was sitting in the pink chair, her hair rolled up in curlers. Elisabeth was pouring a glass of juice in the kitchen nook.

"I met someone," Mia said, swallowing hard. She wished she didn't have to lie, but there didn't seem to be any other choice.

"What kind of someone?" Elisabeth said, her ears perking up. "And does he have good-looking friends?"

"Tall, dark, and handsome," Mia replied, at a loss.

"It's France. Everyone fits that description," Maeve remarked. "Wait. What happened to your face?"

Mia put her hand up to her cheek. "I tripped on the Métro."

"Let me have a look," Elisabeth said, coming closer. She shook her head. "I don't think it will bruise, but you need some ice."

"And a bath," Mia said. "I'm exhausted."

"That's a good idea," her friend said. "I'll figure something out for dinner. It sounds like a good time to have a quiet evening at home."

Mia couldn't agree more. She went into her room to get her things to shower, but as she did, she spied her suitcase under the bed.

For a minute, she toyed with the idea of packing everything and stealing out of the flat in the middle of the night. But Philip was right. Wherever she tried to hide, someone would find her. And the odds were just as good that it would be the Alliance as Philip or one of the Americans. As desperate as she was, she couldn't take the chance.

# 15

Mia woke the next morning after a fitful night's sleep. She sat up slowly, every bone in her body aching, her stomach tied in knots. Philip had left her with more questions than answers.

Who was he, really? He said he worked for the government, but he didn't say in what capacity. And assuming he was telling the truth, it meant that meeting him for the first time in the nightclub had not been an accident. He had been watching her, thinking her a possible spy for Theo Gillette, ready to turn her in if she was caught passing information. She had been in France for such a short time, she couldn't be deeply embroiled in any scandal. And yet, somehow, she was.

She got up and dressed, checking the time. It was only seven o'clock. She had to do something. It wasn't going to be easy to pretend that nothing was wrong, when everything in her world had blown up like a keg of dynamite, but she didn't have a choice.

Pulling open her French doors, she looked out onto the street. Windows were thrown open; people were going about their business. From this vantage point, the world seemed as unremarkable as the day before, yet if everything Philip said was true, nothing would ever be the same again.

At her desk, she took out a slip of paper so she could write him a note demanding information, but as she sat there, she couldn't seem to put words onto paper. He'd told her everything he could tell her for the moment, and she was going to have to accept it.

Mia put down the pen. The others wouldn't be up for hours. If it had been an ordinary day, she would have a cup of coffee and explore for a while before taking her book to the park. However, this was no ordinary day. She had to devise some sort of plan. She couldn't have the Alliance coming after her every time she let her guard down.

She had in her possession only one clue: Rue de Meuniers, number 46. She had been instructed to give it to several people, yet she never knew what it meant. The only way to find out was to go there. Weeks earlier, she'd bought a map of Paris, and she took it out of her wardrobe now, running her finger down the long list of street names until she found it. It was located on the Right Bank, near the Bois de Vincennes. She hadn't been there before, having restricted herself to closer parks, but she had marked it as a place to visit when she felt adventurous. It was dangerous, of course, putting herself in the middle of the case. If Theo caught her, he would know immediately that she knew what was going on. Still, she couldn't wait around for something to happen.

Mia decided to leave her roommates a note. *Gone exploring, back before long.* It was inadequate, but she had already established a habit of going out on her own, so it wasn't likely to arouse suspicion, unless Maeve was as involved in this affair as she was. It was difficult to imagine. As much as she distrusted her roommate, the thought that she was involved in an espionage ring was too much to believe. If she hadn't gone through the trauma of being abducted, she would never have believed that something so outrageous was a possibility.

However, it was true, and she only had a single day before she had to return to work at the House of Rousseau and was once again subject to the scrutiny of Theo Gillette. If she could find something important, she could use it to her advantage.

She took Maeve's sunglasses from a table and slid them into her bag. Then she pulled her hair into a ponytail and tied a scarf over her ears. It was as incognito as she could get. She let herself out of the flat and went downstairs. When she reached the ground floor, she didn't go out the front entrance as usual. Instead, she went down a long corridor until she found a back door, which led into a small empty courtyard. Staying close to the building so she wouldn't be seen from the windows, she made her way around the side and headed down the street.

Mia wasn't accustomed to being guarded as she made her way about Paris, but this time, she walked three blocks and then went into a shop, waiting out of sight to see who passed by. After ten minutes, she left the store and then went back a half block in the direction she had come before turning around suddenly to continue on her way. She didn't see anyone suspicious, but she didn't breathe easily until she found a Métro station and hurried underground to get lost in the crowd. She took the train to the closest station to the Rue de Meuniers. Coming up from the underground, she found herself disoriented for a moment, wondering which way she was supposed to go.

She chided herself for not bringing the map. After walking a couple of blocks east, she turned and headed west, breathing more normally when she saw a sign for the Bois de Vincennes. On a normal day, she would have asked someone for directions, but she didn't want to attract any unwanted attention. From this day forward, she couldn't trust anyone, not even a stranger on the street who might help her when she was lost, as she could have even a day earlier.

Mia paused to recall the map and found her way to the Rue de Meuniers. It was a quiet street, like much of Paris on a Sunday morning. It housed many stores and businesses, all of which were closed on a Sunday, and she kept going until she found number 46.

It appeared to be an empty building. She had hoped it was all a terrible mistake and she would find a legitimate dressmaking factory or inventory warehouse, but she was wrong. Theo had been asking her to give out an address that led to nowhere.

She wandered around the exterior, trying every door, but all were either bolted shut or locked up with chains. It was a street with little to no traffic, and she realized she was exposed, standing there, trying to get into an empty building. Turning, she made her way to the nearest alleyway and hurried over to the park.

None of this made any sense. Had any of the people she had sent to number 46 actually gone there, also discovering that it was an abandoned warehouse? Or had its contents as recently as yesterday been disassembled and moved to another location? It was also possible that no one she had told had taken it as an address at all, but perhaps a code for something else, something to do with 46 perhaps.

It occurred to her that Theo had given her a fake message to see how effective she was at following directions, testing her compliance and ability to follow through. She sat on a bench, leaning back against the seat, trying to stay calm. Somehow, she was going to have to appear easygoing and obedient, the perfect stereotype of a model, all pleasantness and good looks, without enough discernment or intelligence to realize when she was being used.

Suddenly, she noticed a book lying face down on the other end of the bench. Looking around, she reached for it. Prickles came up on her arm as she picked it up. Turning it over, she felt a chill when she realized it was the same one she had given to Philip the day before, *Diamonds Are Forever*.

Mia's heart leaped as she held the book close to her chest. She flipped through the pages, looking for a note, but there was nothing inside it, not even the Italian ticket that had been there the day before.

Although her senses were on high alert, watching for anything unusual, it appeared to be an average weekend morning. It felt like any other day, but as sure as her name was Mia Walker, she knew she was being watched. She forced herself to breathe slowly. Eventually, she slid the dust jacket off the book so that it would be unidentifiable to any passersby. Then she opened the front cover.

She reread the first page several times, aware that she couldn't possibly concentrate on the words on the page. Idly, she flipped a few pages when something caught her attention. It was a word circled faintly with a pencil. Mia frowned, flipping through the pages, when she found another. Suddenly, she closed it and stuffed it into her bag.

It was no coincidence that the book had been left for her on a park bench near the Rue des Meuniers. Philip was obviously aware of her habits. She would have to examine it more closely in the privacy of her room. Standing, she tucked her bag under her arm and then went back to her flat. No one was standing in front of her building, nor was the concierge sitting behind his desk. She went over to her mailbox, but it was empty. Then she trudged up the stairs, waiting to see if anyone was watching. No one was around, not even the cat.

"Hello?" she called when she opened the door.

"Be right there," Maeve replied.

Mia went into her room, leaving the door open. Taking the book from her bag, she slid it under the mattress and pulled down the quilt just before Maeve appeared in the doorway. Her roommate leaned against it and smiled.

"Do we want to go out tonight or not?" Maeve asked. "Because I'm thinking not."

Mia almost sighed with relief. "I could use a night in."

"Me, too," Maeve said. "What do you want to do?"

"I have a book I've been meaning to read," she answered, although she couldn't have concentrated on a book to save her life.

"You always read," Maeve protested. "Let's play gin rummy instead."

"All right," Mia agreed. "Is Elisabeth going to join us?"

"No, she has a date later. A musician, from what I hear."

"Do you want to go out to get something to eat?" Mia asked.

"I picked up a baguette and some ham earlier," Maeve answered. "We can make a few sandwiches and open that bottle of Malbec I bought last week."

"Weren't you saving it for a special occasion?"

"Having a night in sounds like a special occasion enough."

Mia glanced up to see if she was serious or not, but Maeve had already gone into the kitchen and started slicing bread on a platter. She went over to help, and in a few minutes, they had filled the platter with olives and cheese.

She found herself wondering why things hadn't been this companionable before. Nothing had changed between them. Maeve had been her usual critical self the day before, but now they were behaving as though they were friends. Of course, she couldn't trust her, not simply because Maeve had a difficult personality, but because anyone connected to the House of Rousseau was suspect. She was involved in a dangerous game, and pretending to enjoy a friend's company was part of the territory.

They played gin rummy for nearly two hours, talking about the gowns and getting poked with sharp pins and what it was like to be part of a show. Mia struggled to keep her guard up as they drank a couple of glasses of wine.

"This was nice," Maeve said at the end of the evening, gathering the playing cards and shuffling them before putting them in the deck.

"It was," Mia replied. She only wished this had happened a week or two earlier, before she'd heard anything about the Alliance and its implications.

"We should have more relaxing evenings like this." Maeve yawned. "I'm going to write my mother a quick letter and then go to bed."

"Good night."

Mia went into her room and put on a nightgown. She waited nearly an hour, pretending to sleep, long after every sound had ceased in the other room. Eventually, she sat up and got off the bed, lifting the edge of the mattress. The springs creaked as she pulled the book out and took it to the window. She didn't dare turn on a light. She always noticed when there was a light under the other girls' door. Instead, she went to the French doors and pulled back the curtains enough that the shaft of moonlight illuminated the page.

She went through the book again to see if she had missed anything that might have been slipped inside but found nothing. Then she went back to a page near the front of the book where a word was circled in faint pencil. It was the word *next*.

Did that mean something was going to happen next, and if so, what? She flipped through the pages to see if anything else was circled, feeling a slight thrill when she found the second word, *time*, a few pages later.

Next time. Mia shuddered. The words were ominous. What would happen the next time the Alliance got hold of her? Or did it mean that Theo would ask her to pass another message? There were too many variables to know for certain.

She turned back to the front of the book and went through each page until she came to the word *next*. After taking a pencil from her bedside table, she turned the pages, jotting the word whenever one was circled. When she had finished, she looked down at the paper, stunned. It read:

*Next*

*time*

*tell*

*him*

*it's*

*at*

*the*

*Ritz*

*number*

*six*

*seven*

*three*

Once again, she went through the pages to make certain nothing was missing. When she was certain she had found all the circled words, she put the book in the middle of a stack of them that sat on the floor, and folded the paper, tucking it among her undergarments.

The following morning, she slid the note into her brassiere. She would have to take care that the tailors and seamstresses didn't detect it, but there was no other choice. She couldn't leave it in the flat where it might be discovered.

Mia dressed carefully for the day and pulled the book from the stack and slipped it into her handbag. She wasn't certain how, but she was going to have to find a way to dispose of it.

She waited for an opportunity all morning, but there was a flurry of activity in the building, and she couldn't manage to find herself alone. She had hoped to hide it among the *passementerie*, but the only time she made it near the doorway into the hall, someone spoke to her and drew her back in.

Theo called her into his office late in the day. She had her handbag with her, keeping it clamped shut with both hands.

"I have another assignment for you tonight," he said pleasantly. "But I need to give something to my secretary for a moment first. Have a seat."

Mia nodded, waiting until he left the room. Then she leaped to her feet and went over to his expansive bookshelves. She pulled the book out of her bag and tucked it behind a few tall volumes of interior design. The books on his shelves were never disturbed and it seemed a safe place to put it where no one would find it. She was sitting in the chair when he returned to the room.

"We're sending you to a dinner party tonight," he remarked as he went around his desk. He lifted a piece of paper and examined it for a minute before looking up as if suddenly realizing she was still there. "Georgio has the dress for you. I think you'll like it. It's a rich plum color. It will look good with your complexion."

"Yes, sir," she answered.

"Give them the same address," he said. "Any questions?"

"No," she replied, shaking her head.

"Good. Have a nice evening."

She stood to leave, marveling at how trusting she had been ever since she had come to France.

Some things were too good to be true, and a career at a fashion house was precisely one of those things. What a fool she was to have believed him. She should have cashed in the ticket, taken the three hundred and fifty dollars, and started over in the smaller apartment. She could have gotten a job as a salesclerk at any of a hundred stores or asked the manager at the bakery for more responsibility. She could have dated a nice man and bought flowers for her kitchen table and spent weekends in the park, just as she did here, without fear or regret or danger lurking around every corner. But she hadn't done any of those things. Instead, she had set herself up for a life of danger.

That evening, she dressed in the gown Georgio had given her and was picked up by Luca outside her flat. This time, she didn't even

THE KENNEDY GIRL · 195

bother to try to make conversation with him. Her contact, when she finally saw him, was a middle-aged man with foggy glasses and a tic of pushing them up on his nose again and again. He had a large bald spot on the top of his head and had fussed with his tie enough that it was hanging askew. Nothing about him looked suspicious, and yet, like the others, he leaned in and breathed a single sentence in a low voice.

"What is your address, Mademoiselle?"

Mia opened her mouth and closed it again. She almost gave him the address at the Rue de Meuniers. Instead, she took a breath and repeated the sentence formed by the words that were circled in the James Bond book.

"It's at the Ritz, number 6-7-3."

He paused and looked at her, regarding her carefully before leaning toward her once again.

"Watch out for the diamond," he said.

He turned on his heel and left the room. Mia stared after him, not moving until a minute later, when a waiter bumped into her, his tray nearly collapsing onto the floor. She took hold of herself and made polite conversation with the host for ten minutes before making her way to the door. Catching a glimpse of herself in the hall mirror, she noticed her face had gone white. Pinching her cheeks to draw back the color, she pushed the button on the elevator and waited until it arrived. She didn't know which side Luca was on, but she had one job now: to look as normal as possible. However, it was getting harder with every passing day.

# 16

Raphaël Bellamy was born in 1886 in a small village in Normandy, about a hundred miles from the Belgian border. His family owned a farm, raising sheep, poultry, and rabbits for the table and, like everyone else in his family, he was put to work as soon as he could walk. Farming, he knew from experience, was hard work. During years when his father was more flush than broke, they hired help with the work, but even as a child, he had duties and responsibilities, always aware of his position on the farm. As an eight- and nine-year-old child, he would feed livestock, clean pens, and carry out all of the backbreaking chores a man was expected to do. There were ten mouths to feed in his family and everyone had to do their part. His sisters, Rose, Mariette, and Chloë, scrubbed the house like char-women alongside their mother. They made pottage and rabbit stew with the thinner, weaker of the specimens, because the best of the animals on the farm were sold for money. His brothers mucked stalls, mended fences, chased and captured the chickens and sheep that managed to flee their enclosures, and were general drudges around the farm. They spent their youths covered in sheep dung and growing out of shoes and trousers faster than they could be replaced. There was never a day off, never a break from responsibilities, and never a word of encouragement or thanks for a job well done for any of them. They were little more than slaves.

As Raphaël got older, and money grew even more tight, he decided he wanted nothing to do with the farm. Once he turned eighteen, he planned to leave. Of course, he had no money. The few francs he managed to cobble together were taken by his father to buy more feed for the livestock. A mutt had once turned up at the door and he wanted to keep it, but after seeing his father give it a swift kick in the ribs, he waited until dark and then walked it as far from the farm as he could get. He was tempted to join the poor creature, but at that time, he was only fifteen, and if he left too soon, his father would surely hunt him down.

Raphaël was expected to stay forever. The girls, at least, could marry boys from the village, not that it would be much improvement for their lives. They would still scrub floors and cook weak stews and have six or eight children and perpetuate the cycle of life, just with different masters. His brothers were all expected to marry a village girl and bring her back to the house, where she would take the place of a missing sister and help the farm scrounge through another year.

Raphaël was having none of it. By the time he was ready to leave, with a mere six coins in his pocket, he tied an extra shirt and a loaf of bread into a knapsack and took off into the night, much like the mutt that had left years before. He left no note and said no goodbyes. He wanted nothing more than to forget every one of the 6,570 days—which amounted to eighteen miserable years—and get as far away from the farm as was humanly possible.

The night he left, it was cool and damp, but he was thankful for it, plodding one foot after the other in the trenches along the side of the road. His first thought had been to go north to Lille, or perhaps Belgium, where French was also spoken, where he might look for work. However, as luck would have it, a road was closed and he found himself tracking southeast, bringing him closer and closer to the sea. Without a map, and never having traveled before, he had no idea where he was headed, but when he happened upon a beach on the third night, he was elated. It was deserted, but even if it hadn't been, he wouldn't have cared. He tore off his scuffed shoes and his shirt and trousers, and walked toward the water, mesmerized by the sound of the waves on the shore and the ripple of moonlight on the water. Tentatively, he stepped into the sea, feeling the joy that occurs when a man meets the moment when he knows who he is and what he wants. He sputtered and splashed about in the water for a long time before crawling back onto the shore, and then lay back with his hands behind his head, looking at the moon as long as he could keep his eyes open. It was as if he was seeing it for the very first time.

The next morning, he dressed and ate the last of the bread, and went on his way, looking for a village. In fact, he found more than a village. He stumbled upon Honfleur.

Honfleur, in 1904, was a bustling port town, and he decided to find a job on the docks to be near the water. The work didn't matter, not in the beginning. He was used to long backbreaking days. He could roll up a blanket and sleep anywhere. And in short order, because he was honest and trustworthy, he was hired by a fair-minded man named Giraud who owned a small vessel and taught him everything he knew about fishing from the bank of the Seine River estuary to the open waters of the English Channel. Under the man's tutelage, Raphaël learned how to steer a boat and how to catch cod, herring, sole, and scallops. His skin became tanned from a life on the water, rather than dung-encrusted from the filth of farmwork. His light-brown hair bleached blond in the sun.

He eventually rented a room and kept his meager possessions there, buying good rubber boots for the job and a proper set of shoes for evenings when he had a jingle in his pocket and a desire for a beer. He was happy for the first time in his life, because he was free.

One day, he noticed a young woman buying fish from one of the other vendors. Her beauty stopped him in his tracks. She was petite and feminine, with dark hair and a wide mouth, which, to his shock, he could suddenly imagine kissing. He didn't get the chance to speak to her, but he began to notice her at the dock with some frequency.

After a few weeks, he realized she appeared every Thursday morning like clockwork.

He watched her from afar for several weeks. After a while, he noted several things about her. She had a preference for pretty dresses, prettier than any garments he had ever seen before. She was sensible with her money, as well, arguing, albeit pleasantly, when she thought someone was asking too much for their catch. Also, she didn't flirt with any of the men. She came quietly to the dock, chose the best fish she could find, and placed the wrapped parcels in her basket before going on her way. She had been close to him on several occasions, but they had never made eye contact, and Raphaël was eager to rectify the situation.

It was the first Thursday in October. She was wearing a shawl over a blue flowered dress, and a sensible pair of rubber boots in case it was going to rain. He smiled when he saw her and jumped off the boat onto the shore, arranging the barrels of scallops and cod carefully, hoping she would walk just far enough down the pier so that he could catch her eye.

For once, she did. They stared at each other for a moment until he could stand it no longer.

Then she did something that surprised him. She approached him and smiled.

Her smile was friendly and good-natured. He had never talked to a girl his own age before and had no idea what to say. Fortunately, however, she was accustomed to social interaction and spared him the anxiety of speaking first.

"I've never seen you before," she remarked. "Are you new here?"

"I've been here a few months," he replied, shrugging.

She came closer and inspected the two barrels seriously. "These are good-looking scallops. What are you asking for them?"

He gave her the fair market price, and she laughed.

"You couldn't possibly ask that much," she said. "Knock off a few francs and I'll take some home for supper."

He could only imagine the joy of sitting across a table from this vision and eating a plate of scallops slathered in butter. Without being able to help himself, he looked down at her hand, drawing in a quick breath when he saw the ring on her finger.

"You're married," he stammered.

This was a complication he had not expected. His life, so full of promise that morning, shattered about him like a glass dashed to the floor.

"Six months," she replied, watching his face.

His heart broke even more than it had a moment before. He had been in Honfleur for six months. Why hadn't he abandoned the farm even a month sooner? Surely, even in a town of this size, he would have found her. Her luminescence was such that he would have noticed her anywhere.

She returned the following Thursday and the next and the next. In fact, she seemed to seek him out. He had no idea what to do with his emotions. He was literally living for the five or ten minutes a week that this young woman spent in his presence. There was only one thing to do about the situation, he decided. He must befriend her.

He saw her during winters and springs. He saw her through pregnancies and births. He saved the best of his catch for her and charged her less than the going rate every time. In fact, he would have given her anything she wanted for free if she would have taken it.

And so, the years passed. He remained single, eventually inheriting the boat from his generous employer and continuing in the man's footsteps. He bought a house when he was thirty, simple and plain but clean, and a bicycle to ride about town. Without intending to, he saved his money, having no one to spend it on. He went to the cathedral and prayed for her happiness. Raphaël never looked at another woman. How could he when his heart was already promised to another?

By the time he was forty, he knew a great deal about her life and had nothing but contempt for her husband, who obviously did not appreciate the woman he had married. She never said a word about the man, but behind her good humor, there was always a touch of sadness. It was clear to him that she looked forward to seeing him as much as he did her. Yet nothing was ever spoken between them until the day that he read in the newspaper that her husband, Noel Fournier, had died.

By then, they were both sixty years old, still bantering on Thursdays, still making each other smile. So he sat down one evening and poured out his feelings on paper, sealing it in an envelope.

He waited six weeks, out of respect for her late husband, and then he put it in the mail.

It was two months before he received a reply, and during those two months, she hadn't come to the dock a single time. He had ruined it, he thought. He had driven her away. However, it turned out that wasn't the case. She had fled Honfleur and moved to Paris. She told him a little about her life and, whether intentionally or not, provided him with a return address.

His first instinct was to get on a train, but he managed to rein in his emotions. She was grieving. She was alone. It wasn't proper to insert himself into her life. However, he did continue to go to the cathedral and pray for her happiness, and then he wrote her another letter.

For fifteen years, they exchanged them—letters full of carefully restrained feelings, but feelings, nonetheless.

Chantal, having made a stout cup of tea, pulled out his last letter. It was more urgent than any of the ones he had sent before. For more than fifty years, she had been in love with Raphaël Bellamy, who had shown up six months after she married Noel. Now it was too late anyway. They were seventy-four years old. They had lived their lives, for better or worse. Of course, she would like to run away from the mess that she'd gotten herself into, but she couldn't imagine going back to Honfleur. What would Jean-Louis and Jacques have to say about that? They had been bullies when her husband died. And she was fifteen years older now, so it would be worse. They would treat her as an invalid, rather than a woman who was very much in control of her life and her affairs. No, it wasn't possible.

But Raphaël still wanted her. She knew it from his letters. They had been restrained in the beginning. She had never expected him to write, thinking it impossible that someone would wish to marry a jaded sixty-year-old with a dim view of marriage. Yet he was different. Those moments they had spent together, ten minutes here and fifteen there, standing on the dock in every weather, were all rolled into a ball of longing so strong that she almost couldn't stand it. And yet, stand it, she must. She had a task in front of her, one she had not asked for but must complete all the same. Lives depended on it.

Chantal lifted the box from under her precious table and turned it over, taking the key that had been taped under it. She opened the door, listening for any sound of movement. Of course, there was none. She knew their schedule as well as they did. The silly models next door were early risers on the days they had to be at the House of Rousseau, late risers on every other day, except for Mia. They left the flat between 8:30 and 8:45, when they had to go to work, and on the rare occasion that one of them stayed home, she knew because there were only two sets of footsteps in the hall.

Today, she had even glanced out the window at the car that usually picked them up and watched them get inside. They never came back earlier than three or four, more often five o'clock. So she took the key and went over and unlocked flat 2B and went inside, locking the door behind her.

Chantal was not a curious person. She was interested in the comings and goings of her neighbors, naturally, and even interested to know what sort of persons they were, but she was not a snoop. In fact, she disliked that quality in anyone. However, she had her reasons, as complex as they were, and set about the distasteful task of inspecting the apartment.

Mia's room was neat, as she had imagined it might be. Her bed was made, the curtains drawn back, and her books stacked in a neat pile on the floor. She went through the girl's things slowly and methodically, making certain that after checking them, every garment was folded and replaced exactly as she'd found it. Apart from a few personal items, a pocket watch, a framed photograph of herself with her parents, and a handful of postcards, nothing incriminating was found among her belongings.

The other bedroom was shared by the other two young women, and it was as messy as Mia's was neat. The beds were unmade, clothing was strewn about on the floor, face powder and brushes and nail gloss littering every surface. Stacks of fashion magazines lay all around the room. It was a more difficult task to look through the carnage than in a neater room, but Chantal steeled herself and did it, anyway.

Again, she found nothing of interest. It had been a waste of time trying to find out what they knew. She stood in the main room of

206 • JULIA BRYAN THOMAS

the flat, trying to decide what to do. Then she realized there was one place she hadn't checked: a loose ceiling tile in the small kitchenette.

She took a chair and stood on it, raising her hands to the ceiling. She could barely reach it. It wasn't safe for a seventy-four-year-old woman to stand on chairs, but she wanted to see if they had discovered the hiding place that had been in the flat for as long as it had been there. Easing back the tile, she could feel the weight of something and lifted it down carefully.

It was a large envelope, full of papers and franc notes. She looked through it, page by page, but couldn't identify which of the girls it belonged to. There were instructions, which she committed to memory before putting everything back in its place and securing the tile overhead. When she was satisfied that no one could tell that she had been in the room, she walked out of the flat and locked the door.

Someone knew precisely what was going on, and it was up to her to find out which of them was involved. These three young women might appear to be innocent young models living it up in Paris, France, but one of them—or perhaps two—were a danger to them all. She would pass on the information when the opportunity arose, but in the meantime, she would keep her eyes and ears open. She locked the flat once again and crept back to her own, as stealthily as the cat who lived in the corridor. It was time to make a decision about what to do next.

# 17

---

Mia was a quick study, just as Philip had known she would be. She'd grown in a few months from an insecure girl into a woman who could make split-second calls with sound, reasonable judgment. He had left her specific instructions on many occasions, and she had followed each of them to the letter. She even looked older and more capable than she had when she first showed up on his radar and he was glad to see it. It might be the one thing that would keep her alive.

The young woman walking toward him now was a completely different person from the one he had first shadowed months ago. Gone were the flowery frocks that pegged her as an American. Instead, she wore a woolen suit that was snug in all the right places, with a matching cap, a walking replica of another famous American, Jacqueline Kennedy. Her hair was shorter now, too, a smooth bob brushing her shoulders, making her look even more like her idol.

He almost smiled when she walked right past him without making eye contact. Taking a last, leisurely sip of his coffee, he folded his newspaper and stood, jingling the keys in his pocket as if he were undecided which way to go. Of course, he turned to follow her, at a slower pace, wondering where she would take him.

He had to have faith. After all, she'd had plenty in him when he'd dragged her down to the Catacombs and across the city, trying to avoid being caught. She took him on a chase around Paris now, too, through tunnels and back alleys until she came to a hidden café on the Rue St. Charles, a place he had never been before. Fortunately, Paris is chock-full of secret haunts, one of the reasons one can conceal one's identity so easily. She took a seat inside, away from the gaze of passersby, and he nodded to the waiter as he went up to her table.

"That was quite a walk," he said, pulling out the chair across from her. "I definitely got my constitutional for the day."

"It keeps you in shape," she replied coolly. "You don't want to get a pudge around the middle."

"I remember a time when you were nervous to talk to me," he said. "Too bad you still aren't."

She raised a brow and paused as the waiter set two cups of coffee in front of them. She took a sip of hers, turning it on its saucer when she set it back down. It was the only betrayal of her feelings that she couldn't control.

"How did it go last night?" he asked.

He had to admit a certain feeling of apprehension when she did these gigs. Her driver, Luca, escorted her to and from each event, so he wasn't concerned for her well-being, but as she gained more confidence, he was more than a little unsettled about not being able to control what was said, who it was said to, and how the person receiving information was going to respond. In the early days, he was feeding her false information to one of his own informants to see if she was following protocol or if she was too afraid to go against Theo's orders. Turns out, she wasn't. She trusted him, and he couldn't blow it by letting his feelings be known. They were both cogs in a wheel at this point, each with a job to do. His, to feed her information—or misinformation, depending on the circumstance—and hers, to deliver it convincingly to complete strangers who could easily mean her harm.

"It all went according to plan," she said, of the last assignment he had sent her on. "I know very well that if there is a variation in response, I am to leave a message at once."

"Good," he replied.

She was the right person for this job, he knew, even if it was going to change her forever.

"There's something I need to talk you about," he continued, eyeing the croissants that sat on the counter before deciding not to get one. She was right about getting a pudge. "We need to discuss the diamond."

She gave him a sharp look, recognizing the subject from the James Bond book. It wasn't subtle, but it was effective. He had deliberately avoided mentioning it until the last possible moment.

"What is it?" she asked.

"Everything we're doing is because of a diamond," he explained. He spoke in a low voice, even though they were the only people in the back of the café. "Or rather, a diamond-sized chip that contains nuclear information, which was smuggled out of the United States. The Alliance is desperate to get their hands on it in order to take a front seat in the arms race."

"What does that have to do with me?"

"They're pushing their contacts for information on how to obtain it. Operatives in Bulgaria and a few other Eastern European countries have teamed with Soviet Russia to try to attack France's democratic system. They don't know how yet, but with the fringe far right sentiment still alive in this country, they know a big event could bring the radicals out in droves."

"What does that mean?" she asked. "Are you saying France could fall again with the right push?"

Philip nodded. "That's exactly what I'm saying. There's even a growing fear that the U.S. could be destabilized as well, through bombs or an assassination."

Mia looked suitably horrified, suddenly aware of the gravity of the situation. Most people didn't sit up nights worrying about the arms race unless they worked either for or against their national government. The feds sat in dark little quarters, sometimes even the White House SCIF room, with the most important leaders in the country boasting the highest-level security clearances. That was the Sensitive

Compartmented Information Facility, of course, a safe room that couldn't be bugged, a World War II invention created to safeguard the nation's top secrets.

And then there was the other side of the coin, the individuals who wanted to steal whatever it was the feds were working on. And it wasn't just in the U.S.; it was all over the industrialized world.

In 1960, there were plenty of them on both sides, monitoring all the major cities of Europe for rumblings of unrest. There was always trouble in some form or another, and with hundreds of goons on both sides of the aisle, one had to be careful not to attract attention.

Mia got dragged into it, unbeknownst to her, because of a single connection she had with a high-profile Alliance asset. Sometimes that was all it took—one interaction with one person, and one was suddenly in a desperate situation over their head.

She had come so far in just a few short months. Philip wanted to have confidence that things would work out according to their plans. However, one could never tell when things were going to go spectacularly wrong, no matter how much one worked to insulate oneself from the worst possibilities.

"What about Maeve and Elisabeth?" he asked.

They were still uncertain if either or both were involved with the Alliance. His gut told him that at least one of them had to be. Theo Gillette wasn't stupid. He had to have multiple girls working different angles to achieve maximum results. The more impressionable the young woman, the easier it would be to coerce or encourage her to act in his interests.

"I haven't found a single thing in the flat that implicates them in any antigovernment activity," she continued. "Not a letter, a note, nothing that might suggest their involvement. Of course, I won't stop looking."

She was handling her roommates better—listen, don't talk so much—as well as looking the part more than she had when she'd first begun. Obviously, she was young, but she didn't appear quite as corn-fed as she had when she arrived. She carried herself differently now. She had learned, perhaps instinctively, to reveal as little of herself as possible to strangers. He had to give it to her, she had developed a sophistication that he didn't think was possible.

In the coming weeks, it would be time to deal with the situation head-on, and he had to say he was looking forward to it. He knew there was a thrill when a cat catches a mouse and knows it can't get away. It brings a paw down on the rodent's tail and watches it squirm. They were going to have the human equivalent of that situation in the not-too-distant future, and he was planning carefully. He also knew to never, ever make a move until one can predict all possible outcomes. It's a major trick of the trade.

Of course, it wasn't personal. He had seen it all before. First, she'd be shocked, then angry, then downright violent if that's what it came to. But there are always two sides in every war, and everybody has to choose which side they're on.

"I have an assignment for you," he said, watching her closely. "It's going to be the most difficult so far."

"I can handle it," she said, although he didn't know if she meant it or if she was trying to talk herself into it.

"You're going to have to burgle Theo Gillette's apartment."

He waited for a shocked reaction, but there was none. One point for her.

"What do I do?" she asked.

"We have to find out what he knows and how he knows it," Philip continued.

Mia narrowed her eyes. "Why don't you send in a ghost?"

She was smart. He had to give her that. They often used a trained operative in a situation like that, but this was more than just a quest for information. It was the ultimate test of her loyalty. She had to prove once and for all that she was a trusted operative of the CIA.

"The reasons are above your pay grade," he answered, in all seriousness. "Here's what I need you to do. Look for cyphers, codes, numbers, symbols, words—anything that could tip us off to how close they are to getting what they want."

Mia nodded.

"And here," he said, drawing something out of his pocket. He handed it to her, watching her frown.

"A lighter?" she said. "I don't smoke."

"You might want to take it up for a few weeks," he replied. "Or just carry a half-empty pack of cigarettes in your handbag. But this is not a mere lighter. It's a camera. Anything suspicious you find in Theo's flat can be photographed so we can make decisions about what you've seen."

She took it and examined it to figure out how it worked.

"There's an inscription on it," she remarked.

"*To Cyril, with love from Maggie,*" he quoted. "I came up with it myself. If anyone asks about it, tell them you found it on the ground in the park."

She nodded, tucking it in her handbag. He took a few bills out of his wallet and threw them on the table.

"I'll leave the particulars in the usual place," he said. "But be careful, do you understand? Careless spies give themselves away."

# 18

———

Philip's "particulars" weren't as fleshed out as Mia would have liked. It would have been easy to give her an address and full instructions—she was good at following through on specific tasks, whether at the House of Rousseau or anywhere else—but the piece of paper she retrieved from her mailbox and subsequently destroyed provided no such thing. Instead, it merely gave a date two days hence and the message, *Files to the usual place.*

Mia took *files* to mean the lighter, as well as any pertinent notes about anything she found. However, she had to figure out where to begin. First, she had to locate Theo's flat. Then she had to figure out how to get into it in order to search the premises.

She was gaining confidence. For months, she had been watching for instructions from Philip, and her assignments from him were as frequent as those she had received from Theo. None, of course, involved anything like breaking into her employer's home to search it from top to bottom. She had also been examining her own motives. It was true, Philip had given her no choice but to get involved, and every act she undertook went unacknowledged. However, she trusted him, and she knew she had to follow the directives for the good of the country, even if it put her in danger.

For two days, she mulled her options. She had to find out her employer's address, for one thing, and then figure out what she was supposed to be looking for. But how would she discover where Theo lived? She thought about following him home after work, but that was far too risky. If he spotted her, she couldn't explain what she was doing. Even worse, she couldn't do it after a day of work because Maeve and Elisabeth would find her behavior suspicious. She wandered freely around Paris in the mornings on weekends and her days off, but she had never gone off on her own during the evening rush hour, when it would be difficult to track someone, anyway. This was a job that had to be done without raising suspicion from her roommates or anyone else.

Following him was out of the question. Neither could she hire someone else to do it and report back to her. She had no network of informants, and she couldn't trust something like this to a stranger. She considered asking one of the girls at the fashion house if they knew where Theo lived but dismissed the idea at once. Surely, none of them knew, but if one of them surprised her by saying yes, it would put their reputation on the line. As far as she knew, Theo had a record of complete respectability at Rousseau, and he didn't seem to be the type of man to jeopardize it by having a dalliance with one of the models. No, she had to come up with another idea.

In the end, she decided there was only one possible solution: she would have to find access to his address when she went to the fashion house the following day. Then she would feign illness so that she could leave without being accompanied by her roommates and proceed to carry out her mission.

The only two places where she could possibly find that information were in his personal office among his things or in that of the secretary, Mademoiselle Arnaud. Searching his office was the more difficult proposition. He kept irregular hours. He had a tendency to come and go during the day, taking long lunches with colleagues or, for all she knew, attractive women, but two or three days a week, he ate at his desk, immersed in the newspapers. He never left for the day at the same time, either. She had noticed him leaving rather late in the afternoon and still coming back to get something before locking his office for the evening. She couldn't take the chance. Even if Theo himself didn't find her, someone else might and she would be dismissed on the spot.

The only alternative was Mademoiselle Arnaud's office, where employee files were kept. If, for some reason, Theo's wasn't among them, she would have to take her chances and try one of the riskier alternatives.

On the assigned morning, she went down to the office at 9:40.

Mademoiselle Arnaud was known to take a coffee break every morning at 9:30, and Maeve had recently mentioned that she often spent her time with Claude in *passementerie*. In fact, her roommate had been scandalized because Mademoiselle sometimes took him a cup of coffee as well. There were strong rules about fraternization at the House of Rousseau. If Theo got wind of it, she might even be sacked.

Letting herself into the secretary's office, Mia shut the door behind her and took a quick look about the room. Moving to the filing cabinet, she pulled out the drawers one by one until she came to the one with employee files. Most were thin, but a handful were quite thick. Mia wanted to take them out and look at what sort of information they contained, but she couldn't linger more than a few moments. She flicked through the files until she found Theo's, lifting it a few inches. Pulling the front edge of the folder back, she found his address at once. 10 Rue de la Clef, number 503. She repeated it to herself three times and then pushed the file back into place. Then she took a deep breath and left the office.

"Where have you been?" Elisabeth asked when she returned to the fitting rooms.

Mia's hackles rose. She couldn't disappear for a moment without raising someone's suspicions. However, she mastered her emotions and gave Elisabeth a wan smile.

"Actually, I'm not feeling terribly well."

Elisabeth turned, putting her hands on her hips. She was wearing a pink dress with a tulle skirt, looking more like a ballerina than a model. "Could I get you a glass of water or something?"

"No, thank you," Mia answered. "I just drank one, and it didn't really help."

"If you're not well, you should probably let Miss Larson know," Elisabeth said. "She's very understanding. Maybe you should go home and get in bed for the rest of the day. You may be coming down with something."

"I suppose I should," said Mia. "Thank you."

Three months ago, she would have felt upset about lying to her friend. Now she could do it without a second thought. She went downstairs to Miss Larson's office and knocked at the door lightly, opening it when the woman called her to come in.

"Miss Larson, I'm afraid I have the most awful headache," she said to the directress. "I'm terribly sorry, but I don't think I can continue to work today."

The woman's face immediately showed concern. Mia was considered one of the most reliable of the girls. She never called in sick, she never complained. She thanked the tailors and seamstresses whenever she worked with them, aware that she wasn't above them. The couture was the star of every production, and she never forgot it. She had seen others with a haughty arrogance or manner that was less than appropriate, and she didn't want to be one of them.

"I'm sorry to hear it," Miss Larson replied, standing. "Are you running a fever? You do look a little peaked."

Mia shook her head. "No, I don't believe so. But I feel very much like I need to lie down."

"Shall I try to get word to Luca?" the woman asked. "We could get him to take you home."

"He's probably out on errands," Mia said, hoping that was indeed true. "I don't mind getting a taxi."

"I hope you feel better soon."

"Thank you, Miss Larson."

She gathered her things and went downstairs, not even looking in the direction of Theo's office. She flagged a taxi with no difficulty and took it straight to her building in case any questions should be asked. She paid the driver and got out, walking inside. The concierge, Monsieur Dubuc, was discussing something in a low voice with her neighbor, Madame Fournier, whom she hadn't seen in a couple of weeks. The older woman nodded at her and continued her conversation while Mia went up the staircase.

She let herself into her flat, repocketing her key. After changing into a brown suede skirt and matching turtleneck, she went into the small bathroom and pinned back her hair, tying a scarf around her head. After letting herself out of the apartment, she went to the back staircase, which led into the alley.

The Rue de la Clef was less than a mile from her building in an elegant neighborhood. It was more refined than her own area, with decorative wrought-iron edging around miniature flower beds. The streetlamps were ancient, and the buildings even more stately than the ones on the Rue des Écoles, although she was still as enthralled with her Paris flat as she was when she first arrived. For all its small size, it was far nicer than anywhere she had ever lived. Theo's building, however, was much like that of the mysterious Madame Laurent. It was the home of someone with a great deal of money.

She did not approach the building from the front, but walked down the street looking for an alley, which she found. She went around the back, where it sat back-to-back with another building that faced the street behind it. Letting herself in a small gate, she walked up to the building and up to the door.

It was unlocked and she let herself inside. The back entrance was comprised of a long hallway with a handful of doors. Two were broom closets and storage rooms obviously used by the person who saw to the upkeep of the building. At the far end, she found a service elevator, which she was tempted to take, but stairs were safer. It was easier to avoid detection without a bell signaling one's arrival. The staircase was empty, and Mia began her ascent to the fifth floor.

The corridor was silent. She crept to the door, where she pulled the scarf from around her head and tucked it into her handbag. Then she tried the knob, which was locked. Pulling a hairpin from her hair, she poked it into the keyhole several times to release the push-button mechanism.

Twice during her father's illness, she had gotten locked out of her apartment when the super was not in the building. A neighbor had shown her how to get in if she ever got locked out again. She had no idea that it was a skill she would ever use, let alone in an elegant apartment building in France.

After a few attempts, she took a deep breath and tried again, this time hearing the mechanism turn, and the door opened when she turned the knob. She let herself in and locked it behind her.

Theo's flat was several times the size of the one she shared with Elisabeth and Maeve. In fact, it felt cavernous. She slid the hairpin back into place and removed the lighter from her bag before tucking the bag behind a chair. Then she slipped off her flats and set them next to the bag. She wanted to turn on a lamp but decided not to risk it. Instead, she glanced at the clock over the mantle. It was a quarter to eleven.

In case he came home for lunch, she had to be out as quickly as possible, and she made her way around the room, getting her bearings. There were thick cushioned sofas and chairs, and tables that cost more than a year of her salary. She moved to the large Regency desk and examined the items on the top: a magnifying glass on top of a copy of Shakespeare's plays. It seemed more of a decorative element than an actual book that he might read, although she did not underestimate him. There was also a small gilt clock, a fountain pen in a wooden holder, a lamp, a small stack of files, and an antique stereopticon in a stand.

She went back to her bag and took out a pair of white gloves. Then she lifted the stereopticon to see what images were on the slides, afraid she might find images of half naked Pigalle dancers. Instead, it contained bland antique photos of the Eiffel Tower in various stages of completion. She ran through the entire set of images and then set it back the way she had found it.

Likewise, the files contained nothing useful. Some were applications for the House of Rousseau by various young women—models, she assumed. Two held receipts for repairs that had been done on the apartment. Nothing was important enough to photograph for Philip.

She decided to have a look around the flat to determine how many rooms there were. In addition to the large living area, there was a decent-sized kitchen, a dining room decorated in dramatic black and red, two bathrooms, a book-lined study, and two bedrooms. The principal bedroom was the largest and, like the rest of the flat, was decorated in expensive antiques. The smaller of the two was still far larger than her own room, and it appeared to be a simple guest room, although she would have to go through it carefully.

She went back to Theo's room. The door had been closed, and she made certain it was shut behind her as she inspected every surface. She wasn't sure what she was looking for and thought back on what Philip had told her: cyphers, codes, numbers, symbols, words. It didn't have to make sense to be important.

With the door shut, she felt freer to turn on a lamp and she searched the drawers methodically, making certain everything was left as she found it. Her frustration was growing. Surely if Theo were involved in international espionage, there would be some sign somewhere, but of course, information could be kept in a flat like this if the person hiding it were clever. She got down on her knees and once

224 · JULIA BRYAN THOMAS

again pulled out the drawers of the dresser, running her hand along the bottom of each one.

She felt something. Closer inspection revealed it to be a piece of paper taped to the bottom of the drawer. Pulling the lighter from her pocket, she opened the secret compartment and saw a miniature camera lens pop out. Then she lay down on the floor so that she could hold the lighter up to it to take a photo. Three of the nine drawers had something affixed to them. Like Philip had suggested, all contained indecipherable messages.

After getting the photos, she ran her fingers along the inside of lampshades and the back side of each drape. She was just about to leave the room when she heard a sound coming from the living room. She switched off the lamp and hurried to the far side of the bed, where she dropped to the floor and squeezed herself underneath.

The door opened and Mia held her breath. She could see two pair of shoes as two men entered the room. They were speaking in low voices. At first, she thought they were speaking French. She still wasn't fluent—she had decided she never would be—but she knew enough from listening to it every day that it wasn't French, nor was it Italian. She could identify it as a European language, but she had no idea which one.

Actual government employees who worked in the espionage field were trained in these areas, she knew. They could recognize languages and patterns of speech, as well as dialects and the nuances of each spoken word. She was a mere twenty-year-old, with no experience and no business trying to conduct covert activities, particularly surveilling her own boss. If caught, she would be in serious jeopardy, possibly arrested or even killed.

One of them suddenly reached down and picked something off the floor. She stifled a gasp as she realized it was the lighter. She must have dropped it on the carpet as she tried to squeeze herself under the bed. She watched in a panic as he stood there, tossing it in the air and catching it a couple of times before placing it on the dresser. If he had bent down any farther, he would have seen her and life as she knew it would be over.

They pulled open drawers, just as she had, and then shut them quickly again. After a minute, they left the room, closing the door behind them.

Mia didn't move. She tried to calm her breathing so she could hear what they were doing in the outer rooms. They lingered for a while. She went cold when she realized her handbag and shoes were tucked behind a chair, and the bag contained her identification. She didn't remember how far under the chair she had set them, but if they were discovered, they would come looking for her at once. Instead, she listened to them opening kitchen cupboards and looking under the crockery. She even heard them lifting the bottles of the liquor cart, inspecting them and commenting on them to one another. One of them laughed, and then she heard the door of the flat open. After it closed, the apartment was silent.

Still, she waited another few minutes before gingerly squeezing out from under the bed. She rubbed her neck, which was stiff from lying there for too long. She rose and went over to get the lighter, thankful it was still there, wondering who had just broken into Theo's apartment. She was starting to think that no matter what side one was on, there was treachery to be found.

She wanted to leave, but she had to do a thorough job, or she could miss something. In his closet, she took down hat boxes and rifled through jacket pockets until she came up with another possible clue: a photograph of a man and a note written in a foreign language. She set them on the dresser and photographed them with the lighter, returning them precisely as they had been.

She found nothing else suspicious. There were no secret compartments, and none of the paneled walls gave way with a push or nudge. She went over to the chair where she had hidden her things and slipped on her shoes, letting herself out of the flat. Looking up and down the corridor, she made her way quietly to the stairs and retraced her way to the back door of the building. Glancing at her watch, she saw that she had been inside Theo's flat for almost three-quarters of an hour.

There weren't many clues, but as far as she could tell, he was definitely hiding something. She hurried to the nearest café and wrote down all the details she could remember and then stuffed the note along with the lighter inside an envelope and sealed it.

When she made it to her own building, she left the message and lighter for Philip and went upstairs, changed into pajamas, and crawled into bed in case Elisabeth or Maeve suddenly showed up, concerned about her. They had plenty of reason to be, she thought. Her life was entirely out of control.

As she lay there, she thought about Philip. Was he who he said he was? Would an actual agent of the U.S. government rely upon untrained young models when they had at their disposal the services of professional spies? She had no answers to any of her questions, and neither was he around to reassure her that she was doing the right thing. She hadn't come to France to become involved in espionage or to be abducted or coerced into surveillance and counterintelligence, yet that was exactly what happened.

Yet, when it came down to it, he must have been honest with her. Anything else was unthinkable.

# 19

Mia didn't hear from Philip after delivering the photographs. Two weeks passed, and she began to wonder if she had imagined the whole thing. Everything, that is, except the interior of Theo Gillette's flat, which was burned into her brain. Every time she looked at her employer, she struggled not to let her emotions show. She wondered at the significance, if any, of the documents that had been secured to the bottom of the dresser drawers, specifically, if any of them contained clues regarding Theo's involvement in surreptitious Cold War activity. Even though she wanted to know what the papers might contain, she didn't expect to find out. Whatever information they held would never make its way to her, even if they had put her life in danger to get it.

She used the time to focus on her job. Rousseau had sent ten models to the Galeries Lafayette for a public event. Each model only wore one dress, but they had practiced their choreography for two weeks prior to the occasion. They all agreed it was one of the best experiences they'd had at Rousseau.

Later that afternoon, Luca drove Elisabeth, Maeve, and Mia back to their flat. He had been in better spirits lately. In fact, twice he had caught her eye and smiled as warmly as he had when they first met. Perhaps she had been too hard on him. He was a professional; it wasn't his place to get too friendly with any of the girls if he intended to keep his job, one that he obviously enjoyed. He dropped them at the door, where she followed Maeve and Elisabeth inside. Maeve approached the concierge and asked for their mail. He handed her a couple of letters.

"One for me, and one for you, Mia," she said, holding out one of the envelopes.

It was the first time she had gotten mail since she had been in France, and both of her roommates knew it. Mia took the envelope, wondering who sent it. She looked at the postmark, which read *Brooklyn, New York*, and then at the return address. The name Mary Goodwin was written in a neat, feminine script. Mia puzzled over it for a second before she realized that it wasn't a personal letter at all. It was a message from Philip. She could feel it in her bones.

"Who's it from?" Elisabeth asked. "You never get mail."

Mia looked up. "An old friend from high school. I left my forwarding address with my landlady. It's nice that someone decided to look me up."

"She probably heard you were in Paris and wants to visit," Maeve replied as they walked to the staircase. "But there's no way we can accommodate another body. You'll have to tell her there's no room in the inn."

"It's not like we have time to entertain someone, anyway," Mia said, nodding. "We're far too busy."

"Speaking of busy, what are we going to do tonight?" Elisabeth asked, tossing her handbag into the pink chair. "Any ideas?"

"Natalie said some of the girls are going to Chez Claude," Mia answered. "They're going to have a jazz band tonight."

"Look who's suddenly interested in going out," Maeve remarked. "I'd never believe it if I hadn't heard it for myself."

"Come on," Mia said. "You know I like music."

"Let's do it," Elisabeth said. "I'll get ready."

They dispersed into their rooms, Mia shutting the door behind her. She sat down on the bed, kicking off her shoes. Turning away from the door, she slid her finger under the flap of the envelope.

No letter fell out. She pulled it open wider and saw that there was only a newspaper clipping dated 1953. The headline read *Rosenbergs Executed*.

Mia froze. She knew generally of Julius and Ethel Rosenberg, but she had been a child during their notoriety, and had no real knowledge of their case. She straightened out the folded yellowed article, and began to read.

Julius Rosenberg, 35, and his wife, Ethel Rosenberg, 37, were executed yesterday at Sing Sing Prison in Ossining,

New York, after being convicted on charges of spying for the Soviet Union. Longtime members of the Communist Party and former members of the Young Communist League, Rosenberg and his wife had been involved in espionage, filtering information to the Soviets on jet propulsion engines, radar and sonar technology, and confidential U.S. nuclear weapons designs. Nuclear espionage, the act of giving state secrets to foreign governments or agents without authorization, includes any information shared on design, stockpiles, delivery systems of weapons, or deployment of such weapons. The Rosenbergs were executed by electrocution after all appeals had been exhausted.

Mia dropped the clipping to her lap, trying to imagine how this information pertained to her. According to Philip, she was involved in counterintelligence, which she understood to be any activity designed to protect an agency's intelligence program from attack by groups like the Alliance, who wanted to gain access to top secret information for profit and power. It was the most critical conflict in the postwar world, one that could bring nations back into the fray if they succeeded. The Cold War could escalate into a ticking time bomb if nuclear secrets got into the wrong hands.

Still, she was concerned about the meaning of the article. Was it a reminder from Philip that everything she did to protect the interests of the United States government was an act of patriotism? Or was it a warning from the Alliance that people seen to be traitors would be rounded up, tried, and executed?

She read the rest of the article, folding it as tight as it would go and stuffing it in the strap of her slip. She had to dispose of it, but not here in the flat where it could be retrieved by a snooping roommate.

Once she'd tucked her shoes into the wardrobe, she hung up her dress and chose another for the night ahead, a burgundy-colored evening dress with long sleeves and buttons to the waist. She rarely wore red, but it suited her coloring. There were invariably compliments from men whenever she wore it, and she needed to bolster her confidence. Much was expected of her, far more than if she were an ordinary model. Both sides could be watching whenever she was in public, and she had to project an air of self-assuredness that she didn't always feel. She was examining herself in the mirror when her door opened. Maeve leaned through the doorway, smiling.

"How are we doing with potential houseguests?" she asked.

Mia managed a laugh. "It's not a visit, thank goodness. She got engaged to the butcher's son. She wants me to come to the wedding next summer."

"Everything depends on our schedule," Maeve replied, raising a brow. "Spring and summer are our busiest seasons."

Mia nodded, although she didn't appreciate Maeve telling her what she could and could not do. She was supposed to be an employee at Rousseau, not a prisoner.

"Are you ready?"

"Almost," Mia answered. "I'm switching to my black heels."

Maeve left the door open when she went back into the other room, and Mia took the pumps from her wardrobe, sitting on the edge of the bed to slip them on. She picked up the envelope again and looked at the return address: 37 Blixen Avenue. She had lived in Brooklyn all her life, and though she didn't have every street name memorized, she was certain she had never heard of Blixen Avenue. Her instincts told her it was a fake address, and if so, the number or street name might have significance for her here in Paris.

"Here," Elisabeth said when Mia came out of her room, holding out a plate of bread and cheese. "Eat a little something before we go out. It will mitigate the effects of all the martinis we'll be drinking."

A few minutes later, they set out for the club. They crossed onto the Île de la Cité and then the narrow pedestrian bridge that took them to the Île Saint-Louis, the smaller of the two islands. Mia preferred the former, where Notre Dame presided over the parks and squares and buildings, rather than the Saint-Louis, which seemed darker, with its narrow streets and tall buildings, which blocked the sunlight in the daytime. At night, it was nearly pitch black. They walked a few blocks until they found a door that Elisabeth pronounced was the right one.

"Are you sure this is it?" Mia asked, pulling her coat closer around her shoulders.

Elisabeth didn't answer, but turned the knob, where they found a steep set of stairs. Music drifted up and Elisabeth nodded, starting down the steps. Mia and Maeve had no choice but to follow. The room was dimly lit, swirling with smoke. A ten-piece band was playing on a stage at the far end of the room, and there were tables scattered throughout. Maeve found one and sat down.

"Will someone order me a drink?" she asked. "I can't walk another step in these heels."

"I'll go," Mia said, wanting a chance to look around.

She made her way to the bar and ordered three vodka martinis from the bartender, who looked hardly older than she was.

"Vodka?" he asked.

"Yes," Mia replied. She was able to hold her own far longer with vodka than with gin. "With a lemon twist, please."

He nodded, and she leaned against the bar, watching him mix the drinks for a moment before scanning the room. The music was good, as she often found in these venues, and the crowd was sedate. All in all, it wouldn't be a bad way to spend the evening.

"Here you go," he said, setting three glasses in front of her.

She took two of the glasses. "I'll be back for the other in a minute."

At the table, she set one in front of Maeve and the other at Elisabeth's elbow before going back to the bar. She lifted the glass and began to turn when the bartender cocked his head and smiled.

"What's your hurry?" he asked.

Mia shrugged, facing him. "There's no hurry."

"Most people in this place are twice our age," he replied. "It would be nice to talk to someone like you for a while."

"Where are you from?" she asked, taking a seat on a barstool. She hadn't placed his accent.

"Austria," he replied. "I was visiting Paris with friends, and we decided to stay for a year or two."

"That seems to be the case for a lot of people," she observed.

"You're American, I see," he replied. "But your friends aren't."

"How do you know that?" she asked.

"They look European," he said, shrugging. "You're more… What's the word? Wholesome. That's a compliment, if you're looking for one."

"I'm not," Mia replied. "But thanks."

She drank her martini and pushed the glass toward him. He nodded, getting a fresh glass and making her another while she listened to the music. It was a classic set that evening: Glenn Miller, Count Basie, and Benny Goodwin. She knew most of the songs, tapping the toe of her pump in time with her favorites.

"You should be dancing," he said. "What are you doing later?"

"Not dancing," Mia said, standing. For a second, she felt almost wobbly. Normally, the small amounts of alcohol she drank didn't affect her much, but she could certainly feel this one. She would have to switch to water when she returned to the table. "Excuse me."

She turned and walked to the ladies' room, locking the door behind her. Setting her handbag on the counter, she pulled the newspaper article from the strap of her slip and read it all the way through.

The Rosenbergs had been executed in 1953, nearly a decade

after the end of the Second World War. There had been a campaign for clemency, particularly for Ethel, whose role was not as clearly defined as her husband's. There were demonstrations across Western European on her behalf, and President Eisenhower received pleas from every corner of the world, from Albert Einstein to the Pope. He'd turned a deaf ear to all of them, refusing to stop the inevitable.

Julius Rosenberg died at the first electric shock. His wife, however, did not. After three attempts, she was still alive, and the executioners tried twice more before they were successful. After the fifth electrocution, when she was finally pronounced dead, smoke was rising from her head.

Mia leaned against the bathroom door, looking at her image in the mirror. It was deadly serious, this foray into espionage. One way or another, it could end in death or imprisonment. If she weren't careful, she would end up in the same situation as Ethel Rosenberg, even if she were on the right side of the government. Someone was coming after her, either way. Because of what had happened with her father, she felt a keen sense of responsibility to the United States, but she knew it didn't protect her from the consequences, however deadly they might be. The stakes were too high. People like her were surely expendable.

She tore the article into shreds and flushed it down the toilet, wishing she could remove the image from her brain permanently. A twenty-year-old was supposed to be enjoying her life, not worrying that every move she made was going to land her in danger.

She powdered her nose and went back to the table, where Elisabeth smiled.

"There you are," she said. "I was about to come after you."

"I'm fine," Mia replied. "I had two drinks and I think that I may already be over my limit."

"Don't be silly," Elisabeth said. Her roommate looked up. "Oh, look, Natalie is here. Maybe they'll want to get out of here. There's hardly any action."

However, when Elisabeth suggested going to another bar, her idea was dismissed.

"We just got here," Natalie protested.

Two of the other models from Rousseau were with her. Mia had never had more than a passing conversation with either of them, but they seemed to agree with Natalie. Mia hated nothing more than being dragged from place to place, looking for the right man or the right music, both of which were almost impossible to find. She liked the band, and after Elisabeth brought her a third martini, she sipped it far more slowly than she had the others.

With the murmur of conversation around her, Mia turned toward the music, thinking. She gripped the stem of the glass, deciding she would go back to the library and look for a Brooklyn map. She was certain there was no Blixen Avenue there, but she wanted to check for herself. If, as she suspected, there was not, she would have to try to figure out the significance of the address.

They left the bar just past midnight. Mia took one last look around the room as she was walking toward the exit. There, in the corner, were two men she hadn't noticed before, chatting and smoking. She didn't have to look twice to know the one with his back to her was Philip.

# 20

The Bibliothèque Nationale de France did contain a map of Brooklyn, New York, as Mia expected, but there was no Blixen Avenue on it. After scouring it for nearly an hour, Mia returned the map to its drawer and left the library even more bewildered. Just as there was no street of that name in New York, neither was there one in Paris, which meant she had no leads whatsoever. The number 37 was found in so many addresses in their own arrondissement, not to mention throughout the city, that it wasn't a viable option to investigate. She buttoned her coat and sat down on the steps, resting her elbows on her knees, thinking. Perhaps the address had not been a clue at all, merely designed to quell any interest Elisabeth and Maeve might have in its sender. Certainly it had allowed her to come up with a story on the spot.

"What are you doing here, stranger?" a voice called, interrupting her thoughts. Elisabeth walked up to her, smiling.

"Just looking at some maps in the library," Mia replied, standing, wondering what Elisabeth was doing there. She always told the truth whenever possible. It made her lies all the more believable.

"Sounds utterly boring to me," Elisabeth answered. "I think we should go shopping instead."

"All right," Mia agreed. "Where do you want to go?"

"I just saw a little place around the corner," Elisabeth said. She pulled up her collar and looked at the sky. "It looks like it might start pouring, so we don't want to go far."

The weather was mild, and they had endured several wet days in a row. Mia followed her to the shop, which she hadn't noticed before, although Paris was like that, with so many shops and cafés set back among others.

Elisabeth led her to the back of the room, away from the door, where the cool breeze rushed in every time it was opened. She took her time examining the dresses on the rack, sometimes taking one down and inspecting it closely. Working at Rousseau had taught them about craftsmanship.

"So, what's so interesting about maps?" Elisabeth asked, putting a dress back on the rack. "I can't imagine wasting a day off looking at them."

Mia pulled a hanger from the rack and touched the fabric of the dress, shrugging.

"My father had a huge atlas when I was little," Mia replied. "Maps seem to say, 'Adventure's waiting.'"

"Well, that's a romantic view," Elisabeth said.

"What sort of books did you like when you were young?"

"I liked *Heidi*, of course. But my mother also had lots of lovely books on plants and gardens. Sometimes I'd even take them out to the garden and see which flowers I could identify. But then, once I left one outdoors before it started to rain, and I got a scolding I'll never forget. You can imagine, I never did that again."

Mia smiled. "Sounds awful."

"By the way, I've been meaning to ask you what you're doing for Christmas," Elisabeth remarked. "I'd love you to come home with me if you haven't any other plans. You'll love Sweden. It's magical this time of year."

"What about Maeve?"

"She's going home. She hasn't seen her parents in ages." She looked down for a moment. "I wouldn't mind a break from her, I don't mind telling you. She can be a little intense sometimes."

Mia glanced up, surprised.

"You feel it, too, don't you?" Elisabeth continued. "There's something going on, I'm sure of it. She's been acting so strangely lately."

"I didn't realize," Mia said. She couldn't voice her opinions, no matter what she thought. However, she was relieved that Elisabeth thought something was going on with Maeve as well. It bolstered her opinion that Maeve, like Mia, was involved with the Alliance. One had to be careful whom to trust.

242 • JULIA BRYAN THOMAS

"Come on," her roommate insisted. "Surely you've noticed something."

"I haven't noticed her being any different than usual," Mia finally answered, alarm bells going off in her head. She had no business talking about either of them.

Elisabeth frowned. "Well, she is. Just watch her when we get home. I know it's not my imagination."

"I'd love to come home with you, really I would," Mia said, changing the subject. "But I may be doing something else for the holidays."

"Is it a man?" Elisabeth asked, suddenly interested. "That Pierre you were seeing?"

"It's not a man," Mia answered, turning her attention to the next rack.

For one thing, Philip hadn't contacted her once in the last few weeks. She wanted nothing more than to go back in time before anything had ever happened, when he was simply a man she was interested in. Of course, it was far too late for that.

"What about you?" she asked Elisabeth. "You've been out several times with someone, but you haven't said much about him."

"He's nice," she answered, shrugging. "No one I'd get serious about. Look! What about this one?"

She held a dress up in front of her for Mia's opinion.

"I like it," she said. "You should try it on."

"I will," Elisabeth answered. "Here, hold my bag."

"Le Mistral is having a poetry reading tonight," Mia remarked, following Elisabeth into the fitting room, where her friend went behind a curtain to change. "You wouldn't be interested in coming with me, would you?"

"I wouldn't mind, actually," Elisabeth replied. "I like poetry."

"Really?" Mia asked, surprised. She'd never seen her friend reading anything other than magazines.

"Why not? We don't have any other plans tonight, anyway." Elisabeth pulled back the curtain. "What do you think of this?"

Mia nodded at the dress, which was a brown knit with a fitted belt. "It looks great on you."

"Perfect," Elisabeth said. "I'll wear it tonight."

That evening, Mia wore a black dress with a pleated skirt. Elisabeth met her at the door, fastening a necklace about her throat.

"Thank you for asking me along," Elisabeth said. "You can be a little antisocial sometimes, you know."

Mia blushed. "I'm used to being on my own. Crowds of people can be overwhelming sometimes."

"You'll get used to it, sooner or later."

They walked to the bookshop and found a small room filled with folding chairs. To their surprise, Luca was sitting in the back row.

"What are you doing here?" Mia asked. "I didn't know you liked poetry."

He shrugged. "It sounded like a good thing to do on a cold, wet night. What about you?"

"The same," she replied.

They sat next to him, waiting for the reading to begin. Instead of a local poet or well-known writer, one of the booksellers eventually came and sat in the seat in front of the room. She was perhaps thirty, with long plaited hair. After clearing her throat, she began to read classic poems. The room went silent as she spoke the verses aloud.

The beauty of Wordsworth and Coleridge washed over them, and Mia was especially moved by the Shakespearean sonnets. However, it was a line from an Anne Bradstreet poem that caught her attention and held it long after the verse was finished. "*The world no longer let me love; my hope and Treasure lies above.*"

What chance did she have of finding love and living a normal life after getting swept up in the murky politics of the Cold War? It was impossible after all that had happened. There was no escape, nowhere to run. Her loyalty was to Philip and the United States government, and there was no choice but to follow through to the bitter end, whatever that may be.

She was roused from thought by the sudden applause around her, and the woman got up and gave a slight bow. Mia joined in the clapping, and when it had died down, she turned to Luca and Elisabeth.

"I enjoyed that so much," Mia remarked.

"So did I," Elisabeth admitted. "Thank you for letting me tag along."

"I'm afraid I can't stay," Luca said, glancing at his watch. "Can I give you two a lift back to your building?"

"Thank you, but I thought I'd look at books for a little while," Mia said. "Elisabeth, you can go with him if you want."

"That's all right," her friend replied. "I'll walk back with you when you're done. See you Monday, Luca."

He said his goodbyes and made his way through the crowd. After he left, Mia detached herself from Elisabeth, who was looking at gardening books, and found the map section. It was small, contained on a single shelf, and most of them were books on Paris or France. She had no idea where to begin. However, one protruded farther out on the shelf than the others, and she instinctively reached for it, pulling it toward her. When she lifted it, a thin folded piece of paper fell out. Mia lifted it and unfolded it, reading the message scribbled inside. *You're on the wrong track. It's not an address at all.*

Mia refolded it carefully and slipped the note into her coat pocket. How did he know, she wondered? But a larger question loomed. If it wasn't an address, what did 37 Blixen Avenue mean?

Minuscule flakes of snow began to fall as they walked home. By the time she changed for bed, the drops had become wetter and fatter, and soon a layer of glistening white covered the street below. She lay down on the bed and pulled the comforter over her, puzzling over the note, but nothing came to her, not even the next morning.

"It's the week before Christmas," Elisabeth said one evening to Mia.

"I was hoping you'd changed your mind. I'd love you to come home with me for the holidays."

"I'm sure it's beautiful right now," Mia said.

"It is. You'll love it."

"I appreciate the offer, but I can't this time," Mia replied.

"Oh, but you should," Elisabeth protested. "We can't leave you all alone here."

"That's right," Maeve said, sitting down next to her. "And if it's too cold for you in Sweden, come with me to Dublin. There's always a crowd there. You wouldn't stand out at all."

"Actually, I was thinking of flying home to New York for a few days," Mia answered.

The thought had not occurred to her before that very second, but it gave her the perfect excuse to stay in the flat alone for a few days and search it again. There was nothing to go home for.

"New York!" Elisabeth said, as if she'd never heard anything so shocking.

"I've saved up some money," Mia said truthfully. "I've been here almost seven months. I thought it would be nice to go back and see my friends at the bakery and catch up after all this time."

Maeve looked at her skeptically. "You hardly ever get any letters."

"Well, they'll be glad to see me all the same."

Elisabeth shrugged. "If you change your mind…"

"I know. Thank you."

Two days later, Maeve took the train to Calais. The following morning, Elisabeth hugged her and took a train heading north. Mia went with her to the Gare du Nord, seeing her onto her train.

After it pulled away, she left the station, wondering what she was going to do now.

If only she could find Philip, she thought, although she was unsure of which manifestation of him that she wanted. She would have given anything to get back the easygoing, uncomplicated man she had been interested in, who seemed so promising at the beginning of their relationship. On the other hand, she would have given her last dime to sit down with Philip, the expert in espionage, to explain what was happening and to try to convince him to get her out of it.

The House of Rousseau was closed for the holidays. Luca, who had been increasingly friendly, had left for Italy, and the building was closed as members of the staff took off for various parts of the country for Christmas with their own families.

It occurred to Mia that this was the first Christmas she had ever spent alone now that her father was gone. It was true—she could have gone to Brooklyn and her friends at the bakery would have taken her in, even allowing her stay with them and enjoy the turkey dinner that her employer's wife would invariably make, but she couldn't impose on them like that. She had moved on with her life, and they with theirs, and she couldn't go back. Nothing would ever be the same.

Paris was most beautiful in December, dazzling with lights strung across shop fronts and streets. Christmas markets appeared at the Eiffel Tower, Notre Dame, and the Champs-Elysées. Several evenings, she went to watch the locals ice skating at the rink in the Trocadero. Fir wreaths hung from every door, and shops had displays full of tempting items. The Galeries Lafayette erected their famous tree in the cupola, a tradition that dated to 1912. Yet, with no one to buy a gift for or to share a meal with, the holiday would prove to be the loneliest of her life. One evening, she found the cat lurking in the hall and went over to pick him up.

"You're alone, too, aren't you, little fellow?" she asked.

She brought him into the flat and gave him a saucer of milk, vowing not to let him out of her sight until her roommates returned. But, of course, that didn't last. He scratched at the door within the hour, wanting to reclaim his freedom. Mia let him out once again and stood against the doorframe, watching as he crept down the corridor.

Glancing at Madame Fournier's door down the hall, she went over and stood in front of it. She had only seen her neighbor occasionally over the last few weeks, but she knew sometimes the older woman went upstairs to care for an elderly neighbor.

Mia raised her hand to knock but then stopped herself. What would she say? *Do you want company for Christmas? Can I make you a meal? Could we have a few minutes of conversation so that I don't have to spend the entire day in a silent flat with no one to talk to?*

Every question she could think of seemed ridiculous. How had she gotten to a place in her life where she was so isolated that spending an hour with an elderly woman sounded so good?

Sighing, she went back inside and shut the door, then sank into the pink chair.

The only thing she wanted to know was where to find Philip. If he would relieve the emptiness, she would forgive him anything, even involving her in a dangerous game of espionage.

# 21

By the day after Christmas, Mia was mind-numbingly bored. She had wanted some time alone, but the silence in the empty flat was almost more than she could stand. She sat in the pink chair, tapping the envelope, looking at the address from the nonexistent Mary Goodwin, 37 Blixen Avenue.

It had to mean something, she thought. It couldn't have just been a throwaway line written to hide the identity of the person who had sent her the article about the Rosenbergs, which remained another mystery.

Mia drummed her fingers on the edge of the chair, thinking. The number 37 had come up one other time since she had been recruited by Philip. Le Mistral bookshop was found at 37 Rue de la Bûcherie. With nothing else to do but go mad in the empty flat, she folded the envelope in half and put it in her pocket and slipped on her coat.

This time, she took no precautions. If someone wanted to stop her or follow her, she didn't care. She sloshed through the wet pavement, soaking the hem of her trousers. The streets were quiet as she made her way several blocks north. When she reached the bookshop, she stamped the drizzle from her shoes and stepped through the door.

"Bonjour," she said to the young man behind the counter.

He looked precisely like someone who would work in a bookshop in Paris on a winter day: dark hair, dark glasses, and a permanently dour look on his face.

"Bonjour," he replied, barely looking up from his book. "Feel free to look around."

It was unnerving how the French could always tell she was an American by a single word. She watched as he went back to his reading, wondering where she should start looking among the rows and rows of books. Then an idea came to her.

"Do you have any books by an author named Blixen?" she asked.

"Blixen?" he replied, pushing his glasses up on his nose. "I can't think of any."

"It was a long shot," she murmured, more to himself than her.

She walked to the nearest row, wondering what to do when he suddenly spoke again.

"Unless you mean Karen Blixen."

"What section is it in?" she asked.

He shook his head. "You won't find it under Blixen. She published under the name Isak Dinesen. Her most famous book is *Out of Africa*. We have a copy in the biography section."

"Thank you," Mia replied.

She roamed the shop until she found the correct shelf and studied the spines of the books. When she found the right one, she pulled it from the shelf, having a sudden premonition. It was fulfilled when she opened the front cover and found a note had been slipped inside. She was alone in the shop apart from the bookseller, but still, she moved to the corner of the room to look at it, as if a million eyes were watching her. Unfolding it, she read the message.

*I knew you'd figure it out. What happened to them will not happen to you. We're in this together. See you in the new year.*

Mia wanted to cry with relief. Philip hadn't forgotten her. He was simply reminding her of the stakes of the game. All she had to do was to carry on with her job and await instructions. Take each day as it comes; focus on one task at a time. It wasn't her task to plan the endgame. She was only a bit player in the wider scheme. Mia took a deep breath, feeling a renewed vigor. Maeve and Elisabeth would be back soon, and Rousseau would be up and running again, putting her back to work. She just had to steel herself for what lay ahead.

Both of her roommates arrived the day after the new year, the second of January 1961. Mia was shocked at how relieved she was to see them.

"I've missed you," she said to Elisabeth when she helped her get her luggage up the stairs. "Next time you offer to take me to Sweden, I'll definitely come with you."

"Did you go to New York after all?" her roommate asked.

Mia shook her head. "I changed my mind and decided to appreciate Paris at the holidays. It doesn't disappoint."

"Hello, everyone!" Maeve said, appearing in the stairwell behind them. "It's nice to be home!"

"I'm glad you're back," Mia answered. "It's way too quiet here without you. Let me help with your bags."

"I brought you something from Ireland," Maeve continued. "It's too bad you had to spend the holiday alone."

"It was the first Christmas without my father," Mia replied. "It was never going to be a good one."

"We understand," Elisabeth said. "Come on. Let's get unpacked and I will tell you all about Christmas in Sweden."

Winter took a firm hold on Paris. Temperatures dropped, with chilling wind, but it wasn't until February that a thick layer of snow blanketed the city, stalling traffic and delaying trains. Crowds huddled in the steamy underground platforms, and fewer people braved the frigid air to walk to work or the market, instead hibernating in their four walls, waiting for a break in the weather.

Mia had never liked winter. She was well acquainted with the unforgiving cold and bitter winds that made her trek to the bakery unbearable, and it was just as bad here. Even in Luca's car, they never truly felt warm, and she developed a chill she couldn't shake. She noticed that her roommates weren't coming and going as much as normal. Everyone's rhythm had slowed to a standstill.

At Rousseau, there was talk of spring and the new collection, although the immediate concern was a winter gala planned for late February in Belgium. Theo had discussed sending four of his girls to model for the occasion. He hadn't announced who he was sending, but Mia had the feeling she would be chosen.

As it turned out, she was correct. Maeve, Natalie, Isabelle, and Mia were also selected for the Belgium job, and the fittings and preparation took most of a month.

"I'm sorry you weren't asked to come with us," Mia told Elisabeth. "I thought for certain Theo would send you, too."

"That's all right," Elisabeth replied. "He mentioned a show in Amsterdam later in the year, and he said I'm right for that one. You can't do everything. It just means that I'm here to help you both get ready."

"Did you know Luca will be driving us?" Maeve asked, sewing a button on a blouse. "He'll be staying in Brussels the whole week. We should take him out and plan a few things together while we're there."

"I thought we'd be taking the train," Mia said. "After all, there are four of us, and there will be luggage, too."

"We'll send our trunks on the train with Isabelle and Natalie, but Theo thought we should have Luca around in case we need to get around the city during the week."

Mia nodded, trying to ignore the unease she suddenly felt. The last time she had taken a trip with Luca, it hadn't worked out well. She would keep her distance. She had no intention of repeating the same mistake.

The gowns that were chosen for her to wear in Brussels were among the most beautiful she had ever worn. Although she had liked the bright, attractive styles she had worn in the summer and the sleek, tailored looks of fall, the winter styles were by far the most romantic. Dressers would be accompanying them to make certain their ensembles were perfectly coordinated, and Diana Larson would also be there to manage their time on the catwalk. Natalie would go first, followed by Maeve and Isabelle. But the all-important final gown would be worn by Mia in a dramatic display of her ensemble. She practiced diligently to perfect each move and consider every variable. It took concentration and skill to focus on precision moves and even her facial expressions.

The drive to Belgium was uneventful. Mia chose the back seat, allowing Maeve to sit next to Luca and to keep the conversation going. She contented herself with looking at the scenery. She hadn't been north of Paris before and wanted the opportunity to see something new. Now and then, he caught her eye in the mirror, and she gave him a faint smile before turning away to watch as the villages disappeared behind them.

"Have you been to Belgium before?" Maeve asked him.

"No," Luca replied. "Theo usually sends me south."

Mia tried not to think about the day they spent together. It didn't matter, anyway. Her life had taken such a drastic turn, she would never feel normal again.

They settled into their hotel later that afternoon, Maeve and Mia sharing a room. It was a jewel box of a place, more glamorous than their modest flat, overlooking a beautiful square.

"I didn't know Brussels was so pretty," Mia said, unpacking her things.

Their trunks had been taken to the venue, where Miss Larson and the dresser would be taking care of each gown, repairing creases and laying out the accessories that went with each one. She had a system, marking them by number so there would be no confusion.

"Tomorrow's the big day," Maeve said a couple of days later. "It's too bad we won't be here longer. At least we have tonight. What do you want to do?"

As it happened, they went out together, the four models and Luca. They had dinner at a café lit up with strings of lights, the windows frosted over from the cold. Mia sat between Isabelle and Natalie and kept the conversation going by asking them about the holidays and their hometowns, something each of them were eager to discuss.

The evening passed uneventfully, and they made it an early night to be fresh for the gala the following day.

This was what she lived for, the experience she had nearly missed out on due to fear of the unknown. Yet, this was also what had led her to become involved in an international plot. The next afternoon, as Mia sat in the hairdresser's chair, she couldn't help but think that all the good things in her life and all the terrible were colliding at a single point in time. At least this was a chance to immerse herself in fashion and beauty, and a break from the struggle of being vigilant every moment, wondering what would happen next.

The show began, a parade of elegance and an escape from the bleakness of winter. Even Diana Larson looked pleased as each rotation of the girls went smoothly and effortlessly, a testament to their preparation. The audience was large and refined, clapping at each of the designs being shared with them at such an exclusive event.

Mia modeled her first two gowns, and as she was being helped into her final one, her confidence was at an all-time high. The dress, an ice-blue evening frock of pure silk, had a deep V-neck in front and a band of satin around the waist over an expansive skirt. The back, also created with a V design, dipped nearly to her waist. She didn't know how many yards of fabric had been used in the skirt, but it swirled deliciously with every movement. Rousseau had paired the voluminous sleeveless gown with a snow-white fur muff and stole, with a matching beret. It was the most beautiful ensemble she had ever seen, much less had the opportunity to wear, and was certain to be a showstopper.

The matching ice-blue shoes had a perilously high heel and a pointed toe. She took a step and twirled before beginning her walk down the runway, aware of the delight of the crowd. Even the most sophisticated women in the room were leaning forward, lips parted, eyes wide at the luxurious furs and light-catching dress.

She kept her eyes on her marks: the back of the room beyond the end of the runway when she was moving forward, and similar spots to the left and right as she turned and paused, lowering or raising the stole to show a little shoulder and then covering it up again, only to let it slip dramatically when she turned her back to the room.

Theo encouraged them to have a three-point stance at the end, allowing the left, right, and center to have a last, impressive look at the front and back of the gown. It was only in those final moments that she allowed her gaze to sweep across the audience, allowing herself a moment to appreciate the admiration of the crowd. Of course, the attention was for the dress. However, she knew that certain models were more adept at garnering the interest and approval of the attendees than others. She had the look. Theo had told her on several occasions, and the other girls noticed it as well. It was why she knew she would be going to the most important events on the Rousseau calendar, and why he had chosen her all those months ago.

This time, however, when she looked across the crowd, she saw a face that looked familiar. More than familiar, in fact. It was one of the men to whom she had been instructed to give information from Theo, when in reality, she was passing something altogether different from Philip. She mastered control of her smile and her gaze, but inside her chest, she could feel her heart start to hammer. What if he knew she had passed false information and had come to confront her, or worse? In Paris, she felt safer because she allowed herself to believe that Philip was keeping an eye on her, however distant he was at times. But she was in Brussels, in an entirely different country, and he wouldn't have been likely to shadow her for something as insignificant to the American government as a fashion show.

He stood and began to walk toward the stage. Mia panicked. What did this man want? If he were aware of what she had done, was he trying to seek retribution? She turned her back to the crowd and glided slowly off the stage as she would have on any other night, all too aware of how it had felt to be abducted from the steps of Montmartre. She hurried backstage, shrugging off the stole and handing the hat and muff to the dresser who accompanied them.

"Unzip me, please," she said, placing her hands on her hips.

The other girls, including Maeve, were clustered in one of the rooms, laughing and talking about how well the evening had gone. Mia, however, changed quickly into her dress and coat and slipped from the building, in search of Luca. She found him in his car, leaning back with his eyes closed and his arms crossed.

Mia rapped her knuckles on the window and waited as he rolled it down.

"Can we get out of here?" she asked.

In answer, he started the engine as she went around and slid into the passenger side.

"Is everything all right?" he asked.

"It's fine," she replied. "I just want to leave."

He pulled out and in minutes, they were across town.

"I assume you don't want to go back to the hotel yet," he said.

"I don't, if that's all right," she answered.

He drove into the Grand Place, the central square in Brussels. Tall beautiful buildings, City Hall and the Maison de Roi towered over them, their Gothic spires illuminating the night sky. The facades were festively lit, and Luca found a parking spot where he wedged the car in and opened the door.

"Come on," he said.

Mia stepped out of the car and looked around. "Where are we going?"

"To blend in with the crowd."

It was a good choice. They were far from the gala, and even though it was a cold evening, they walked among the crowds who were taking photos of the buildings and posing in front of City Hall.

Luca took her hand. "This way."

They wove through the tourists, catching up to a small group who was entering a pub. Following them inside, Luca led her to a table and then went to get them each a beer.

"Drink this," he said. "You'll feel better."

She didn't ordinarily like beer, but it was cold and invigorating.

She took a sip and then another, and then set it on the table in front of her.

"It's got to be exhausting," he mused, looking at her. "Being the center of attention all the time."

Mia nodded, relieved that he had drawn his own conclusions.

"I'm not used to it, you know," she answered.

"Sometimes I love the pace of it all," he continued. "Other times, it's difficult."

"I have a question for you, if you don't mind."

Luca looked up. "About what?"

"What happened with you and Victor Perdreau?"

He looked uncomfortable for a moment. "A girl happened. What else? I went out with a girl he liked, and he has never gotten over it. That's why he tried to make a move on you. He thought we were together."

Mia gave him a look. "Then why didn't you say something?"

Luca shrugged. "I was trying to figure out what I thought about you, myself."

Mia took another swig of beer. "I'm not sure that makes sense."

"Does anything about life make sense?" he asked.

She had to agree. "Come on, let's get out of here."

"Where do you want to go?"

"I thought I saw a cinema on the next street over."

Luca nodded, relieved to be finished with the conversation. They left the pub and walked around the corner, finding the theater.

"They're playing an American film," she said, pointing at the marquee. "Let's go inside."

They bought tickets and slipped inside the theater. The movie, *The Apartment*, was already in progress. Shirley MacLaine was flirting with Jack Lemmon in a wholesome sort of way. Mia and Luca took their seats and settled in to lose themselves in the plot. However, Mia couldn't concentrate.

She wasn't sure how much longer she could keep this up, no matter what she had promised Philip. She wanted to disappear. She didn't know how or where, yet, but it was inevitable. Her bank account was growing. She had learned that models in the 1940s had made as little as ten dollars a session and she made four times that. But her compensation for weekly work was low because she was provided living accommodations, so she was still counting every penny. In the meantime, she was getting better at getting around undetected when she needed to. Her second decision was to avoid entanglements with the opposite sex. She glanced at Luca, who turned to her and smiled. She had no idea how to respond. She couldn't be herself anymore. Everything was weighed under the possibility of whether someone could be trusted or not.

They'd sat through the first half of the film when Mia leaned over to Luca.

"I'll be back in a few minutes," she murmured.

"Do we need to leave?" he asked.

"No, I'll be fine."

She stood and made her way out of the half-empty theater to go and reapply her lipstick and to take a few minutes to think. She'd been so rattled at the end of the show. This was all too much. There was enough pressure trying to do her job without the fear of people coming after her.

As she headed for the ladies' room, someone suddenly grabbed her arm and pulled her into a small room, closing the door behind them. The face glaring down at her was the man she had spotted earlier.

"What are you doing?" she asked, trying to keep her breathing even.

"A better question is, what are you doing, Mia Walker?"

He stood unnervingly close, his fingers still biting into her arm.

She shook her head. "I don't know what you mean."

"Who are you working for?"

"I work for the House of Rousseau."

He scowled. "That's not what I mean."

She tried to jerk her arm away, but he held it fast. "Let me go."

"You can't get away with it, you know. We're watching every move you make."

"Mia!"

She turned when she heard Luca's voice in the hall, breaking free of the man's grasp and stepping out into the hall.

"Here!" she said, not daring to look behind her. "I must have gone in the wrong room."

"I'm tired," he said. "Why don't we go back to the hotel?"

"All right," she said. "I'm tired, too."

Now she had another problem. Someone suspected her of working against the Alliance. When she got back to Paris, she would leave a message for Philip. If he didn't answer, she would figure out what to do on her own. There were spooks and spies around every corner now, no matter where she went. She didn't know when one of them might come after her.

# 22

---

The blackest part of winter comes just before it's over, before the thaws and the drip of melting snow, before the winds cease howling and while the sun is still obscured behind murky, gray clouds. It's the part of the year when one's bones have been so cold that they feel like they will never be warm again and the hibernation of December has grown into a stubborn unwillingness to step one more foot outdoors until the situation improves.

Chantal was not alone in her dislike of winter, as was attested to by the lack of activity out of her window. She spent much of her time reading in front of the fire, glad that she had plenty of books to keep her company. Yet too much time spent alone allowed one to dwell on the most difficult aspects of life. She still hadn't answered the letter from Raphaël, nor had she attended to the matter with Monsieur Lindsay, who had no doubt grown tired of waiting for her reply. She was stiff and sore from days and weeks without physical exercise, and her mind was rebelling from a lack of stimulation, though she tried to maintain hope. *Things will improve,* she told herself. *It can't be long now.*

There were other matters that needed her attention, although even the urgency of some seemed to have waned in the dullness of winter. She was in no mood to handle anything. In fact, she had taken to pacing, something she rarely did. It indicated a mind that was not at rest, and one thing a seventy-four-year-old woman—soon to be seventy-five—needed was a mind at rest.

Several things kept her busy, however. Madame Bernard required more care than usual. The old woman had developed a cough in January that still plagued her weeks later, and it was more difficult than ever to get her to eat. Madame's daughter had threatened to take her into her own home if she didn't improve, but Chantal was determined to get her through winter in the meantime. It was unfair to die when life was at its most cold and grim. Better to live until the spring, she always thought. Even when one can no longer venture out into the world, spring finds a way to make it into one's home, lifting the spirits and warming the bones.

She was deep into the book *Dr. Zhivago.* Perversely, she read winter books during the coldest season, this time commiserating with Yuri Zhivago on the heartaches of loving two women while simultaneously suffering the vicious rule of the Bolsheviks, who were destroying life as he had known it. Chantal knew something of this herself. She had gone from a woman with a large estate and children and grandchildren to a woman alone, navigating the city as though she were half her age, handling her grief in a different way.

There, at the very end of winter, in the excessive hours she spent alone with her own thoughts, she was aware that she had made mistakes. That she even, dare she say it, had regrets. If only things had been different.

No one gets through life without regrets, but some are more stinging than others. She thought of Raphaël in 1904, when she had been a young wife in Honfleur. When she met him, she was already pregnant with Jean-Louis, though she hadn't known it yet. Her first instinct upon meeting him was to run away with him and become a fisherman's wife. Throughout the years, she imagined the cottage where they might have lived, wondering endlessly what their life would have been like.

However, she loved her sons. She cared, too, for Noel, as cantankerous and demanding as he had been through the years. She stayed with him because she had made him a promise, even though she never stopped loving someone else. Like Zhivago, she was torn between duty and love, and to see it so brilliantly written on the page was nearly a defense of her own actions. Divorce, neither during the Bolshevik Revolution nor even earlier in 1904 when she met the love of her life, was simply not done. If one made a commitment, one was true to that commitment. Never mind the impulses of the heart.

Restless, she got up and went to the window. It was pouring rain, but she had to do something. She wouldn't venture out in a storm, but perhaps she could go downstairs and check the mail, as well as chat with the concierge, who like her, was forced to stay in one spot and simply wait for something to happen.

There were other things she could do in the building, things she told no one, tasks she preferred to do early in the morning or late at night, when there was little chance of running into someone who might be curious. It wouldn't do to attract attention. At least for now, most of the residents were either grimly pulling on rubber boots and heading to work or hunkering down in their flats like a hunter at dawn. Chantal appreciated the comparison. In some ways, she was a hunter herself.

As far as she could tell, the building was silent. The girls next door had not gone in to work that morning and no sounds were heard from their side of the hall, which meant they were taking the opportunity to sleep the day away. One had to occasionally if one kept such a great number of late nights, she supposed. She didn't begrudge them their youth if they weren't too noisy.

Chantal opened her door and stepped into the hall. One of the hall lights had burned out; she would have to tell the concierge about it. It was dangerous to prowl around a dim corridor. Pulling her jacket closer around her, she went down the stairs as nimbly as a sprite.

"Madame Fournier," he said when she appeared at his desk.

"Monsieur Dubois," she replied. "And how are you on this very wet day?"

They paused to look out of the window at the downpour. The

large urns had been dragged under the awning, to protect the small trees that grew in them. In the spring, yellow and violet pansies were planted around the base of the trees for color, but that pleasure was still weeks away.

"No one has come to my desk all day," Dubois replied with a gloomy expression on his face. "If I were a different sort, I would pack it in and let everyone pick up their own mail."

"But you are not," Chantal answered. "And we are thankful for that."

"As you say, Madame," he said. "I'm afraid even the postman has been delayed today. I wonder if it may be tomorrow before we see him again."

"So, there have been no movements to note," she said.

He shook his head. "None whatsoever. How is your book coming along?"

"*Zhivago* is very good," she replied. "Have you read it?"

"I read it when it first came out."

"Then you should read it again. What are you reading now?"

"A little Proust."

"You can never go wrong with Proust."

"Would you like me to ring you if the postman arrives?" he asked.

"No, thank you," she answered. "I'm not expecting anything. By the way, there is a light burned out in our hallway."

"Thank you for letting me know, Madame," he replied. "I will take care of it."

"Good afternoon."

Chantal went up the stairs, the unused muscles in her calves protesting. She hadn't gained an ounce from inactivity over the last few months, but she was out of shape. She decided to take the stairs twice a day to be ready for the day when the weather broke, and she could resume her normal schedule.

The cat appeared at the top of the stairs, staring down as she approached. He looked fatter than usual, and she wondered who had been feeding him.

"Where've you been, you scamp?" she demanded.

He licked a paw in response, and she shook her head at him. She hadn't seen him in over a week. Even Madame Bernard had commented on his absence. Chantal had assured her friend that the creature had likely found shelter with Monsieur Lindsay, being no more interested in climbing up and down the drafty staircase than the residents were. But one couldn't make friends with a cat. They were too capricious.

She hurried her step and then gasped as she lost her balance and fell hard against the railing. Pain bloomed in her hip and elbow on the right side, and she shifted her weight slightly to see if anything was broken. She moved her leg a couple of inches and sighed with relief. There would probably be a bruise, but nothing was fractured. Rubbing her elbow, she moved to sit up when the door opened on her floor and Mia Walker came rushing out.

"Madame Fournier!" she said. "I thought I heard someone. Can you stand?"

Chantal nodded and allowed Mia to take her arm to help her up before making her way up the last few steps. She went to her flat and opened the door.

"Thank you, Mademoiselle," she murmured.

"I think I'd better go in with you," Mia answered. "If that is all right."

Chantal had dreaded the moment something would happen to her. However, she allowed her neighbor to come inside. The wretched feline followed behind and had already crawled into a basket in the corner before Mia shut the door.

"Is anything broken?" Mia asked, looking at her seriously, her brows furrowed. "Should we get you to the doctor? Or is there someone I can call?"

"No," Chantal replied. "No doctor. And no need to bother anyone."

She didn't mention that there was no one to call. As far as she was concerned, she was the one who helped others, not the other way around. A sudden thought struck her, that she was to take Madame Bernard a container of soup. In fact, she was expecting her any moment.

"Let me help, then," Mia said. "I'll make an ice pack for you."

Without permission, the girl went into her kitchen, finding a heavy cloth and chipping ice from the freezer to put inside it. She tied it in a knot and brought it to Chantal.

"What hurts the most?" she asked.

"My hip and elbow are quite sore," Chantal admitted. "I'm sure they're just bruised."

"I'll get another ice pack," Mia said. "And you should elevate your leg."

Although she was unaccustomed to anyone telling her what to do, Chantal obeyed orders. She leaned back on the settee and stretched out her legs.

"I feel so foolish," she said when the girl returned. "I never fall."

"In case you don't remember, the first time I met you, I'd tripped on the stairs and dropped packages everywhere," Mia replied. "You came to my rescue."

Chantal nodded. "Thank you for the compresses. You did that quite efficiently."

"My father was ill the last two years of his life," Mia answered. "He hated to ask for help, but as his health declined, it became harder and harder to manage on his own."

"Not everyone has the patience and ability to help others," Chantal said. "It's an admirable trait to have."

"You're cooking," Mia remarked. "Do I need to check on something in the kitchen?"

Chantal tried to move, but it was too painful. "You may turn off the stove if you don't mind. I make dinner twice a week for Madame Bernard in 4B. She's expecting me anytime."

"Why don't I take it up there for you?"

Chantal looked at the girl with fresh eyes. This was unexpected, perhaps even welcome, considering the situation.

"Are you certain you don't mind?" she asked.

"Of course I don't mind," Mia replied. "What do you put the soup in to take it to Madame Bernard?"

"I usually use the red bowl with the matching lid in the cupboard," she answered. "Fill it to about an inch from the top. When I take it to her, I always dip her a bowl and ask if she needs anything else. If you'll hand me the telephone, I will tell her you have kindly volunteered to bring her soup this evening."

Mia moved the telephone closer to Chantal, pulling the cord out of the way. "I'll get it ready, Madame."

Chantal waited until Mia went into the kitchen to make the call and explained to Madame Bernard what had happened. As she did, the cat abandoned his spot in the basket and jumped up to sit next to her on the settee, watching her with one eye cracked open. He was a curious little thing.

"Oh, no, *chérie*," Madame Bernard exclaimed when Chantal had told her what had happened. "I hope you will be all right."

"I'll be fine in a day or two," she assured her friend. "It is very nice of Miss Walker to come to our aid in the meantime."

She didn't tell Madame Bernard everything she knew about Mia, but of course, she didn't tell Madame everything about herself. One only needed to know so much about someone or it might cause alarm. The important thing was that, in her opinion, the girl could be trusted with this particular task.

Mia delivered the soup and returned to the apartment fifteen minutes later, convincing Chantal that she had done the right thing. Obviously, the girl had taken care to make certain Madame's needs were met, a kindness she couldn't repay.

"Join me for supper," Chantal told her when she returned.

"Oh, Madame, I didn't mean to impose on you," Mia protested.

"It's not an imposition," she replied. "In fact, I could do with the company. Oh, and while you're in the kitchen, would you mind getting a saucer of milk for the cat?"

In spite of herself, she reached out and scratched the cat between the ears. He submitted to the affection tolerantly before slinking into the kitchen to see what the fuss was about. After his saucer of milk, he returned to his spot on the settee, edging ever closer to Chantal while Mia took the cold compresses to the kitchen.

She unbuttoned the cuff of her sleeve and pulled it up to inspect the damage. There was a bruise, but it didn't throb quite as much as it had thanks to the attention of her young neighbor.

Perhaps it was true that one cannot exist in the world without the help of others, but it was difficult for her, after being on her own for so long, to admit it. To do so was to embrace the idea of her own frailty, something she preferred not to do. It was difficult enough to think of Madame Bernard's fragility and dependence upon her and others; it was impossible to think of her own.

Mia made a tray for her and then brought another bowl for herself to the table. It was quite companionable, Chantal thought. She never ate with Madame Bernard and was unused to company during a meal. Perhaps that was why she had hesitated to form an answer for Monsieur Lindsay downstairs. She had no wish to hurt his feelings, but when someone has been on their own for a very long time, it is difficult to allow someone else in.

"How do you like modeling?" Chantal asked. "You're at the House of Rousseau, isn't that right?"

"I like it very much," Mia replied, although she didn't quite meet Chantal's gaze.

"I've seen the advertisements in the newspaper. Their gowns are stunning."

"I never imagined having the opportunity to do anything like this," Mia continued. "I feel very fortunate."

The girl lowered her eyes to her bowl and finished her soup. Her comments had been bland, certainly the rote response one might expect if one were trying to hide something. And Mia Walker was definitely hiding something. It was her job to find out precisely what that was.

# 23

---

"Mia, do you have a few minutes?" Diana Larson said shortly after their lunch break.

"Of course," Mia replied.

"Meet me in my office, please."

The request was innocent enough, but Mia knew every change in routine was a potential complication. After the Belgian gala, there were a handful of events and social evenings where Theo had asked her to share information, different messages than she had passed on before, but she knew the pace would pick up as soon as the season began. The potential for danger was higher, too, now that someone suspected her of answering to someone other than Theo.

Rousseau was in full swing preparing the spring collection, and Mia, like all the other models, tried to focus her attention on her duties. Every seat for the hotly anticipated show was booked, and each department at the fashion house was working day and night to get the designs ready. The doldrums of winter were swept away with the arrival of warmer weather and the schedule full of opportunities to share their upcoming line of couture. Each model eagerly awaited her upcoming assignments and fittings. Winter was over and spring, at least on the calendar, had arrived.

Mia followed her into the office and Miss Larson stepped behind her desk, lifting a handwritten note. "We'd like you to run an errand for us this afternoon, Mia. You will have a meeting at the Hôtel de Crillon. Do you know it?"

"Why, yes," Mia answered, surprised.

She'd seen the extraordinary building several times when she had explored the city. Although she had been in Paris for less than a year, she knew its reputation for impressive clientele, from movie stars to presidents. Situated near the Arc de Triomphe, it looked more like a palace than a hotel. She had long wanted to see if the interior was as grand as its exterior but had never been so bold as to walk through its doors. Now she would have her chance.

"You are to go the bar. Instructions will await you there."

Miss Larson did not appear to think the arrangement was out of the ordinary. In fact, she looked rather bored, as if this sort of thing happened every day. Mia, however, felt a flutter of nerves.

"Yes, Miss Larson."

"Luca is outside. He'll drive you."

Mia stood and nodded. She gathered her things and left the

building. It was chilly outside, and she was glad she had brought her coat. Luca was standing on the pavement, holding the door open before she could do it herself.

"Thank you," she said.

"The Hôtel de Crillon?" he answered, raising a brow. "That's interesting. And in the middle of the day, too."

"You never know where they're going to send you," Mia replied, shrugging. She could be as vague as he was. "It's just another meeting, but I can't wait to see the lobby. I'm sure it's beautiful."

"Tomorrow's Friday," he remarked. "Are you doing anything special?"

"Maeve hasn't told me yet," she said in a light voice, as if it were a joke between them.

"Of course, there's still tonight…"

"I'd love to," she lied. "But I have no idea how long this meeting is going to last."

He pulled up in front of the hotel, waving off the valet. Then he turned to her, drumming his fingers on the steering wheel. "Shall I wait?"

She shook her head. "No, thank you. We'll be discussing ribbons and lace all afternoon. You've got more important things to do."

"I don't mind."

"I appreciate it, but I'll see you in the morning."

As she reached for the door handle, the valet pulled it open.

"*Merci*," she said, as she got out of the car.

She nodded to Luca and walked into the hotel. As she suspected, it was grander than she had even imagined. Glass chandeliers sparkled overhead; marble floors were covered in Aubusson rugs. Sofas and chairs in various shades of cream and gold were arranged around the cavernous room, against a backdrop of gilt walls and a fresco on the ceiling. It was welcoming and luxurious, and entirely empty. She looked around until she found a large, highly polished desk with a man behind it, approaching it with as much composure as she could muster.

He looked up and nodded at her. "May I help you, Mademoiselle?"

"I am looking for the bar, please."

"You must be Mademoiselle Walker," he said. "There is a table for you in Les Ambassadeurs. Let me get someone to take you there."

He lifted a bell and rang it twice. A moment later, a bellboy appeared out of nowhere.

"Matthieu, Mademoiselle Walker has arrived. Please escort her to her table."

The bellboy gave his superior a slight bow and then held out a hand to gesture to the right. "This way, if you please."

She followed him through the lobby, where her heels sank into the plush carpets with every step, wondering who was awaiting her in such a place. She couldn't fathom who it might be. Every time Theo had sent her out to speak to someone, she had been given a specific phrase and instructions about whom she was going to meet. This time, he hadn't even sent her himself. Diana Larson had been the one to do it.

They walked through the enormous lobby until they came to a smaller room. Like the lobby, it was covered in gilt and frescoes, but this one was full of dark mushroom-colored chairs and sofas against a backdrop of marble walls. The lighting was dim, with candles burning on every table. In the far corner of the room, a pianist was playing "Stardust" at the baby grand. She took a deep breath, wondering what was about to happen.

"This way, please," the bellboy said, leading her through the empty room to a table at the far end.

She sat in a chair facing the piano as the music swept over her, trying to relax. There were two realities in her life at odds with each other. In one, she was a model living in Paris, wearing some of the most beautiful clothes in the world. It didn't matter that she wasn't making a huge salary. The benefits outweighed the lack of money. Besides, one didn't need a fortune to enjoy the most beautiful city in the world. Walking the parks, exploring the monuments and buildings, having coffee at a sleek French café were life-changing experiences.

The second reality, however, was devastating. Even though it had been months since she had been abducted at the Montmartre Stairs, that day had changed her life. When Philip had shown up—the Philip she had been so attracted to—life had become more confusing than ever. She couldn't go back to the days of being an innocent in Paris. There was a noose about her neck, whether she kept up the charade or not.

"There you are," Theo said as he approached. "Right on time."

Mia tried to smile as he took a seat across from her. Neither of them spoke for a moment as the waiter came to their table.

"May I get Sir or Mademoiselle a drink?" he asked.

"I'll have a bourbon and water," Theo replied. He looked at Mia. "What can he bring for you?"

Mia felt like she was facing a test, but she would not order alcohol in front of her boss. "Just water, please."

Theo made no comment, waiting for the young man to leave.

"You're probably wondering why I asked you here," he said.

"It is out of the ordinary," she admitted.

"That's because I have something out of the ordinary to discuss with you, and I want it to remain confidential. The only person who knows you are here is Luca. What did you tell him?"

"I said I had a meeting about fashion," she answered. "I wasn't specific."

"Perfect," he said. "I knew I could count on you."

The waiter brought their drinks and then turned to leave. The long empty room, which had been so attractive to her a few minutes earlier, now seemed sinister as she waited for Theo to continue.

"This discussion requires the utmost discretion, do you understand?"

"Of course," she said.

She lifted the glass and took a sip to calm her nerves, hoping he couldn't tell how unsettled she was.

282 · JULIA BRYAN THOMAS

"A very special event is being planned by the French government," he said. "It's a dinner to be hosted by President de Gaulle
and his wife. You will be a guest on this occasion. For obvious
reasons, I do not want the other girls learning about it before the
event."

"I understand," she answered, shocked. It was as momentous as
he had built it up to be. She had a million questions. "Who will I be
going with?"

"You'll be the guest of an ambassador who would like someone
charming to accompany him," he replied. "State dinners can be rather
dull when one is in a foreign country and doesn't know anyone, as I
am sure you are aware. His identity will be revealed to you closer to
the day of the event."

"I see."

"There will be foreign dignitaries present, all of whom must
be protected from gossip or interference, some of whom are very
important on the world stage. Do you understand what I'm saying?"

"Yes, sir."

Theo put his glass down and leaned forward. "You've been loyal
to Rousseau, Mia, and we are entrusting you with this very important
assignment. However, that is not all."

He stopped to take another drink of his bourbon, swirling it
in his glass. Mia was aware of the pianist, who was playing a slow,
melodic version of "Moonlight Serenade." It was incongruous, sitting
in a snug, romantic hideaway with an attractive man, knowing that

it was all a sham. As she waited for the details, Theo set his glass on the table and smiled.

"A special gown is being created for this event," he continued. "You will be wearing it at the Palace of Versailles."

Mia couldn't conceal her surprise. She hadn't been to Versailles, but she knew of it, having even looked at books in the library on the palace, which had belonged to Louis XIV and Marie Antoinette before the French Revolution. It was the home of kings, the most important palace in France.

He cleared his throat. "There is more. You will be wearing a priceless Cartier diamond necklace. It is currently the world's most expensive piece of jewelry. Naturally, there will be security provided for you during the event to ensure the safety of both you and the necklace you'll be wearing."

"I don't know what to say," she stammered. "I never imagined something like this would ever happen."

"It will be a glittering night, probably the most exciting of your life. And yet, you have to remember that, like every event of this kind, you are there as a representative of the House of Rousseau. We expect your usual professionalism. When Monsieur Rousseau asked my opinion about which of our girls could do it, you are the only name that came to mind."

"Thank you, sir," she said.

"You have a reputation at the House, Mia," he continued. "You're our 'Kennedy Girl,' you know."

Mia colored.

"It's a term of endearment," he said. "Your dark hair, your coloring, your preference for Jacqueline Kennedy suits. It's quite charming."

"I'm not sure if I should be flattered or not."

Theo leaned in closer. "I told you this for a specific reason. The Kennedys are the guests of honor at the state dinner. You'll have the chance to see your namesake."

Mia gasped.

"Of course, you will not speak to her nor, indeed, any of the dignitaries involved other than the ambassador, but I thought that might make this event even more appealing for you."

"It will be a dream come true to see Versailles," she murmured.

He smiled. "I'm glad you're pleased. Just a reminder, do not speak to anyone about this. I'm counting on you."

"Yes, sir."

"Well, I'm off," he said, standing. "Feel free to listen to the music a little longer if you wish."

Mia waited for twenty minutes after he had gone to avoid seeing him in the lobby. As she sat there, she toyed with the napkin, wondering why he had brought her here to tell her about de Gaulle and the Kennedys and a state dinner at the Palace of Versailles. It was possible he expected her to tell someone. Perhaps it was another test of her loyalty. A few months ago, she knew the rules of the game: find the person Theo described and give him a message from Philip instead. But over the last couple of months, Philip had disappeared. She was on her own now, with no one to go to for help.

When she was satisfied that Theo had gone, she left the hotel and walked to the Concorde Métro station. It was ludicrous, stepping out of one of the finest hotels in the world and into the crowded underground. The station was crowded, as she so often found them during the day, hundreds of people walking left and right and waiting on the platform.

She was starting to feel paranoid. Men in suits with crisp leather cases, young men walking in gangs of eight and ten, even the blue-collar workers who had come back into Paris after a day in the fields: everyone looked suspicious. Anyone could be coerced into cooperation by the Alliance. Anyone could be a danger if one didn't see it coming.

She got off the Métro at the closest stop to her flat and walked to her bank. When she approached the desk, she took out her wallet. Just the day before, she had counted the equivalent of twenty-five dollars and folded the bills she planned to deposit in her savings account. She took out the money and counted it once again. Every dollar was hard earned, and she was saving every penny for the day that she could leave France and start over somewhere else, some-where far away from the House of Rousseau and the international ring of spies trying to get their hands on nuclear weapons.

"May I get my balance, as well, please?" she asked.

"*Oui*, Mademoiselle. I just need to see your identification," the clerk replied.

Mia took her passport from her bag and held it out for the woman's inspection. When she nodded, Mia tucked it back into her bag once again and then slid the franc notes across the counter.

"One moment, please," the woman said.

Mia nodded, relieved that for once there wasn't a line. She was ready to get home and kick off her shoes. After a moment, the woman returned and slid a piece of paper across the counter.

"This is your deposit receipt with your balance on it," she said.

Mia took the paper. Each time she made a deposit, she checked the balance, watching the amount grow. Last week, she had added ten dollars to her account, and after this deposit, she would have saved close to four hundred dollars. Looking at the slip of paper, however, she did a double take.

"Madame," she said, handing it back. "This can't be right."

"It is correct, Mademoiselle Walker. I double-checked."

"I have trouble converting francs to dollars," she confessed. "Can you do it for me?"

"*Oui*, Mademoiselle." The woman took out a pencil and a piece of paper and, in a moment, handed it back to her. "This is the American dollar amount."

Mia stared at it, unable to comprehend the sum. One hundred thousand U.S. dollars was sitting in her bank account, the one that should only have four hundred. Instinctively, she knew she couldn't press the woman any further.

"Thank you, Madame," she replied.

She left through the front doors as if nothing had happened, but instead of heading home, she found a bench and sat, trying to stop shaking. Someone had deposited a huge sum in her account, perhaps to have some sort of leverage over her. Only one person could help her understand what was happening, and it was the very person she couldn't reach when she needed him most.

# 24

Philip spent half the winter in Moscow, with one of a dozen passports and identities that he put on and off with the alacrity of a tightrope walker. January and February were cold in the Soviet Union in 1961, -12° Celsius for a high some days, which is 9° Fahrenheit to the rest of us. His alias, Tom Burroughs, was an agriculture minister, ostensibly there to talk wheat and barley with the appropriate sources. By day, he called on his knowledge of grains, imports, and exports in order to discuss potential deals; by night, he went undercover, working with his contacts to learn how far the Soviet government was progressing in their quest to get their hands on a nuclear bomb, or more likely, the recipe to build it.

Before Christmas, he had wandered around Eastern Europe, taking the political temperature there as well. Unrest was everywhere, dulled temporarily in the bustle of the season celebrating Hanukkah and the birth of Christ, as ubiquitous in the towns of the East as it is in the West. The holidays were a facade, however, hiding the political tensions that were as obvious to him as the nose on his face.

After the first of the year, he took the train from Warsaw to Moscow, to a place called Borovitskaya Square on the opposite end of Alexander Garden, where there was a statue of Vladimir the Great. Vlad was prince of all Russia, and during his reign, he extended Russian territories to include parts of Lithuania and Poland, in a way that would influence the geopolitical landscape for decades to come.

Philip wouldn't have known anything about the man at all—after all, he died in 1015—except for this statue of the man holding a huge Orthodox cross in the middle of Borovitskaya Square. A longtime fellow operative, Evgeny Petrov, whom Philip had known for years, liked to meet there whenever he was in Moscow. It was unnervingly close to the Kremlin, only a few minutes' walk away, and not far from Saint Basil's Cathedral in Red Square, which draws traffic throughout the year. But Petrov, whose father was also named Vladimir, preferred it to any other meeting place in Moscow and Philip allowed him his sentimental choice.

They met on January 18 on a mercilessly wet and cold evening, and Philip had walked two miles from his hotel in the rain so that no taxi driver, should he have even found one at that hour, could have thought him suspicious and reported him to the authorities.

He looked a little worse for wear, Petrov, and as they lit a couple of cigarettes in the shadows of Vladimir the Great, Philip tried to get

290 · JULIA BRYAN THOMAS

answers out of him in short order. In those days, he was in Moscow two to three times a year, meeting his contacts to compare notes. No other form of communication was safe. No letter, no telephone call, no coded telegram were free from prying eyes. They had direct contact or none at all.

Things weren't going well. Two spies had been captured and executed in Russia in the few weeks before Philip arrived, and the previous year, 1960, saw a lot of political activity in the Soviet capitol. In May, the U.S.-Soviet summit collapsed after the Soviets downed a U.S. spy plane and captured the pilot, which led to a confrontation between Eisenhower and Kruschev. Parties in both countries had held out hope that they were about to embark on a period of peace, possibly even an end to the Cold War, but the die was already cast.

The International Meeting of Communist and Workers Parties had convened in June. The meeting was in marked contrast to the capitalistic values of the West, and one of the fears held by the government was that so many democratic nations had groups that participated in it, from Australia to Denmark to Spain. Philip knew the president was desperate to get the upper hand in the situation.

He wondered how long people could ignore the growing strain between the two most powerful nations in the world. There were also rumors of the Soviets having secret talks with Cuba, which was fewer than a hundred miles off the coast of Florida, and the last thing the Americans needed was to have the Soviets on their doorstep. At the time, however, Americans were lulled into believing they were mostly in a time of peace, and they had no desire to reawaken the beast of Communist politics.

That didn't mean there was no threat to the U.S., and neither did it mean there was true peace, as was evidenced by the "duck and cover" air raid drills. Nevertheless, people went about their business, happy to let the dark forces and agent provocateurs go about the dirty Cold War business. They didn't want to know as long as they could purchase a new car or television set and sit in the ballpark on a nice summer evening.

Philip knew he was jaded. It would be hard to be involved in international espionage without feeling disillusioned in one way or another. But that didn't matter. What did was the fact that an embedded layer of moles and plants spread out through the nation and the greater world beyond, were keeping a close eye on the rumblings that went on below the surface.

Petrov, a disreputable-looking soul with shaggy hair and worn clothes, was one of those moles. His contacts in the Kremlin kept him apprised of the plans: woo Cuba—bribe them, if necessary; establish a deeper network throughout the sympathetic countries in Eastern Europe, those who could benefit from Soviet influence; and finally, get their hands on the diamond, which was said to be passing through France by early summer.

It was Philip's job to find out how this was going to be done, and his job to figure out how to prevent it from falling into the wrong hands.

He hadn't been back in Paris for a week before he received word that Petrov was dead. A fellow colleague brought him news that Evgeny had been shot in a bar in Krasnogorsk while collecting information. Philip was furious because Petrov was a truly good man, one he had trusted a thousand times. He kicked a concrete wall when he heard the news, nearly breaking his foot. But he had bigger problems now. If his suspicions were correct, Mia was going to come into direct contact with the diamond, placing her in even greater danger. They were running out of time. Things, he knew, were about to spiral out of control.

# 25

---

Weeks had passed, and then months, without seeing Philip. He hadn't even responded to her last several messages. Mia tried to concentrate her energy on the upcoming launch of the spring collection, allowing herself to get more involved in it than usual. It was a relief to have something to focus on. All of Paris seemed gray, from the buildings to the houseboats on the Seine to the incessant rain. Even the covers of *Vogue* had been dull. In February, the magazine had featured a plain belted two-piece beige ensemble, and in March, a black-and-white-tweed suit with a jacquard-print bow blouse with a matching bucket hat. Neither piqued her interest. Like her friends, Mia was ready for livelier, brighter spring couture, something to break up the doldrums in the fashion world, hoping the new collection wouldn't disappoint. Just as Coco Chanel had shaken up the fashion industry when she popularized the little black dress in 1926, Mia was hoping the House of Rousseau would create something revolutionary to inspire the women of the 1960s. Of course, the one bright spot was the news that Jacqueline Kennedy was coming to Paris in June, and Mia couldn't wait to see what she would be wearing.

She hadn't confided in either of her roommates about the upcoming state dinner at Versailles in part due to security issues, but also to avoid scrutiny. While she hadn't had any conflict with any of the Rousseau models herself, she knew that, from time to time, jealousies developed among the girls about the opportunities some of them were getting rather than others. Of course, that wasn't the reason she had been given this assignment. Theo was using her, and so far, she hadn't been caught betraying his trust. That day would come soon enough, and she wasn't ready for the fallout. In the meantime, she couldn't help wondering about the Cartier necklace. Twice, she had stood in front of their shop windows to view their displays, but nothing so priceless was available for show. It was kept under lock and key, getting as much security as any national treasure in France.

In April, the weather improved, and spring made its way into Paris. The linden trees began to sprout leaves, the greenery awakening the city from the somber days of winter. By the end of the month, pink and white cherry trees were in bloom. Restaurants reopened their terraces and street markets put up tables to display their wares. Store windows were decorated for Easter, and queues formed everywhere, from the *chocolateries* in Saint-Germain-des-Prés to the long lines at Poilâne for steaming baguettes. The world was coming back to life.

It was May before she knew anything about the gown she would be wearing to Versailles, and then, only the color, a rich royal blue. She had seen the bolts of fabric in the atelier. The design, however, was kept secret, although she couldn't wait to see it. To compete with the most elegant women in the world, it would have to be stunning.

"There's going to be a party for the Rousseau staff this weekend," Elisabeth said one evening when they were out at a club. "Did you hear about it?"

Mia nodded. There were signs tacked to the doors of each dressing room at Rousseau. "I assume that means we're all invited."

"It's the twentieth anniversary of the launch of the House of Rousseau," Maeve added. "We have to talk about what to wear!"

"Speaking of what to wear," Elisabeth remarked, "we heard about your news."

"My news?" Mia repeated, setting her drink on the table.

"Don't be dense," Maeve scolded. "You've been chosen to represent Rousseau at a state dinner. What else could we be talking about?"

"Why didn't you tell us?" Elisabeth demanded. "I'd be shouting it to anyone who would listen if it were me."

Mia stood and walked over to the window. "It doesn't seem real if you want to know the truth. Honestly, a state dinner?"

She left out any reference to the Kennedys or world leaders. The less they knew about it, the better.

"When is it?" Elisabeth asked.

"Sometime next month," Mia replied. "How did you find out?"

"Miss Larson mentioned it to the group while you were still dressing. It's probably the best job any of us will have until the fall collection is released."

"It's more pressure," Mia said, trying to downplay its importance. "I'll be nervous every minute. Ordinary shows on the runway are so much easier. You just walk, spin, and show off the clothes."

"And flirt with the audience," Maeve said, raising her drink.

"Here's to flirting," Elisabeth answered.

Mia raised her glass, and they clinked them together. Then Elisabeth set hers on the table and looked around the darkened room.

"Speaking of flirting…" she said.

She smiled and grabbed her bag, leaving the table.

Maeve shrugged. "Well, we almost had a moment."

"It's fine," Mia insisted. "A good end to the week."

"Are you really nervous about the state dinner?" Maeve asked. "You never seem like it when you're on the runway."

"A little. Don't you get nervous, sometimes?"

Maeve laughed. "Never. The dress is the star, not me. As long as I tell myself that, I'm fine. You know, your anniversary is coming up, too."

"My anniversary?" Mia asked.

"It's been almost a year since you arrived in Paris," Maeve said, nodding. "We'll have to celebrate."

"I can't believe it's been a year," Mia replied.

Elisabeth waved from the doorway, where she was stepping

outside on the arm of an older man. Mia and Maeve stayed for another hour and then walked back to the flat. No one knew what time Elisabeth came in, but she was there the next morning making coffee when Mia got up.

Both of her roommates were more pleasant than usual, but Mia couldn't take her mind off Philip. As far as she knew, he had gone back to America and left her to face the consequences of her actions alone. She had nearly been caught searching Theo Gillette's flat and never even heard from Philip if the information she found was useful. The state dinner at Versailles put her under even more scrutiny.

Mia watched Maeve pour the coffee, trying to remember if she had seen Maeve alone with Theo or going into his office, but she couldn't recall it if she had. Elisabeth had gone in to talk to him last week, but all the girls did from time to time. Now she wondered if Maeve knew something she wasn't telling. One of them was likely another agent for the Alliance, although she hadn't been able to uncover a single incriminating piece of evidence. Sometimes Mia felt as if she would never know everything that was going on, and she would certainly never understand it.

On Friday evening, they dressed for the party, which was held in the ballroom of a hotel near Rousseau, and it was the first time Mia had seen all the other models at an event. The mood was festive. Paper lanterns hung from the ceiling and candles burned on every table. A band was playing, and many were taking advantage of the

298   ·   JULIA BRYAN THOMAS

opportunity to dance. Mia stood apart from the crowd, wondering if she would have wanted to join in if things were different, if Philip had been the Midwestern businessman he had professed to be and wanted to take her dancing. But there was no way to know. He was gone, and she might not ever see him again.

She turned and found herself staring into the eyes of the man who had escorted her to the first social event she had attended for Theo. He was devilishly handsome and, she recalled, mischievous as well. It took a moment to remember his name, but suddenly it came to her. Jack Carr. He was one of the most attractive men she had met in France but also one of the most aggressive. She could see that hadn't changed when he began to walk toward her.

"Mia Walker," he said, looking her up and down. "I wondered if I would run into you again one of these days."

"Mr. Carr," she replied.

"Oh, come on," he answered. "We're old friends now. It's Jack and Mia. We have to catch up, my dear. It's been too long."

"What are you doing here tonight?"

He shrugged. "The same as you, most likely. Seeking companionship and entertainment in this cold and lonely world."

Mia raised a brow. "I doubt you'd have any difficulty finding either."

"Neither would you," he replied. "Particularly since I'm here."

"Do you work in Paris?" she asked.

On the one evening they spent together, she had been too uneasy to ask him anything. Now she wanted to learn as much as she could about any of the subjects who came into her life.

He raised a shoulder. "I dabble in this and that. Investments, mostly."

"What brought you to the House of Rousseau for the show that day?"

"That's an excellent point of conversation," he said. "But first, we must find a table where we can discuss things more comfortably."

He took her elbow and led her to a table away from Maeve and Elisabeth, who were involved in conversations of their own. After pulling out her chair, he signaled to a waiter.

"A glass of champagne for me," he said. "And for the lady...?"

"The same, please."

The waiter placed two glasses on the table in front of them. Jack was sitting close enough that they were almost elbow to elbow.

"I must say, Paris isn't as bright when you're not around," he remarked.

"I bet you say that to all the girls."

"You know you have a special place in my heart."

"What sort of investments are you in?" she asked, trying to change the subject. "Bonds? Commodities?"

"Are you looking for a job?" he teased. "Or financial advice?"

"I'm just curious," she said.

She took a sip of the wine, setting it back on the table. It wasn't a coincidence seeing him again, she was certain. She no longer believed in them.

He cocked his head toward her. "You know, right now, I'm interested in jewels."

"Platinum, gold," she murmured, wondering if he knew about the Cartier diamonds. "Those hold their value over time, I'm sure."

"Maybe I wasn't clear," he said, knocking back a gulp of his scotch. "I'm more interested in pretty things, if you get my meaning."

"I'm sure your wife will be happy to hear it."

"Oh, we parted ways a long time ago," he answered. "I've been looking for a suitable replacement."

"How flattering for your future love interest," she said, looking him in the eye.

"I know about the diamonds, Mia," he said. "And I can just imagine how perfect they will look on you."

"I don't know what you're talking about."

"Of course you do," he replied. "I'm just trying to finagle a way to get to see you wear them for myself. Gillette's being overprotective of you."

"The jewelry we wear for modeling events is not valuable enough to warrant any attention," she argued.

"Must I spell it out for you?" he asked. "I'm talking about the Cartier necklace."

"I don't know what you mean."

He looked at her intently for a moment and then smiled. "Good girl. I expected no less of you. Keep up the good work."

The band struck up another number and he stood, holding out his hand.

"Shall we dance?"

Mia allowed him to lead her to the floor where several other couples were already swaying to the music. Maeve noticed them and nudged Elisabeth, who looked up and raised a brow. In fact, the murmurs around the room stilled as they caught everyone's attention. Jack was a wonderful dancer. Even though she was less than skilled, he made her look better than she was.

"They're watching our every move," Mia remarked in a low voice.

"They aren't the only ones."

With that, he proceeded to let go of one of her arms and spin her around. When he pulled her back, he held her a little too closely.

"Let's get another drink," she said.

She didn't want one, but she wanted to end the spectacle, although it was clear that they had delighted the crowd. However, he agreed, and led her off the floor.

"Thank you for the dance," he commented in her ear. "I wasn't certain I would get one."

"Who taught you to dance like that?" she asked.

"You learn a lot in love and war," he replied.

"Which is this?" she asked, against her better judgment.

"Only time will tell. If you'll excuse me."

He bowed, and then walked away. She couldn't help but notice that he avoided Marcel Rousseau and Theo Gillette.

"Who was that man?" Maeve asked, coming up behind her. "He's the dreamiest thing I've seen since I've been in France."

"He works in investments," Mia answered. She couldn't tell them he was a suspected member of the Alliance, as involved one way or another as she was in international affairs.

"Well," her friend replied, raising a brow, "I wouldn't mind letting him invest a little time in me."

# 26

———

Two weeks later, Mia sat glued to the television, watching the Kennedys' motorcade as it traveled from Porte d'Orléans to the Boulevard Saint-Michel. Even on the small screen, she could see thousands of people lining the streets, hoping for a glimpse of the American president and his glamorous wife. Screaming crowds waved American flags, a sea of red, white, and blue against the backdrop of the most beautiful city in the world. *Vive le président!* and *Vive Jacqui!* signs could be spotted among the throng. Mia watched their progress as the motorcade turned onto the Rue de Rivoli and continued along the Tuileries Gardens. When the parade entered the Place des Pyramides, they were accompanied by a hundred Republican Guards on horseback in full ceremonial uniforms, navy coats roped with gold braids and white sashes, their black and gold hats plumed with red feathers. Despite the revolution, which had occurred nearly two hundred years before, they were a spectacle fit for a king. Gooseflesh came up on Mia's arm. Never had a procession affected her like this, and judging by the crowd, she wasn't alone in that opinion. There was something electric in the air, and all of France could feel it.

The car carrying the Kennedys, the announcer explained, had been fitted with a plexiglass roof so that the president could be easily seen by onlookers. When the camera zoomed in on them, Mia could even see that Jacqueline was wearing a three-strand pearl choker. She recognized it, having seen it on another occasion. She longed to know the color of the First Lady's suit, but she would have to read about it in tomorrow's papers, from which she had already learned that Jackie had arrived on French soil with numerous steamer trunks full of gowns. Speculation was rampant as to the nationality of the designers. Mia assumed that she would wear some American evening dresses in recognition of the fashion industry in her own country, but privately she hoped there would be a nod to French fashion with a Paris-designed gown as well.

Enclosed in the plexiglass-topped vehicle, Jacqueline Kennedy looked exactly like what she was, the most famous woman in the world. No matter how many silk gowns and hand-embroidered frocks Mia had worn, no matter how many lessons on comportment she had been given, she would never achieve that level of glamour. One was born with it. Such an innate sense of style transcended mere fashion.

Of course, Mia was competent at her job, but it was only a facade. Suddenly she wondered the same about Jacqueline Kennedy. Was her life a facade as well? Had she been chosen for the role she embodied so perfectly simply because she could carry out whatever task needed to be done, rather than for the simple reason that her husband loved her? If that were the case, Mia thought, perhaps love doesn't exist at all. It wouldn't surprise her now. Nothing could anymore.

"Are you nervous?" Elisabeth asked, sitting down beside her. She sat forward, studying the screen in front of her.

Mia shook her head. "No."

Whether it was true or not wasn't important. She knew better than to betray her feelings to anyone, even Elisabeth. It was simple. One needed only to look elegant enough to promote a Rousseau gown, and innocent enough not to arouse suspicion. She had the ability to do both.

She suddenly wondered how much Elisabeth knew, and if she were involved in the subterfuge that Mia had been dragged into. Was Maeve? Or was Mia the only Rousseau pawn in a high-stakes game? As much as she wanted answers, it was dangerous to ask them of the wrong person.

"Who is doing your hair tonight?" Elisabeth continued.

"Julien."

"He's the best. I hope he gives you the French twist, like he did last time. It suited you perfectly."

"What are you doing tonight?" Mia asked, trying to change the subject.

Elisabeth shrugged. "Nothing as fabulous as a state dinner at Versailles with de Gaulle and the Kennedys."

"It's only a boring dinner," Mia replied, trying to keep her voice light. "The chicken will probably taste like rubber."

Six months ago, they would have laughed about it. Now Elisabeth merely shrugged, never taking her eyes off the screen. Everyone was affected by the majesty of it, even her roommate, who was rarely impressed.

Mia glanced at the clock before turning her attention back to the television, straining for another glimpse of Jacqueline Kennedy. She had less than an hour to report to the House of Rousseau to get ready for the evening. Not long ago, she would have been beside herself at the opportunity; now it was another dangerous strand in the web in which she was caught.

Elizabeth watched for another few minutes and then announced that she was going to take a walk. As soon as she left, Mia turned off the television and went to take a shower. Afterward, she brushed out her hair, and chose a cotton dress with a cardigan before slipping on a pair of sandals. She took a taxi and arrived at the atelier early, where the team was ready and waiting for her.

"Come with me," Micheline said. "Makeup first."

She led Mia to her station and turned on the bright lights to inspect her face. Ordinarily, Mia was in the chair for ten or fifteen minutes, but this time, Micheline was doing an entire makeover. Her face was scrubbed and cleaned and moisturized before Micheline set out the items she would use to transform Mia into a glamorous figure. While she worked, Mia fell silent, thinking about what sort of night lay ahead. Panic gripped her. Something was going to go wrong. There were too many uncontrollable variables: the dress, the priceless gems, the intimidating feeling of walking into Versailles in a room full of presidents and dignitaries. After what seemed like an eternity, Micheline turned Mia toward the mirror and nodded.

"What do you think?"

Mia sat forward in her chair. She always looked elegant after a makeup session, but this was different. Her skin glowed. She looked like a perfect version of herself, one she had never seen before.

"It's wonderful, Micheline," she answered. "I don't know what you did."

"Now, on to Julien, my dear," the woman answered. "Have a nice time tonight."

*As if this were an ordinary night*, Mia thought. She knew better, but she murmured her thanks and proceeded to the salon, where Julien was waiting. He nodded to her before turning her head this way and that with his fingers, making the occasional note on a slip of paper.

"Something different tonight, I think," he said, in a voice so low, it seemed he was talking to himself. "This will be an occasion to remember."

Mia knew better than to ask. He was an artist with a blank canvas of hair, and he immediately began to massage something onto her scalp.

She closed her eyes and relaxed. Nothing could happen to her here. The evening wasn't ruined yet nor was the gown soiled. She tried to remind herself she wasn't important in the overall scheme. In fact, she was scarcely more than a mannequin being styled for a window display. It suddenly seemed a great deal of work for so short an evening, for no matter how long she would sit at a table in the grand Hall of Mirrors, it hardly seemed worth the time that was being put into the occasion. In the end, her hair was woven and then braided with a thin blue ribbon and then pinned in a long, low bun at the nape of her neck.

"It's a work of art, Julien," she said when he handed her a mirror.

He smiled. "You look wonderful. Do us proud tonight."

For the occasion, Monsieur Rousseau had selected a gown of the richest blue with a strapless bodice with gathered folds and tucks that hugged her slight frame. A thin veil of tulle in the same shade of the dress was positioned over her shoulders and secured at the front of the bodice to avoid any semblance of impropriety. The dress had a narrow fitted skirt with a voluminous see-through layer of tulle over it, giving it the appearance of a sweeping skirt without the attendant difficulties. As had been her experience with some of the other couture gowns she had worn, she would be zipped into it and additional stitches would be sewn into the seams to prevent any chance of slipping.

She couldn't eat before being dressed in such a garment, nor would she be able properly eat while wearing it, although she would have to give the appearance of doing so. It was her responsibility to make certain the dress arrived back in the atelier in precisely the same condition she received it.

As she stood in front of the tall mirror of the atelier, she regarded her appearance. Without the shadow of espionage, she might have felt as pampered as a bride, but now she felt like she was trussed up like a turkey, ready to be devoured.

She knew nothing about the man who was escorting her to the event, other than that his name was Aleksandar Dimitrov and he was the ambassador to France from an Eastern European country. No one had mentioned which country. She didn't even know if he spoke English or if she would be merely a decoration on his arm. As she tried to pull herself together, Theo and a contingent of men in suits came into the room. Her employer gave her a cold smile as he approached.

"The vaults have been opened at Cartier this evening," he said, indicating the men who followed behind him. "This is Jacques Touret, the director of the Paris branch of Cartier."

The tall bearded man stood next to her with a large velvet box in his hand. Behind him stood six burly individuals who appeared to be guarding the jewels.

"This is Raoul," Theo said, indicating the tallest one. "Cartier has assigned him to accompany you to the event this evening. He will not be with you during the dinner, but he will escort you inside the building and then back to your car when the evening is concluded."

"I understand."

"There's more," Theo remarked. "You must not touch the necklace, if at all possible, and you certainly may not remove it. It is worth more than a million American dollars and is on display to some of the wealthiest women in the world, who might be interested in owning such an item. If anyone asks about it, merely say that it is from Cartier."

Mia gasped as he opened the box. She had wondered what it would look like, and she was not disappointed. The diamonds sparkled like stars in the summer sky. No one would be able to take their eyes off it.

The necklace, Jacques Touret explained, was constructed with more than four hundred and fifty diamonds. The main circle was lined with diamonds and there were twenty-five strands fanning down from it at quarter-inch intervals, like raindrops falling from the sky.

"I can't believe that I get to wear this," she murmured.

Touret nodded. "It is a great honor as well as an enormous responsibility. Maintaining the safety of the jewels is of utmost importance."

"What about my escort for the evening?" she asked, looking at Theo.

"He is an ambassador, as you are aware," he replied. "He has been told that you will be in possession of a priceless diamond necklace and that no one may touch it at any time."

Mia nodded.

"Turn around, please, Mademoiselle," Touret said.

After a moment's hesitation, she obeyed. She felt the touch of his fingers against her neck, trying not to recoil. The necklace was cold on her skin, and she had to resist the impulse to reach up and touch it.

"It's heavier than I expected," she said.

He didn't answer. Instead, he fastened the clasp and then came around to face her, reaching up to straighten it perfectly against her collarbone. For a moment, she couldn't breathe. Then she turned and faced him, forcing herself to smile.

"You are beautiful," he stated.

Mia wasn't certain how to respond.

"Let's wait downstairs," Raoul said. "We will take the elevator. The ambassador's car is en route and should be here any moment."

"Take care of that necklace," Theo said one final time.

Mia nodded and lifted the skirt of her dress as she made her way to the elevator, taking her matching silk handbag from the table as she passed. Because the underskirt was so snug, there was no way she could have moved quickly. She could hear Raoul behind her, thinking she felt less safe with him than if Luca were accompanying her.

When the elevator doors slid apart, she stepped out. The front door was open, and a tall middle-aged man with a beard and mustache stood in the middle of the foyer. He wore an ornate diplomatic uniform of black with gold, with a wide gold sash tied about his waist. A cross medallion was pinned to the front of his jacket alongside several medals. He cut a fine figure, the sort of man Mia believed was more handsome in middle age than he had been when he was young. The two of them would catch the eye of everyone in the room.

"Miss Walker," he said.

She gave a small bow. "Ambassador."

He walked her to the car, where the driver opened the door, allowing her plenty of time to carefully fold her dress into the vehicle. When the door closed, Dimitrov came around and got into the car beside her.

They drove in silence. To still her nerves, she almost initiated a conversation, but he seemed preoccupied. Raoul followed in the car behind them, but even though he couldn't see her at that moment, she didn't touch the necklace. She noticed the ambassador looking at it and averted her eyes. It was a long drive, but it allowed her the opportunity to think. Perhaps this evening could give her the chance for some reconnaissance of her own. She would make note of who the ambassador spoke to and who spoke with him in turn. There was no way to know his political leanings, but she doubted that she would have been chosen to attend the event if he weren't involved in some way or another.

The Cartier necklace was protection from something happening to her, she was certain. She would be the object of everyone's curiosity, and too many eyes would be on her. She might even be used as a distraction from any covert activities in which Dimitrov might engage. That was the most likely scenario, she decided, in which case all she had to do was to avoid as much conversation as possible with the ambassador and to appear graceful and enigmatic to the other guests, the very job she had trained for over the past year. She would have to be vigilant, making a mental note of who took interest in the diamonds.

As the car approached Versailles, Mia strained for a glimpse, taking in its astonishing size and scope. The palace was long and wide with a grand canal separating the building from a grand park, and a parterre garden bloomed with thousands of asters and holly-hocks among acres of boxwood hedges. In the canal was an enormous fountain with statues of Greek gods. There was an air of unreality to it all. It seemed impossible that it had once been the home of Marie Antoinette, whose life seemed more legend than fact. Mia had thought her story little more than a doomed fairy tale. But as they stepped from the car, she realized her life and death were far too real. Outside the gates stood a golden coach, and music and the murmur of voices could be heard inside. Mia lifted the hem of her garment as they made their way across the cobblestones.

"You may not speak to anyone unless I tell you to," Dimitrov said, grasping her wrist.

She turned to look at him.

"Do we understand one another, Miss Walker?"

"Of course," Mia replied, her voice steady as she replied. She was getting better at hiding her emotions.

Her heart began to race. A year ago, it would have been a dream come true to have been invited to such a prestigious event. However,

Mia could only hope she was mere window dressing on a night such as this. Certainly, there were more armed guards that night than at any other location in France, perhaps all of Europe.

She took a last glance around before they stepped inside. The sun had begun to set, wrapping the palace in a dusky pink glow. Surely nothing terrible could happen in such a place, she thought. Or perhaps she was wrong. Perhaps this was precisely the place where the unimaginable could happen.

# 27

———

Inside the grand entrance to Versailles, a reception area awaited where guests were greeted by a long line of French dignitaries. Aleksandr Dimitrov took Mia's elbow a little too forcefully and guided her through the procession. She did not react. The only thing she knew about him was the fact that his diplomatic ties had allowed him to be invited to a state occasion, and while she wasn't intimidated by his position, she understood her role in the event. She followed him from dignitary to dignitary down the endless line. He shook hands with each of them, exchanging pleasantries as Mia bowed to each one and took a step back to allow Dimitrov to conduct his conversations without her interference.

It soon became clear that she, not the ambassador, was the object of everyone's attention. To a man, whomever was speaking to Ambassador Dimitrov had his eyes firmly fixed on her. First, the

Cartier necklace caused a raised brow. Then the eyes traveled up to hers, forcing her to acknowledge him with a nod. Finally, his gaze traveled back to the necklace and then perhaps still lower, causing her to avert her gaze.

"Stunning, Mademoiselle," one of the men remarked, taking her gloved hand and raising it to his lips.

"*Merci*, Monsieur," she replied, without a hint of a smile.

She wasn't churlish, but neither was she there to encourage inappropriate behavior nor to stir Dimitrov's irritation, which was lurking just below the surface. However, it happened again and again. She kept her eyes fixed as much as possible upon Dimitrov himself, as if she knew him, and was perhaps even in love with him, though she would never be interested in a man like him, no matter his wealth or position. That was one of the difficulties of being a model: people assumed she was in the business for money, attention, and prestige, a stepping stone to a glamorous, privileged life. Mia knew if none of this had happened, she would have been satisfied to have seen Paris and to have had even a small part in the fashion industry. She had gotten more than she'd hoped for, though it had come at great cost.

She followed Dimitrov down the line, nodding and bowing and keeping her thoughts to herself. Ten minutes later, they had completed the receiving line and were ushered into an enormous room. It had tall grand ceilings, full of luminous lights shining overhead. Mia stood next to the ambassador, listening to him speak to a fellow diplomat about the Algerian War. It was in all the newspapers. The country had been under Vichy control during the Second World War, causing Roosevelt to deploy American troops, who fought and regained control of Morocco and Algeria. After the war, calls for independence from France grew stronger. More than eight thousand villages had been destroyed, and two million Algerians taken to prison camps. In the early '50s, Truman had sent a committee to evaluate the situation, but now it was Eisenhower's problem.

"What do you think of the prospects of the Algerians winning the war?" the man asked Dimitrov.

Mia looked at his medals, wondering if she could divine what country he represented, but found she could not. She avoided his gaze, feigning interest in the beauty of the room as he glanced at her every few moments.

Dimitrov scoffed. "I doubt they can do it. They're a bunch of ragtag soldiers. The whole lot of them are demoralized. I shouldn't expect anything from them, myself."

"The National Liberation Front has killed tens of thousands," the man remarked, suddenly turning to Mia. "But I'm afraid we're boring the young lady. This is a night for enjoyment and pleasure, not thinking about war."

Dimitrov gave her a dismissive glance. Inside, she bristled over the implication that a woman wasn't capable of understanding world conflicts and international affairs. That was one of the reasons she was useful to them, she knew. No one put any stock in the intelligence of a mere model. It was infuriating, although it gave her some cover when people believed she was unable to comprehend their conversations.

A waiter came by with a tray of champagne and Dimitrov took one.

"Miss Walker?" he enquired. "Would you care for a glass?"

"No, thank you," she replied.

He nodded, satisfied, and turned his attention to a gentleman on his right. From where she was standing, she couldn't hear their conversation. He spoke in a low, unhurried voice, appearing to know his counterpart well. They leaned toward one another, nodding as they spoke.

Mia was aware of the tenor of voices around her, particularly when someone caught sight of the Cartier necklace. A few women even gasped at the sight of it, and she noticed one nudging another and nodding toward her. She kept her eyes focused as much as possible on the ambassador, feigning interest in his conversations.

Across the room, she caught sight of Charles de Gaulle and his wife, Yvonne Vendroux. The Kennedys had not yet come into her field of vision, though a ripple of chatter told her that they must be nearby. Like his American counterpart, de Gaulle had only been in power a short time, having taken over the French presidency a year earlier than John F. Kennedy. She had seen him on television numerous times, but in person, he had a particularly commanding presence. He was the tallest man in the room, six feet five inches, towering over everyone around him. His face was thin and long, and he was speaking animatedly with an acquaintance. His eyes were deep set, and his forehead was high, and he held a drink in the hand he used to gesture while making his points. His wife was by no means a handsome woman any more than he was an attractive man, although they seemed suited to one another. Mrs. de Gaulle wore a scoop-necked, sleeveless dark velvet dress for the formal occasion, with opera-length gloves. She had a faint smile on her face. It accompanied a pinched look, which Mia suspected was always present.

The crowd moved slightly, and Mia felt a tingle in her spine when she realized that Jacqueline Kennedy and her husband were standing to the left of the president of France. A moment passed before she realized she was holding her breath. The woman she admired most in the world was standing in her field of vision. The crowd appeared to notice, and the buzz of conversation hushed, apart from the ambassador, who glanced at the pair of presidents and went back to his own conversation.

After a couple of minutes, Dimitrov moved closer to the Kennedys and de Gaulles, as intrigued as everyone else. They came within ten feet of Mrs. Kennedy when he suddenly stopped and turned to speak to an acquaintance. Mia looked up at Jacqueline, realizing with a start that the president's wife was staring at the necklace around her throat. Then she looked up at Mia and smiled, nodding slightly in acknowledgment, before turning to Madame de Gaulle.

Mia's spirits soared. She had shared a moment with her idol. Even Dimitrov couldn't dampen her mood now. Some minutes later, when glasses had been collected on silver trays and the men adjusted their ties and offered an arm to their female companions, everyone began to move into the Hall of Mirrors.

Having been in France for a year, Mia had read about the Grand Baroque–style gallery and seen photographs in glossy magazines. However, that hadn't prepared her for the sight of it in person. The first thing she noticed was the long bank of seventeen windows looking outside onto the grounds. Dusk had fallen, the sky a velvety blue punctuated with stars and lanterns from outside the palace. It was breathtaking. Above, thirty murals adorned the ceiling, encased in frames of gold, each telling the story of a historic event that had occurred in France in the 1600s. Seventeen gold mirrors, each directly across from one of the windows, reflected light, which sparkled from the numerous crystal chandeliers. Greek and Roman statues—some gilt, others made of marble or granite—lined the walls in silent sentry.

In the center of the long room was a table long enough to accommodate each of the many guests. White tablecloths, crisp and perfect, went on as far as she could see. When she approached, Mia took in the sheer beauty of the table: crystal glasses for wine, priceless Sèvres china collected by the last kings of France, along with Grand Vermeil from Napoleon. Candelabras had been placed between each place setting, alongside low sprays of roses. It was a sumptuous display.

Dimitrov pulled out her chair, and Mia gathered the tulle of her skirt and sat, feeling the unnecessary brush of his hands against her bare arms. It took immense willpower not to flash him a look. Instead, she focused on the pink and white roses, which were as fresh as if they had just been picked a moment before from the enormous rose gardens outside.

A sharp popping sound pierced the room, causing some of the guests to jump. Mia glanced at President de Gaulle, who gave a wry smile.

"Ah, the champagne!" he pronounced, causing a ripple of relieved laughter to float through the room. "My apologies. We wouldn't want to frighten the president of the United States. Otherwise, he wouldn't bring his charming wife back to see us again."

Kennedy laughed good-naturedly, and everyone went back to their conversation. Mia couldn't see Jacqueline well from where she was sitting. A Rousseau model couldn't crane her neck for a glimpse of someone famous; she herself was the object of admiring looks and interest, not only for the necklace about her throat, but for the poise and beauty she was there to project in the name of her employer. However, she took the opportunity now and again to reach for the pepper cellar to steal a glance in the First Lady's direction.

The table was wide enough that she could not make conversation with the guest across the way, who happened to be a heavyset leering envoy far too interested in Mia and the diamonds about her throat. That left Dimitrov to her right and another gentleman to her left. He was charming, and within minutes, he began a conversation with her.

"Good evening, Mademoiselle," he said, taking hold of his napkin. "How are you enjoying your night so far?"

Mia gave him a closer look. He was tall and blond, with a short beard, cutting a trim figure in his uniform, which boasted a long row of medals across his left lapel. She didn't know the significance of them, but from his looks and bearing, she could see that he was well decorated for his service to his country.

"It's lovely, thank you," she replied.

If it had been any other night in any other circumstance, that would have been true. Versailles was the most elegant building in all of France. Nothing could possibly match the superior beauty of this palace.

"If I may say it, that's quite a lot of diamonds you're wearing," he continued. "You have the eyes of the entire room settled around your throat."

"It's Cartier," she replied, just as she had been instructed, although she was uncomfortable with his remark.

"Ah, the finest jewels for the most beautiful woman in France," he replied. "Allow me to introduce myself. My name is Emil Wachter, and I am the envoy from the wonderful country of Liechtenstein. And you are?"

"Mia Walker," she replied.

"I see you are a guest of Ambassador Dimitrov," he said, leaning closer. "Are you well acquainted with him?"

She blushed at the question, all too aware that he had noticed as well. "We have only recently met." It was less damning than if she had told him she had met the man only a couple of hours before.

"Let me guess: you are a model."

Mia looked at him and then quickly glanced away. "I work for the House of Rousseau."

Wachter nodded. "A very good house, if I may say so."

"Thank you," she replied.

She tried to keep her gaze on the roses on the table in front of her, so that Dimitrov wouldn't take exception to her speaking to a stranger, although he was caught up in an animated conversation with the gentleman on his right.

"How long have you been in France?" Wachter asked. "I assume from your accent that you are an American."

"I've been here a year," she replied.

"Everyone should spend a year in France," he remarked. "Have your travels taken you to Liechtenstein yet?"

"No," Mia said. "Although I hear it is lovely."

Wachter smiled. "It is, indeed. I would personally love to show you around, should you ever have the occasion to visit."

"You might want to rethink your kind offer," she said, suddenly coquettish. "I'm afraid I come without diamonds."

He laughed, and then he gave her a long look. "A beautiful woman is worth far more than diamonds, you know."

Mia turned and picked up the goblet of water in front of her and took a sip, returning it to its place on the table, all too aware that his eyes were trained on her. Suddenly, he turned and answered a question that had been put to him by the officer on his left. Mia took a deep breath, wishing the night was already over. Dimitrov felt no need to entertain her, confining his attention to the people at his right. Occasionally, he looked in her direction, took stock of the Cartier gems, and then returned to his conversation. She tried to listen, but the acoustics of the room made it difficult to make out what he was saying.

Wachter turned back to her every few minutes, as if aware that she had no partner with which to while away the long dinner as the consommé and fruit and steak au poivre and each of the other courses were seamlessly set in front of them and then removed as if by magic. He stabbed at his steak and then smiled at her.

"What a waste," he complained. "Sitting for an hour being plied with food when one would rather be dancing. Don't you agree?"

"I have to admit, this does feel like a night for it," she replied.

"They should take away all of these tables and just have the orchestra and moonlight," he continued. "That's what a room like this was made for."

Mia smiled. For a moment, she imagined a different night altogether, not as the model who was sent along to attract the attention of the rich and famous, but as a woman in a stunning gown with a man who wanted nothing more than to dance with her. Everything sparkled: the glittering candles of the chandeliers, the diamonds, the sequins and crystals, even the stars glimmered outside the immense windows. Wachter was right. This night was indeed being wasted.

President de Gaulle interrupted her line of thought, making the first toast of the evening. It was answered by a toast from President Kennedy and then echoed by others one by one around the room. The mood among the guests was high, every guest thrilled to be entertained at the Palace of Versailles, with its rich food, stunning backdrops, and esteemed attendees. It was a night never to be forgotten.

Three courses later, Mia sensed that the meal was nearing its end. She reached for her glass of champagne, which, until now, she had not tasted, and took a sip, careful with her dress and the jewels. The alcohol might help her relax, and she took another before setting it on the table.

"Shall we adjourn and take ourselves to the concert hall for the entertainment Madame de Gaulle has arranged for us tonight?" de Gaulle said in a loud, clear voice a few minutes later as the final plates were taken away. "We are fortunate enough to have a performance of the Paris Opera Ballet tonight. I understand it is one of Mrs. Kennedy's favorites."

Jacqueline smiled and leaned toward him, murmuring something in his ear. It appeared to amuse him, and he laughed.

Everyone rose from their seat and followed the guests of honor out of the Hall of Mirrors. Mia saw many of the women separate from their partners and wander in the direction of the powder room. Although she had only had a few sips of the champagne, she felt woozy when she stood. She wasn't supposed to leave Dimitrov's side, but a sudden lightheadedness overtook her, and she decided to follow the other women. She caught Dimitrov's eye and nodded, heading that way before he could stop her.

In the lounge, a half dozen women were perched in front of mirrors, touching up their lipstick. Even this room was astonishingly appointed for such a humble purpose, and the colorful gowns of the women around her were as diverse and beautiful as the roses in the gardens outside.

She opened her bag to extract her compact, but her heart suddenly started racing. Her body went cold and clammy, and a wave of dizziness came over her. She froze when she realized she was going to faint. Glancing up in the mirror, she saw that she had gone pale. She tried to breathe and then collapsed to the floor.

By the time she regained consciousness, the other guests had been escorted out of the room, and the bodyguard was standing over her.

"What happened?" he asked. "Where's the necklace?"

Mia gasped, putting her hand to her throat. She sat up, reaching for her bag, which was lying on the ground a couple of feet away, and opened it, somehow expecting the priceless Cartier gems to be there. Instead, as before, it held only her compact, the lipstick, and her father's watch.

"I said, what happened?" he demanded. "Give me the bag."

She handed it to him and watched as he looked through it, tossing it on her lap when he was done. The attendant helped her up and straightened her dress as Mia stood rigidly, waiting for what was going to happen next.

A gentleman came into the ladies' room, and when Mia looked up, she realized it was Emil Wachter. He turned to the bodyguard and barked at him.

"Have the car ready at once," he said. "Miss Walker needs to be escorted out of here before anyone notices that the diamonds are missing."

As she watched Raoul leave, she turned to Wachter. "Who are you?"

"Someone whose job it was to keep an eye on you," he replied. "Let's say I'm doing it for a mutual friend. Tell me exactly what happened."

"I felt unwell," she said. "Right after I came in here, I knew I was going to faint."

"You didn't eat much at dinner," he said.

"I was afraid of spoiling the dress," she admitted. "But I broke the rule. I had a little of the champagne just before I stood up."

"Something may have been put in your drink," he remarked. "But I'm afraid to be certain, we will have to search you."

Wachter waved over a woman who waited in the corner. He stepped back as she unzipped the gown partway down Mia's side.

"I'm stitched inside the gown," Mia said. "They always put a few extra stitches in to keep the seams from showing."

Wachter reached into his pocket and took out a knife, handing it to the woman. She slit the stitches carefully and then removed the dress. Raoul returned and watched as two men did a full search of the fabric and her handbag, making certain nothing was concealed in the folds of the gown. At the same time, the woman searched Mia's slip-clad body. She shook slightly, trying to remain calm. When nothing was found, she was helped back into the dress and the woman left the room.

"I apologize for the indignity, Miss Walker," Wachter stated. "No one thinks you would pull off a million-dollar heist in the middle of a huge crowd of diplomats and presidents, but the people we report to would have insisted upon it."

"I understand."

"Hand me your bag," he said. He removed the lipstick and handed it to her. "Repair your face. I will be right back."

With a shaky hand, she reapplied a light coat onto her lips, trying to decide what to do. If she had understood him correctly, he'd all but said he was working for Philip. She had to trust him. She tried not to catch Raoul's eye as she finished. A moment later, Wachter came back into the room.

"Here's your bag, Miss Walker," he said, handing it to her. "Everything has been examined."

Mia realized at once that it was heavier than it had been when she had given it to him. Instinctively, she left the tube of lipstick on a console to avoid opening the bag.

"Thank you," she said.

He walked her into the hall, and they approached Ambassador Dimitrov, who was waiting for them.

"I'm with Versailles security, sir," he said to the ambassador. "It appears that something was put in Miss Walker's drink. She's not feeling well and will need to be escorted home right away."

Dimitrov nodded.

"Everyone has gone into the North Statue Gallery for drinks before they move into the auditorium for the ballet," Wachter continued. "You can leave undetected if you go this way."

"What about the necklace?" Dimitrov grumbled. "We were responsible for the safety of the jewels."

"That's what insurance is for," Wachter replied, shrugging.

Pursing her lips and dabbing at them with the corner of her finger, she clutched the bag tightly, nodding at Wachter, panic seizing her. In front of all the guards and half the gendarmes of Paris in attendance to protect Charles de Gaulle and John F. Kennedy from threats such as herself, she was about to leave Versailles holding a silk bag full of priceless jewels.

There was no way to escape. She wouldn't get far in the blue silk stilettos she was loaned for the occasion, and neither could she kick them off and run across the cobblestones. She had no choice but to follow through with the instructions she had been given and hope she could extricate herself before anything else happened.

Dimitrov escorted Mia out of the building and toward the car where Raoul was waiting, his eyes locked on her bare throat. She slid into the vehicle and waited as he came around to join her. A

330 • JULIA BRYAN THOMAS

movement in the darkness caught her eye and she realized that Luca was standing beside a nearby vehicle.

She froze, wondering why he was there. Why had Theo sent him when another driver had been hired for the occasion? She turned away from the window as the driver got into the car. They started down the road when suddenly Dimitrov turned toward her.

"You've ruined the evening, Miss Walker," he said. "What do you have to say for yourself?"

She didn't reply, lightly placing her hand on the bag, which rested on her lap, wondering when she would ever breathe normally again.

# 28

---

By the time they arrived at the House of Rousseau, chaos had broken out. Monsieur Rousseau, Theo Gillette, and Diana Larson were pacing the lobby, engaged in a high-pitched argument. Swear words colored the air when she and Dimitrov were ushered into the building.

"What the hell happened?" Theo boomed as Mia came through the door.

"Someone put something in my drink," she replied. She had to stay calm. No one else was going to. "It made me sick, and I passed out in the powder room."

Monsieur Rousseau turned to Raoul and Dimitrov, his temper flaring. "You were supposed to watch her every move."

"We could hardly follow her into a women's lounge," Raoul said. "There was an enormous crowd of people present."

"We'll have to search your dress," Theo said, turning to Mia.

"I was searched on the premises," she replied. She clutched the bag, holding it to her side, its bulk disguised by the folds of the dress.

"She was," Raoul admitted. "I was present. The stitches in the dress were even slit by a knife to get her out of it."

"Dear God," bellowed Monsieur Rousseau. "Get that dress off her now."

Mia narrowed her eyes. "Miss Larson, would you please come with me and allow me to remove it with your help?"

After a beat, Theo nodded helplessly and allowed the two women to leave the room. Mia followed Diana to the atelier. As they went inside, she tucked the bag behind another garment, which was sitting at a station to be altered. Without missing a beat, she went up to Miss Larson and allowed her to help her out of the dress. She stood perfectly still in the middle of the room as the dress was examined.

"You're right," the woman said. "Nothing has been hidden here, and the dress doesn't appear to be damaged. I'd better get it down to Monsieur Rousseau so he can see for himself. You might as well get dressed."

Mia nodded, waiting until she had left the room. Then she took the silk bag from its hiding place and brought it with her into the changing room. She pulled on her dress, kicking off the heels she had worn for the evening. Then she opened the silk bag and took out the diamond necklace. She stared at it for a moment and then looked at herself in the mirror. With a shaking hand, she reached up and clasped it about her throat, tucking each of the twenty-five diamond-encrusted strands under her collar. Pulling a scarf from her pocketbook, she wound it around her neck, making certain that it covered the diamonds to prevent them from being discovered. Then she put on her coat, turning up the collar, and went back downstairs.

"We're deeply disappointed in you," Monsieur Rousseau reiterated as she came into the lobby where they were waiting. "The dress wasn't harmed, young lady, but you have caused us incredible embarrassment. I don't care if you think it wasn't your fault. You were uniquely responsible for it. I wouldn't be surprised if the police don't come looking for you. Right now, we're evaluating your future at the House of Rousseau."

It was the first time he had ever spoken to her, and she was shocked that it came as a reprimand, although she refused to rise to the bait. "May I go?"

Theo sighed loudly. "Report to my office at eight o'clock tomorrow morning on the dot. Is that understood?"

"Yes, sir," she said. She looked at Raoul, wondering if he was going to drive her.

"The escort service is over for the night," Monsieur Rousseau said. "You will have to find your own way home."

Mia nodded and let herself out of the building, shocked that she had eluded their grasp. No one had thought to search her again. On the street, she made her way to the nearest Métro, glancing at her watch. It was after nine o'clock, and the sky was dark, the clouds obscuring the moon overhead. With a quick step, she entered the tunnel-like entrance, not allowing herself to make eye contact with any of the characters who, like her, were waiting for a late train— miscreants all, from the look of them. However, it was even more dangerous to wander the streets at night alone than to try to make it back to her flat quickly. A stout man wedged himself into the seat next to her. She kept her eyes trained forward, ignoring him as well as she could, relieved when they reached the Cluny stop and she had made it out of the station.

It was a three-minute walk to her building, although it felt much longer in the moonless night. The necklace felt even heavier around her throat than it had throughout the evening with the eyes of every well-known person in France taking it in. With every step, she was more shocked that no one at Rousseau realized she was the one who had it. When she finally arrived home, the lobby was empty and she went upstairs, pausing at the old walnut console down the hall, where someone had placed an oversize basket for the cat, who often slept there. She unclasped the necklace and slid it off her neck, then wrapped it in the scarf, pushing it far enough behind the basket that even the cat wouldn't notice it was there. Then she let herself into her apartment.

All the lights were out. She listened at her roommates' door and realized that they must have gone out for the evening. Then she went into her room and sat on her bed, trying to figure out what to do. Philip had deserted her, and she was going to have to make her own decisions now.

She would probably be fired tomorrow. Even after Rousseau and Theo calmed down and realized she wasn't responsible for having something put into her drink, they would have to deal with the humiliation she had brought to the company. And if she were being fired, anyway, it was the perfect time to leave.

But there were so many unanswered questions. Why had Philip given her instructions throughout the winter and then disappeared? Was he even still alive? Who was Emil Wachter, and was it possible for her to find him and ask him about his role in the events at Versailles? And Luca was another complication. He had been outside the palace, as if he were there to pick up someone himself. Could it even have been her? She had to talk to him, but it would have to wait until morning. Whatever had been put in her drink was still causing her to feel weak and somewhat ill. She dressed for bed, then pulled the covers around her and fell into such a deep sleep that she never even heard the door open when Maeve and Elisabeth returned.

The sun was shining the next morning, as if she hadn't just had the second most terrifying day of her life. Her hand went instinctively to her throat, as though she expected to find the diamonds still there. She sat up, relieved to remember they weren't, and quickly got ready. The kitchen and sitting room were empty, but Maeve and Elisabeth had tossed their jackets on the settee before turning in. There was no telling how late they had gotten home, but they would sleep for hours. Mia slipped on her jacket and let herself out of the apartment.

Luca had driven them countless times up and down the streets of Paris, and once he had pointed out his own building. She would go there and demand an explanation. She walked briskly, pausing now and then to see if someone was following her, although she didn't detect any movement. Traffic was light, and she darted across the road to get there faster. When she found Luca's building, she went in and looked at the mailboxes for his flat number. Within two minutes, she was rapping on his door.

"Who is it?" he called.

She could sense the tension in his voice, wondering if Monsieur or Theo had called him and threatened him, too.

"It's Mia."

The door flew open and he stood there, staring at her.

"What are you doing here?" Luca asked. "You need to leave now."

"Why were you there last night?" she demanded. "What's going on?"

Suddenly, she heard a sound coming from the other room.

"Who is it?" she asked.

She assumed it was one of the models. That would explain why he was behaving so strangely. He was playing all the angles, though she was surprised to find that she didn't care. She only wanted to know why he had been at Versailles.

"No one," he said. "But you must get out of here now."

"Not until you tell me why you were there last night," she snapped. "Did Theo ask you to follow me?"

"Trust me, Mia, it's better if you don't know."

Suddenly, a man walked into the room, and Mia took a step back. Emil Wachter was coming toward her, holding a gun pointed directly at her.

"Emil," she finally choked out.

"Mia," he answered. "What a surprise to see you this morning."

They stared at each other for a moment, and when Luca glanced at her, she noticed that Wachter gave her an almost imperceptible shake of his head. She stared at him, realizing that he didn't want her to reveal to Luca she had the necklace. Neither did he want to alert Luca to the fact that he was really working for the United States government.

"What's going on?" she asked.

"We were having a discussion," Luca said. "And you need to go."

"First tell me why you were there last night," she said, turning to face him. "I saw you beside your car when we were leaving Versailles."

"That's a good question," Wachter said, nodding. "I'd like to know the answer to that myself."

"I was a backup for Raoul in case anything happened," he said. "Monsieur Rousseau sent me to make certain nothing went wrong."

Wachter shook his head. "I don't believe you."

"I don't care what you believe."

Luca lunged at Wachter, knocking him to the ground. They wrestled around for a minute before the gun went suddenly off. For a moment, both men went still. Then Luca rolled off Wachter, holding the gun.

"Dear God," he said.

Mia instinctively reached for the hairpin in her hat, even though it was a useless defense against a pistol. When she held it out in front of her, he gave a grim laugh.

"Don't be ridiculous," he said. "Take this and get rid of it as fast as you can."

He thrust the gun into Mia's hands. Her mouth flew open as he ran out of the apartment. She looked at Emil's lifeless body, dropping to her knees beside him. He was bleeding from a wound in his chest. His eyes opened momentarily, and he looked as if he were trying to form a word. Then his head rolled to the side.

Mia thrust her fingers to his neck to check for a pulse, but there was none. She stood, her body shaking.

It was too late to save Wachter, who she believed was trying to warn her, and Luca was gone. She bent down to check the dead man's pockets, finding nothing, and then stood back up. Slipping the hatpin back into her hat, she tucked the pistol into her handbag.

When she left the building, Mia walked to the boulangerie, stood in line to buy croissants, and took them to the Jardin du Luxembourg. There, she fed bits of the bread to the pigeons, trying to think.

Wachter was dead, Luca had likely gone straight to Theo, and a priceless Cartier necklace was tucked behind a basket on the floor of her building where the cat liked to sleep. Philip had disappeared, possibly forever. Despite the note he had left for her at Christmas, she hadn't seen him in months, and she was suddenly afraid he was dead, too. The thought filled her with a deep, violent grief.

There was nowhere to go. Either her roommates were involved in the plot to steal nuclear secrets or they were innocent, and she couldn't put them in the way of danger. It wouldn't take long before someone found her, too. There was no choice about what to do. She would have to steal back into her building, take the jewels, and disappear.

Once she had made the decision, she stood, disposing of the gun in the closest bin. She turned in the direction of the Rue des Écoles, making her way down alleys instead of walking down the street. When she reached the back of her building, she opened the service door and went inside, going up the back steps. When she reached her floor, she opened the door a crack and listened for any sound coming from her apartment. It was silent.

She went to the console in the corridor and moved the cat's basket to get the scarf, but it wasn't there. She dropped to her knees and pulled the basket from the bottom shelf, searching behind it, but it was gone. Mia froze, realizing that the priceless Cartier necklace had been found, which meant she was in even more danger than she had been before.

Suddenly, the door to her neighbor's flat opened, and Chantal Fournier appeared in the doorway.

"Mademoiselle Walker," she said, holding up the diamonds. "Let me guess. Is this what you're looking for?"

# 29

---

"Madame Fournier," Mia said, unable to take her eyes off the diamonds. "What are you doing with that?"

"Come inside," the older woman insisted.

When the door was shut, Mia noticed that the customary fire in the fireplace was not burning, and no aroma drifted in from the kitchen. It had been a week or two since she had seen her neighbor. She couldn't remember exactly when, but they had said a quick "Bonjour" as they passed on the stairs a few days ago. Now she held in her hand a scarf containing a million dollars' worth of diamonds, as casually as if it were a book she had plucked from a shelf.

Madame Fournier turned to face her. "We are leaving now. There is no other alternative. In fact, your bag is already packed."

"What do you mean, 'packed'?" Mia asked, shocked.

Madame shrugged. "I've had a key to your flat for years. I knew that one day it would come in handy."

"Did anyone see you?"

"No. Your flatmates were out."

"Give me the diamonds, Madame. They do not belong to you."

"Neither do they belong to you, Miss Walker. We're wasting valuable time. We must leave."

"Where are we going?" Mia asked.

"You have to trust me," Madame answered. She gestured to two bags and an enclosed wicker basket that sat on the floor beside them. "We are not safe here."

"What's that?" Mia asked, pointing to the basket.

"It's the cat."

"But, Madame…"

"There is no time for *buts*."

Madame opened the door and lifted her bag. Mia took her case and then lifted the wicker basket. The cat pushed his nose to a small opening, mewing to be released. Once they were out of the building, Madame began walking across the alley. Mia clutched her case, wondering if the diamonds were inside it, and followed with the cat. In the nearest street, Madame raised her hand, and a taxi arrived a moment later.

"Madame," Mia said, once they were inside the cab. There were so many questions.

Madame shook her head.

"Gare du Nord," she told the driver.

When they arrived at the train station, Madame Fournier went to a window and bought two tickets. She spoke so quickly that Mia couldn't make out the words. Neither could she get a look at the tickets to reveal their destination. She followed the woman across the huge station to the platforms, where Madame stopped in front of one of the trains. Mia caught her breath. She might be young, but she had difficulty keeping up with a seventy-four-year-old woman.

Madame Fournier nodded. "Follow me and say nothing until I tell you it is safe."

For some reason, Mia trusted her. Perhaps it was because there was no one else to trust, or perhaps it was because she insisted they bring the cat, but there was no other choice. She had to get out of Paris, and this was the most expedient way to do it. Madame went to the most isolated corner of the train, and they took a seat across from each other, the cat's basket on the seat next to the old woman.

"Where are they?" Mia asked in a low voice.

"Don't worry. I didn't leave them sitting around so that someone could find them. They are in my bag."

"Why did we bring the cat?"

Madame Fournier crossed her arms. "Because we cannot go back."

Mia was shocked. "Who are you, and what's going on?"

"Young lady, you are in a great deal of trouble, and it is my wish to make certain you get out of it. In the meantime, we are going somewhere safe."

The train was more than half-empty, most of the passengers sitting near the front. They were alone in the back of the car, but Madame turned away from her, watching as they pulled out of the station. It was a gritty view, as rough as any part of Paris that Mia had seen. However, within a few minutes, they had left the city and its seedier parts for a destination unknown.

"We're going west," Mia remarked, checking the position of the sun.

"I will tell you more when we are closer."

Mia could see she was in no mood to talk. In fact, she needed some time to make sense of the situation herself. So much had happened in the last twenty-four hours that she couldn't have stayed in Paris for another second. She was the last person known to have seen the diamonds and the focus would quickly turn to her as a suspect.

Mia leaned back in her seat, everything weighing heavily on her mind. She could still see Emil Wachter's body lying in a pool of his own blood, the gun in Luca's hand. Who was Emil, and why had he given her the jewels? Why had Luca given her the gun and left the scene, and why had she disposed of the gun instead of going to the police? She wasn't protecting Luca. Her own fingerprints were on that gun.

She glanced at Madame Fournier, who was clearly lost in her own thoughts. More than fifty years separated them in age, but their situation was the same. They both knew more than was safe and had become involved in a jewel theft, if not murder. But nothing would be discussed now, no matter how she tried to force it. Instead, she, like the older woman, turned her attention to the valleys and plains passing under the wheels of the train. The cat was lulled to sleep by the rocking motion, but Madame remained impassive throughout the trip, leaving Mia the chance to contemplate every act she had taken in the last year, from the moment Theo asked her to take this job to the incongruity of sitting on a train with a priceless necklace in a bag at their feet. What happened now she could only imagine.

Hours passed; signs came into view. Mia realized they were headed toward the English Channel. She looked in her handbag, making sure her passport was still there, wondering whether they would need it. Before long, the train came to a stop at a station.

Madame lifted her case but did not move until the car was empty. Then she nodded at Mia, who took her own bag and the cat's basket and followed her off the train. Madame found a taxi at the queue, and they got inside. She leaned forward and gave the driver an address. A moment later, they were moving.

"I see we're in Honfleur," Mia said. "But why are we stopping here?"

"I know the area well," Madame replied. "We're near the coast, not far from Le Havre. There is a place we can stay while we discuss our next move."

Mia opened the basket to allow the cat to get out of its cage. He nimbly jumped out and sat between them on the seat, licking his front paw as if he hadn't spent the last four hours in a wicker hamper. After they had driven for about ten minutes, Madame turned to her.

"I'm afraid you'll have to put the cat back into the basket."

As she did, the taxi came to a stop in front of a small stone house. Madame Fournier paid the driver, and they took their things and got out of the car. The house was on a quiet street, and there were few signs of life. However, Madame walked up to the door, her bags in her arms, and reached up a hand to knock. A moment later, an older gentleman opened the door and stepped back, staring at her with complete astonishment.

"I decided to come instead of write," Madame Fournier said.

He came forward and took her by the shoulders, delivering a kiss to both cheeks. Then he looked at Mia.

"Mademoiselle," he said, nodding. Then he turned to Madame. "Here, let me take your things."

He led them both into the house, where he placed the bags on a table, including the cat's basket.

"May I?" he asked, opening the lid. Without waiting for permission, he lifted the cat out of the basket and scratched him between the ears. "What is his name?"

"He has no name," Madame replied.

"Nonsense," he replied, looking at Mia. "We all have a name. By the way, mine is Raphaël Bellamy."

"Mia Walker."

"Well, Mademoiselle Walker, what do you think of Beau as a name for the cat? He's a handsome fellow."

"It's fine."

"Raphaël, Miss Walker is in trouble," Madame Fournier said. "We have come seeking refuge."

"You are welcome, as always. Have you been to the house?"

"We are going to take a look at it now."

"First, you will have something to eat, and then you must let me drive you."

Mia had given up trying to predict what would happen next. After a bowl of stew, they got into Monsieur Bellamy's car. Madame sat in the front seat with him, holding her bag of jewels on her lap; Mia and the cat sat in the back. They had only driven for a few minutes when the car slowed down and turned onto a small paved road, which was nearly obscured from view by the trees and hedges all around. The building that eventually came into view behind the arbors of elms was no mere house. It was a manor, situated in the grounds as if it belonged to a count or earl. Mia turned curiously to Madame.

"Where are we?" Mia asked, bewildered to be in such a place.

"This is my house," Madame answered.

Monsieur Bellamy parked the car and helped them bring the bags through the front door. Mia followed Madame Fournier and her friend as they walked through the rooms, all of which had been undisturbed for years. Madame lifted sheets from the furniture while

Monsieur opened the shutters to let in the light. Then they went into the kitchen, where Madame tested the tap and found it working, so she set about putting a kettle on the stove. Raphaël found a dish on a sideboard and filled it with water, putting it down for the cat, while she took cups and saucers from the oversized dresser and rinsed them before making a pot of tea.

"There," she said. "Now we can talk in a civilized fashion."

Mia couldn't broach the conversation she wanted to have with a stranger present, so she sat back and allowed them to talk. They knew each other well, and she tried to guess their relationship. It was warm and intimate, leaving her to realize he was more than a friend. After he finished his cup, Chantal lifted the teapot to pour him another, but he shook his head.

"I'm going to check the house and grounds to make certain they are secure," he said. "Then I shall return with some supplies for you."

"Thank you, Raphaël," she said. "I would come with you, but I must talk to Miss Walker first."

"I don't understand, Madame," Mia said, after he had gone. "Who are you and what are we doing here?"

"I am a simple French woman who has been enlisted by the French and American governments to keep an eye on subversive activity in our building, specifically, in your flat," Madame Fournier replied. "There are movements afoot by foreign governments who want to get their hands on vitally sensitive information, of which you have been made aware."

"How long have you been working for the government?"

"For about a year before you arrived," Madame said, pouring them both another cup of tea. "National security interests must be guarded at all costs. Our government had suspicions that the House of Rousseau was being used as a means of delivering information to enemy hands. There are many people working around the city with an eye on the administrators of the fashion house, but it was well known that a handful of eager young models anxious to make a name for themselves would make easy targets for Rousseau to use for their own ends."

"A year!" Mia replied. "Then you suspect Maeve and Elisabeth of subversion and espionage."

"Only one of them is involved."

"Which one?"

"That, we shall discuss in due course."

"Why did you bring me to Honfleur?" Mia asked.

The cat jumped onto the chair next to her and stretched out on the cushion, unconcerned about the change in his environment.

"There are so many reasons," her companion replied. "We had to go somewhere I knew, and where we could be undetected. Also, I have some personal things to take care of that I have been putting off for far too long."

"Who is Monsieur Bellamy?"

"That is a story I will tell you tomorrow," she replied. "For now, we must get some rest."

She led Mia upstairs into a room overlooking a pond with a four-poster bed and a desk and chair.

"I'm assuming I can trust you," she said to Mia as she took linens out of a cupboard.

"Of course, Madame."

"However, in the meantime, the jewels will be put into a safe." Madame pulled a feather pillow from the cupboard and handed it to Mia. "We'll be up early. Be ready to take a walk."

It was a fitful night's sleep. Mia tossed and turned throughout the night, wondering what was going to happen. She was tempted to look for the safe while Madame Fournier slept, but she had no way of getting inside it. Even if she did get her hands on the diamonds, there was nowhere to go. Soon, both the government and the Alliance would fan out from Paris to track her down. What should have been the most exciting experience of her life had turned into the deadliest. Long before dawn, she was sitting up, staring out the window, wondering if they could stay in the safety of this large estate, where no one would think to look. She couldn't go back to Rousseau, nor would she ever model again. And if the government began to investigate her, they would find the hundred thousand dollars that had been deposited into her bank account, which implicated her in ways she couldn't even fathom.

At six o'clock, there was a light rap on her door. "Are you up?"

"Yes, Madame."

"Good. Let's make breakfast together."

Mia made the tea while Madame cooked eggs and sliced bread, spreading a thick layer of butter on top. The cat had been fed and had commandeered a laundry basket sitting in the corner, which was preferable to the cold tile floor.

"What will happen to Madame Bernard?" Mia asked when Chantal sat across from her at the large farmhouse table.

"I've contacted her daughter, who is coming to get her today," Madame Fournier said. "She is not able to live on her own any longer."

"I'm glad," Mia answered. "But that leaves another question. What is going to happen to us?"

"We're driving into town and taking a walk," Chantal replied.

A quarter hour later, they had arrived at the Honfleur dock. Madame Fournier led her to an area where fishermen had set up barrels to display their catch. The sky was overcast, and the wind had picked up. Even at that early hour, it was a busy scene.

"The docks are a special place for me," Chantal said. "I used to come here every Thursday to get fish for supper."

"It looks like an Impressionist painting," Mia replied.

"You are correct. Many impressionists have painted in Honfleur," her companion replied. "Monet, Pissarro, Renoir. But that's not the reason I love it. I met the man I would fall in love with on these docks."

"Monsieur Fournier," Mia replied.

"No," Chantal answered. "Monsieur Bellamy. I was a young, pregnant, newly married woman when I met him."

"Madame!" Mia said, surprised.

"It's not what you think," Madame answered. "We never spoke of our feelings, not once. Then my husband died fifteen years ago, and we began to write letters."

"Why did you leave Honfleur?"

"My sons were being difficult," she said, shrugging. "I was done letting a man run my life, no matter who it was. I had to live on my own terms for a while."

Mia watched the boats bobble on the water below. "But now you're back."

"We none of us know how much time we have left," Chantal said. "I've decided to spend what is left of mine with the man I love."

"What will your sons say?"

"I love them, of course, but it doesn't matter what they think. One must do what is right for oneself."

"But what about your work for the government?"

"My dear, what more can they ask of me? I have provided evidence to them for twelve long months. There are others equally willing to be of service to their government."

"That explains why you are here," Mia said. "But I still don't understand. How did you find the jewels? What do you intend to do about them?"

For a moment, Madame Fournier didn't speak. Mia watched as she looked out over the river at the vessels that arrived in the harbor. It was a perfect morning. The sun was shining, and the activity on the boats and in the harbor attested to life that would go on far longer than anyone there at that moment. Ropes slapped against the side of the boats; barrels were dragged out onto the pier. The murmur of conversation was bandied about on the wind. She reached into her coat and drew out the scarf. For a terrifying moment, Mia thought she was going to throw the Cartier diamonds into the sea.

"All of your questions have answers," Madame Fournier replied. "However, I am not the one to give them to you."

Mia looked up, suddenly aware that someone was approaching. She took a step back when she realized it was Philip, watching him stride across the pier with a confident step, as if he had never been gone. She didn't even notice Madame walk away, only aware of the look on his face as he came near.

He hadn't forgotten her. He had trusted her to deal with whatever came her way. And from the look in his eye, she could see he was about to ask her to trust him once again.

# 30

---

"What are you doing here?" Mia demanded. She took a deep breath, vacillating between relief and anger.

Philip didn't immediately reply. She held the scarf of diamonds in her hands, weighing her options.

"I needed you yesterday," she said, anger finally boiling up to the surface. "I'm implicated in a murder."

"And you disposed of the murder weapon," he parried. "Quite neatly, too. Where did you come up with that one?"

"First tell me how you found me."

"Do you plan to give me the diamonds?" he asked.

Mia shrugged. "I'm thinking about it. First, you have to explain everything."

"I followed the diamonds," he replied. "They were fitted with a tracking device by the government. As a matter of fact, I was only one train behind you. I just barely missed the one you were on, but I knew you were with Chantal and that you wouldn't leave her sight as long as she had the jewels in her possession."

"Philip, you need to tell me what's going on. Who was Emil Wachter? Why did Luca kill him? And where have you been all this time?"

Philip cocked his head, indicating a spot farther down the pier, where there was a bench overlooking the water. "Come on. We need more privacy than this."

Mia glanced around to make certain they weren't being followed. Instead of going to the bench, he walked to the railing and looked out over the water.

"It's nice here," he said. "I can see why Madame Fournier likes it."

"You owe me answers. Stop stalling."

"Sit down," he said. "This is going to take a while."

Mia sat down next to him, leaving as much room on the bench between them as she could. She couldn't forgive him for leaving her alone when she needed him most.

"Start with Versailles," she insisted.

Philip shook his head. "It started long before Versailles. You know that I am an agent with the United States government. As you know, it came to our attention that Marcel Rousseau or his director, Theo Gillette, was using the fashion house to gather and send information to foreign agents on behalf of the Soviet Union and their satellite countries. Their aim was to break the deadlock in the Cold War and get their hands on sensitive nuclear information."

"Which is why Rousseau was sending me out with cryptic messages that I didn't understand." She looked down at her hands. "I thought it was innocent, Philip. I really did."

"Which is why you cooperated with us when we asked for your help." He crossed his arms.

"It doesn't make sense, you know. The coded messages, the assignments. Yours, theirs. I've been doing it all blind."

Philip leaned back on the bench. "The less you know, the safer you are."

"Why was I abducted that day? You've never explained it, and you haven't explained how you were there."

"You were being watched by more than one party," he said, touching his nose. "Chantal Fournier, for one. Others whom you haven't seen, on both sides. The day you were taken, we had a man shadowing you. Unfortunately, in this line of work, you're in danger more than you're not. When the Alliance got their hands on you, our man on the inside gave me a call so that we could get you out. He convinced them that you weren't important enough to bother with and couldn't offer them any real information."

"I hope that's true." She held out the scarf that contained the diamonds, and he took it, placing it in his bag. She didn't want them anymore.

"You were still useful to us, but when Rousseau decided to use you to represent the house with the Cartier diamonds, you were once again a target. Even though Rousseau is a front for the Alliance, there are many different factions all trying to get their hands on that necklace. I'm surprised one of them didn't kill you to get them."

Mia took a deep breath. "It was terrifying having a million dollars around my neck. It felt like every eye in the world was on me that evening. So, who was Emil Wachter, and why was he killed?"

"Emil was precisely who he said he was, a Liechtenstein diplomat. He was also working with the U.S. government against the Alliance. It was his job to keep an eye on you during the event. We were sure they would go after the diamonds. Do you remember when I told you about the chip that contained nuclear information?"

"Yes, but—"

"That chip was attached to the Cartier necklace. The Alliance was alerted to the fact in the hope that they would make a play for it that evening."

Mia gasped. "You knowingly put me in danger?"

"You're in danger, no matter how you look at it. You were passing information meant for Soviet ears, which makes you a spy against the United States government. When you agreed to help us, you were in danger of being found out." He looked out over the river at the boats bobbling on the surface of the water. "There are some roads in life you can't get around, Mia. You have to go through them to get to the other side."

"But they didn't get the necklace, so what happens now?"

"You're going to give it to them."

"What?" Mia asked, shocked.

"You are going back to Paris and you're going to march into Marcel Rousseau's office to give him the diamonds. You're going to say you took them."

"Why would I take them?" she asked, incredulous. "Someone put something in my drink, and I felt ill. When I woke up, they were gone. Then, as we were leaving, Emil Wachter handed me the bag with the diamonds in it. How am I supposed to explain this to Monsieur Rousseau?"

"I'll give you the story you're going to tell them."

"You're trying to get me killed."

His face softened. "Trust me. We know what we're doing. I wouldn't let anything happen to you."

"The record begs to differ." She took a deep breath. "How did you enlist Madame Fournier?"

"She was perfectly placed to collaborate with the French government when she was chosen, at least a year before you arrived on the scene. No one is going to notice the movements of a seventy-year-old woman."

"She's going to stay in Honfleur."

"Good," he replied. "That's the best place for her right now."

"If what you're saying is true, it leaves me more vulnerable than ever. She got me out of Paris after the shooting. How is Luca involved? Why did he kill Wachter?"

"No one expected Luca Rossi to show up that evening at

Versailles. Security was tight, but Gillette and Rousseau somehow got him through, obviously to keep an eye on you. Was he present when Wachter gave you the bag of diamonds?"

"No," Mia answered. "Several people were there when I was being searched, but I didn't see Luca until I was taken outside to the car."

"I believe he was there to discover what, if any, role Wachter played in the evening's events. After your car left, Wachter was followed. Now we know it must have been Rossi."

"That doesn't explain why Wachter was in Luca's apartment, or why he was killed."

"Wachter was a double agent," Philip said. "He was caught by the Alliance, and they decided to do away with him."

"If you're expecting me to walk into Rousseau and tell them I took the diamonds, without knowing what will happen to me, you've lost your mind. What will they do to me? And what will happen to the diamonds?"

"You're going to give them to Rousseau and tell him he can trust you. He won't, of course, but he'll be so relieved to get his hands on them, he won't care."

"This is a huge mistake, Philip."

"Believe it or not, the mission was a success," he said. "For one thing, we've been able to identify some of the Alliance players, and now we're going to crack the entire ring."

"I'm not sure I can do this."

"You can. You're going to tell Rousseau he can trust you."

"After I stole the most valuable necklace in the world."

"First, I want you to tell me exactly what happened when you went to Luca's apartment," he ordered. "Why did you go in the first place?"

"I wanted answers," she replied. "You'd gone AWOL, and I wanted to know why Luca was there that night. I thought he had probably been asked to be another pair of eyes on the diamonds to make sure we got them back safely. But, of course, I wasn't sure."

"What happened when you arrived?"

"He tried to get rid of me. I was only there for a minute before I realized someone was there with him. I thought it was one of the other models."

"And then?"

"A door opened, and Emil came out," Mia replied. "He was pointing a gun at me. But he had given me a look when he handed me the bag the night before. I was certain he was on our side. Then Luca began to argue with him, and before I knew it, there was a scuffle and Wachter was shot. Luca handed me the gun and told me to get rid of it. I didn't know what to do."

"That explains one thing," Philip said. "Luca was definitely there to keep an eye on Wachter. I'd bet every dime I have that Emil was onto him and went to talk to him, to convince him he was with the Alliance. When he heard that you had entered the apartment, he drew his gun with the intention of getting you out of there, whether he pretended to be a strong arm for the Alliance or not."

"He died trying to save me, then," she murmured. "But why did Luca ask me to get rid of the gun?"

"Either he trusted you or he used it as a way of finding out what you'd do." Philip crossed his arms. "That's why you did the right thing, Mia. As far as they're concerned, you protected Luca and didn't run to the authorities. If you had, you would have been eliminated as soon as possible. That buys us time and will strengthen the argument that you had a plot of your own going on regarding the diamonds."

"I hate this," she remarked.

"We'll get through it," he said. "Nothing lasts forever."

"Are you sure?"

"Come with me," he said, standing. "We have things to talk over."

# 31

---

"You made coffee," Mia said the next morning as she came into the kitchen.

"I did," Philip answered. He took down two cups from the dresser and proceeded to pour one, handing it to her.

"It's better than Maeve's witch's brew," she observed after tasting it. "That stuff can kill you."

They had talked long into the night, joined at times by Chantal, who brought them cups of tea and sandwiches by the fire before returning to her tête-à-tête with Raphaël in the kitchen, each of them making their own plans.

The kitchen was Mia's favorite spot in France. It was a large room, once meant for a bevy of servants and cooks, and later home to Chantal's family, which she managed with a smaller staff. Mia couldn't help comparing the estate to the flat Chantal had chosen in Paris, marveling that the same woman could be as comfortable in three small rooms as in a manor house. She wanted to know more about her neighbor, but this wasn't the time to ask.

"Good morning," Chantal said, when she arrived in the kitchen, Raphaël behind her.

"Good morning," Mia replied, wondering what would happen to them all now.

Raphaël made eggs for breakfast, and the four of them sat at the table in the kitchen together, talking only of the weather, the long summer ahead, and Beau, who had taken to his new home as if he had always lived there. Anything but the matter at hand. It was a relief. Philip had drilled her for hours on their next series of moves, and at the end, there was nothing left to say except goodbye.

"A car will be here for you in a few minutes," Philip told her as they cleared away the dishes. "The driver is Armand. He will take you to the place where your journey begins."

"You're not coming," she stated.

"I am, but you won't see me again for a while," he replied. "Don't forget what I told you."

"Come with me, my dear," Chantal told her. "We have to get you ready."

They went upstairs to the room where Mia had spent the night, and Chantal had draped strange clothes across the bed for her. Mia changed into them quickly and turned to the older woman when she had finished.

"Will I see you again?" she asked.

"Of course," Chantal replied crisply. "Things will look much different to you when today is finally over."

Chantal, who had seemed so remote for the last year, had been ensuring her safety the entire time. So many things she hadn't understood had been made clear over the past few hours. It was hard to take it all in.

They went downstairs, where Philip walked her out to the car that had pulled up in front of the house.

"This is Armand," Philip said. "He'll be driving you back to Paris."

Mia nodded at the driver and got into the car. Philip leaned toward the open window for a moment and then nodded, tapping on the top of the vehicle to signal to the driver that it was time to leave. As the car pulled away from the house, she resolved to return one day when all of this was over, to sit in that kitchen with them once more. If, indeed, this was ever going to be over.

As the villages of Normandy and then Île-de-France appeared and passed from view, Mia thought about everything she had discussed with Philip, rehearsing her lines in her head again and again. The plain shift dress she wore was a size too large. It had been purchased in Honfleur along with an out-of-fashion tapestry bag with the jewels placed inside. Everything was chosen with the intent to not attract attention to herself.

Armand let her off in an unfamiliar area of Paris, at the Nanterre

Ville Métro Station, where she took the underground as instructed to the Réamur Sébastopol. Philip had given her an address and a key, which she removed from her handbag. The building was close to the station, an unassuming residential block with no front desk, no concierge, and no traffic. She let herself in and took the stairs to the fifth floor, where she let herself into the small flat. It was tidy and clean but clearly unoccupied. The only personal possessions in the place belonged to her. Her blue Jackie Kennedy suit, a high-necked silk button-down blouse, the matching pillbox hat, her best pair of heels, her gloves, her white handbag, even her undergarments. One perfect outfit for the most difficult task of her life.

She changed clothes slowly, transferring the diamond jewels to their hiding place. Then she folded the borrowed clothes and shoes, tucking them into the tapestry tote and placed it by the door. Making a final sweep of the apartment to make certain nothing was left behind, she took a deep breath, lifted the tapestry bag, and locked the door behind her. She went back down the three flights of stairs and out the back door, where she tossed the bag of borrowed clothes into a bin. Two blocks down the road, she spied a window box full of flowers and casually stopped in front of it, pretending to admire them. As she leaned in to smell the miniature roses, she removed a glove and pressed the key into the soil.

"Taxi!" she called when she spotted one on the next street.

She couldn't take the Métro in her best suit, at a time like this. The driver skidded to a halt when he saw her, and she folded her long legs into the back seat, giving him the address for the House of Rousseau. It took half an hour to get to the fashion house, and when they arrived, she opened her bag, finding several bills folded neatly in her wallet. She extracted three of them and got out in front of the tall elegant doors of the House of Rousseau. Taking a deep breath, she settled her handbag over her arm and walked in with all the poise she could muster.

Heads turned when she went through the lobby to the main office, but she ignored them, walking directly to Monsieur Rousseau's office.

"Miss Walker!" Marcel Rousseau exclaimed when she walked through the door. He stood at once, his height and girth making him even more formidable than usual. His voice was loud enough to attract Theo's attention in his own office down the hall, and a minute later, he rushed into the room as well, looking from one of them to the other.

"Where have you been, Mia?" Theo demanded.

"I wasn't certain I had a job any longer," she said smoothly. She had the urge to remove her gloves, but of course, she couldn't—not yet. "I needed some time to think."

"Close the door, Theo," Monsieur instructed, coming around the desk.

She turned to face the two of them, who were obviously wondering what gall she had to come strolling in after two days and stand in front of them like she belonged there.

"Speaking of your job, I'm not certain you do," Theo replied, having gotten over the shock of her sudden appearance.

"I have something you want," she told them.

The two men looked at each other.

Marcel Rousseau broke the silence. "Which is?"

Mia didn't answer. Instead, she unbuttoned the top five buttons of her blouse, while they watched in astonishment. Then she pulled it open, hearing them both gasp. From her throat dangled the Cartier diamonds, glistening as brightly as they had on the night she had worn them to Versailles.

Theo was the first to recover. "What are you doing with those diamonds?"

"I brought them to you," she answered.

"How did you get them?" Rousseau demanded.

"I walked out of Versailles, holding them in my hand."

"Impossible," he snapped. "Raoul was there. He said you were searched down to your undergarments."

"That's true," she admitted. "Nevertheless, someone handed my bag to me right in front of him, and the diamonds were inside. When we came back that evening, your only concern was for the condition of the dress and the implications about the loss of the diamonds. I had them around my neck when I walked out of this building."

A flash of anger came over Theo's face. "Why didn't you give them to us then if you had them? Why bring them back now? Surely you're savvy enough to figure out how to sell them on the black market."

"They're not mine to sell," she answered. "The Alliance wants them, you know. And who is better placed to get it to them than you?"

Marcel Rousseau shook his head, trying to comprehend what she was saying. "I see you realize the stakes, Miss Walker, but I don't understand why you would bring them to us. If you're aware of the Alliance, you know there is a chain of command, and there are others who want them even more than we do."

"That may be true," she conceded. "But who else could I trust?"

Theo went over to the bar in the corner and poured himself a scotch, downing it in one gulp. Then he turned to Rousseau, who nodded. Gillette poured two more glasses, handing one to his employer.

"This is more than just the most expensive necklace in the world," Mia said.

"What do you mean?" Theo asked.

"As you know, there's a microchip hidden in this necklace. It needs to get into the right hands."

Rousseau eyed her for a long moment. "And whose hands are those specifically, Miss Walker?"

"That's what I'm counting on you to know."

There was silence for a full minute as they mulled what to do. Eventually, her employer turned to her and nodded.

"Your loyalty to Rousseau is commendable, young lady." He gave a slight cough. "May I have the necklace now?"

"What's going to happen to me, gentlemen?" she asked without moving.

"Your position here is assured, my dear. You have made the right decision." He went to his desk and picked up the phone. "Luca, we need you here in ten minutes to drive Miss Walker."

Mia watched as he replaced the phone in its cradle. Theo set his glass on the console and came over to unfasten the necklace. It was an eerie sensation, having his hands around her neck and feeling the heavy jewels being lifted from her throat. She swallowed, trying to keep her breathing calm. As Theo removed the necklace, Marcel Rousseau took out a swath of black velvet fabric, setting it on his desk. Mia watched as Theo took the jewels and arranged them on the velvet. The three of them stared at it for a few moments, each knowing they would never see it again once it left this room.

Theo put his arm around Mia, running his hand along her waist. She resisted the urge to move away, aware it wasn't merely an inappropriate gesture. He was checking to see if she was armed or wearing a listening device.

"Let me walk you downstairs," he said, reaching over to pick up her bag, opening the clasp and inspecting the contents before handing it back to her. "You understand, I had to check."

Mia nodded and went to the door, feeling his presence just two steps behind her. She had hoped he would let her walk out of the building on her own now that they had the necklace. If he didn't accompany her out of the building, she could tell Luca she felt like walking home instead, per Philip's plan. She wanted nothing more than to disappear. She had returned the diamonds, which was her primary task. However, the familiar Citroën came into view just as she and Theo exited the building. He took hold of her arm and escorted her to the vehicle, reaching out to open the door of the back seat when the car came to a stop.

She had no choice. If possible, she would bolt whenever traffic brought the car to a stop. Whatever happened, she couldn't let Luca take her back to her flat. As she bent down to get in the car, she realized someone else was sitting in the back seat. Elisabeth smiled at her as she got in, and a feeling of relief came over her.

"Theo said you were in the hospital with stomach pains after the Versailles dinner," Elisabeth said, reaching out to touch her on the arm. "I was afraid it was appendicitis."

"It wasn't, thank goodness," Mia replied as Theo shut the door and waved them from the curb. "Just a false alarm."

"It's the worst time of year to get sick, with the season heating up," Elisabeth said. "I'm glad you're feeling better."

Mia nodded. "I just need to rest for a couple of days. You know, sip tea and read magazines."

"Then that's what we'll do," her roommate assured her.

Luca was silent as he drove through the streets, and Mia glanced up at the sky, which was overcast and dreary. Of course it would rain when she was in her best suit, although that was the least of her problems. Luca turned down the next couple of streets and then onto one where she had never been before.

"Where are we going?" Mia asked, trying not to let the concern seep into her voice.

"I just have to make one stop," Luca replied, avoiding her gaze in the rearview mirror.

"I was hoping to get out of these clothes," she continued. "I want a hot bath and a very long nap."

"And after that, I'll get you that soup from Agnelli's that you like so much," Elisabeth said. "That will make you feel better."

Luca turned the car down a side street and went down a few blocks, turning in at an alley. He got out of the car and came around to open Mia's door.

"Do you mind if I just wait here?" she asked, relieved that Theo had given her a reason to avoid going anywhere with him.

"Just come in for a minute," he said.

"I really don't feel like it, Luca."

"There's a chair inside where you can rest," he argued. "It's far more comfortable than sitting in this cramped car."

She turned and looked at Elisabeth, who nodded. "Let's go. He's not taking no for an answer."

The three of them went inside the building, and Luca pressed the button for the elevator. Mia thought about not following the two of them into the lift, but Luca stayed behind her, and they all got in when the doors opened.

There were eight floors in the building, and although Mia was behind Elisabeth in the small elevator, she could see that Luca pressed the button for the eighth. No one spoke as the doors closed and they began to ascend. The elevator opened onto a dimly lit floor, and Luca stepped aside, making sure Mia and Elisabeth got off first. He pressed the button for the ground floor and waited until the doors closed.

There was no light in the room apart from the windows at the far side of the room. He walked them over to a door, which he opened with a key. Inside was a steep flight of stone steps, leading, Mia realized, to the roof.

"Let's go," he said.

"What are you doing?" she said, turning to him. "You don't want to ruin your life, Luca. It's not too late to stop this."

"Do as you're told," he growled.

"You could get right back in your car and head to Italy," she insisted. "You'd be with your family within hours. Trust me, if you do this, you're making a big mistake."

Luca pulled out a gun and aimed it at her. Then he waved toward the staircase.

"Upstairs, both of you."

Mia and Elisabeth went up the stairs and opened the door to the roof, where she scrambled up to assess the situation. They were eight floors aboveground in a business district. There were no trees to block a fall, and although there were stairs leading down the side of the building, they were narrow and completely vertical. It would be nearly impossible to escape. Besides, Luca had a gun. Even if she could scale down an eight-story building, she couldn't dodge a bullet from a gun aimed directly at her.

"Why are you doing this?" she asked, looking Luca squarely in the eye.

"Orders, of course," he replied.

"Let Elisabeth go, at least," she said. "She hasn't done anything."

No one spoke for a moment, and then Luca began advancing toward her, the gun still aimed at her chest. She took two steps back, and he nodded.

"That's right," he said. "Keep going."

She took a few more steps back, her eyes never leaving the gun.

"Almost there," he remarked. "I'll get a bonus for this."

"I brought the Cartier necklace back to Rousseau," she said. "And trust me, Luca, if I'm dispensable, so are you. He's using you to erase the evidence. You're going to lose everything if you do. Even your life."

"This is just an accident, Mia," he said. "A curious girl peers off the edge of a tall building and leans out just a little too far. But it doesn't matter anyway, because there's a bomb that will detonate in the next few minutes, and when your body is found, it will look like peripheral damage from the blast."

"Elisabeth," she said, turning to her friend. "Talk some sense into him."

"I can't, Mia. It's for your own good."

Mia stared at her roommate. "But I thought Maeve—"

"You were wrong," Elisabeth replied. "Maeve has nothing to do with this. She never has."

"Jump, Mia," Luca ordered. "You'll never know what happened."

She stood rooted to the spot.

"How did you get involved?" she asked Elisabeth, ignoring Luca entirely.

"The same as you," Elisabeth answered. "Although, frankly, I believe in the Alliance and all that it stands for."

"Sweden was neutral during the war."

"A mistake that will have long-term repercussions, in my opinion."

"You can't get out of this, Mia," Luca said. "None of us can. I have to do what I can for the sake of my future."

"What you're saying is, it's nothing personal," she replied. "My death doesn't matter. None of it matters as long as you get what you want."

He took another step closer. She lunged at him, grabbing his arm. Shocked, he pulled back, and they wrestled for control of the gun. Then he reached out and slapped her so hard, she was knocked to the ground. In one deft movement, she reached for the Beretta M 1951 that was strapped to her inner thigh, the one that Theo had missed when he tried to frisk her. She aimed it at Luca's chest and pulled the trigger, knowing she wouldn't have a second chance.

He stumbled back, dropping his gun as they all froze. A second later, he brought a hand to his chest and touched the spot where the bullet had entered his chest, and then shook his head before falling forward onto the ground. Mia dragged herself to her feet as Elisabeth lunged toward Luca's gun. Her roommate, whom she had considered the most beautiful of the models, grabbed it and rolled over onto her back, trying desperately to aim it at Mia. However, Mia lifted her pistol, hoping she would back away. Instead, Elisabeth came at her. With her heart in her throat, she raised the gun and shot her, shuddering as Elisabeth fell back and went still.

Dropping the gun, she ran to her side, letting out a cry when she realized Elisabeth was dead. She had never believed she was capable of killing someone, let alone someone she cared about. Mia blinked back the tears that were threatening to fall. She didn't know what to do now, but she was running out of time.

Mia ran over to the door of the building, only to find it was locked. Knowing there was a bomb set to go off, she dropped onto the ground next to Luca's lifeless body and searched for a key. However, she couldn't find it. She walked to the side of the building, evaluating the fire escape stairs. She felt dizzy just looking at them. Kicking off her shoes, she wiped her clammy hands on her suit. She put a foot on the rungs, willing herself not to look down. She couldn't wonder how much time she had before the bomb detonated or what she would find at the end of the stairs. She marshaled all her energy into one infinitesimal movement at a time, trying not to die from a fall onto the hard pavement eight stories below. It didn't matter that Luca had tried to kill her or that Elisabeth had wanted to finish the job he couldn't complete. It only mattered that she take slow, deep breaths and inch her way down the side of this building, one terrifying second at a time.

# 32

---

Mia edged her way down the narrow fire escape ladder as quickly as she could. She knew it didn't extend all the way to the ground, but she couldn't tell how far it went. However, she had no choice but to keep going. Inside this building was a ticking bomb that would soon blow the entire block sky high. Her knees were scraped and bleeding, but she kept going. She was more than halfway down when she reached down with her foot to place it on the next rung and found she had run out of ladder. Trying not to panic, she assessed the situation.

She was approximately three stories above ground. Although the ladder had ended, there was a fire escape platform the next floor down. Mia looked to the left and the right, wishing someone would come along who could help, but the only sound to be heard was the flapping wings of ravens in the distance. There were windows to both the left and the right, neither close enough to reach from the ladder.

No help was coming, and she had run out of time. She pulled herself down as far as she could and let go, dropping onto the platform below.

She landed hard, wrenching the platform to the left and right for a minute before it finally stopped moving. Her breath was ragged as she pulled herself up to a sitting position. Her right knee and ankle had taken the brunt of the fall, but nothing appeared to be broken. She had another story to go and leaned over the platform, trying to gauge which way to lean. If she went left, she would land on the hard pavement. Bones would be broken; there would be no walking away from it when the bomb went off. On the right, however, were the remains of an old garden bed with ancient straggly boxwood hedges. She took a deep breath and jumped, landing in a tangle of bush.

She immediately felt a piercing pain in her left side, possibly a broken rib, and her left arm was suddenly numb and hanging at an odd angle. Despite the pain, she stood and began to move as quickly as she could away from the building. She had barely rounded the corner when she heard the bomb go off. The explosion shook the ground like an earthquake, and she was knocked to the ground, causing her to cry out. As she did, a huge of plume of smoke and ashes rose into the air.

She could smell the fire before she saw it. Still, no one came running. The darkened sky didn't aid them with a drop of rain. Mia stood on the street in her bare feet, with cuts and bruises all over her body, cradling her left arm in her right. She dragged herself down the street and then another until someone finally spotted her and came running. Before she knew it, she was being loaded into an ambulance and taken to the nearest hospital.

She was admitted with a broken arm and two broken ribs, along with dozens of cuts and contusions. Word of the explosion had gotten out and it was assumed by the hospital staff that she had barely gotten out of the building with her life, the only way to explain the fact that she was found wandering near the area with no shoes and no identification. As far as the officials were concerned, she was a victim of a mysterious local bombing. Her wounds were cleaned and dressed, and after X-rays were taken, her arm was set in a long cast, from her fingertips to her upper arm. She would have called Philip but had no idea how to reach him. She thought about calling Maeve, but that, too, wasn't possible, certainly not as long as she didn't have an official story to tell her roommate.

When she awoke, Philip was sitting in a chair pulled up next to her bed, watching her.

"You're awake," he remarked. "I would have brought you flowers, but I rushed over to make sure you were all right."

"Am I?" she asked, giving him a look, wishing the morphine would start to dull the pain.

"You're alive, Mia, and that counts as all right in my book. Actually, you're lucky it wasn't much worse."

"It would have been if I'd fallen off that building."

"You're very resourceful, when it comes down to it."

"I didn't have a choice." She tried to move, touching her bandaged side as she shifted position. "Tell me what happened."

"What do you want to know?" he asked.

"Why did they blow up the building?" she asked.

"After losing the necklace, and the valuable microchip, they correctly surmised that their mission was compromised," Philip answered. "The Paris branch of the Alliance was based there. Before you happened into their offices, Rousseau and Gillette had planned to destroy the building to conceal their involvement with foreign governments. When you arrived, it would have meant a different course of action, but by then it was too late to stop their plan. They decided that they might as well be rid of Luca, Elisabeth, and you as a way of burying the evidence. If you hadn't returned, they would have decided to lie low and then start up again next year with another recruit or two. Instead, you brought them what they thought they wanted, and they saw it as their chance to finish what they started."

"What do you mean, 'what they thought they wanted'?" she asked.

"They wanted the Cartier diamonds and the microchip."

"Which I gave them."

"No," Philip said, shaking his head. "You gave them the decoy necklace. The 'chip' implanted in it was merely a listening device."

"It was a fake!" she exclaimed. "You let me walk right into their offices with a fake! What if they had realized it?"

"You didn't, and you were one of the few people who has ever seen it close up."

"What's going to happen to Theo and Monsieur Rousseau?"

"The Sûreté swooped in to arrest them."

"The Sûreté?"

"The criminal investigation branch of the Paris Police Department."

"What happened to the real Cartier necklace, or was I wearing the fake when we went to Versailles? Has none of this been real?"

"No, you were wearing the real thing that evening. The fake could never have caught the eye of so many people. Emil Wachter and his team made the switch, giving you the substitute necklace in the bag when you left that evening."

"What do you mean?" she asked. "Was he the one who put something in my drink?"

Philip nodded. "He was, indeed. It was his job to make the switch, with the aid of the woman posing as an attendant in the powder room. He put something in your champagne, causing you to have to feel dizzy, and she was a member of the French Police. She took the necklace, hid it in her uniform, and slipped away without ever being questioned. Wachter substituted the necklace and gave it to you. We needed you to have it to convince Rousseau and Gillette that you had something they wanted."

Mia frowned. "Did it really have a microchip in it?"

"No," he replied. "There was a chip made for it, but it was never put into the necklace. In fact, the man who created it has been arrested and is awaiting charges."

"They might have brought down the Paris headquarters, but

they haven't brought down the entire Alliance. What's going to happen now?"

Philip nodded. "It's true, there are bad actors all over the world, trying to get their hands on nuclear information. However, as I said before, we were able to identify many people involved in the scheme and managed to have taken out their main center of operations in Europe. It will take years to put it all together again, assuming they can recruit at the same level as they did after the war."

"I still have so many questions."

"Such as?"

"Who was Madame Laurent?"

"She is better known as Sylvie Gillette."

"She's Theo's wife?" Mia exclaimed. "But I was in his flat and there was no sign of it being shared with a woman."

"That was his pied-à-terre in Paris," Philip answered. "The two of them own a house in the sixth arrondissement. She wasn't really there to help acclimate you to France. She was the first tier in a system of deciding which girls to recruit to assist them with passing information."

"You mean, she saw a flaw in me that caused her to believe I would turn against my own government?"

"Don't look at it like that," Philip cautioned. "I'd say she was looking for trusting young women who were separated from everyone they knew. She didn't have any idea how smart and resourceful you would prove to be."

"I don't feel so smart and resourceful," she said, trying to lift the heavy cast.

"The fact that you survived this day is a testament to it."

The next three days were spent in the hospital. Sitting in a quiet room in a clean bed, even with bland food brought on trays felt like heaven. Philip visited twice, bringing her a small bouquet of flowers on his second trip, but he hadn't been able to stay long, and nothing was said about what happened between them.

On the third day, there was a knock on the door, and Maeve entered, carrying a small bag.

"Are you up for visitors?" her roommate asked.

"Come in," Mia replied, trying to sit up. "I'm glad to see you. It's been far too quiet the last couple of days."

"Well, you were involved in an explosion," Maeve answered. "You were due for a little quiet."

She set the case down beside the door and pulled up a chair. She looked worried and worn.

"Are you all right?" Mia asked.

"I've received a visit from the French government, as you can imagine. I'm sure you already know that Elisabeth and Luca were involved in some sort of scheme. Even Monsieur Rousseau and Theo are involved. I don't understand what happened."

Mia knew it wasn't her place to tell her. "What are you going to do?"

"I'm getting you ready to fly home tomorrow, and then I'm packing my bags and heading back to Dublin. The House of Rousseau is closed until further notice."

"What will you do when you get there?" Mia asked.

Maeve shrugged. "I have choices. I can get a job, or even go and stay with my cousin in London. She's got connections. I just can't believe Elisabeth is dead. I went home with her, you know. I met her family. They're going to be devastated."

"We're all devastated."

"Come on," Maeve said. "Enough of this misery. Let's get you changed into some real clothes and break you out of here."

"Thank you, Maeve," Mia replied.

"The only thing we can do is try to put this all behind us."

The next morning, Mia packed her belongings with Maeve's help, taking extra care with the framed photo of her parents and her father's pocket watch. The file of clippings was the last to go into the case. Mia couldn't bear to open it. It once represented all the promise of the future. Now it was a reminder of the tragic events of the last few days. Sighing, she dressed and went down the street to her favorite café, where Philip was waiting. After they ordered lunch, they sat, stirring sugar into their coffee.

"What are you going to do now?" he asked.

She glanced down at the cast on her arm.

"Nothing much, until this heals," she admitted. "Although I know what happens after that. I'm going to put in an application for college."

"That's great," he said, nodding. "Although I'm a little surprised. Are you sure you don't want to try to get work in one of the other fashion houses?"

"No," she said, shaking her head. "I've had all of the fashion I can take for a while."

"Where are you going to apply?" he asked.

"I'm going to try to get into NYU," she replied. "I want to go back home, where things are familiar. I've even written a letter to the bakery where I worked, asking if I can have my old job back."

"You worked as an agent for the federal government, you know," he said. "And in case you don't recall, a sum of money was deposited in your account to help you transition to the next phase of your life."

"I don't know what to say," she murmured.

"There's nothing to say," he answered. "We just want you to be able to get on with the rest of your life. Do something good with it, Mia. You've earned it."

"What about you, Philip?"

"You know me," he said, shrugging. "I'm never too far away."

"I should know better than to ask you questions. You never answer them."

"This case is wrapping up. Lives were lost, but that was unavoidable. We managed to thwart one of the biggest Cold War threats since World War II. I may have to take an extended vacation. I'm way overdue."

"I don't like to think of you in harm's way," Mia said.

"Nor I you," he answered. "Come on. We need to have lunch, because in about two hours, you have a plane to catch."

# 33

---

Four years had passed since Philip had been in France, four long years of sitting behind a desk in DC like a regular working stiff, although he never got the case out of his mind. Not every federal agent gets the chance to have a role in bringing down an entity like the Alliance, intent on stealing nuclear secrets in a quest for world domination. He knew there would never be another event like that during his career, but he was fine with it. He had served his country in other ways, glad that he'd had the opportunity to be at the center of one truly big case that safeguarded democracy and freedom in the Western world.

In the intervening years, he often wondered about Mia Walker. Of course, he knew precisely where she was, at New York University, getting a double major in psychology and political science, a girl after his own heart. He kept loose tabs on her, of course; he checked with NYU admissions from time to time to make sure she was still pursuing her degrees, nothing more serious than that. He didn't know where she lived—although he could have found out easily—but after such a high-profile case, he realized some things are better left unknown. She'd served her country and deserved the right to build a life of her own.

No doubt she was doing all the things normal college students did, like dating a steady stream of eligible young men and making friends, that is, if she were able to trust anyone again. They had all used her in one way or another, but Philip hoped she was able to resume a normal life once she left France. He liked to imagine her with her arms full of books, tacking up her grades on a bulletin board behind a desk in her dorm, bent over a desk in the library writing term papers. In other words, having the typical college experience, which she richly deserved.

His own life was something of a mess. He drifted between work and his Georgetown apartment a little aimlessly. Cases were worked on and solved, and he was occasionally loaned out to assist whenever a state government needed federal intervention, but nothing of note occurred. After a couple of years, he began to write a book about stopping a nuclear theft and an assassination attempt during the Cold War. Fiction, of course. No one would ever believe the truth.

He dated off and on. No one really captured his attention like a certain dark-haired model, but that was all right, he figured. Government jobs can be all-consuming, and while his current work wasn't as dangerous as taking down the Alliance, there was enough travel that it justified his staying single. He adopted a dog, a scrawny golden retriever named Sam who became his constant companion and kept him from being too lonely. The two of them lived the bachelor life, content to have each other's company, particularly on weekend mornings when they headed out to their favorite corner coffee shop on O Street. The waiters all knew him and brought him a little something from the kitchen whenever they were there, a scrap of sausage or a slice of bacon. Sam wasn't as scrawny after a few months and filled out nicely, his thick golden fur gleaming in the sun. He liked to lie under his master's chair, keeping a lazy eye out for interlopers, who, of course, never came. Philip ordered coffee and a croissant, the one time a week he let his thoughts drift back to Paris and think about the stunning girl who'd done her part to stop the most dangerous event of the Cold War, the Bay of Pigs notwithstanding. The girl who deserved a normal life after all she'd gone through.

It was September and the weather was still good. Philip and Sam walked several blocks to the coffee shop, stopping along the way to buy a copy of the *Washington Post*. They snagged their favorite table under the elms and Sam crept under the chair, his snout resting on his front paws, doing a very good job of pretending to sleep. Philip couldn't have taught him better himself.

He opened his paper and snapped open the crisp pages, flipping through until he found the sports section. It was interesting, full of stories about the Los Angeles Dodgers, who looked on track to make it to the World Series. He was betting on the Orioles to win the

American League pennant, although the White Sox and the Twins were giving them a run for their money. A light breeze rustled the edges of the paper, and he moved so that it wouldn't land squarely in his coffee, when he realized someone was sitting across the table from him. A woman, in fact. At least, she was now, no longer the girl he had last seen in France four years earlier who was planning to start over.

He folded the paper in an attempt at composure and frowned down at Sam. "Some guard dog you are."

The retriever twitched his ears, unconcerned, and Philip looked back at the woman staring at him. She had a slight smile on her face as if waiting for him to acknowledge her presence, but he waited for a beat, as if she were a mirage and would disappear the moment he spoke.

"You're in Washington," he finally said, stating the obvious.

But surely she hadn't come with the intent to see him, he thought. He represented one of the most stressful times of her life. She had to be visiting and must have noticed him and come over to see what he was doing.

"Yes, I'm in Washington, and I've had my eye on you," she said, dispelling that notion. "I know all your usual haunts. This café, for one, where you like to order croissants smothered in French jam. It reminds you of Paris."

"Too easy," he answered, gesturing at his plate. "You have evidence right in front of you."

"You walked down to the Wharf last night," she continued. "You were leaning against the railing, watching the boats. I imagine you'd like to sail, but you've never made the time. Either that or you were thinking of Honfleur."

"Well," he said, impressed, if nonplussed. "It sounds like you were following me."

"Turnabout is fair play."

"It is, at that," Philip replied, unable to hide his smile. "Is that all?"

"I'd work on my diet, if I were you. You're eating far too much ice cream and not enough vegetables. You should take better care of yourself."

"Who's going to notice?"

"Someone," she replied. "Someone will notice."

"How's your diet?" he asked.

"Terrible," she admitted. "I need someone to notice what I'm eating, too."

"We should do something about this."

"We should probably have dinner tonight," she said. "That way, we can keep an eye on each other. You know, to discourage any bad habits."

Philip nodded. "Where do you want to go?"

"Do you trust me?" she asked.

He laughed, remembering that he had asked her the same question four years earlier.

"I do," he replied.

"Then meet me at the Wharf and I'll take care of you."

"What if you pick something I don't like?" he asked.

"Ah, but you need to try new things once in a while," she answered. She gave him a look. "And for the record, I hope I'm going to be one of those things."

Sam got up at that moment and went over to inspect her more closely. He had good instincts, Sam.

"Seven o'clock?"

Mia nodded. "Seven o'clock. I've missed you, by the way."

"Don't worry," Philip replied, leaning forward to look into the most beautiful eyes he had ever seen. "I'll never let that happen again."

# 1

---

"Dread remorse when you are tempted to err, Miss
Eyre; remorse is the poison of life."

—CHARLOTTE BRONTË, *JANE EYRE*

It had been raining for hours and still a light pattering soaked the
cobbled pavement, fallen leaves swimming in puddles all around.
Alice Campbell walked down Simpson Street in one of the oldest
parts of Cambridge, Massachusetts, not looking left nor right but
straight ahead, waiting for the redbrick building to come into view.
It was a beautiful place, the Cambridge Bookshop, her pride and joy.
Lifting her umbrella, she took it all in: the cherry-red door set at
an angle at the corner; the glossy, black facade and trim; the simple,
faded gilt letters spelling out BOOKS. When she opened the shop,
there hadn't been room to put the entire name on the plaque, leaving

it perhaps a little nondescript. But Alice hadn't minded. The people who were meant to buy her books would find their way inside.

A few titles were exhibited on shelves in the window, newer books that had just come out in the last few years: *The Catcher in the Rye*, *The End of the Affair*, and her favorite, *From Here to Eternity*. The store, however, was located on an unremarkable street without a dress shop or comfortable café nearby, leaving pedestrians to walk past without giving it a second glance. Nor did the titles displayed to passersby reflect the true nature of the bookshop, where both old and new books rested on the somewhat crooked shelves. That, too, did not matter. She had chosen her entire catalog herself. The bookshop and the books in it were her refuge, her life, her mission.

Two windows, also framed in black, were above the shop on the second story, where Alice had made a flat out of an old bookkeeper's office. At night, she read there by lamplight; by day, she organized and ordered and occasionally sold a few books in her little shop downstairs. It was more than she had ever hoped for. Sometimes she wondered at her good fortune.

Stepping around puddles, she made her way to the door, fishing in her pocketbook for the key. It turned in the lock and she pushed the door open, the musty odor of books lingering in the air. After closing the door behind her, she folded her umbrella and slipped it into the stand, setting her bag on the counter. Every time she entered the room, she was overcome by its beauty. The walls were paneled in oak and the window casings were wide and generous, allowing a great deal of light into the room. The secondhand desk in a corner was made of mahogany and was quite grand, she thought, though Jack would have called it wormy. It's true, it had seen better days, but she had polished it until it had a lustered sheen, and as far as she was concerned, the worn places only gave it character.

Alice removed her gloves and unbuttoned her raincoat, then hung it on a hook near the door. Before she locked the shop and went upstairs, she would choose a book to take with her to while away her evening. A box from Doubleday had arrived earlier, and she took a sharp knife from the top desk drawer and cut it open. Unfolding the stiff cardboard, she pulled back the flaps to find copies of a du Maurier novel, *My Cousin Rachel*, which she had been expecting. Nodding in satisfaction, she closed it again and wandered over to a nearly empty shelf where she had stacked several new copies of *Jane Eyre*. She took the one from the top of the pile and tucked it under her arm, wondering who would read it with her.

All around the world, she knew, were kindred spirits who reached for the same book on the same evening for comfort or affirmation, souls who found themselves in the pages of a book. But there were other readers too—readers who didn't yet know who they were and how much a particular novel would mean to them. Alice felt it was her job to find them and give them a book.

She bolted the shop door, took her pocketbook from the desk, and turned off the lights before making her way upstairs. It had only been a few weeks since she had moved into the building, but already she knew the familiar creak of every stair.

The flat above was simply furnished: a bed against the far wall, a wardrobe, a table, and chair. She hadn't a television or even a sofa, but there was an old chaise with cushions one could sink into and a trunk she had found at a secondhand shop that functioned as a perch for a teacup. In the second room, there was a makeshift kitchen, where she plugged in the electric kettle and set out a cup and saucer as she did at the end of most days.

Alice had never lived in Cambridge before. In fact, she had never even been to Massachusetts. After Jack, she had taken a map and traced her way as far from Chicago as she could get, loading her few possessions into suitcases and boarding the train to Boston. It was the most frightening, exciting thing she had ever done. It had taken her three weeks to find an empty shop and then another two as she cleaned it up sufficiently to house the books she had selected and ordered from publishers and used bookstores around the city.

After pulling a dressing gown from the wardrobe, she slipped it on over her dress as the kettle whistled. She brewed a cup of tea and took it to the chaise, where she sat down with her book. It lay unopened on her lap as she contemplated the silence. It was good to have a space to oneself where one could think and dream and plan. And there was much to plan, for it was to be a busy year if things turned out as she hoped.

Taking a sip of her tea, she leaned back into the cushions, lifted her new copy of *Jane Eyre*, and held it to her breast. It was hard to imagine it had been published in 1847, as fresh as it felt to her each time she read it. She understood the loneliness Jane must have felt has a child and even more the struggle to find her way in life. Brontë's heroines, like so many women before and after, were often dependent upon the humor and indulgences of men. Alice's sister lived in a twenty-room mansion in Chicago, but at what expense? To have such a home meant to be as dependent as a child, and that was one thing Alice would never be again.

She opened the book to the first page, content in every way with her situation, and began to read.

The following day was Friday, a good day for a bookseller in Boston. In fact, it was a good day for booksellers everywhere. Readers came in with wages in their pockets and the desire to have a book companion for the weekend. She sold two copies of *Catcher*, a Hemingway, a Nancy Mitford that had only been in the shop for a few hours, and four used books she had picked up at a book stall a week earlier for a quarter apiece.

Around three o'clock, a young woman walked into the shop, and Alice glanced up from her seat behind the oak desk, where she was shuffling papers, writing down accounts. She nodded in greeting, loath to disturb anyone browsing through a bookshelf, though the girl didn't respond. She was likely one of the college girls around town. They were near Radcliffe, after all. The girl wore a plain dress, with sensible shoes and a pair of dark tortoiseshell glasses. Alice tried to turn her attention back to the accounts, but she was interested in which shelves the girl explored. For a moment, she thought of handing her a copy of *Jane Eyre* and then stopped herself. This was not a kindred spirit, she could tell. This was a girl who wanted *A Tree Grows in Brooklyn* or another popular book of its ilk. Not that she disparaged readers of any sort, but she was looking for someone different.

Eventually, the girl turned away from the shelves and brought a book up to the desk. It had been previously owned, a slim volume of poetry, an altogether nice choice.

"That will be one dollar, please," Alice said.

As the girl took a bill from her handbag, Alice placed the book upon a sheet of waxed brown paper, folding it carefully and tying it with a length of string. When she was finished, she took out an ink pad and stamped an image upon the package. "The Cambridge Bookshop" looked elegant in formal, ink-dipped letters. One might not know the name of the shop when one went inside, but if one came out with a purchase, it was stamped upon the paper for everyone to see.

The girl glanced at a flyer on the desk and back at Alice.

"You're having a book club?" she asked. "How does that work?"

Alice nodded. "Once a month, a small group will meet and discuss a different book."

She picked up the flyer, which read:

## THE CAMBRIDGE BOOKSHOP

is proud to host a Reading Club

Last Thursday of each month

Serious book lovers only

*Inquire if interested*

"Will it be a classic?"

"Most of the time, yes," Alice replied. "In September, we'll be reading *Jane Eyre*."

"May I take this?" the girl said, reaching for the paper. "I'll talk to my friends and see what they say."

"Of course," Alice replied, wondering if she had misjudged the girl. "Let me know by next week if you're interested."

The next few days were unremarkable, although satisfying in their own way. Alice loved having a routine, and her days had little variation. Coffee, toast, and the newspaper, in which she read only the fashion page. Selling and ordering books in the morning. Exploring Cambridge during her lunch hour, walking through parks and peering in shop windows until she came upon the luncheonette, where she usually ordered a ham on rye or chicken salad at the counter. Afternoons were spent going over the accounts, followed by no small amount of daydreaming over what to read next. She was anxious about only one thing: to know with whom she would share *Jane Eyre*, wondering if the girl who took the flyer would return with her friends. Fortunately, she didn't have to wait long.

She knew them the moment she saw them. The weather was as sunny and bright that afternoon as it had been rainy the previous one. Alice was washing the windows, which looked as if they hadn't been cleaned in years, when four girls, smiling and talking, arms linked, came down the street and stopped at the door. A moment later, they stepped inside and Alice smiled in greeting, as if they were very old friends. They were young—not even twenty, if she was correct—and obviously Cliffies. One, a beautiful blond, even wore a sweater with the Radcliffe emblem on the front. She couldn't have been happier to see them.

"Hello!" Alice said in greeting. "Welcome to the Cambridge Bookshop."

# 2

---

Tess Collins sat primly on a bench in front of her college dormitory, a light breeze ruffling her skirt about her knees. A copy of *Byron's English Composition, First Edition* was perched on her lap, though she had some difficulty concentrating on the page in front of her. She had been a formidable student back at home in Ohio, but while writing a thesis statement and constructing a topic sentence were familiar territory, she didn't intend to let the grass grow under her feet. She was first in her class in Akron and planned to be first in her class at Radcliffe as well. Ordinarily, she studied for exams in a library, behind a wooden carrel to block out the world. One didn't excel in the academic setting if one was distracted by blue skies and unseasonably warm weather. On the other hand, she thought, she was eighteen now, a college student. A mature young woman could both familiarize herself with the crux of her studies and enjoy the last of the summer air.

The dormitory behind her, Duncan Hall, was a grand-looking building with two tall white pillars on either side of the long porch, where weathered gray benches were lined up in a row. Inside, it was as refined as one might expect from its exterior. A large, comfortable sitting room, full of upholstered sofas and chairs covered in chintz, was flanked by walls lined with shelves and shelves of books. They weren't standard textbooks or dry nonfiction tomes either; someone had filled them with novels and mysteries and volumes of poetry in a heroic attempt to appeal to the varied tastes of the girls who lived there. She'd only been at Radcliffe for two weeks but had yet to see anyone peruse the titles, and though she herself had, she was looking for a book in particular that couldn't be found on the shelf.

The second and third floors housed the inhabitants of the building: two girls to each room, sixteen to each floor. It was overwhelming in its way, and she was glad she hadn't chosen one of the larger dorms, trying to navigate her first year of college in a sea of nameless faces.

Tess pulled her sweater around her shoulders and pushed her tortoiseshell glasses up higher on her nose. She almost smiled. It was a little thrilling to have a book in hand and the opportunity to sit outside to read it. She had just turned her attention back to the page when a blue-and-white Bel Air convertible careened into the drive and came to a sudden halt in front of the dorm, the brakes squealing on the pavement. Her roommate, Caroline Hanson, was in the passenger seat, sitting next to one of the best-looking young men Tess had ever seen. He leapt from the vehicle and came around to open the door for Caroline, who laughed when he leaned in close. Tess sat forward, wondering if he was going to breach all decorum and kiss her in front of God and everyone, when Caroline pushed past him with a laugh and walked up the steps.

"Tess," she said in her breathy voice. "This is Carter Gray."

Tess locked eyes with him for a second, blushing. Like Caroline, he was obviously wealthy. He wore a pair of well-fitting white trousers and a white cable-knit tennis sweater with red and navy bands along the V-necked collar, which emphasized his tan, making him look like he had stepped straight out of an advertisement in a magazine. After a quick nod in her direction, he took Caroline by the hand.

"When do I get to see you again?" he asked, massaging her knuckles with his forefinger. "We could go to the pictures tonight."

Tess closed her book, all hope of studying now impossible. She should have expected such an interruption and studied for her exam in the safe harbor of her dorm room at the minuscule desk, although it was possible there would be distractions there too. Caroline was a vision, an eighteen-year-old Grace Kelly, who would no doubt be engaged by Christmas, and their dorm room seemed to have a revolving door, as everyone wanted a glimpse of the Rhode Island beauty. Her major was art history, but she was so popular even in such a short time that Tess doubted her roommate would finish the year. In the meantime, she realized with a sigh, it would be back to the library and wooden carrels if she wanted to keep to her goal of being first in her class.

"I'm busy tonight," Caroline told Carter Gray with a smile. "Tess and I have things to do, don't we?"

She unexpectedly took Tess's hand and led her inside, closing the door behind them. Curious, Tess followed Caroline up the stairs.

The dorms had large but plain rooms. The college had provided two twin beds and mattresses; two plain wooden desks; and tall, matching wardrobes standing side by side. There were twin closets, none too large, but because they had a corner room, there were double the amount of windows, including two over the beds that swung open from the bottom to allow them to listen to the birdsong and the rustle of the wind in the trees.

# READING GROUP GUIDE

1. Amelia "Mia" Walker, a bakery worker in New York City, finds herself approached by a stranger and is suddenly whisked away to Paris to begin a career as a model. What did you think of Mia's decision to go abroad? If you were in her shoes, what choice would you have made, and why?

2. The prologue shows Mia holding a gun over the body of a dead man. What effect did these opening pages have on you as you continued the rest of the story? As you read, did you form any ideas about what happened in that opening scene, and if so, were you right?

3. As the story progresses, we learn that the House of Rousseau is involved in a Cold War espionage scheme. What were they trying to accomplish, and how were the models a part of their plans? Then, think about the Cold War as a whole. Is this a period of history you're familiar with, and if not, what did you learn from this story?

4. Mia earns herself the nickname "The Kennedy Girl" among

her peers in Paris. Why do they call her that? Then, think about the ways Jacqueline Kennedy inspires Mia throughout the story. Do you have someone in your life who you look up to in the way that Mia looks up to her?

5. Much of the story shows Mia adjusting to her life as a fashion model. What is her modeling experience like at the House of Rousseau? Did you learn anything about the modeling world of the 1960s, and if so, what?

6. Interspersed throughout Mia's narrative are chapters from an unnamed narrator who seems to be spying on her. Who does this turn out to be? What do these chapters add to the story?

7. Mia is asked to model couture at social events and soon learns that her presence is for far more than fashion. What does the House of Rousseau have her doing, and how does she feel about it? What would you have felt if you were in Mia's position?

8. Mia finds herself living with two roommates, Maeve and Elisabeth, both models at the House of Rousseau. What is the dynamic like between the three girls? Think about your own experiences with roommates. How might they have compared to Mia's?

9. Mia's involvement in the Cartier diamond scheme is not only a crucial moment in the events of the story but also for the growth of her character. What was the House of Rousseau trying to do with the diamonds, and how is Mia able to stop them? Were you surprised by how this all played out and by Mia's decisions in the end?

10. Mia doesn't know much about modeling when she begins her journey, but by the end, she finds that it is so much more than just clothing. In what ways do fashion and politics intersect both in the novel and in our current world? After reading this story, do you feel differently about the world of fashion than you might have felt before? Why or why not?

# A CONVERSATION
# WITH THE AUTHOR

**This novel is filled with intrigue, glamour, and unforgettable characters. What inspired you to write _The Kennedy Girl?_**

I'm a lifelong Francophile and have long wanted to write a book set in Paris. In fact, I had been developing characters for a while without knowing what book they would be in. Chantal Fournier was one of those characters because I am interested in strong, dynamic women of a certain age and what they can contribute to a story. I also love studying history, especially about World War II and the Cold War, so I decided to use it as the basis of this book. Once I created Mia, the plot came together quickly. Fashion and politics felt like a match made in heaven.

**What does your writing process look like? Are there any ways you like to find inspiration?**

I'm fortunate to be able to write full-time, which means I can schedule my day easily. I like structure and keep to a morning writing schedule whenever possible. My trusty laptop can go with me from room to room for a change of scenery. For inspiration, I enjoy watching classic movies set in whatever era I'm writing about and studying nonfiction books for background and detail. I also keep a

Pinterest board for fashion, clothing, and other information I need to reference for the book I'm writing. Having those visuals at my fingertips keeps me inspired and eager to write.

**This novel is set in Paris during the Cold War. What kind of research did you do for this book? Did you find anything unexpected while writing?**

I drew on my first experiences in Paris for this book: the sights and sounds and the feeling you get when you see it for the first time. I can still remember how it felt to wander into the Père Lachaise on a rainy day and to stand outside the Sacré-Coeur, where you can look out over the entire city. Of course, as someone who enjoys studying history, I've visited memorials and museums dedicated to World War II, and I've read a great deal about the war and its aftermath. For this book, I delved into the dark and murky race to steal nuclear secrets and was surprised at how many different factions and countries were trying to destabilize the world and gain power.

**What do you hope readers take away from Mia's story?**

So many endings in life can really be beginnings if we allow ourselves to think about it that way. Mia couldn't imagine a world without her father but eventually discovers an inner strength within herself that she didn't know she had. There is always hope and a chance for a new chapter in life.

**How did the novel evolve over the course of writing?**

I couldn't quite nail the beginning at first. It wasn't until I decided to write Chantal's point of view (and later Philip's) that I realized where I was headed. I absolutely loved the way the Kennedy family history aligned with the events in the book, lending authenticity and glamour to the story. It was a privilege to take so much of what I have learned about the Cold War era and spin it into a tale that could be just as relevant today.

# ACKNOWLEDGMENTS

*The Kennedy Girl* was a book that required years of research, from learning about the fashion industry to Cartier diamonds to the intricacies of the Cold War. My husband, a former librarian and author of fifteen mystery novels, assisted me in finding some of the research materials that I was able to use to provide rich detail for the book. Likewise, our travels across France allowed me the opportunity to learn more about one of my favorite countries, which helped bring the story to life. Countless people we met in Paris and beyond, from waiters to historians to the staff at Versailles, inspired and informed me as I wrote this novel.

Thanks are also due to my fabulous editors, Shana Drehs and Liv Turner, whose enthusiasm for the project meant so much to me. They guided me through the editing process so smoothly, it never felt like work. Liv, your cheery editorial notes made me laugh and brought so much fun to the process. I'd like to also express my appreciation to the whole team at Sourcebooks, including my publicist, Anna Venckus, whose work behind the scenes makes the launch of the book so enjoyable.

I am blessed with a wonderful agent, Victoria Skurnick of Levine Greenberg Rostan, who is as much a friend as an agent. Her support, as well as that of everyone at LGR, is immeasurable.

And of course, I am grateful to the family and friends who are always in my corner. Thank you, Lori Naufel, Leslie Purcell, Connie Miller, and Patti Long, along with so many others, including Jana Watters, who explored Paris and Normandy with me one very hot summer.

Love and thanks to my husband, Will Thomas, and my daughters, Caitlin and Heather, as well as my son-in-law, David. You provide encouragement, inspiration, and a much-needed sense of humor along the way. This book is for you.

# ABOUT THE AUTHOR

Julia Bryan Thomas is a graduate of Northeastern State University and the Yale Writers' Workshop. She is married to mystery novelist Will Thomas.

# THE RADCLIFFE LADIES' READING CLUB

*Never underestimate the power of a woman with a shop full of books...*

Massachusetts, 1954. Alice Campbell escapes halfway across the country and finds herself in front of a derelict building tucked among the cobblestone streets of Cambridge, and she turns that sad little shop into the charming bookstore of her dreams.

Tess, Caroline, Evie, and Merritt become fast friends in the sanctuary of Alice's monthly reading club at the Cambridge Bookshop, where they escape the pressures of being newly independent college women in a world that seems to want to keep them in the kitchen. But they each embody very different personalities, and when a member of the group finds herself shattered, everything they know about one another—and themselves—will be called into question.

A heart-wrenching, inspiring, extraordinary love letter to books set against the backdrop of one of the most pivotal periods in American history, *The Radcliffe Ladies' Reading Club* explores how women forge their own paths, regardless of what society expects of them, and illuminates the importance of literature and the vital conversations it sparks.

*"A great choice for book clubs."*

—*Library Journal*

**For more Julia Bryan Thomas, visit:**

**sourcebooks.com**

# FOR THOSE WHO ARE LOST

*One woman's split–second decision will tear a family apart…*

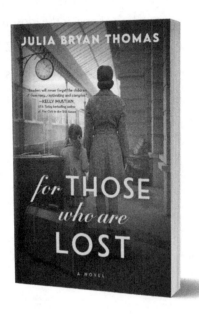

Inspired by true events, *For Those Who Are Lost* begins on the eve of the Nazi invasion of the island of Guernsey, when terrified parents have a choice to make: send their children alone to England or keep the family together and risk whatever may come to their villages.

Ava and Joseph Simon reluctantly put their nine-year-old son, Henry, and four-year-old daughter, Catherine, in the care of their son's teacher, who will escort them on a boat to mainland England. Just as the ferry is about to leave, the teacher's sister, Lily, appears. The two trade places: Helen doesn't want to leave Guernsey, and Lily is desperate for a fresh start.

Lily is the one who accompanies the children to England, and Lily is the one who lets Henry get on a train by himself, deciding in a split second to take Catherine with her and walk the other way. That split-second decision lingers long after the war ends, impacting the rest of their lives.

*"Highly recommended."*

—Historical Novel Society

**For more Julia Bryan Thomas, visit:**

**sourcebooks.com**

.

Made in the USA
Las Vegas, NV
14 January 2025

16383124R00256